# THE
# LAST
# DG
# ON
# EARTH

## ADRIAN J. WALKER

sourcebooks
landmark

Published by Sourcebooks Landmark, an imprint of Sourcebooks, Inc.
P.O. Box 4410, Naperville, Illinois 60563-4410
(630) 961-3900
Fax: (630) 961-2168
sourcebooks.com

Originally published in 2017 in the United Kingdom by Del Rey, an imprint of Ebury Publishing, a division of Penguin Random House UK.

Library of Congress Cataloging-in-Publication Data

Names: Walker, Adrian J. (Suspense fiction writer), author.
Title: The last dog on Earth / Adrian J. Walker.
Description: Naperville, Illinois : Sourcebooks Landmark, [2019]
Identifiers: LCCN 2018005175 | (softcover : acid-free paper)
Subjects: LCSH: Human-animal relationships--Fiction. | End of the
    world--Fiction. | Orphans--Fiction.
Classification: LCC PR6123.A423 L37 2019 | DDC 823/.92--dc23 LC record
available at https://lccn.loc.gov/2018005175

Printed and bound in Canada.
MBP 10 9 8 7 6 5 4 3 2 1

For Bronte, and all the dogs
of Peckham Rye Park

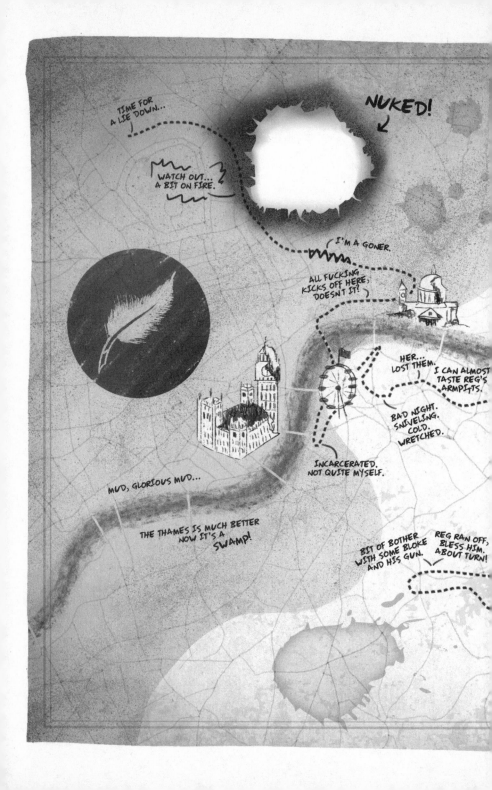

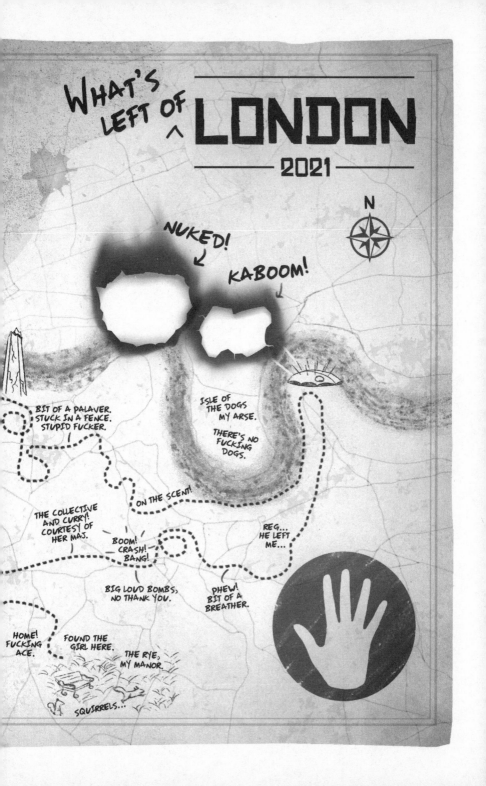

# PART 1

# BOSH

## LINEKER

THE MACHINE GOES ON and—*BOSH!*—we're away. This is a good bit, definitely. I get the smell first—graveyard dirt, burned grass, and old lemons fingering their way up my snout. Then I hear the gurgle and roar of the water, the drip, drip, drip into the pot, and I open my eyes and see the green light in the kitchen. That's another good bit. It's 5:00 a.m., still dark outside, but my head's up, tail wagging, looking at the door, waiting as the coffee fills, waiting, waiting, waiting…

And then, finally, the door opens and there he is. There he fucking is in all his fucking glory. What a body. What a mind. What a man. What a fucking *god*.

I'm skittering and sliding, halfway across the floor before I even know I've left my bed. And he's rubbing his hairy face and scratching that huge arse of his, releasing that heavenly aroma of salt, peat, and tripe that's *all for me*, and before he knows what's happening, I'm in the air and bouncing at him—bounce, bounce, bounce until he gets down and gives me a scratch, both hands behind my ears, face-to-face so I get the sweet fog of his breath, a rich soup of saliva and half-digested food that's been marinating beautifully for the past eight hours. And it's too much, I just have to lick him, so I do, and he lets me, and it's fucking brilliant.

I love him. Reg. My master. Without fail, the best bit.

Reg gets his coffee—UHT cream and three sugars for Reg, being a man of substance—while I scurry in a daze of ecstasy around his frayed slippers. He drinks it and sighs—a good bit because here comes more breath, more bliss for us down here on the linoleum. I'm reminded of what he ate last night, which is usually something hot with meat and a lot of cheese or bread or spices—oh fuck me those spices, like ants exploding up my nostrils—and I'm dizzy just thinking about it. Because I'm hungry. I'm always hungry. This is in no small way down to the fact that our flat smells constantly of food—fermented cow's milk, mostly. It's our very own house of cheese. But it's also because I am a dog, and therefore my throat, my belly, and my tongue are like a single organism; a gnawing, insatiable beast that only lives to consume any fucking thing it comes into contact with. Meat, vegetables, eggs, grain, wood, hair, shit—yes please, lots of that, ta very much—meat, concrete, insects, spiders, chicken skin, fish skin, my own skin, Reg's skin, fruit, old fruit, rotten fruit, rotten meat, oh yes indeed, crockery, bone, leather, plastic, polyester, wool, sock, pant, shoe, skirting board, and did I mention meat?

All of it. Down my gob, bish bash bosh, thank you and good night.

Except apples. I can't fucking stand apples.

Anyway. I'm hungry, and Reg, God bless his fetid socks, knows this all too well. So he fills my bowl.

Now, I will admit that there is an element of tension at this point in proceedings. I have no idea what I'm going to get for breakfast. It could be dry, it could be wet. It could be some delicious slop from a plate in the fridge, or fat-smeared crusts from his bacon sandwich. My belly beast is straining to feed, and it has no idea what it's going to get. I can't control it, and the anticipation is killing me.

Know this about dogs: this is how we spend most of our existence. We are endlessly at the mercy of things beyond our control. Hunger, thirst, heat, sex, sleep, itching, violence, flying objects, scent, *meat*. Something's always there leading us on to the next moment. Act and react, that's what we do.

So I stand on the brink of this new world of breakfast, trembling like a pilgrim father in the waters of Cape Cod.

And then it comes and the smell smashes into me and my mouth's flooded and it doesn't even matter anymore. A *fucking* good bit. My bowl's on the floor and I'm in it, chomping it, inhaling it. By the time it's done, I can barely remember who I am or what it was I just ate, and, quite frankly, I couldn't give a shit.

Nice bit of water for pud—lovely—and I'm off again, spring in my step, belly beast sated for the time being. What's next? Reg has opened the curtains by now, so I get up on my hind legs, paws against the glass of the balcony doors so I can see out. We're so high up I can see for miles. My entire kingdom is laid out before me in the creeping dawn, the roads, streets, and terraces crawling about, knotted together like worms in turned soil. I know it all by heart. Every shrub and hedgerow in The Rye, every crevice and tar-caked trash can on the high street, every piss-stained corner, every burned-out car, every fallen, vine-strewn building, every smashed window and human skeleton. I know it all, and I fucking love it.

My name's Lineker and I live in South London. I don't know what I am. Bit of this, bit of that, bit of the other. Terrier, retriever, hound. I never knew my dad, and my mum's just a big warm, milky memory—her tongue on my brow, pink and wet and smelling of heaven, me crowding against her tits with the rest of them little fuckers, pulling out that rich, white elixir and feeling my strength swell. Ah, me old mum. Probably kicked the bucket now, I expect.

So no, haven't got a Scooby what my breed is, pardon the pun. I used to hear people say I was "Heinz 57," on account of the beans, which, to be completely honest with you, is confusing, not to mention insulting. I'm not beans and I'm not a watered-down version of other dogs—I'm an original. Special edition. Custom shop. Mold broken. One in a fucking million.

What I do know—what I am fairly fucking sure about, as it happens—is that I am the last dog on earth.

I know!

Me and Reg—my master, my two-plates (plates of meat, feet; that's cockney rhyming slang that is, keep up)—we're bachelors. We live alone in our palace—sixth floor of a Peckham high-rise with stairs so dank with urine I could swoon. Forty, fifty years of the stuff, all spread about on top of each other, just amazing. Anyway, it's just us. We don't have time for ladies. Too busy.

Actually, when I say we don't have time, that's not strictly true. Little porky. I *would* have time, it's just, you know, there aren't any ladies to have the old time *with*. No skirt for Lineker anymore, ho hum, woe is my poor old todger, etc., etc.

Reg? Well, I can't speak for him, but I couldn't tell you when he last had a female two-plates back in *Casa del Fromaggio*, even before things got quiet out there. Don't know why. Fair enough, he doesn't match your average Prince Charming photofit, and you wouldn't hear many gussets slapping onto the balcony tiles if he ever crooned up in that voice of his, which I'm afraid has the timbre of a bookish mole—that adenoidal tenor *you* associate with cardigans, electronics catalogs, and notebooks full of train numbers but which *I* think is simply the mark of a man who knows his fucking onions.

Yeah, Reg is prime material in my book. Tall, wide, hairy, lovely farts, and a huge heart—almost huge enough to match his breath, which is *fucking enormous*. It's beyond me why he's not been snapped up, but there you go. What do I know?

Maybe it's because he works so hard. He's a writer, you see. An author. A wordsmith. That's why he's awake every day before dawn, scribbling away in that book of his to crack out a few pages before we head out. I'll wander around and have a snooze somewhere, floating in breakfast's dreams. I'll slumber till he's done, unless he decides to masturbate, of course, in which case I am *very* much awake. It is a privilege to witness this, an honor. So I sit up, back straight, paws together in solemn reflection as this beautiful act unfolds. I tell you, it's enough to make a grown dog weep.

What else about Reg... Oh, yes, Reg's favorite thing is football, or rather, a very short period of football history spanning the late '80s and early '90s, during which the English football team got further than usual in the World Cup. That's why I'm called Lineker, after his

hero, Gary. He watches old tapes of the matches, and one in particular that ends in a penalty shoot-out. Every time he cheers them on
as if he doesn't know how it's going to end. Sometimes even I'm
surprised when they fail, which they always do.

So that's Reg: writing, football, and me.

Now, I know what you're thinking. How does yours truly know
so much about all of this? I am, after all, just a dog. I understand.
You like asking yourselves questions like that, don't you? You clever
little monkeys.

How best to answer? Hum hum…well, couple of ways I could
do it: I could try to explain to you how we think in different speeds,
or how we can tell what you're thinking just by looking at the way
your shoulders slump, or how we talk to you and to each other, not
just with sounds but with smells and looks and the way we position
our bodies (which, actually, isn't a whole lot different to you).

I could try to tell you how dogs don't just pick up fleas and
sticks but *everything*. Things you never see, like the quiver of a cat's
whisker (don't, just don't, get me started) or the flash in a man's
eye that tells me he's nervous, or excited, or that he's about to do
something he shouldn't. I could try to tell you that every little thing
you do, everything you say, every little expression that flickers upon
your chops: it all goes in these furry noggins and that's where it
stays, whether you like it or not. (Me, I like it. I like it very much
indeed, thank you.)

I could try telling you what it's like when we find ourselves
awake in the middle of the night, triggered by nothing more than a
tightening in the air, as if space has been suddenly gripped by some
unknown hand, and that this twist in the fabric of things carries with

it messages encoded in ways that cannot be turned into words, and we have to get up and see what's what.

I could try to explain things in this way, using simple sentences and facts, but sometimes plain language just does not cut the mustard.

Poetry, however—now there's a mustard cutter. That'll chop your Colman's right down the middle.

Now I…ahem…I dabble in the old poetry myself, as it happens—STOP LAUGHING—I do. It's hard not to when you live with a literary giant such as Reg. I've picked up the craft and I practice for hours, looking out of our window at the city and the infinite shapes and colors it makes. I've had a little go at explaining how exactly I know all these things, and so far, this is the best I can come up with.

So here, if you'll humor me, is my poetic meditation upon the mysteries of canine intuition.

*The world howls.*

Yeah. You're disappointed. I'm sorry. Really, I am—I hate it when you're disappointed. Makes me feel fucking awful if you want the truth of it. But…bollocks…what can I say? That's all I've got right now.

Gulp.

Don't worry, I'll keep trying, I promise.

Anyway, the point is I do—know about all this stuff, I mean. So don't be surprised or scared if I happen to know certain things about you; whatever it is you think you've done, you naughty monkey, I still think you're fucking magic.

Now, where was I? Oh yeah, *life*! Our fucking brilliant, stupendous life.

After breakfast, Reg and I hit The Rye.

Peckham Rye Park is where we take our walks, Reg and me. It's what you might call my territory, my turf, my manor. Not exclusively mine, of course. Plenty of other dogs tread The Rye—at least they used to. I can still smell most of them, still tell where and when they took their last pisses before… Well, I'll get to that in a bit.

It's winter now so our walks are cold. I don't mind it. It's not as though summer's much to write home about these days anyway. Winter's all right by me. And the smells. We'll get to smells too.

Quite often I'll lose track of time on The Rye. I'll find myself deep in the tall grass, dodging this way and that, jumping up occasionally so I can get my bearings and see where Reg is, chasing those little wisps of things that have been and gone either the night before or decades past. And then I'll stop and I wonder where I've been. There's nothing but the blades rustling and the heavy clouds brooding above. Sometimes, I swear, I even forget who I am.

And then I remember: I'm the last dog on earth.

Then I hear Reg's whistle, sharp as a magpie, and it all comes back and I'll dart out to meet him.

We usually have to collect a few things afterward. Reg has his favorite haunts, of course; very predictable, my Reg. Doesn't take us into places we've never been before, no shops we haven't already been around a million times, stairways we've not checked, doors we've not already opened. And he's punctual too. Never one to be late, this fella, oh no. If we're out for too long, he gets anxious, quickens his step and lengthens his stride. Got to get back bang on the dot. Solid as a rock, he is. As a *rock*.

Once inside, it's free time, really. He might give me a snack and something for himself. Nice cup of tea for his lordship, usually. Then it's more writing for him and more nap time for yours truly. By now I'm properly pooped, so I slump down on the sofa and drift away to the scribbling of his pencil, already ravaged by the morning, and of the fact that this is and will be a day like every other day of our glorious lives.

# MARVELOUS BINOCULARS

**REGINALD HARDY'S JOURNAL**

**DECEMBER 3, 2021**

Your own problems always outweigh those of the world.

I am looking out at a dead city. A black hole where once a hundred million stars shimmered—the happy lights of homes, offices, restaurants, pubs, and cars. Their absence should dismay me, but, in fact, it is only the absence of one which does.

I have a feeling that Beardsley is on the move. Either that or he is dead.

I hope he is dead.

Beardsley is not his real name, of course, just the one I gave him. It could be a man or a woman, or men, or women. He could even be a family, though I doubt it. I cannot imagine the technicalities of raising children here now.

Shilton looks a little dim tonight too. One or two of his bulbs dead, I expect. Either that or he's conserving them for fuel. I wonder where he gets his supplies? Pearce looks all right and Butcher's erratic as usual, but Beardsley...well, he's not been on for five nights now.

*Perhaps you're sitting in the wrong position, Reginald*, I thought to myself when I first noticed. *Unlikely*, I thought back, but I recalibrated, just to be sure.

Always be within reach of a tape measure. That's a good rule for the book.

Diagonal distance from Reginald's left eyeball to left corner of balcony window = 35⅛ inches (I'm an imperial man): *check*.

Diagonal distance from Reginald's right eyeball to balcony door handle = 31¾ inches: *check*.

Seat height = 18⅞ inches: *check*.

Gaffer tape strip on seat matches gaffer tape strip on floor matches gaffer tape strip at base of balcony door: *check*.

Window clean: *check*.

Straight back, head facing forward: *check*.

Commence light count.

Shilton: *check*

Pearce: *check*

Walker: *check*

Butcher: *check*

Parker: *check*

Wright: *check*

Waddle: *check*

Gascoigne: *check*

Platt: *check*

Lineker: that's us, *check*

Beardsley: nothing

So that is a problem.

They're highly satisfactory, these binoculars. My vision is less than

mighty—a moderate myopia of roughly -3.23 diopters has neces-
sitated glasses since childhood—so it is rather a treat to see distant
objects so close-up. There's not much you can do about this ceaseless
fog, mind you; I have not seen a clear skyline since 2018. I acquired
them from a camping shop off Peckham High Street—12× magnification, crystal-clear lens, nice and light but strong and solid, and well
out of my price range, of course. There is no possible way I could
have afforded them before.

They are, primarily, for the wildlife. Peckham is full of it these
days, especially down on The Rye. Rats, mice, pigeons, cats,
woodpeckers, chaffinches, and those bright-green parakeets that
screech through the trees on the southern rim. Jimi Hendrix brought
them into London during the '60s, so it goes. Great fun to watch,
and, what with them and three years of uncut grass and trees left to
grow wild, the whole place looks like a jungle.

The woods are deep and dark now, full of fox stink, and I have
spotted the odd badger there too. The squirrels are still as numer-
ous as ever, and due to the warm winter we have, until recently,
enjoyed, they are all fat and slow after a two-month binge on nuts.
They cover every branch with their whirling, squirrelly blur.

Full of life. Sometimes I just sit and watch it all squirm and jump
and flutter through these marvelous binoculars of mine.

But they are not merely for zoological observation. I use them to
keep an eye on the lights too.

Beardsley was the first of them. It was the evening after I found
my generator, Bertha, just over three years ago. The power had
been down for weeks and, having made my decision to stay by
then, I knew I had to take things into my own hands. Luckily

I had expertise in these matters for I was a trained electrician in another life.

People say that, don't they? *In another life.* As if life isn't a single stretch of time but many of them: a series of befores and afters. We do have a peculiar way of looking at the world.

Anyway, I had just dragged Bertha up ten flights of stairs—and I am no Arnold Schwarzenegger, believe me—so I was having a well-earned rest when I spotted a glint through the window. I thought I was seeing things at first, maybe because of the exertion. But no, there it was: a little glimmer in a dark mass of buildings about a mile north of our block. I took a closer look, thinking it might be just the low sun reflecting in a broken window, but it was definitely a light—steady and orange, electric, man-made. Another stay-behind, just like me.

Foolish of me to believe that I had been the only one.

I circled the light on the window with a marker pen and watched it all evening. When the light turned off, my stomach turned. I did not like to think of whoever had made it out there, moving about in the dark and getting up to things.

It was there the next day, and the next, and the next, like clock-work: same time, same place, right under my mark. I made records in my book and, eventually, when I accepted that he was a perma-nent fixture, I adjusted the boundary on my map.

I had drawn my map long before the lights appeared, long before the fog descended, and long before all of this happened. It marks the streets to which I keep, and we should all have one if you ask me.

You only need a small space in which to live. I calculated it. The surface area of the planet is 197 million square miles, with only

58 million square miles of this comprising land. Much of this land is uninhabitable, and people tend to stick to coasts and cluster in packs, forming cities, like London. London takes up 3,236 square miles and, when I drew my map, was home to 14 million individuals. This means that, if you split it equally, every square mile of London's dirt would contain 4,326 people, with room for a little one.

That comes in at 716 square yards for every man, woman, and child.

Of course, when you factor in public parks, private land, underground parking, tower blocks, and all the places you just can't go, plus the fact that you *do* have to give a bit of wiggle room, the equation for how much space you should move about in gets a little complicated. Plus I had a dog, so he needed space too.

In the end, the borders of my map ran from Ada Road in the northwest to the bottom of Bremmington Park in the northeast, running south to Homestall Road and west again to Calton Avenue. Two square miles. I consider this generous.

When I spotted the lights, I brought the northern perimeter in a few streets, just in case I bumped into anyone.

I cannot touch people, you see? If I do, well, I get the heebie-jeebies.

This has not always been the case. For thirty years of my life, I was perfectly normal, but then…well, when my affliction took hold, I could see that it had the potential to make my life rather difficult. Two reasons:

(A) I lived in London, an enormous city full of people, all with skin, all moving, all liable to get close enough to *touch*, and

(B) I was an electrician, so I had to meet people fairly regularly.

But actually, in a place like London, people keep their distance anyway. The only ones I had to be on the lookout for were handshakers.

Handshakers were mostly men in middle-class houses who offered you tea and cookies while trying to talk to you from the corner. Quite why you would want to welcome a stranger sent to fix your fuse box in such an effusive way is beyond me, but there you go.

Whenever I sensed a shaker, I would stand well back from the door, tools in one gloved hand and a laminated sheet in the other explaining my condition. Once they had assimilated the information written thereon—generally with some amount of awkwardness—we would be safe to proceed.

So I stay within my boundary and I do not touch people. Those are my rules, and, happily, the world in which I now live makes sticking to them rather easier than before.

Oh, and I cannot go near water either.

Before you ask: no, I am not insane. Water is dangerous; that is merely a fact. I can assure you, I am no lunatic.

Something has come over me lately, though, I will admit that. I do not really know what it is, but it is close. I can feel it, like breath down my collar. My thoughts keep winding themselves up in knots, the same ones again and again, reminders, things that might never have happened, or maybe they did, I don't know, I just…

This is why I am writing my journal again. I had a therapist, way back.

"When your thoughts get too much," she said, "try writing them down. It might help, especially since writing is one of your hobbies. How is that novel of yours going?"

I did not like that word: *hobby*. Bird-watching, that is a hobby.

Dog walking too. Anything that takes your mind off things for a while. Eighteen years I have been trying to write this book of mine, and it does not feel like my mind is off anything. I just cannot seem to finish it; I do not know how. There's this Duchess, you see...

But I digress. The lights.

Beardsley and I, it appeared, were not alone. Over the following weeks, nine additional lights appeared, and I marked each one on the window and in my book. One night, as I worked on rigging the generator up to my flat's electrical supply, I realized—with some amount of dread—that I was a little light too. They would see me, as I saw them.

I had to have a little sit down at that.

Would one of them come to call? Thankfully, the answer, so far, has been no.

The first light, the other nine, and me: eleven lights in total. A bit of a gift, that number; I knew instantly how I would christen them. We would be the England squad from the 1990 World Cup semifinal against West Germany, 8:00 p.m., July 4, Stadio delle Alpi, Turin—a game I have seen many times. We took Lineker's namesake, of course.

But now, with Beardsley gone, it looks as if we are down to ten men. One less stay-behind. He shall have to be rubbed from the window.

You would probably say I was mad for staying. There is no electricity, no water, no refuse collection, little in the way of fresh food, and no people. Mad—I know that's what she would have said.

So why did I stay?

Because leaving would have meant change, and that is something I like to avoid at all costs.

It came slowly, with little chinks appearing as if another reality that existed behind the curtain of our daily activity had decided to crawl through. It was nothing spectacular. You saw more heads raised than usual. More nervous eyes met on the street. Bus conversations went on louder and longer than was deemed normal and rang with words that made the ears of other passengers prick.

It was the year of an election—the last of its kind, as it turned out—and amid the usual distant Westminster rhetoric, you heard other voices closer to home. These were the fringe campaigners, supporters of strange causes echoing from a past most thought had been buried for good.

One day, after walking Lineker, I passed a long trestle table on the pavement that was piled high with leaflets and taped with printouts and photographs. I glanced at the middle-aged woman sitting behind it in her shawl and boots and, suspecting some kind of left-wing activism, quickened my pace.

"Well, hello, little Reggie H!" came a familiar voice.

My boots scuffed to a halt and I looked back. The woman was standing now. She raised an eyebrow.

"Don't you recognize me?"

I frowned. Then it hit me.

"Angela?" I said, turning to face her. "Angela Hastings?"

I had grown up with Angela. At school, she had been the heavy-set girl with a loud mouth who commanded playground games. She had an unusual blend of precocious authority and mischief, and grew into an early developing, make-up-wearing, fierce-eyed teenager who tried everything before anyone else would dare. We were in the same year but different social groups—which is to say, she *had* a social group, whereas I had none. She made fun of me. It was only when we were fifteen and she started going out with a friend of my brother's, four years her senior, that we started moving in the same circles. She became a regular at the Wheatsheaf, where my brother took me when Mum needed privacy. As with most other boys my age, Angela represented a version of female sexuality you could not hope to attain and would be terrified of if you did. But we all thought about it anyway, sometimes, deep in the night.

She grinned and winked, and with a sigh, she plunged her hands into her cardigan pockets.

"It is you, then," she said. "My, my, it has been an age, Little Reggie. I think the last time I saw you was…"

She stopped, and an awkward ripple crossed her face—a transitory expression which I had long ago learned to recognize as pity. She shook her head.

"I was so sorry when I heard, Reggie," she said. "Really, I was. How have you been?"

"I am just fine, thank you, Angela," I said. "Just fine."

She nodded, smiled hopefully, and looked down at Lineker.

"Oh," she said. "I see you have a dog." She kept her eyes on Lineker. There was a change in her countenance then, a tightening of her jaw which I remember considering extremely odd. "That's good," she said. "I've heard that can help."

Lineker gave a low growl.

"Lineker," I warned.

"Don't worry," she said, looking up. "He can probably smell mine. I've got three at home, for my sins!"

She let out a raucous laugh—the same laugh I had heard many

times from the corner table of the Wheatsheaf, where I had spent countless evenings sitting quietly in the shadow of my brother's social life.

I looked at the table in front of me. "So, er, what's all this about then?"

She sniffed and cleared her throat. "We're campaigning to overhaul Rye Lane," she said, straight-necked and beaming.

"What, you mean structurally?" I asked. "Rooftops, roads, that kind of thing?"

"No. I mean we want to completely change it. Rip out the phone shops, pound shops, stinking fish markets, the places selling substandard African goods... We want to restore it to its former glory, Reggie. Make a fine British street out of it again."

I watched her, chin raised and face pinched with an unsettling mixture of pride and disgust. I hardly knew what to say.

"That is quite an ambition, Angela," I said at last.

She shrugged. "We need to be ambitious if things are going to change."

She motioned to the table.

"You should take one, Reggie. Educate yourself."

I picked up one of the garish pamphlets and looked it over. On its cover was a cheap photograph of a man in a suit, smiling.

"And who is this?" I asked, referring to the stranger who would soon be known the world over.

"That, Little Reggie, is our future," said Angela in a tone I had never before heard her adopt. It chilled me.

"Is that so?" I said. I was beginning to suspect that Angela Hastings's sanity had, somewhere along the line, taken a wrong turn.

"Why don't you join us?" she said with a welcoming smile, as if she were offering nothing more sinister than membership at a local church. "We can always use an extra pair of hands. Plus, we're a sociable lot, you know."

There was that awkward ripple again, followed by an encouraging nod. "It would be a great way to meet other people."

I placed the pamphlet carefully back on the table. "I don't think so, Angela," I said. "Thanks all the same, but I think I'll stick with Lineker here. You could say I, er, prefer the company of dogs to people right now."

I ventured a smile, but her expression had already darkened. Her sympathy, her brightness, her hope—it all fell away like dust. Beneath it was a stonelike glare. Lineker growled and this time I did not stop him.

"Change is coming, Reg," she said. "Whether you like it or not. You can't hide from it."

*I can*, I thought. *I can and I will.*

"Goodbye, Angela," I said and left.

"Bye, Little Reggie!" I heard her call after me, her brightness somehow restored. "I've always remembered you—stay safe, now!"

Less than a year later, a crowd watched as that first tank rolled into Peckham—its buffoon of a driver careering into the rail arch and bringing down the train that is still there to this day, covered in mud and creepers. By that time, I had already lived in my flat for twenty-five years. I would not have been able to tell you the last time I had escaped the M25's snaky coils, and I had not been north of the river for almost a decade. I wore the same clothes, read the same paper, watched the same telly, and drank the same brand of tea every single day, without fail. Then it all happened. I watched people howl and run from tanks and bombs and those chest-beating brutes in their purple jackets and golden plumes. I watched it all and stayed quiet; it was just another change, like a hurricane—devastating and treacherous, but it would pass. I would not let it take me with it. Not this time.

Change: something to avoid at all costs.

I was born in 1969, at almost exactly the same time that Mr. Armstrong's feet settled upon the moon. My mother said I should have been called Neil, but unfortunately, my brother had already claimed that name. So Reginald it was, after nobody in particular. My dad had hightailed it for Ireland long before I was born, so it was just me, Mum, and Neil, and our Nunhead flat.

I have lived in London all my fifty-two years so have witnessed half a century of change swirling about its streets. I have seen roads break apart and snap together like a child's train set. I have witnessed buildings rise and fall like dominoes, big and fat or sharp and spiky like broken bottles. Fashions have changed too—clothes, shoes, haircuts, scraps of colored fabric slapped over each other, each one screaming it's the best of the bunch, but it never is. Music, film, and theatre—the next big things arriving in limos and tripping down red carpets with their faces all shiny and their nails as sharp as razors. People—they change the most. Friends become strangers, lovers become distant memories, children…children do what they do. Voices change. People's accents, the words they use and the things they say. Opinions, minds, feelings. Those things change faster than light.

Month after month, year after year, fad after fad, it all just goes on and on and on. Change, change, change.

It is simply not for me.

That is why I stayed, so things would not change anymore.

You need very little to live. Shelter, food, and water—they are the staples. You might argue that you need a bit of company now and then, maybe even a bit of the other. I need nothing of the sort and, in any case, sexual conquest is a young man's game.

The basics, that is all you need; everything else is just dust.

We're doing all right, Lineker and me. Bertha is thrumming away, the fuel store is healthy, plenty of bulbs, food, and water, and the heating is doing a cracking job, even if I do say so myself. Good thing too because it is finally getting cold.

And I have my writing to keep me busy. Although this Duchess, she's really starting to give me a headache. If I could just find a way to… I don't know.

Like I say, something's come over me lately. I don't know what it is, but it's drawing in.

# PACK

### LINEKER

Squirrels are cunts.

They are, though. Cunts, the lot of them.

Ooh, if I could get my claws on one, what I wouldn't do to that stupid, vacant, twitching, little *cunty* face... It's enough to, I tell you, it's enough to...

I know, I know, I need to relax. It's just...my head, calm down, Lineker, come on mate, chill out.

I'm fine. It's all good. I'm sitting down. Calm, calm, calm...

This is my most favorite spot: by the window, looking out. It's long and tall with a view of countless buildings stretching away into the fog. Sometimes I can see gulls flying between them in great flocks. They seem to move slowly from so far away, not like individuals caught up in their own instincts—squawking, pecking, fluttering, and stinking like salt rats—but as a single thing, a tide rolling in slow motion. They're not themselves anymore. They're part of something else, a bigger unit with instincts of its own.

The best time to watch them is late afternoon when the sky bleeds orange. I lie with my chin on my paws and let my eyes go free, soaring out through the dirty glass to find them. I'll look for vegetation—tree branches poking out through windows, or vines wrapping around pillars; that's where you'll usually see them first, as a dark patch rippling on the green. If I look harder, I can see them fidgeting, making themselves ready. I imagine I can see their beaks glinting in the falling sun and hear the deafening caw of a thousand ideas, all trying to find the same one. Then suddenly, they'll rise up without warning, first like an arrowhead hooked in a ragged cloth; then like an animal trapped in a sack, a blob pulsing and struggling to find a common direction, and then they find it and become it—a swooping, swirling wash of shadow, a song with no words and no tune. A howl. They're part of The Howl.

I try to find one, just one to follow, and I get lost in the beat of its wings against the air, and I wonder what it would be like to fly, or even just to run beneath them all. To one day follow them through those strange, lonely buildings out there and through streets I've never seen, just once. Just once, to go out a bit farther.

And then they fall, as if whatever has been carrying them has dropped them, and they swoop down and lose themselves through the hole in some giant rooftop, and I imagine them fluttering about finding perches on rafters thick with their own rich, creamy excrement, and the wonderful din they're making, and hearing, together, as a flock.

And then I hear sighs and whines and I realize that it's me making them. Sometimes when I make these noises he'll come and ruffle my ears or scratch my chin and my tail will start thumping, even though I'm still out there somewhere, lost with the birds. Then he'll go back to whatever he was doing, and I'll watch him do that instead, and gradually I'll find myself drifting back inside and off to sleep. And I'll dream of those filthy gulls in their shit-packed rooftops, and what it's like when you forget yourself and become something else.

It wasn't always like this. I had a flock of my own once, my pack. Dogs are social animals—a bit like wolves but not quite so up themselves, know what I mean? Bit self-important, wolves, if you want my opinion. Your average male wolf takes himself *very* seriously. No room for fun or frolics with these fuckers; it's all nose-to-the-wind, paws-cracking-bracken, flesh-is-the-life, blood-is-the-creed kind of stuff. And all that breathy grunting; fuck me, you don't need to make that kind of racket when you're running. And your lady-wolves— even worse. Fucking hippy earth mothers, the lot of them.

Not that I'm against all that, you understand, not that I don't feel that electricity when I'm deep in the woods, not that I don't like a good howl; it's just, you know, have a word with yourself! Have some fun for a change.

I wouldn't say that to their faces, of course. Wolves are scary. They're also armed to the teeth (and I do mean the teeth—these little canines of mine have nothing on their flesh-tearers), not to mention highly unpredictable. You do not want to get on the wrong side of a wolf, or any side, for that matter. I can tell you that from personal experience.

That's called *foreshadowing*, that is. I learned that from Reg. Basically, there's going to be a wolf somewhere in this story, so you want to read on.

Where was I? Oh yes—despite our difference in outlook, dogs and wolves do share a common heritage. Somewhere along the line, probably about the time you lot got interested in moving dirt around and growing things, whatever existed before us split into factions.

We—us dogs—crept a little closer to you, intrigued by the warmth of your flames and the smells of your cooking meat, the nice little noises you made with your voices, and the safety of your settlements.

We heard howls from the mountainside: *Fools! Come back! They'll kill you! Eat you! Murder you with their spears! They'll betray you like they've betrayed The Howl! They're not fit for this earth, brothers and sisters! Come back and be saved, do not abandon your sacred creed! You'll be gone! Doomed! Damned! Awrooooooooooooooo!*

Yeah? Well, look who's laughing now, sunshine. Have you ever heard of bacon? Chew sticks? Chicken korma leftovers? Ever had a belly scratch? Ever played with a ball? Have you ever even *seen* a ball? Do you know what they're capable of? Have you ever sat by a fire— INSIDE—and drifted off, safe within four walls you don't have to look after and a roof that keeps you dry and a floor that isn't crawling with worms trying to get up your arsehole and eat whatever pitiful shreds of rotten deer meat are gargling away inside your scrawny little innards? Have you? Have you ever stuck your face out of a van window and let the wind drag your tongue out and hope it never stops? Have you ever touched sand? Drank seawater until you puked? Have you ever had someone else clean up your shit? (Actually, not entirely sure why that happens and, to be perfectly honest with you, wouldn't mind if it stopped.)

Have you ever gazed up into a hairless face haloed with sunshine and wondered if it was possible to love anything more? Eh? Have you?

Have you fuck. You still have to skulk about in forests, sleep in the snow, and count your dead children every morning. How do you like them (yuck) apples?

Again—not to their faces. No fucking way.

So we diverged, us and the wolves. We went our own separate ways. But we still hang out in packs; that's not changed.

I haven't seen my pack for three years.

There are two bits I remember from back then, back before it all went different. The first was a good bit, one day in winter.

It was a cold one. February. Clear blue skies, frost on the ground, and my shit almost freezing solid before it hit the crunchy grass of The Rye. We were there early, sun still a red blister bursting over the Peckham rooftops. That time in the morning was lovely and quiet before all the traffic started up, very peaceful on my ears. Quite a different story going on in the old conk, though. The morning air was already a cacophony of different scents, and I could smell each and every one, clear as day.

We moseyed through the gate and Reg unhooked me and then I was *off*. My paws scrabbled at the concrete and the universe soared past, the air like arctic seawater rushing over my face and a thick mist billowing in my wake. I was off into The Howl.

I'd caught the scent, see. Unmistakable. Like oil and eggs. I could already smell its filthy claws fidgeting, its stupid tail twitching.

My heart was in overdrive and I was already up the path, left onto the common, and shooting into the bushes. And there in the clearing he stood—the daft prick—bold as brass, that brainless face on him, looking at me as if this had never happened before. He dropped it—nut, twig, pebble, whatever the fuck he'd been fiddling with— and darted off. *But*, I thought, *I've got you this time, you little tart. I had a head start, didn't I? The mist gave me some ground. This time, you're mine. I'm going to sink my teeth into your trembling little rump and drag out your... Fuck, he's gone up a tree.*

I skidded to a halt and leaped up at the trunk a few times, barking uselessly. He stared down at me with those vacant brown eyes.

"Ar 'ey, Lin, did you get it, mate?"

I turned to see a familiar black shape loping through the mist. Wonky.

"You what?"

"That squirrel," said Wonky. "Did you get it or what?"

Wonky sat down next to me and looked up at the branch, all panting and expectant, staring right at the squirrel I had just failed, yet again, to catch. The squirrel rippled its tail and relaxed.

I'd met Wonky a few years before when he and his two-plates moved down from Liverpool. He'd seemed a bit nervous, right leg in bandages after a run-in with a Staffy back home—hence the name; he developed a limp that stayed with him after the bandages came off—so I'd taken him under my wing a bit, you know, looked after him. We'd got close after that and, well, I suppose you could say he was my best mate. After Reg, of course.

He was a good dog, our Wonkers. Loyal, good-natured, good laugh, typical Labrador. But I tell you this right now: there was fucking nothing going on in that thick black head of his.

"Do you see anything in my mouth, Wonk?" I sighed.

"Ey?" he said, eyes darting at me, then back at the branch. Clouds of his breath were pumping into the mist. "No, why?"

"Do you see anything on the ground? Fur, blood, entrails, that kind of thing?"

Wonky glanced down.

"Er, no. Why? Come on, Lin, tell us. Did y'get it or what, lad? Hey!"

Wonky suddenly jumped up at the tree and started barking. The squirrel watched him for a bit and wriggled up out of sight.

"Come back down here, y'little bastard!" shouted Wonky. "I'll 'ave you, I will!"

By the way, you should know I'm doing this for your benefit. Dogs don't talk—not in the way that you think—although if you think you've cornered the market where communication's concerned just because you make that wonderful noise you call talking (and it is wonderful, believe me, I could listen to it for hours) then think again. You've only been here for a few hundred thousand years. Do you think the world got to where it was before you turned up without a bit of natter? You're having a laugh. You only have to listen for a few minutes. Shut your eyes and open your ears—the world is one big chin-wag. One big howl.

But going back to Wonky and me, although this happened as I say, we weren't speaking. I'm making it up. Poetic license—learned that from Reg too.

"I'll fookin' 'ave you!"

I shook my head and went to leave, but I felt a snout in my tail.

"Well, good morning to you too, young lady," I said, looking around at the black-and-white Border collie currently engrossed in my hind quarters. Scapa withdrew and gave a happy sniff.

"Morning," she said. She nodded up at the tree. "Miss another one, did you?"

"Afraid so," I said.

"Bonny one too, by the looks of it."

"Bonny? There's nothing bonny about those little twats."

"Ach, I think they're nice." She wagged her tail. "Furry wee rascals."

"Yeah," I growled. "Well, I'd like to rip their furry heads off."

Scapa clucked. "You're so *angry*, Lineker."

"I'm not angry. I'm just… I mean, have you *seen*…"

'Ar 'ey, Scap!

Wonky bounded down from the tree and lolloped over.

"Good morning." Scapa laughed as he ran around behind her. "And how are you, then?"

"I'm all right, lass, thanks for asking, how about you? 'Ey, your arsehole smells lovely today, by the way."

"Ah, thank you, Wonk. That's really nice of you. I'm all right."

We could tell she wasn't.

"What's up?" I said. "Your two-plates not letting you up on the bed anymore?"

Scapa frowned, indignant.

"I'll have you know, my master *always* lets me up on the bed. No, absolutely nothing wrong in the bedroom department. Just…he seems a bit worried. Don't know what's wrong."

"Hey!" shouted Wonky, wagging his tail. "Me an' all!"

"Really?" said Scapa.

"Yeah! He almost forgot to fookin' feed me this morning. Just sat there listening to that radio, didn't he, shaking his head, rubbing 'is brow. I 'ad to bark as loud as I could just to get 'is fookin' attention!"

"What about you, Lineker?" said Scapa.

Reg *had* seemed a bit gloomy, come to think of it. I shrugged.

"Time of year, I expect. *Dos Platos* always get the doldrums in winter."

"Aye, 'spect you're right there, la'," said Wonky. "Come 'ead then, let's be off."

We made our way out of the clearing and found Reg with Wonky's and Scapa's owners in a huddle of bleary-eyed, serious faces, hunching their shoulders against the cold. Then we ran off, tumbling against each other as we went.

A voice met us at the crest of the hill. "What ho, chaps!"

The silhouette of an Irish setter stood proudly against the sky, tail sweeping in fine, slow arcs. Jeremy. He beamed at us as we approached. His chestnut coat shone and steamed in the rising sun.

"Top of the ruddy morning to you all!" he announced.

Jeremy liked to draw on his Irish lineage a little too much, but the truth was he was as posh as the queen's knickers.

We said our good mornings and circled around. Pebble was there too, a charcoal greyhound with a slender snout and a clipped tail. She was sitting patiently by her owner as she talked urgently into a phone. I noticed Jeremy's owner shaking her head at the ground.

"Your two-plates acting weird too?" I said.

"Well," said Jeremy, putting on a brave face. "I don't know about weird, but Mildred's certainly upset. She could barely get out of the door this morning for crying, poor love."

He looked wanly across at the stout woman in a wax jacket, who was patting Pebble's owner on the shoulder.

"Fuck me," I said.

"Quite," said Jeremy. "Fuck you indeed, and fuck me also, old boy. Fuck us all, in fact. Any sign of improvement, Pebs love?"

Pebble padded over and nosed Jeremy's midriff.

"Nowt," she said. "She smells like dead voles. That's fear, that is. Fear and dismay."

We all agreed that was exactly what fear and dismay smelled like.

"This is no good," said Scapa. "No good at all. I feel nervous."

Jeremy brightened.

"Not to worry. Probably just something going around, what? Wonky? Wonky, what's wrong, old sport?"

"Lineker," said Jeremy. He raised his eyes over my head.

"What?"

"Watch out."

*Boom!*

Stars flying, ribs heaving, the earth spinning, as if a hundred-pound boulder had just slammed into my side at forty miles an hour. Which, as it turned out, was almost exactly what had happened. Except the boulder was Wally.

"Hurr hurr hurr!"

His voice bellowed behind as I landed in a heap by a tree.

"Gotcha! Hurr!"

I raised my head and shook off the impact. "Fuck me, Wally, bit of warning, eh?"

"Nah, where's the fun in that? Hurr hurr hurr!"

Wally was a Staffordshire bull, face like a bear trap, coat the color of mud.

I tried to catch my breath. Through the mist and my winded haze I saw Scapa and Pebble darting off in a game of chase. Wonky and Jeremy were up in my face, barking their advice.

"Get up, man!" said Jeremy. "Give him what for!"

"Come 'ead, mate! Come 'ead!"

I heard Wally's chops slavering and his throat thick with grunts and wheezes, but before I could get to my feet, he'd charged me again and rolled me over. I'm ashamed to say I yelped, but I was ready for him on the third attack, leaping to one side and springing onto his back, clamping my mouth around one of his gristly ears.

"Get off! Get off me!"

Wally bucked and swayed, but I tightened my jaw, growling. Heinz 57 I may be, but there's definitely a terrier in there somewhere; I'm a tenacious cunt.

Jeremy and Wonky were still barking their support, and somewhere in the distance I saw Scapa pin Pebble. The mist was rising, dawn giving into the day. I tightened again, just a bit more pressure and—

"Ow!"

Wally yelped like a little pup and I let go, laughing. With the game won, I jumped off and took a piss.

"Good show, good show!"

Jeremy was virtually clapping. Wonky ran up and nudged me in the shoulder.

"Nice one, lad! That was well good that was."

Wally snuffled in the dirt and pawed at his ear. Then he was up again and after a few snorts he was standing, grinning from ear to ear, which, let me tell you, is a considerable distance.

"That was good," he said, out of breath. "Good. Good fun. Hurr."

He smacked his lips and looked about, eyes landing on Wonky. A funny look crept across his big mug. Wonky anchored himself, worried.

"What are you looking at, Wall?" he said.

"Nothing," lied Wally. He licked his lips.

"Wally," growled Wonky. "Don't even think about it."

"Come on." Wally winked. "Let's have a go. Just a bit."

"Wally!"

Now, you must remember that Wally was a full-fledged, paid-up pack member. He was our pal and we would have died for him, as he would for us. That's just the way it goes. But I would have been the first to admit that he did have a few strange habits. Things he took an interest in, things he liked to, er, *do*.

One of them, the main thing, in fact, what you might call Wally's guilty pleasure, could be a little unsettling. You'd have been forgiven for making certain assumptions about him if you didn't know him, but you'd have been wrong. I know for a fact he was not *like that*. Not that I would have minded if he was, you understand—if you prefer the tradesman's entrance of a well-endowed mastiff to the front door of a pretty little spaniel, that's your own business—but that wasn't Wally's thing. I knew this because I'd seen him balls-deep in every type of bitch that dared to flounce within a hundred yards of his considerable snout. He'd had everything—bassets, Danes, Chihuahuas, Afghans, the lot. No, Wally was most definitely not a woofter.

But he did like to do things. And the thing that Wally most liked to do, if he was of the right mind, was lick your balls.

And right there and then, he wanted to lick Wonky's.

I stood with Jeremy and watched the pair of them race around the common—Wonky terrified, Wally delirious with pleasure. Jeremy sighed.

"Beautiful thing to behold, isn't it?" he said. "The hunt and the chase. Wild and free. *Predator and prey*."

"You're right there, Jezza," I said. "Beautiful."

And it was beautiful. There and then on that cold, frosty day with my pack on our turf, with everything just the way it should be. Beautiful. We'd almost forgotten about our two-plates when Pebble called us over.

"Look," she said. "Over here."

We all turned to see. Our owners had formed a circle, and not just with themselves, but with others too. You usually see dog walkers having little chats together on The Rye, but this was something else. There were twenty of them, thirty, maybe more, some with dogs— even those we knew had no business being on The Rye—those without dogs, runners, parents with children, every color face you like: black, white, brown, yellow, pink, red, all congregating together, all talking, some with their arms flying, some arguing, some consoling the ones who'd lost it.

And swarming from them all in icy tendrils on the breeze was the thick smell of voles.

Sirens sounded up the street, then from far away I could hear voices floating in, roaring.

"What the devil?" said Jeremy.

And suddenly it wasn't so beautiful anymore. Suddenly it felt like everything was about to change. And take it from me, for a dog, that's just about the worst feeling in the world. We have to know where the lines run. Where things are, when things happen, the good bits and the bad bits. That's what makes us happy—nice, neat lines and no changes, thank you very much. But when those lines get mixed up or removed, it's no joke. It feels like someone's taking a piss in your soul.

Our tails went down, and we all just wanted to be at our masters' legs. We all wanted to be in that safe space we called home.

The second bit I remember was much worse.

The year had dwindled, winter letting spring have a go, then summer yawning in with all its promises of long days and snoozes in the sun. Except this time there were no such promises. My lines had been taken away. Life wasn't the same anymore.

The days were full of the sound of shouting, mostly from outside, but also from the television, which was permanently on. Usually I didn't mind this, but now I hid from it. It was just a blur of the same things again and again—that flag waving, and those purple jackets, bold letters, and loud voices telling people how things were going to be from now on, and pictures showing what happened to those who didn't agree.

Down on the street, there were loud engines and gunshots that made me dive beneath the sofa, where I spent much of the time in those days, it has to be said. My skyline—my most favorite thing— changed beyond recognition. There was always at least one explosion a day, sometimes more. A distant boom, the windows rattling, and Reg looking out as flames and a black plume rose in the sky. Then, as the smoke cleared, either a ragged scar in a rooftop, or another building falling. Soon, Reg kept the curtains closed. It was hot, and stifling, and dark. Most of the time, we just stayed inside, and on the rare occasions when Reg took me to The Rye, I hardly ever saw the others.

This last day I did, though, if only for a second.

It was June, and a warm drizzle swept down from the leafy canopies of One Tree Hill as we reached the park entrance. The air was full of mist—or smoke, it was hard to tell anymore. I could feel the electricity before we saw anything, the unmistakable fizz of humans with purpose, meeting a turning point. Like before, there were more gathered there than usual. Someone had set up a makeshift stage by the picnic area, and a West Indian woman with long braids and a rainbow hat was talking on a megaphone. I could smell meat cooking, and there were cups being handed out. The woman's words were urgent, full of kindness and strength. I could taste the steaming crowd around her, surging with citrus, blood, and steel. No voles anymore—this was the smell of fresh hope.

Before long the southern field of The Rye was packed, the long grass, untended since the previous summer, stamped down by the boots of those marching toward the podium and scurrying with the feet of children, and dogs.

"Lineker!" I heard a familiar voice calling. I looked up and saw a gaunt figure trotting through the mist. He looked so thin I hardly recognized him at first, and his coat was dull and shabby and crusted with filth.

"Jez," I said, sniffing his backside. "Blahdy 'ell, mate, what's happened to you?"

Jeremy looked me up and down and offered his nose half-heartedly at my rear.

"Lean times, old friend," he said. "Lean times. I can see you're struggling too."

Dogs don't do mirrors in the same way as you do, so it had been a long time since I'd given myself a once-over. I did so then and saw that he was right. I was thin too, and the hair on my paws seemed a little sparser than I would have liked.

There was a cheer from the crowd, and we looked up to see hands in the air. Some of the two-plates had banners and flags. And smiles too. Hungry smiles.

"Any idea what's happening?" I asked.

"No, but it feels good, doesn't it? Smells good?"

I barked in agreement.

"Half of ruddy Peckham must be here, wouldn't you say?" said Jeremy. "Not to mention East Dulwich, Nunhead, Forest Hill. It's packed. Something's happening, definitely."

We looked at each other, having arrived at the same thought.

"Find the others?" I said.

Jeremy looked up at his owner, who was shuffling forward, trying to get a closer look. Reg was doing the same.

"Don't expect they'll mind if we're gone for a minute," said Jeremy. He looked back at me, tail wagging. "You're on."

We darted through legs, following scents, trying to pick up on something. Sure enough, it wasn't long before we got the waxy, veal-like aroma of Scapa, followed by the tripe of Wally. Before we knew it, we'd found them all sitting in a clearing by a log at the edges of the crowd. They looked just as skinny as us.

Joyous barks, tails wagging faster than I thought possible, sniffing and bounding and rolling. What with all the excitement of the roaring crowd, and that smell of lemons and metal and blood, and the sound of laughter coming from the stage, and the shaft of sunlight that broke through at the same time, the sight of each other was like heaven falling down upon us all. We scampered about the clearing, yelling for joy, certain that this was the end of something and the beginning of something else, that things would get back to normal soon.

But the feeling only lasted a moment. I stopped to sit down and catch my breath, and as I did, I looked between them—Jeremy, Pebble, Wally, Wonky, and, finally, Scapa. But when my eyes landed on hers, she did a strange thing. She jumped and cowered in fright, looking up and to the right, as if some invisible hand had struck her. Within the space of a second, we were all doing the same. Sometimes, when you're deep in The Howl, events have a way of making themselves known before they've arrived.

I could feel the air tighten and relieve itself of noise. The crowd seemed to hush, the roars of approval silenced in an instant, like a trapdoor opening beneath them. They turned toward the city skyline, and the woman speaking turned to look upward too.

We took one last look at each other, my pack and I, one last look to keep close, but it wasn't long enough, and it never would be. I wanted to scream, to run, to burst through it all and escape from the moment as it drew nearer. But there was no escape.

The sky lit up in a furious blaze of white light and shuddered with an upside-down thump as if all of the air was being sucked from my ears. And then I was running, falling, tumbling away down the hill, away from the pack, away to find Reg, as the ground rumbled beneath me.

# ANOTHER LIFE

## REGINALD HARDY'S JOURNAL
### DECEMBER 4, 2021

I AM AFRAID I may have spoken too soon; Bertha is struggling. I have been trying to ignore the jiggering sound all night, but there's no getting around it—the generator needs some attention.

It is a fairly simple fix, of course; a couple of new bearings should do it. The only problem is that I have a feeling the only place I shall find such bearings is on the outer reaches of my operational boundary—an extremity to which, happily, I have had neither the necessity nor the desire to stray since before the bombs.

The first was only tiny by all accounts. From what I heard it was 100 tons, just a fraction of what landed on Hiroshima. Ground zero was Kings Cross Station, the resulting blast and fireball taking out most of Regent's Park, Camden, the British Library, the British Museum, Great Ormond Street...

The second one was a touch bigger and aboveground too, so it packed more of a punch. It made short work of Westminster, removed a hefty slice from Buckingham Palace, and turned St. James's Park into a swamp. A third and fourth—little ones again—detonated near Canary Wharf. I saw those from the flat: spectacular to watch those banks crumble like dust.

They were not enough to flatten London, but they did rob it of power. The grid was still running then (just), but down on the ground we had frazzled substations, melted cables, and blown fuses by the bucketload. So, for electricians like me, business was booming. Every mushroom cloud, you might say.

I remember those few weeks running around trying to get to every job. Absolute pandemonium. Most of the work was impossible to complete, but I saw it as my duty to try. It was easy at first because the streets were suddenly quiet, as if the shock had made the population shrink inside like mollusks. To some extent I expect it was a misplaced fear of fallout that kept people indoors, but the prevailing wind was from the south and I knew enough about blast zones and radiation levels to know that the chances of being affected were fairly slim. I took a calculated risk.

Either way, the streets were mine, and I whizzed my Transit around them like a pinball on an open table. It was a joyful time, really—if you leave aside the threat of nuclear cataclysm and social collapse, of course.

My freedom was, however, brief. The panic, confusion, and fear those dirty great bombs caused—what they were *designed* to cause, in retrospect—soon set in. Reality ensued, plans were formed, and somewhere within that woeful, muddled aftermath, an exodus began; the good people of London fled their homes.

I was turning onto Queen's Road when I saw the first car leave. The driver—a worn-out looking chap with bags under his eyes and hair like a wind-ravaged haystack—was hunched by necessity over the wheel, the rest of the vehicle bulging with his family and their many possessions. Two mattresses were strapped to the roof, and perched upon them, lashed down with two bungie cords, was—of all things—a washing machine.

I watched them roar past, looking rather comical as they careered around the corner and sailed off to whatever new life they had planned—presumably one in which automatic garment cleaning was still a high priority.

Such sights grew in regularity as the idea spread. Panic exploded exponentially as more and more people loaded up and took to the streets—a chain reaction as unstoppable as the ones that had caused the whole mess in the first place.

After a week or so of clogged roundabouts and the air thick with fumes and car horns, the streets gradually grew quiet. Tower blocks and tenements were drained of life. The shops and offices were shut, unguarded. The mansions of Dulwich were locked up and boarded against looters as if the owners had merely taken an extended break to Barbados or whatever tax havens they kept their second homes in.

Three years on and those windows are still covered in planks.

People ran away. And you might say they were perfectly right to—I know she would have—because those bombs really were just the start.

Everyone knew who was behind it. Deep down they did. At first there was all the pomp and flag-waving from that mob down the Wheatsheaf. "Effing terrorists!" they shouted out on the streets, beers in hand. "Effing Muslims! Enough is enough!" and all that tripe. But they knew. We *all* knew. It was him.

For the life of me, I could not tell you what that man stood for or what he wanted. I will be the first to admit that I am not a great political mind—*each to his own* is about as much of an opinion as I can muster—but I will listen to them, these people who get it into their heads that they can run things better than the last, or that they have thought of some bold, new direction for us, or that they care more than the others, or that they understand the common man, or that they won't take it lying down anymore. Or any of that twaddle. I will listen to them, just to give them a chance and see if anything they say chimes with me.

But not that man. I switched him off whenever I saw him on the television, which was all the time toward the end. There was something about him that made my blood run cold, him and that haircut of his, and that smile like a bank manager offering you a loan, and those gorillas lining up behind him in their purple jackets and gold plumes. Remote, off, gone.

I ran into some of his boys a few times. They called themselves the BU, but most just called them Purples on account of their jackets. It was after the exodus and I was doing my rounds, seeing if I could pick up some spare parts in Denmark Hill—a little close to my border, it must be said, but these were desperate times—and as I turned onto a side street, there they were, blocking the road with their big Purple van. Five of them were lined up in front of it, guns across those ridiculous jackets of theirs. They saw me and I stopped, letting the engine run while I decided on a suitable course of action.

*Run, Reginald? Or remain calm?*

I had no reason to run. But still.

Behind them was a trail of people. Women, children, men, white, black, brown. They were all cuffed together and, one by one, they were swabbed.

Swabbing was their means of assessing us—*sorting the wheat from the chaff*, you might say. They carried these devices like Breathalyzers with a clear plastic probe on the end. If they had a reason to suspect you as an undesirable, then they stopped you, placed the probe upon your tongue, and waited while the machine performed its tests and announced your fate. A green light and a chirp was good news. Red light and a low beep—not so good.

I found a pile of them once, abandoned in a dumpster, so I took a few home to open them up, see what was what. I discovered very little—inside was a circuit board attached to a loose, empty vial, a leaking battery, and a fragile probe all attached to one another with shoddy soldering and flimsy wires. No wonder they had been abandoned. There was nothing I could salvage from them, so I replaced them in the dumpster and went on my way, still none the wiser about what dreadful chemical reactions went on inside, or what an "undesirable" meant.

All I know is I was never selected for swabbing, so I can only assume that my fifty-two-year-old, balding, overweight, white-skinned, male appearance was—somehow—"desirable."

But this lot, unfortunately, were not. Red lights and beeps all around. I watched as they were herded into the van, heads hanging in miserable silence.

One of the guards removed his sunglasses when he saw me looking and made some remark to his friend, who laughed. The others laughed too, but their smiles fell away when the first one took a step toward me. I made my decision, put the van into reverse, and pressed hard on the accelerator pedal, spinning around the corner and whipping it into first, just like they do in the films. I never looked back.

I have not seen anyone with the letters BU on their shirt for a long time. But then again, neither have I set foot near the edge of my domain, so I have reasons to be cautious.

Still, I am a trained electrician and I know full well when a generator needs new bearings. So it is off to the shops we shall go.

# SMELL

## LINEKER

I KNEW SOMETHING WAS up straightaway. First off, Reg was awake before me, which never happens. I heard a bang and jumped up, straight into attack pose I was, growling, thought, *We've got company! Right, then, Lineker, smarten up, son, time to get busy, get involved.* I was a bit excited if I'm honest; intruder or not, it would be the first human I'd seen in ages, apart from Reg, but…no. It was just him. The door was open and he was out in the stairwell banging on that thing with a hammer. His flashlight wobbled in the dark.

Felt a bit sheepish then, I can tell you. Bit useless. Cowered a bit, little whimper, tail down and all that. After all, if there's one thing a dog's supposed to bring to the table, it's a bit of security, isn't it? So what fucking use am I if I can't be relied on to wake up at the same time as my master? Not a good bit to start the day with. Not at all.

Still, I stopped feeling sorry for myself and turned my mind instead to the question of why he might be up so early. I thought I'd take a look, and try to make amends in the process. I had a shake, jumped down from the sofa, and went out.

When he's out there with that thing in the morning, it's usually to start it. A few tweaks, a few switches, nice firm tug on the cord, and it's away. Noisy thing, didn't like it at first but I got used to it, especially once I'd worked out that it meant heat and light. But it wasn't making any noise now, and Reg was hammering away on that thing like he wanted to murder it.

I whimpered and sniffed his trousers, but he shouted at me, so I slunk away into the corner feeling like he must be pissed off at me for sleeping in. Then he shouted even louder at the machine, which made me feel better. It was the machine's fault. Stupid fucking thing, it wasn't even awake yet, even with all that hammering! Must be properly sick, I thought.

After a few more clangs and tweaks and a pull on the cord brought nothing, Reg kicked the side of the machine and stormed back inside. The beast gave a sad wobble in the dying glow of his flashlight. Felt a bit sorry for it, if I'm honest. Then I followed Reg back inside.

It was winter and cold, and I was getting hungry, but I didn't feel like asking him for food. He was busy marching around the flat, opening curtains, looking out and shaking his head, swearing, banging into walls, knocking things over, opening cupboards and shoving supplies into his bag. I watched him, worried about his mood, but also feeling a tingle of excitement in my paws and nose. I hadn't seen him pack like this for a good while.

I looked out through the window. Anemic light was slithering from the sun, and I watched those distant buildings crawl out from the darkness like great, unknowable beasts, and I wondered: Were we going for a little adventure?

Fuck me, wouldn't that be sweet?

It was still dark when we left, and Reg had to use the flashlight to guide us down the stairwell. It's ten flights of stairs past closed doors—doors behind which I can still smell the funk of the ones who'd lived there, like they were in such a hurry to leave they'd forgotten to pack the most important things—*their very beings*—and then we're out onto the street.

Bracing? Fuck me, it was brass monkeys out there. The snot froze in my snout and my hairs crackled with frost. Reg had his big coat on, trudging ahead in great clouds of steam with his flashlight swaying. What a sight, like a machine he was. It stopped me in my tracks, awestruck by the magic of him, the magic of *you* with all your know-how and wherewithal and what have you. Geniuses you are, the lot of you. And there's me with just my shaggy coat and paws. I have to laugh sometimes, I really do. Pathetic.

When it was too cold to stand still any longer, I had another shake and scampered over the planks and masonry lying outside the block and followed Reg out into the morning, still hungry, still cold, but feeling alive.

We passed the Victorian cemetery where we used to walk sometimes. It was always an old place, untended and left to grow over so the graves started bulging up under the tree roots. I used to like going there. I'd dart in and out of the broken tombs, getting good whiffs of all that old, dusty death mingling with ancient wood and dirt.

That cemetery used to look out of place next to the concrete and metal of the roads and estates around it, like an abandoned house gone to ruin on a row of proud homes. But now it's starting to fit in. Everything goes that way; you can hear it. Deep within The Howl, down in the low notes way below the twitters of birds, the cracking of insect shells and the babble of fast-flowing water, is the sound of old wood groaning beneath tons of earth, and of sap rising, and greasy vines creeping into stone like a thousand claws.

Over The Rye we went, northeast this time, which we never do, and then out past the old playground hanging with frayed, swingless rope, and farther, farther, till my eyes widen at the thrill of new scent flirting with my nostrils, farther out to the fringes of everything I'm used to. I can feel it coming—not with my eyes or my ears or my paws, but with my tongue and snout. A whole new world of smells awaits me near the border.

There are no words to explain to you how it is to be a dog.

Likewise, you can't tell me what it's like to be a human. I'd have no chance, would I? Not with all that brilliant stuff banging around in your noggins. Amazing! So much to think about, with all those times and dates and places and appointments. Then you've got your telephones and football teams and what have you; your haircuts and clothes and films, and then all those objects you have to move from place to place like keys and books and cups and plates. Mind-boggling. I can sit and watch Reg for hours with no fucking clue what he's doing. I just bask there, dumb with love, until he's finished.

You've always been a busy lot, you sapiens. Climbing, foraging, skinning, sharpening. Planting, turning, carving, building. Crossing oceans. Waging wars. Looking up. Looking down. But thinking— that's what you do the most. You gaze up and drift away and none of us can guess where you go. Fucking Einsteins, the lot of you.

Take away all that thought and replace it with smell. Yeah, that's the nearest I can get to describing how it is to be a dog.

Smells are like ghosts of the things you once did or felt. Every emotion has its own smell—I've already mentioned vole-like fear, and that zingy metal tang of hope—and every individual has their own version of that smell. Some have feelings that others don't, feelings that are just for them, their own personal blend with its own distinct perfume. You have to be around them for a while before you recognize what it stands for. Like my Reg, he has this one blend I've not smelled on anyone else. It's a kind of desperate terror, deer flesh and urine, with a sadness, dead orchids and crushed chicken bones, but the whole thing's kind of tempered and protected in this film of ice and thistle, like a sack of bones and photographs left to freeze on a winter moor. I don't want to be anywhere near it when it comes because I know how it feels to him, and it makes me feel it too.

You leave ghosts everywhere you go. They trail behind you on buses and streets, in bedrooms and empty stairwells, along hospital corridors and through dense forest. And when you meet others, the ghosts of how they make you feel remain long after you've parted company, so that they merge and create bigger ghosts, like fights and arguments, and laughter, and tears, and fucking. You leave them and they stay there, sometimes forever.

If I seem a little distracted by some tree, or post or corner or other, it's not because I'm just having a sniff; it's because I'm seeing how something played out. So don't get angry if I don't come back when you call—I might just be checking if someone's all right.

That's my world: ghosts everywhere. Ghosts that lead to other ghosts and those to others, trailing off forever in time and space. I could tell you the whole story of this city if you let me. I could describe the taste of Boudicca's sweat as she led the revolt against the Romans, who fled and who fought when the Vikings rolled in, the first lick of flame from the Great Fire, the dying rooms of the plague, the children's fear in the underground tunnels when Hitler's bombs dropped. This snout of mine, it's a time machine. A fucking *time machine*.

Of course, some smells are simpler than others. There are your good old-fashioned, straight down the line, smack on the nose, no questions asked, pleasant smells. Like a nice cunt. Very pleasant indeed. I think we all agree that a nice, strong cunt beats most smells on a good day—pears, seaweed, limestone, and honey, lovely. And cock, equally inspiring when you get a good one, all musky and pelty like ripe bananas and cheese and pork chops, ooh, getting my snout all wet at the thought. And balls—don't forget balls, as I'm sure my dear friend Wally would have said.

Other ones: meat, shit, piss, grass, carrots, dirt, vomit, sweat. All good.

Then there are the more confusing smells; the ones that are hard to categorize. Like fox. If I get wind of a fox, I don't know whether I want to cuddle it, fuck it, or pull out its guts and eat them in front of it. It's extremely confusing for me.

Foxes are close to wolves too, although not like us. They loped off much earlier to go and do their thing, which, as far as I can tell, was to shrink and bury themselves and then skulk about looking all haunted and screaming. Can't say I like them much, apart from the cuddling and fucking bit, obviously. It's not like with wolves. I don't think they're dicks; it's just... Well, they've got that whole cat thing going on, and just, honestly, don't get me started.

There are quite a few foxes about now, much more than before, and they don't just come out at night either. Whole families trot about the place in broad daylight, bold as brass, kids making a right racket with their little, bright faces and fluffy tales and their little legs that you *just want to*... Calm down, son, deep breaths, deep breaths. I'm telling you, though...foxes.

They're fatter now too—not like before when they looked like rotten sacks of pipe cleaners. As Reg and I crossed Dulwich Park, hacking our way through the plain fields and crossing the swamp that used to be the boating lake, I could smell their ghosts. Hordes of them, sets everywhere.

Other confusing smells include spiders, flies, marmalade, and toilet cleaner.

We stopped in the white wooden building that used to be the café, now stained brown and crawling with weeds. It was light by then and ghostly white beams roamed over the tables and chairs strewn with dirty plates. Reg pushed his way through to the kitchen, disturbing a few ducks that were resting there. After a quick search he came out with some bottles of water, one of which he opened and poured for me to lick at. Then he broke up some crackers he'd found and fed the bits to me, one by one.

We pushed on through the park and followed the creepered streets for a mile or two until the smell of foxes began to vanish behind us. As it did, others blew in on the wind, fresh and new. These weren't old ghosts at all, and when we turned onto a thin road with high walls near the station, my hackles rose.

Because there are the bad smells too, like Reg's ziplocked fear-sadness, and voles, and burning hair.

And them.

I'd only seen them twice, though I'd smelled them a thousand times. And I did what I did whenever I caught that smell. I barked until my lungs burst.

# REASONS TO
# BE FEARFUL

**REGINALD HARDY'S JOURNAL**

**DECEMBER 5, 2021**

I GOT LINEKER WHEN he was a pup, ten years after she left.

"You could try a dog?" said the therapist. "The company of an animal can sometimes help you move on."

*Move on* was a phrase I had been hearing rather a lot at the time, mostly from my brother on the other end of a phone line. I am sure he was only trying to help, but the thing is, sometimes moving on is the last thing you want to do. What you want to do is move back.

Still, I had always quite fancied the idea of a dog, so I took a trip to Battersea Dogs Home and spent an hour edging between the cages full of Staffies and pits hammering and yowling at me to pick them. As if I would! Needy, clawing beasts they were, with desperate eyes all looking at me to save them, look after them. Protect them.

Suddenly getting a dog did not seem like such a good idea, and I had almost made up my mind to leave. But then I saw him.

He was sitting at the back of his cage, quiet as you like, while the room howled and clawed around him. We gave each other the once-over. He had a deeply familiar quality, and the way he sat reminded me of something I had once heard about conflict: for every great battle, for every great war between two tribes, there is always a third one sitting up on the hill, watching and waiting to see how the dice fall.

An engaging idea that—keep your head down, stay out of trouble, and wait for the world to blow itself apart. Then enjoy the peace and quiet that comes afterward. I liked it.

*Perhaps*, I thought, *this chap feels the same.*

When we were finished sizing each other up, he gave a single thump of his tail against his blanket, and if I had had a tail and a blanket, I do believe I would have done the same.

Click. That was that.

I bought some books and videos and had a go at training him. A shiny-faced American in a tight tank top grinned from the screen and explained how dogs need to know their place, how they are only happy when they are working *for* you, how one should not coddle them but lay down clear and consistent boundaries. I had to be his *master*. I tried, for a bit at least, but my heart just was not in it. All I could see when I stood there pretending to be all dominant, trying to project the right *energy* and assume the right tone, was that chucklehead on the screen with his white teeth and muscles. And I thought to myself: *You want to be the master, do you? Is that why you got a dog?*

So I gave up. I managed to get him to come when I called him and sit when I told him to, sometimes. Everything else, I thought, would come naturally.

But I stood there on that foggy street with voices snapping from around the corner—some shouting orders and another one pleading, followed by a child's wails. I stood there with Lineker barking at my heels, giving away our location, and I wished to heaven I'd done more.

"Lineker!" I hissed. He kept barking, legs out, fangs bared, snout pointing ahead. Oh to have a special whistle, oh to have a secret command, oh to be the *master*.

"Lineker! Be quiet!"

At this point I had already resigned myself to the strong possibility that one of us might die. I knew who was around the corner and so did Lineker, but we both seemed to have very different ideas about how things would play out if we met them. He was moments from bolting off to check his theory, so I thought, *It's going to be him, not me*. I was ready to run, and if he didn't run with me, then that was that.

But, to my surprise, he stopped. He stopped and sat and looked up at me, licking his chops. I stared down at him for a moment, and he gave an impatient snuffle, as if to say: *All right, so what's next?*

"Good boy," I said, still stunned.

The voices had stopped. I heard whimpering and the sound of boots coming toward us through the fog. I looked down at Lineker again.

"Come," I ventured. And what do you know? He did.

I led him into a side street and tried the first door I found. It was locked. The bootsteps were closer now, two sets of them marching out of time. Gunmetal clinked against their buckles as they walked.

I tried the next door—locked as well—then scurried to the third, but Lineker stayed put with his eyes on the street.

I thought the spell had broken and my brief success at masterfulness had evaporated. Any minute now he'd start barking again and the game would be up. I tried the door and it opened, and was ready to push my way in and leave him. But then—another first—he turned at the squeak of the door's hinges and ran toward me, through my legs, and inside. As the bootsteps reached the alleyway, I slipped in after him and pulled the door shut as quietly as I could.

I backed away and stopped where Lineker was sitting, on a thread-bare scrap of carpet at the bottom of a staircase. We both watched the small, frosted window as deep voices approached. I opened a hopeful, quelling palm to Lineker.

The bright pane darkened purple as heels scuffed to a halt outside. I kept still, frozen as much by my fear of Lineker's response as anything. But he seemed to follow my lead, dropping to the floor with his chin on his paws.

The figures turned this way and that, exchanging words and making slow ripples in the distorted glass. Then one leaned on the door.

It creaked and bulged under his weight, and for a second I thought I might have neglected to close it properly. But it held. Lineker flinched and I dropped to my knees, putting a hand on his head. A lighter chinked and struck. Soon I smelled cigarette smoke. As the first inhaled, he threw back his head and it hit the glass. Another flinch from Lineker. Then he growled.

It was quiet, but it was enough to make the two men spin on their heels. They stood back from the door, and I prepared myself for their entrance, trying to decide whether I should bolt for the front door. But we'd come in through the back; the front led out onto the street where we'd heard the voices. We were trapped on either side. So it was up the stairs and hide, or face them.

I had no real reason to be afraid of them; I had never been picked out for swabbing, like I say. But there was still something about them, something unpredictable that made me want to stay as far away from them as possible. So my preference was for the stairs. I was about to make a dash for it when I heard an engine start in the distance, and through the window I saw the two purple-capped heads turn and disappear.

When I was sure they were gone I stood up, released the breath I had been holding, and looked around. The place was London housing stock, part of a terrace of two-up, two-downs like most other streets. It was quiet and dusty, carpets pulled back, papers on the stairs, and a trash bag with clothes falling out of it halfway down. I walked through to the front, treading carefully in case the old boards creaked.

The sitting room was full of old furniture and newspapers. Dust drifted in a shaft of light squeezing between the closed, maroon curtains. I got down on my knees and crawled to the window, peering over the ledge. Lineker followed close to my hip.

Through the gap in the curtains, I could see a flatbed truck with a small crane at the back. Its flanks were adorned with familiar rippling flags. The engine was running, black smoke chugging from the exhaust, and five Purples stood around the back with guns across their waists. A sixth gripped the hair of a man on his knees who had wild, rolling eyes. It was difficult to tell from the state of his swollen face and bloodied beard, but he looked as if he was—or had been—a fairly average chap. White skin, fair hair, nothing that would have marked him as an undesirable.

A few feet away stood a woman and a child, restrained by a guard.

The woman was dusty-skinned—Middle-Eastern perhaps. She was crying, the girl holding out her hand to her father with her face crumpled in a frown. The man's eyes found hers, and he tried to smile in reassurance.

The Purple was shouting down at him. "What? What did you say?"

The man shook his head. "No, no, please, I don't…"

"What?"

The Purple looked back at the others in mock confusion. "Can't fucking understand you!" he said and spat on his face. To laughter, he then yanked a swabbing device from his belt and thrust the probe into the man's mouth. Looking at his watch in mock boredom, he waited for the result.

Five seconds. Ten. Fifteen. Chirp, green light, all clear.

Released, the man sprawled on the ground as the Purple shepherded his family toward the truck. The man reached out for them.

"Don't take my family, please!"

The Purple stopped, twisting his face as if he was talking to an idiot.

"Does Daddy want to come too?"

He turned to one of his boys, jabbing a thumb at the truck. "Get him up."

Two of the other Purples dragged him by the armpits toward the truck, upon which his wife and daughter now sat. I sensed relief. The man nodded his head, saying "Thank you, thank you," and held his arm up to his wife. She smiled through her tears and reached down to him.

Wherever they were taking this man and his family, I suspected that it was not going to be good. But it was hard not to feel hope for them as I looked out on that quiet street bathed in mist and milky light. I thought perhaps things might turn out all right.

I saw a wavering smile on the man's face as he took his wife's hand. His daughter reached out to help. Perhaps they felt the same hope I did.

We were wrong to. Hope was elsewhere that morning.

Before anyone knew what was happening, the two guards had slapped something around the man's torso. He stammered and cried as they pulled buckles and braces tight.

"What? What are you... No, no!"

His family was now restrained at the front of the flatbed. The woman screamed in horror as they lowered the hook of the crane and attached it to her husband's harness. Then they gave him some slack, laughed, and shoved him away from the truck.

The engine revved and the Purples jumped up on the flatbed, grinning as they rolled away down the street. They were slow at first and the man walked behind, keeping pace. Then, as the wheels turned faster, he broke into a jog. I watched them crawl down the street. Again, hope dawned on me as it clearly did with them, perhaps this was just some humiliation, something to show him off. The Purples jeered and egged him on, and the man played along with a nervous laugh, tripping as he jogged.

But the jeers stopped and one of them banged the roof of the cab. The engine spun, and the truck shot away down the street, wrenching the man forward. His head whipped back as he fell, and I heard thumps, laughter, squealing brakes, and two screams—one high, and one higher still.

When the street was quiet again, I pulled the curtain closed.

This is what happens, is it not? This is what happens when you try to live together. Something always snaps. Someone like that man with the bank manager's smile comes along and puts an end to things. It is not as if it is the first time.

It is change that does it—change and people. So steer clear of them both, I say. Stay out of the way, up on the hill.

# PURPLES

WE FOUND THE BEARINGS, as I expected, in a huge, flat-roofed warehouse lined with pallets of dead plants and rusted barbecues. A society of pigeons had sprung up in its rafters since I had last visited. We took our spoils and wandered homeward, keeping to the smaller streets and avoiding the main roads.

I found a good stick so we could hack through the parklands, and we came across some brambles in Belair that still had a few withered berries deep within the thorns. I plucked them out and threw a couple at Lineker, but he dropped them in the dirt with a cough. I ate mine. I was never much one for my five-a-day in all honesty, but it is foolish to pass up fresh fruit now.

It turned into rather a nice day as we neared home. Something I had never appreciated before London emptied out was the sound of no sound. If you have lived here all your life, then your ears grow accustomed to the noise of it all: the traffic and roadworks, sirens in the middle of the night, thieves hammering the speed bumps, next door's sex and shouting, planes and trains spinning by all day. It never stops. Then, suddenly, you wake one day to this, no sound at all. Just birds and animals and the sound of the day rolling beneath it.

I had only once heard silence like it.

I can remember it, if I choose to—the warm sun on our faces and that dreamy roar of quiet broken only by the buzzing of a bicycle chain and the gentle ripples of water beside us. It was a long time ago. A whole other before.

As we approached the turning to our road, I must say I was feeling pretty chipper. My dog was at my feet, zipping about in the foliage, the sun was high, and we were safe. What's more, I had my bearings, and I was looking forward to working on Bertha. For men like me of a practical bent, there is nothing quite like a closed door, a full set of tools, and an endless project with no distractions. Absolute bliss.

It would give me a chance to clear my head, I thought, and take my mind off that bloody book.

This Duchess, see... No, forget it.

But as we reached the corner I heard a noise. There were more voices, shouts from ahead.

*Again?* I thought. *Surely not.* No sign of anything remotely purple for over a year and then two come along at once. What rotten luck.

I held Lineker's collar and peered around the corner. Exactly 208 yards away (I knew because I had walked and measured the road home a great many times) parked outside Seton Bayley Tower, our block—*right outside it*—was a truck. I pulled my head back and huffed to myself. This was too much. I mean, out in Brixton, fair enough, but here? What were they doing here, in Peckham, in *my domain*?

I extended my neck to get a closer look. *Odd*, I thought. It was a truck all right, but it was not BU. It was green, an old army truck, and standing behind it were—I could hardly believe it—soldiers.

I almost pinched myself. Soldiers. There had been no sign of them since the tanks, and those chaps had not stuck around for long.

One of the tanks is still there, as it happens, lodged in the betting shop window with its turret burst open like a tin of beans speared with dynamite. Five days—one week, maximum; that's how long they lasted before they retreated from those Purple swarms. They left beneath volleys of bullets, hoots, and jeers and never came back.

But now this.

What *was* this?

I lifted my marvelous binoculars, adjusted the focus—lovely action on that dial—and there they were, large as life in helmets and full combat uniform. I counted one, two, three, four, five, six of them, each with a gun and a nervous expression. The back of the truck was open, and they were scanning the street. One of them was talking in a quiet, controlled voice, as if he was trying not to sound too frightening. I crept out to take a look and almost dropped my binocs in shock. There, along the wall, was a row of children going to the bathroom on Seton Bayley Tower.

Children.

Half of them were little boys, bending their knees in an effort to make the streams of their urine reach as high as possible. The rest were girls searching the rubble for a safe place to squat. All wore brown coats, shorts, and hats.

"Quick as you can, quick as you can," I heard the soldier say, like a nervous father on a school run. I turned my binoculars toward him.

He was young, late twenties perhaps, fit but hungry-looking. He exchanged glances with the others, and I could tell he did not want to be there any longer than he had to.

Children being transported by soldiers. And they were relieving themselves on my home. How dare they.

"Come on, Lineker," I said. "Let's go home."

We edged out into the middle of the street and made our approach. About halfway down, as I had expected, one of them saw me.

"Halt!" he cried, dropping to his knees with his gun raised. The children cried in alarm as their six protectors jumped into a well-rehearsed defensive formation, three of them lining up to face me down, with two others guarding the truck's sides and the last gathering the youngsters. Lineker barked, but then reconsidered and let out a submissive whine.

"Stay where you are, hands in the air!"

I stopped.

"This is my home," I ventured.

"Stay where you are," he repeated.

"I live here."

We stayed like that for a while. The children were proving difficult to shepherd, some still in midflow, and a couple of the girls unwilling to leave the privacy and safety of their doorway. One of the other soldiers went to help, but they still seemed a long way off getting them on board. That had to happen before I reached them; I did not want to risk the chance of contact.

"I just want to get to my flat," I said.

"Stay. Where. You. Are," he insisted.

"Please—"

As I spoke, two of the soldiers popped their heads up to see past me. I heard a familiar rumbling, and doom prickled on my neck. I turned to look, afraid of what I would see, but sure enough, speeding up the main road about half a mile behind was a purple truck. A crane hook swayed in its wake. Something was still attached to it.

I turned back, eyes wide, eager to move. The soldiers were directing orders between one another, my mark edging toward me with his gun still raised.

"Stay where you are!" he shouted.

I shook my head and took a step forward. The sound of the truck's engine grew behind me.

"Sir! Do not take another step!"

But I did. I took another step, and another, until I was not just walking but running toward them with my hands still high above my head and Lineker nipping at my heels. By this time, many of the children were safely aboard the truck, but there were still some stragglers, boys crouched with their heads between their knees, girls squealing, fists by their sides.

Now, I am no Usain Bolt, but I do not lie when I say that I had already halved the distance between us and the truck when the soldier made his feelings about my actions known.

"Stop or I'll shoot!" he said. There was sweat on his brow. "Stop!"

I shook my head and maintained my pace, closing my eyes and expecting him to follow through with his threat. But he and the rest of his troop had now turned their attentions to the machine thundering behind me. I could almost feel the heat of its grill as it screeched to a halt, and the soldier's eyes seemed to slide away from me. He swung his gun to the truck and I jumped to the left, landing in a heap within a small alleyway.

Lineker fell in beside me, and I squashed myself against the wall. We were midway between the two trucks—Greens on the left, Purples on the right—and all we could see through the slim opening of our alley was the rubble-strewn ground between them. I heard doors slamming, children crying, and orders to stand down from both directions. Then there was quiet, nothing but sniveling, murmuring, and feet on the concrete.

A megaphone whistled.

"State your business!" crackled a voice from the right, the Purples.

A soldier's voice replied immediately from the left. "Negative. Stand down, place your weapons on the ground where we can see them, and take twenty paces back with your hands on your heads."

There was some laughter from the right.

"*Negative*," mocked the voice. "*You* stand down and state your business. This is a BU-controlled zone."

*No it bloody well isn't*, I thought. I tightened my grip on Lineker's scruff. *This is my home.*

The megaphone squealed with feedback. "Who are you transporting?"

"Repeat, stand down, place your weapons on the ground where we can see them, and take twenty paces back with your hands on your heads. Do it now."

I must admit that the soldier's tone was highly convincing, most masterful. No problem with dogs, I shouldn't wonder.

There was a pause. In the silence I heard one of the soldiers speaking quietly.

"*Come out, it's all right, come out, we have to go.*"

And on the right, the click, click, click of the megaphone's trigger. On, off, on, off, on…

"*Negative.*"

There was a wild report of gunfire from the right, and shot after shot whistled past us. I pulled in tight against the cold brick wall as the Greens returned their fire. Their shots were slow and controlled in neat intervals. I heard the cries of men on both sides, then quiet again, and children wailing. Lineker had escaped my grasp and found a safe place to hide behind a trash can. In the quiet, I crawled to the end of the alley to see what was going on. To the right, I saw two Purples drag an injured one behind the truck. To the left, one of the soldiers was facedown, another lying against the truck, holding his stomach. Almost all of the children were on board now, but three had become separated and were standing in a terrified huddle in the no-man's-land between the trucks. One of the soldiers ran out to pull them back, but before he could reach them the Purples opened fire again. I just had time to see him spin as a slug hit him in the shoulder before I retreated back inside the alley.

Silence again. Then the nervous whimpering of the three children as they edged farther into danger. I saw small, scuffed shoes shuffling past. Then the megaphone whistled once again. "It's OK," said the voice. It was female, wavering, trying hard to be sweet. "Come here, it's perfectly safe."

"Put your weapons down!" screamed a soldier to the left. The children jumped in fright, scattered, and regrouped until all three were standing before me, halfway between the two trucks.

"Weapons down!"

One of the children, a boy of maybe five, was facing me from the huddle. He had both hands to his mouth, nibbling his fingernails and trying to lose himself in his feet. I must have moved because he looked up, and when he saw me, his eyes flashed. It was either fresh fear or hope, or both at once. He looked back at the soldiers, then up at the Purples looming above, then back at me.

"Perfectly safe" came from the megaphone. "Come here, come on."

"Weapons down! Now!"

The boy wobbled between his feet, still chewing at his nails and staring at me. I stared back at him. Then I shook my head, just once.

Boots stamped, metal shook, and gunfire filled the street again. One bullet hit the wall of the alley and a brick exploded above my head. One child dropped like a rag doll and the other two crouched with their arms over their heads as a Purple ran in from the right, snatching them up and leaving the third lifeless on the ground.

A few moments later, amid the shouts and shots still being fired, the engines of the truck to the left growled into life and roared away. The Purples followed, and I just had time to see the torn form of the man still hanging from the crane before the two trucks disappeared, tracing the broken, overgrown streets north.

I sat there for at least an hour watching the dead child with my hair and face covered in red brick dust. It was the boy, I think. He had one arm stretched out above his head and his chin tucked down. *Like Freddie Mercury*, I thought. *In that picture. We will rock you. We are the champions. That tribute concert, when was that? '91, '92, something like that. We watched all of it at her mum's house.*

Lineker came over and put a paw on my belly, but I pushed him away. All I could think of was Freddie Mercury dressed up like a housewife and pushing a Hoover.

Eventually I took a breath and looked around. The sun was dropping and the trucks were long gone, so I got to my feet and banged the fizz from my legs. *No use dwelling on it*, I thought. *What's done is done.*

But still, there it was again—that feeling of something approaching and its terrible breath upon my neck.

As I stepped out onto the street I heard a noise: a tinkling followed by brisk taps on concrete. My eyes shot to the open gate leading to the steps up into Seton Bayley, and I saw a shadow disappear inside.

I froze.

Lineker growled and barked, then flew across the street.

I chased him up the stairs, letting him follow his nose with his paws clattering on the stone and his barks and yelps echoing like springs against the cinder-block walls.

I found him a few flights up with his snout pressed into the corner of a door and his tail wagging, double quick.

"What have you found?" I said.

He growled and pushed his snout farther into the corner. The door squeaked as a gap appeared and he jumped back, looking up at me and licking his chops.

I'd been in this place long ago on my first outings. An old lady called Joyce once lived there. She had her meals delivered. The hallway still smelled of gravy, even though she was long gone and I'd taken all the food from her shelves.

And I remembered that I had closed this door when I was done, as I did everywhere.

I pushed it open and he darted in.

"Hello?" I called.

I heard a scuffle and another tinkle as something broke in the front room. Lineker led me through and stood, pointing at the sofa with his nose. He gave three loud barks, tail still going like the clappers.

The curtains were closed, and the air was dark and damp.

Something moved from behind the sofa.

"Is someone there?" I edged closer, crossing the room sideways like a crab, avoiding unseen furniture. "I'm coming around."

My leg caught the edge of a table. A glass fell and smashed on the floor, and there was a terrific scream. Lineker howled, countless barks crossing over the last, as a cat jumped out from behind the sofa, screeching and spitting with its claws out. It flew past Lineker in a blur, and he chased it out into the stairwell.

I shook my head and left the old place, shutting the door firmly behind me.

It was too dark to work on Bertha, and by the time Lineker had slunk back in with his tail between his legs and a few new scratches on his face, I had lit some candles and was tucking into some cold stew, straight from the tin. He sprang up on the sofa next to me, and I let him have the dregs of it. I watched him cleaning every last morsel, and when he was sure there was nothing left, he dropped down on my lap with a weary sigh. I thought that I should do some writing, but it was too dark, and I was too tired.

No use dwelling on it.

# WORRY

## LINEKER

YOU WORRY TOO MUCH, you do. You always have done. Not that I'm saying you haven't had a lot to worry about, because, yeah, you have. I mean you were *born* into worry, alone on a rock full of horrible beasts and worms and things that wanted to kill you and you had nothing, *nothing* to protect yourself. No proper claws, no proper teeth, shit at running, shit at climbing, shit at fighting, no fur, no horns, no armor, skin that would tear at the scrape of a daisy. You were an ape, granted, but every other ape had something sharp or strong going for it. Never fuck with a monkey and never try it on with a gorilla—that was the advice whispered through the jungle. But you? You had nothing. You were a joke. You sat there shivering in your cave, naked and cold and hungry.

"Fuck me, what have we here?" bellowed Nature as the bears, snakes, and lions closed in.

But, ah, what Nature didn't know…

You can take an ape, strip it of fur, pull out its claws, file down its teeth, dock its tail, and make it slow and weak, but give it a brain? Give it a brain and that ape will fuck a lion right up its arse.

Now you've got Mother Nature wrapped around your little

finger—apart from the odd hurricane and tsunami, of course. *Lovers' tiffs*, you might call them.

And still, you worry.

If the history of planet Earth was a day, then most of that day was just bollocks. Sloshing and swirling, big, gray, biblical seas moaning and groaning all over the place. BORING. The party only really got going at 6:00 p.m., and by the party I mean the fucking (copulation, screwing, sexual reproduction, all that) and even then, it wasn't really what you'd call good sex, just weed and lichen mashing themselves together for a few billion years like a pair of sweaty teenagers. No, the good stuff happened a bit later on, about twenty to twelve, when the mammals turned up.

But the real party started a little later, with you. You're the one who rocked up at midnight with some strippers, a box of pills, and a flamethrower—and now everyone's dancing properly.

Two minutes to midnight, that's you, and look at all you've done with that noggin of yours, will you? Just look what you've done! You should be fucking proud of yourselves! You and your wonderful brains. And still, you worry. You spend lifetimes thinking of new things to worry about, like the tides, and the ice, and the heat, and whether you should have ever crawled from your cave at all. Worry, worry, worry.

Right now, I'm looking at a worried man, and he's sitting on a chair by the door, peering through the eye glass.

Can I just say one thing? I don't want to be a dick, but...fuck it, look, it's like this. You seem like a stable person. You probably have a few hang-ups, you know, things you regret, relationships that went sour and all that, but you still know you're not a lost cause. Right? You know there's good in you as well as bad, and you try your best to find that good in most of what you do, even though you know you'll probably fail. You put yourself out there, and generally you try to make a good impression on everyone you meet.

Now, you might not always see eye to eye with every soul— some people rub you up the wrong way and that's fine—but you recognize that they're fighting the same battles as you, on some level, every day. So you cut them some slack, as they do you.

But now and again, once in a blue moon, maybe only once or twice in your life, you will meet somebody who makes you wonder, seriously, how bad a life sentence would be. It might be at a party, or at work, or on a plane, or on the other end of the phone, but you'll know, just *know,* without them even speaking a word, that you are going to want to kill them. And you can see it in their eyes too, hear it in the crackle of the telephone—they hate you, despise you, the very shape you make in the earth is one which they want to eradicate. They, like you, see this clear and terrible fact—that you are exact opposites. It doesn't matter about evolution, or the brotherhood of man, or common battles anymore. The only thing you have in common is a belief in a single opposing truth: the other one should not exist.

And then they do speak, and it's worse than you thought, and then you don't just want to kill them anymore; you want to destroy them. You want to desecrate them. You want to take every nerve in their body, every fiber, every atom, and collect them together into a nice neat box so that none of them can escape, and then you want to piss all over them. And then you want to take that piss-drenched mush, bag it, carry it way into the desert, and burn it with lizard bones and witch shit and the tears of the damned, and you'll dance around the flames, laughing, until there's nothing left but a stain in the ground which you spit on.

That's cats, that is. That's how I feel every time I see or smell a cat.

So that's why I had to chase that fucker who sprang out of the sofa at us. That's why I had to chase it away until I was sure it wouldn't come back. Eventually it found its way out of a window and onto the guttering, then jumped across to the block next door, and I would have chased it farther—would have chased it back to where it belonged, in fucking *hell*—but I remembered Reg.

I felt bad for him. He'd had a fairly shitty day, by all accounts, and now I'd gone and left him alone. So I went back and found him eating his dinner, and what did he do? He gave me some of it. Love him for that.

Anyway, there we were afterward drifting off to sleep, me letting the taste of that wonderful stew work away the last scent of *that cunt,* when I heard a noise. It was a thump. I sat up, trying to hear over the sound of Reg's snores. Nothing for ages, then…there, a thumping noise again. I gave a little twitch and growl and Reg sat bolt upright because he'd heard it too. We looked at each other in the dying light of the candles, waiting for the same thing. There again— three thumps this time, followed by another sound: a whimper in the stairwell.

Reg jumped off the sofa and I leaped to the door, barking, barking, barking. There's a point where the door and the wall and the floor all meet in a little triangle, and in order for the door to open, I have to bark at it, stick my snout right in there, so that's what I did, as Reg peered through the eye glass into the dark stairwell. Eventually he went to get his flashlight and opened the door.

And when he did, even I froze, because there in the corner, curled up in a ball, was a child.

It was a female. I could smell her before the beam lit up her face, something like new grass and milk. But voles too. I got a lot of voles from that little girl.

I felt my senses tug and went to run for her, give her a little lick, see what she was all about, but Reg caught my collar. He dragged me back inside the door and told me to stay. I'd been listening to him very hard that day, trying to make him happy after my late start that morning, so stay is what I did, despite every fiber in my being making me want to jump across that hall and get a taste of the thing that was huddled there, voles or not.

I looked up at him and waited for his next move. The little girl blinked in the bright light, but Reg just stood there in the doorway, breathing hard. I saw his eyes pulse, and then I realized—voles. Reg was scared too.

He took a step back and slammed the door shut. Then he pulled up a chair close to the door and sat on it. He's been there ever since.

Worriers, you lot.

I have to admit, though: here in this corner, watching Reg, my two-plates, my master, my *world*, behaving in a way I've never seen him behave before—I'm worried too.

# FEAR

SHE IS JUST A child. She is harmless. I have nothing to fear.

I put a chair in front of the door and my flashlight on the floor so that the beam spilled through the gap and out into the stairwell. Then I sat down, and I waited. Every minute or so, I stood up and checked through the peephole to see what she was doing. The beam spread in a dim arc across the stone, so even with the starlight I could only make out shadows shifting.

That is another thing—starlight. Before, all you got was the moon and a few pinpricks here and there in the sky; the glow from 20 million lightbulbs made sure that anything else was obscured by an orange spray. Now the universe wheels above, unmuffled by artificial light. Only the fog muffles it, but if it is low, I sometimes sit on the roof with my binoculars, trying to pick out constellations I can dimly remember the names of, getting lost in the flickering, distant lights and imagining I can see faces and arms extending from them. On a good night, the streets and our stairwell are bright with them all.

Not tonight, though. All I could see was the bundle in the corner. I could make out the pale skin of her tucked-up shins and what I thought might have been her ear. She was quite still, barely breathing.

Later, without warning, her face turned to the door, nodding lightly in time with her heartbeat. In a second, she shuffled and made little grunts as she moved along the wall toward me.

I fell back and pushed myself away from the door on the chair, gripping the arms.

*She is only a child*, I told myself. *Be reasonable, Reginald, you have nothing to fear.*

The shuffling sound had stopped. Carefully, and pretending to myself that I was *not* shaking, I got to my feet and crept to the twinkling spy glass. I pushed my eye toward it, then jumped back in fright as the girl's face filled it. She was standing right there at the door, lit from beneath in my flashlight's glow. Her face was bony and scared, her eyes wide and flitting about like flies. She kept her hands clasped to her chest as if they were her only protection against the dark.

I sprawled back on the floor and Lineker jumped over, licking my face to check I was all right. I pushed him off and stood up, breathing hard, watching the door and listening.

She knocked three times, slowly. I jumped again and Lineker barked, tail wagging, panting as he always used to when somebody came to the door. He snuffled around at the gap where the light was shining through, and I could see the shadows of the girl's feet disrupting the beam.

Then she spoke. It was barely a whimper, half a word croaked and cut short by a dry throat, but I staggered back yet again, terrified. I imagined her there on the other side, moving from foot to foot with her face up against my door, hungry and cold—wanting, needing, demanding. A chill prickled through me, draining all the warmth from my blood. It was already freezing in the flat, it being winter, and Bertha having been off all day.

Bertha. She was out in the hall, and if I wanted to fix her, I would have to go out there, go past *her*. And that was not something I wanted to do in a hurry.

I imagine you are asking yourself why. Why was Reginald so afraid of a lost little girl? The answer is simple: because I knew what she wanted from me. It was what every child wants—protection. That is why I was afraid.

Another knock and another whimpered word. Her voice made a dreadful echo that seemed to rouse the wind outside. It moaned back in despair, worrying its way down the street. I pulled myself straight, telling myself to get a grip. She *was* just a child, after all, and the door was firmly locked.

Lineker barked back at her. His eyes twinkled with yearning in the flashlight. I took a sharp breath and stared at the door.

"Go away," I spluttered. I caught Lineker cocking his head. "Go. Away," I said, this time clearer.

She shuffled, her shadow still dancing beneath the doorframe. Finally it stopped, and I sensed her departure. My lungs emptied. Lineker dropped and padded away, stopping as he reached me and looking up, tail still.

"Don't," I said. "Just don't."

I made for the window, opening one curtain. Outside, the city's ruined geometry rose from the fog and blocked itself up against the galaxy's white spray. I saw the nine lights flickering. Still no Beardsley. The presence of these lights had been a comfort, like a border of the human world. As long as they stayed where they were—distant and static—I was all right. But now they just seemed to make the presence of real company all the more terrifying. I gave a fresh shudder when I thought of her still behind the door.

I let the curtain drop and rested my head against the frame.

Then, from out in the stairwell, I heard footsteps moving away. I walked to the door, looked out, and saw her creeping between the other flats. She knocked on one, waited with her hands clasped, and moved to the next. I wondered how long it would be before she realized.


I only go through open doors. That's my rule. I keep the locked ones shut.

About half of Seton Bayley Tower cleared out in the first few days of the exodus. By then the streets were crammed with cars, buses wedged across junctions, and families trudging south carrying too many things and dragging their squealing kids behind them. When we got wind of the road attacks and others in the north, most just left their cars and walked.

I do not know how far they got. Every day it seemed there was something else—another little smoke plume on the horizon or a whisper of an incident abroad. I saw a plane take a dive once; a passenger jet's engine exploded over The Rye as it was making its descent into Heathrow. I watched it bank into the black smoke, screaming and sliding away from the sky like butter melting off an invisible pan before disappearing north. A distant boom sounded and the resulting smoke lasted two days.

Then there was the conflict, of course, the lackluster tanks and the proud Purples and all that. More civilians left or were taken during that week, and many more in the wake of it.

After that I lost track of things. But I knew I was never leaving.

Some of my neighbors locked their doors, either through habit or design, but most left them banging in the wind. One day I woke up to the sound of a fly buzzing in the window and nothing else. I listened to it for a while, marveling at the silence in which it played, then got up and wandered out. To my surprise, the whole block was empty, and it wasn't long after that the rest of the streets went the same way. Me and Lineker—we were on our own.

I enjoyed the peace. I enjoyed the space. There was more room to move around in and nobody to get in the way, no pavements I could not move on, no cars to watch out for, no angry faces behind windows. And the quiet let my thoughts move around too. Modern life is a peculiar thing. All that stuff happening out there outside your head—all that progress, all that change—you think you can blot it out and close the door, but it seeps in. The buzzing, the bubbling, the noise of it all gets caught in your head too, and soon you don't realize that you've been walking around with a head like a wasp's nest.

But then it settles. When everyone goes, your thoughts go too, and they leave you with something else entirely. Your head opens up and empties out, leaving a shell of new shapes and opportunities. Just like London did.

But it does have its downsides, this space in your head. After a little while, all those other thoughts—those ones that had been keeping quiet in all that noise—they come crawling out of the woodwork again. And when mine did, I knew I had to turn my mind to something new.

I waited a few weeks to see if anyone came back. Even then it felt unusual. The silence made what I was doing seem worse, as if the building itself was looking down on me with judging eyes glaring from every corner. I prowled the silent stairs, feeling like a child in a room he should not be in.

My first was number 517: fifth floor, seventeenth flat. The door was chipped and, when I gave it a push, something rustled. Squeezing my way inside, I saw a black trash bag squashed between the door and the wall, with papers and bottles spilling from it. There were others like it about the place, tied or open like this one, and the floor was strewn with rubbish. A child's doodles decorated the wall above a skirting board—faces, flowers, and a hopeful sun scrawled in Biro on the chipped paint. Beneath it, torn comics and plastic toys from fast-food meals mingled with cigarette butts and bottle tops, like a nursery scrapyard.

Through a door was an unmade bed with a single boot sitting on its pillow.

"Hello?" I called. Perhaps that sounds foolish, but you would have done it too. There was no reply, of course, so I turned my attention to the kitchen. Some of the drawers were open and one was hanging from its runners with the cutlery falling out, but the cupboards and fridge were closed. My boots crunched on broken glass and dirt.

I remember all this detail only because it was my first. I had never been someone who took things from other people, not because I thought it was wrong or anything; I had nothing against it, in its right place, and I had once known people who made a living from it, the ones who walked the streets nightly in July to scope out the empty houses, checking the timings of the lights and the strength of the fences and which ones had dogs. No, I had no moral objections to burglary; it was just that the idea of poking around the lives of other people made me distinctly uncomfortable.

So the last time I had done anything like this I had been nine. I had watched as my friend Jason, with his shock of yellow hair and gawky grin, broke into the upstairs of a furniture warehouse and poked his head out brandishing a drill. I had run off when I heard his dad approaching, just left him there and hid behind the trash cans, from where I watched him being dragged away by his ear, beaten as he went.

Jason is in prison now, so I believe. Or at least, he was.

In that first flat, I found a jar of pasta sauce, half a pot of marmalade, some plain cookies (had been hoping for chocolate), and some concentrated apple juice. I left them there—there was no need to take anything yet since the supermarkets were still reasonably well stocked—but I wrote down what I had found. I do not know why, something just told me to, so I got out a little notebook and scribbled it all in, dated and marked with the flat number. The next day I searched the other flats on my floor, and then I started on the rest. Soon, I had cataloged the entire block and was doing the same with the others in the area. The gaps in my map filled with each day, and with every new door I opened, the reality of my solitude became more apparent. Everyone was gone.

I stood frozen to the spot, listening to her as she made her way down the corridor and imagining her feeling along the walls between the doors. She knocked on doors and I counted each one, matching them against each empty flat until she stopped. There was a moment of silence before the familiar squeak of the door to the stairwell. It thumped back into the frame and slow, uncertain footsteps disappeared down to the floor below.

*Brave*, I thought.

About half an hour later as I lay in bed, shivering in the cold, the stairwell door squeaked again, and the slow shuffle of her footsteps returned. She knocked on my door and I squeezed my eyes shut, willing her to go away, which she eventually did. The last I heard of her was a slide and a thump as she found her corner, followed by distant, fractured sobs.

Since my catalog of the flats first began, three weeks after the exodus, I have slept like a baby, every night.

But I will not sleep a wink tonight. Not with the girl outside.

# SHIT BIT

**LINEKER**

THIS IS NOT A good bit. This is, quite frankly, a shit bit. The shittiest shit bit I can remember for ages. In fact, the last time there was a bit as shitty as this shitty bit, I was a pup. And that's saying something.

I'm well pissed off.

I love Reg, you know I do. I love him like nothing in the world. I would walk this great green earth of his twice around backward on my hind legs balancing a steak on my nose if I knew it meant a cuddle with that man. I trust him to do the right thing, and sometimes that means putting up with a fair bit of unusual behavior. Like all that fucking about he does before we leave the flat. What is that? My nose is at the door as soon as I hear the jingle of my lead, but this one, he's back and forward, picking things up, putting them down again, opening and closing drawers, putting on his jacket, saying things to himself, dropping keys. Very odd indeed, but I know he has to do it all for some reason. I trust the mysterious ways in which he moves.

But really, honestly, I do think he's lost the plot this time. We have been inside this fucking flat for TWO DAYS STRAIGHT, and if I don't get a walk soon, I'm going to go properly mental.

I have to piss in a saucepan. IN A SAUCEPAN. And don't get me started on shit. You might think it's all right to take a dump on a piece of newspaper, but me? No. Just no. No, no, no, no, NO.

Going to the lav is a rather important and sensitive issue for me, as it is with most dogs. It is not OK to just go anywhere you like; it matters where it goes. That's just common fucking decency in my book. I have to go where I've gone before, or rather, where not many others have gone before.

Think of it this way: If you're busting for a shit and you walk into the bathroom to see someone else's floating there, what would you do? You wouldn't just sit down and coil one out on top of it, would you? You'd flush first, probably giving one of your little tuts as you do it. *People are so disgusting*, you'd probably say to yourself, eyes lifted to the angels as you wait for the offending item to spiral away before laying down your own eye-shuddering cable as you flick through *Heat* or *Twat* or *Men's Washboards* or whatever stupid fucking rag you've… I'm sorry. I'm a little worked up. Love the flat. Love Reg. No concerns there, just, you know…*properly* mental.

Anyway, as I was saying: you flush. But we dogs don't have flushes, do we? No, we have noses; noses that tell us exactly where some other animal has done its business. And not just in the last day, either, nor in the last week, month, or year. Our noses tell us exactly who has done what where SINCE TIME IMMEMORIAL.

I'm exaggerating perhaps. But you get the idea. It's important to choose the right place, and I can't do it where he wants me to do it, I just can't, though fuck knows I've tried. I've already disgraced myself twice in the kitchen, once next to the television, and three times up against the bedroom door. This has only made Reg even madder (and he's pretty bonkers right now, let me tell you) and me more confused. But I can't help it. Some things just don't go the way you want them to.

Kitchen, telly, bedroom door—these are all places I've done it before, back when I was a pup and knew no better. But right now, with every passing second I spend locked up in here, I feel more and more like that frightened little runt taking those first wobbling, piss-pawed steps into his new home.

I'd been in Battersea since birth. All the others had gone, my old mum too, so it was just me in the cage, the bare floor and the endless parade of faces. Christ, I can still remember the racket. Those wankers had no hope—*no hope*—of getting picked with all their slavering and howling and mad eyes rolling about.

Me, pick me, please pick me I love you I love you I do I do I won't bite you I'm nice I'm sorry about that thing on the floor I won't bite you honest PICK ME, YOU WON'T REGRET… HEY! COME BACK HERE! COME BACK HERE AND STOP CRYING! STOP CRYING, YOU LITTLE PIG-TAILED CUNT!

Who wants to look after something like that?

I didn't know the gig at the time, of course. I thought this was the world, like anything that's born in captivity. I didn't even know there was an outside.

Strange then, isn't it, that I felt sad? Strange that I somehow believed things could get better, that these paws and this snout and these springy muscles were telling me that they were born for something more.

Ever get that?

That's The Howl, that is. The Howl tells everything where it's supposed to be and what it's supposed to be doing. The Howl tells everything when something's just not as it should be. So rather than curl up in a ball and cry, I stood up, held my snout to the air, and learned to be patient.

Face after face passed my cage and I watched each one drift by. The screams of the others became the noise that filled my days, and their whimpers and whines became the nights. And in those nights, I'd dream of wide places I'd never been that swarmed with huge animals, and my feet would be buried in mud. Battersea was a desperate place, full of fear and anger.

I tried to keep my thoughts on the only memory that made any sense, which was my mum, all milky and warm and soft. Every day she seemed further away, a part of her disappearing like a jigsaw breaking into pieces. And the others—I couldn't remember who or how many there were. I kept telling myself I could remember the shape their bodies made against mine as we flumped about at Mum's tits, or the sound of their voices trying to speak, but I couldn't, not really. The only feeling I had was the hardness of the floor, and the only sound was the yelling of those pricks around me.

Then Reg came along, and it was like a window opening. The Howl spoke to me: *This one*, it said. *This one's yours, and you're his. That's how things are supposed to be.* It was a good bit, so my tail wagged. And the rest, as they say… An entire history of good bits.

Not a good bit now, though, not at all. You're not supposed to lock yourself away. You're not supposed to hide from the world. You're not supposed to be alone. Even the wolves know that.

That's the other thing you had, as well as that magnificent ape mind of yours. You had you. Lots and lots of *you*. You looked after each other, cared for each other, watched each other's backs. You did this right from the start and you did it without question because the feeling was something so raw and deep that you didn't know how else to be. You did it because The Howl told you to. And the way The Howl told you to was by giving you that wonderful thing called love.

Real love. I'm not talking about roses or cherries or fluttering looks. I'm not talking about beating hearts, swollen cocks, or throbbing cunts either. I'm talking about the thing that binds you—that messy glue that hardens on contact, that shatters when it breaks, and even then leaves bits of it behind.

I'm talking about the thing that you feel when you're screaming through a car window or arguing over a phone or throwing plates or shaking fists or about to throw one—the feeling that tells you no matter how much you hate this person, if you saw them in some foreign place where the signs made no sense, or shipwrecked on a far shore, or fleeing for your life on some alien planet, you would seek them out. Because deep down you're the same, and your only hope of survival depends on sticking together.

Even with that mind of yours, the odds were still stacked against you. Forget your lone hunter standing proud on a hill—nothing lasts long on its own. Wolves know it, foxes know it, squirrels know it, birds know it, cats…

(Cats are a different matter. Cats, and I'm positive on this, do not know the meaning of the word *love*. This is because they are from a place where love does not exist and that place is called hell, where the Dark Lord himself, who is a cat, will roast the soul of every pussy that has ever scratched or hissed or purred or sprayed in a monstrous pile of flaming kitty litter for ALL TIME.)

Apologies. Not myself.

I'll admit it, there are a few animals out there who like to go it alone. Spiders, for example. Not great at parties, spiders. Bears like to keep to themselves too, mostly because they're too fucking stupid to find their way out of the woods, and when they do, they go berserk and start killing everything. Jaguars, leopards, tigers, cheetahs (all cats…I rest my case), pandas (just not fucking), and koalas, who probably would be all right at parties if they weren't so off their faces most of the time.

And even then, these animals are not the most cheerful lot, are they? Not happy campers, by and large. The only time you see a bear smiling is when it's fucking another bear.

We're not supposed to be alone. *You're* not supposed to be alone. But try telling Reg that.

I have. I've tried whining and pawing and even—I'm ashamed to admit this, but I'm desperate—even making noises close to human words. But he just shouts or pushes me away. He paces around and spends most of the time in his room or looking out of the window through those binoculars of his.

I know it's because of her. I can hear every move she makes out there, and I smell her constantly. I'm latched onto her, everything she does. It's weird. I know she uses the stairwell as a toilet, and I know she hasn't eaten for four days because her stomach acid is making it smell like her insides are turning in on themselves. I know the smell she makes when she's about to come to our door again. I swear I can smell her thinking. She's found water from somewhere with a metal tang that makes me think it's from one of the dripping pipes downstairs, but it's not enough. Her mouth is dry and swollen, and it hurts. I can smell her pain and her woe and the little shreds of hope, like flesh on barbed wire, that keep making her return to our door. And when she does, she knocks, and Reg covers his ears and shuts his eyes and takes huge, wet breaths through his nose until she stops.

She wants our help and I don't know why he won't give it to her. She's just a pup, alone, on a cold, hard floor.

# TARGET

SHE STOPPED CRYING SOMETIME early this morning. It had not really been crying by then—just a series of croaks and whimpers that had kept me from sleep for a third night.

Her surrender brought a wretched mixture of relief and guilt, a poison that numbed me toward some hateful version of sleep. But before it took me, something yanked me back to consciousness. A voice inside of me, an actual voice, and I knew at once who it was. The warmth, the swift upward inflection, the crack as she said my name.

It said: *This is not how things are supposed to be. Get up now, Reginald, and take a look.* So, weary and ragged, that is what I did.

I stood at the door and looked out through the spy glass. She lay engulfed in her coat with curled limbs and clawed fingers, perfectly still. Again came that rotten wave of dull comfort accompanied by sinking failure. Thoughts came quickly to help me out: *What kind of world was this for a child, Reginald? She would have died anyway, and*

*what would you have done with her if she had lived? Could you have made*
*her happy? It is over now, she is at peace...*

But the way the bones showed in her fingers and the way her
head was pressed into the corner, trying to seek some bubble of
warmth—she looked anything but at peace.

Lineker growled at the door. Then suddenly he spun around and
ran for the window instead.

"What is it?" I said, but he just stood there with his paws up, back
stretched, and tail down, staring out at the silent morning.

Her voice again.

*This is not how things are supposed to be, Reginald. You know this.*

I opened the door.

I got the light smell of her doings on the wind whistling through
the hall, and a rat scuttled past my feet.

"Lineker," I called, but he was still there at the window, ignoring me in favor of the view. I watched the rat weave between the
skirting boards and dart beneath the stairwell door. Then it was just
me and her.

I walked to the corner and stood over her. Her face was as bony
and drawn as it had been before, ghoulish in the flashlight on that
first night. Now her eyes were closed, their long lashes interlocked,
and her mouth was parted, showing two oversized front teeth and
a gold one beside them. Her features were fine and taut, as if still in
whatever fretful dream had accompanied her into death. I bent down
and pulled back her hood. Her hair was dark and curled in tight
ringlets, like oil against the moon of her face.

Around her neck was a piece of string and, attached to it, a brown
tag. I pulled it from a crease in her coat. It read:

NAME: Aisha Gray

AGE: Unknown, roughly 7 years old

ORIGIN: Streatham

DESTINATION: HM Military Stronghold Kestrel 24-C,

Wembley, N. London

PARENTS/GUARDIAN: Deceased

SIBLINGS: Deceased

RELATIVES: Unknown

ENDANGERMENT STATUS: Target

I let the tag drop and fell on my backside, holding my head and staring at her face. My right leg began to wobble as if it belonged to someone else. I heard somebody breathe hard and realized it was me. My lungs were sucking and squeezing like giant, flapping bellows— huge gulps of air I neither wanted nor needed. My vision swam, dizzy in the tide of oxygen surging in my blood. I was somewhere else, in another time, another place.

This was not what I had wanted.

*What was it you wanted then? You left her out here. You could have saved her. You could have looked after her. You were supposed to look after her.*

Somewhere else. Another time, another place.

*She needed help. You failed her.*

I jumped to my feet and tried to pace off the panic, this swarm of shrieking ghosts that had descended out of nowhere.

Then two things happened.

The first was that Lineker started barking from the window. It was proper barking too—rapid, loud, and aggressive—and beneath it, from the street below, was the sound of engines approaching.

And the second thing that happened, as I stood there drenched in my own doom, was that the girl's cheek twitched.

I staggered back, then forward again, as if on the lurching deck of a ship. I looked behind at Lineker springing and snapping madly at the window, and then back at the girl. With my legs still wobbling, I took a few hesitant steps toward her, rubbing my fingers like an old man at a horse race as I tried to decide whether what I had just seen I had actually just seen. I watched, waited, and chewed my lip as the engines outside throttled. Brakes squealed. Doors slammed. The girl's pale face remained still. My shoulders slumped—this time in despair, with no shred of relief.

The sun broke through a cloud and struck her with its ray. As the cloud swiftened away, the light traveled up her face, and when it hit her right eye her cheek twitched again. This time her entire body followed with a gigantic spasm that made me fall to the floor. She took one mighty, rasping breath and coughed. I scrabbled backward, watching her stockinged legs wheel against the air.

She sat up, still coughing, looking about as if the place and time in which she had found consciousness was not the same as the one in which she had lost it. Her eyes darted between the walls as she fought for breath and pulled her coat around her tiny frame. Then her breathing suddenly steadied. In the jolt, a black ringlet fell from behind her ear and hung there, trembling. Her face flickered with a memory, and very slowly, she turned it toward me.

We watched each other from our respective corners. I heard a voice from outside and Lineker barked. It was a different sound to the one he usually made, wary and low, not quite sure of itself. I went to see.

Down on the ground there were two trucks, both BU. Their drivers were outside arguing about something, nose to nose, fists clenched, gloved fingers pointing.

I did not know what to make of this. Whether I had accidentally drawn them here or whether they had resumed sweeps in this area, I had no idea, but either way, it did not bode well at all. Then there was the army truck from earlier, and now this child. Too much company. Far too much.

The argument below was blustering to a climax when all of a sudden a terrific roar tore through the air and ended in a distant thump. The drivers stopped bickering, grabbed their guns, and looked up. A tight fist of black smoke spiraled from the north. The men snapped a few more words and returned to their cabs, spinning off in the direction they had come.

I watched the smoke plume dissipate and waited until I could no longer hear the trucks. Then I turned to the door. She was standing there, watching me.

I seated her at the table and gave her a blanket, a bottle of water, two tins from my store (one peas, one ravioli), a tin opener, and a spoon. Lineker positioned himself on the floor beside her, snout up and tail wagging. She drained the water and thrust the bottle back at me. As I fetched another from the kitchen, she picked up the tin opener and looked it over, trying a few combinations against the side of the can of ravioli before dropping it and attacking it with her teeth. When this didn't work she banged it against the table instead. I took it from her, opened both tins, and let her go to work on them, scooping the contents out with her fingers and mashing it into her mouth. Lineker watched with excitement, and I left them both to fix Bertha.

It didn't take long to fit the new bearings, and after a bit of tinkering, the old girl came back to life with a furious roar.

When I returned to the flat I found the girl sitting at the table, staring at the empty cans. I got things going—fire, lights, water filter, pump—and ran a bath. It was tepid, but the water was clean, and I put a towel in the bathroom for her. She understood, closed the door, and returned fifteen minutes later looking and smelling a little less like the grave. I gave her more food and water, and watched while she inhaled it.

It was almost midday but there was still a hard frost outside, stiffening the vines and creepers that covered our balcony, the street—everything made of brick or concrete—into glistening white cables. The fog was relatively light, so you could see how far the creepers stretched and how high they'd risen. A dense web of sap and sinew spread out as far as the eye could see, attaching itself to anything its tendrils touched and clawing it imperceptibly back into the Earth. *How long would it be?* I wondered. *How long before those empty shells crumbled? How long before Seton Bayley, my home, fell?*

The girl placed her last empty can on the table and let a little burp escape from her lips.

"Your name," I said. "It's Aisha, isn't it?"

She stared into the fire, her face orange in the electric glow.

"I read it on your tag," I went on.

She blinked and said nothing.

"You were going to Wembley, correct?" I asked.

Still nothing.

"Those men you were with, and the children. They were taking you somewhere safe. You have to stay with them, not the other ones. You know that, don't you?"

Her eyes drooped, but still she said nothing.

"You have to get back to those men. The green ones, they're the army. They'll keep you safe. A home or something. Maybe…maybe new parents."

She took a little breath, then reached inside her coat and pulled something from her pocket. Without taking her eyes from the fire, she lay it on the floor beside her. I picked it up. It was a photograph, faded and out of focus, of something that looked like a farm or an old country house. There was a hill in the background, streams, rivers, sheep, all that countryside business, and a woman at the gate wearing boots and work clothes, carrying a stick. I could see other people in the background, a few children and adults carrying things. Beyond them was a white tent, and others on the hill behind.

I turned the photograph. On the back were written the words:

*Gorndale, Bistlethorpe, Yorks.*

MAGDA. X

It was something she had found, perhaps, or something from her time before. Maybe it had belonged to her parents. I set it back on the carpet and she took it, eyes still trained on the fire.

"You must get back to those men," I said.

I left her with Lineker and went back to tinker with Bertha.

When I returned it was dark and the girl had found a place on the floor next to the fire, where she huddled with Lineker. Open upon her knees was a book which, with fury, I recognized as my photograph album. I leaped forward and snatched it from her hands.

"How dare you!" I yelled. "How dare you look at this!"

She flinched and looked up at me, eyes wide.

"This is mine! Nobody is to touch this, do you hear? Nobody!"

My hands were shaking. My blood thundered. I looked down at the open page awash with overexposed, badly focused memories dotted with red eyes and spots of age. Me, my brother, my mother, a whole array of faces I barely remembered.

And her. Of course, her.

Half of one page was taken up with a group photograph. It was our corner table in the Wheatsheaf, full of leers, grins, cigarette smoke, and headlocks. There was my brother, rabbit-ear fingers hidden behind one of his friends. There was me at the end, nursing a half-pint of something weak, trying my best to smile for the camera.

And there at the other end, eyes in midturn toward me, was her. We had kept this photograph—not because of the people in it, but because it was the evening it happened. Almost the moment, in fact: July 4, 1990.

I once heard someone say that we're all born a natural age, and when we reach that age, that's the time in our life when we're the happiest. Some are just waiting for the time their old souls feel happy in their skins whereas others carry the glow of their twenties throughout their lives, or never stop being children. I don't know if that's true, but there's definitely a part of me that still lives in that summer.

I was twenty-one but far from happy. Although my life was

supposed to be just beginning—I had just finished my electrician's apprenticeship, a momentous occasion that brought everyone on the street to offer their congratulations—I felt like I was watching it slip away. I had wanted to be an engineer, but a profession like that required a university education, which was out of the question. There were no savings or second jobs or "we'll make do somehow" promises; it simply was not up for discussion. The mention of a degree brought only laughter and tuts from my mother. So the dream slid back in its box, I smiled at the endless back slaps, and took the path that was offered.

Neil said nothing, but those arm jabs of his, which I had endured since learning to walk, were harder than usual. I realized that all they ever had been was tacit encouragement, his only means of fathering me in place of a real dad. Mum was proud but I'm sure those carefully hidden tears peeling spuds at the sink were just as much of relief. She had raised her boys and now they could look after themselves, and those expensive dreams of further education were now firmly in the past.

They were happy days for everyone, so I buried my thoughts and smiled at the smiles. Even if I had not, nobody would have noticed, for there were much more important things afoot than a young man's future.

*Italia '90.* The World Cup. England flags, pizza, and Pavarotti everywhere. Heaven for football fans, but not so much for me. Neil had tried his best to get me, into the sport as a boy, dragging me out to those dreary West Ham matches. *The beautiful game*, he called it, but for the life of me, I could see nothing beautiful in spending an afternoon chewing cold pies and cheering on millionaires.

The tournament was nearing its conclusion, and it seemed that the whole country was preparing itself for an important match.

"Come on, Reggie," said Neil. "You need to get yourself out of the house for a change. You'll never meet any birds stuck up in your room. Stop moping."

"I am not moping."

"Well, come on then! It's fucking England, Reg. England and West Germany! The semifinals! Why would you want to miss that?"

I capitulated, as I always did. The best I could hope for was that Neil and his friends would get drunk so quickly that they would not notice me slipping out halfway through the first half. I certainly was not expecting to meet my future wife.

It was midafternoon on a Wednesday, and the whole of South London, it seemed, had either taken the day off or left work early. The pubs were full and car horns honked as I traipsed through the streets after Neil. At the Wheatsheaf, we pushed our way through the crowd and made for a table in the corner, which his friends had managed to keep since starting drinking two hours before.

"The match doesn't start until seven," I said.

"What?" said Neil. "Speak up!"

"I said it doesn't start till seven. Why are we here so early?"

He cuffed me with a *don't be daft* look on his face. "To get a few in, of course! What do you want?"

"I don't know. Shandy, I suppose."

"Shut up, you muppet, you're having a pint. Keith, what you havin', mate?"

I never really got the hang of pubs. Couldn't see the draw—all that squashing and shouting and trying to have a good time. It all felt forced.

Right then, as Neil got the orders and I tried to find a space among all those booming, beer-breathed hooligans, all I wanted to do was slip out and go home. I was considering doing just this when I heard a voice.

"There's a seat here, if you want?"

I looked down and there she was. Bangles, curly hair, dungarees, and a tight white tank top that I made a mental note not to stare at. Girls can see you looking, I had read, even when you think they cannot, so you should always keep your eyes at a respectable altitude.

She smiled and patted the battered chair next to her. "My friend was sitting there, but I don't think she's coming back."

She nodded at the end of the bar, where a girl with long, black hair was engaged in a canoodling embrace with a plumber I knew called Mark.

"I won't bite," said the girl beside me.

"Thank you," I said, sitting down.

"I'm Keith's cousin, Sandra. What's your name?"

"Reginald Hardy," I said. "But everyone calls me Reg."

She sucked on her straw and her eyes danced over my face. "I like Reginald," she said at last. "I think I'll call you that."

That's what love is, in my book—calling someone by their real name.

Neil brought my drink, which I nursed for an hour, much to his consternation and Sandra's delight. Things settled down a bit and Mildred, the landlady, wheeled a small portable television into one corner. This drew a small crowd who argued over the best way to tune it in properly. Mildred danced about in the space behind the television, holding the aerial aloft with a look of mystical awe, like a medium trying to contact the dead.

Neil stood up and weighed in with his own advice. I watched with a modicum of amusement, the watery lager having achieved a certain lubrication of my spirits. I noticed Sandra smirking at the spectacle too.

"Put it on the window, love," Neil shouted. "Up there. Oi! I said up on the fucking… Christ, you can't hear yourself think in this place, know what I mean?"

"You can hear your name," I said.

"You what?" said Neil, landing heavily on his seat and scooping his pint.

"I said you can hear your own name. It's called the Cocktail Party Effect."

Neil frowned at me, glass halfway to his lips. "What you fucking on about? Jesus, 'ere, boys, Reggie wants a fucking cocktail!"

The table jeered and returned to lobbing volleys of advice at poor Mildred. I looked down into the yellow froth of my beer, but I could feel eyes still watching me. "What do you mean?"

I looked up at Sandra, who had her head cocked to one side and her hands folded neatly on the table. "Oh, nothing," I said. "Just ignore me."

"No, tell me, what's the Cocktail Effect?"

"The Cocktail *Party* Effect," I corrected. "It is an auditory phenomenon. Your brain is able to pick out meaning in a mass of sound. For example, if you are in a noisy room, like a cocktail party or a pub like this, the sound of a hundred people talking makes no sense, but if you hear something related to you, like your name, it leaps out. Sorry, I read a lot. I'm not very interesting."

Her eyes, which had been watching me intently, seemed

suddenly to despair. She straightened her back. "Don't say that," she commanded. "Don't ever say that again. I think you're extremely interesting, Reginald Hardy, extremely interesting indeed."

With that, she stood up and faced the television. "Mildred O'Connor!" she shouted, and Mildred's haunted face snapped toward her. "Up on the window ledge, love!"

Mildred raised a finger and nodded, then swept the aerial up onto the window ledge. The television crackled and fizzed, and a great cheer filled the pub as the screen lit up green.

Sandra sat down with a wink. "It's still very busy in here," she said.

"Would you like to move nearer the front?"

"No. To tell you the truth, I'm not that much into football."

"That makes two of us."

She drained her drink and fiddled with the straw as if something was occurring to her. "Reginald?" she said, setting the empty glass down.

"Yes?"

"I do hope you don't think me too forward, but would you like to walk me home?"

I hesitated. "What, now?"

"Yes. I thought perhaps we could watch the game together in my flat. Even though we don't like football that much. What do you think?"

"I—"

"It's all right. I understand if—"

"Yes," I said. "I think I would like that very much."

We snuck out onto the hot streets, eerily quiet now that the game was about to begin. After picking up some beer and a takeaway curry, she led me to her flat in a block a few estates north of our street. She stopped at her battered blue door and turned. I realized we were the same height.

"What's wrong?" she asked.

"Nothing. It's just that I've never…you know, never been invited back to a girl's place before. Not that I'm suggesting it's anything like… I mean, I know it's just to watch the football, but…"

"Are you nervous?"

I paused, then shook my head. "No," I said. "I know I sound it, but I'm not. I'm happy."

"Why are you happy?"

"Because I'm not in that place anymore. I'm here with you."

Her eyes fluttered, and she put her hand on my cheek. "Reginald, you don't have to let the world eat you up, you know. Some people like to lose themselves in crowds; others need their own space. Staying in's all right."

Then she opened the door, took my hand, and led me inside.

It was a studio flat with a kitchenette. A wardrobe and a single bed took up one wall beneath a cracked mirror and an open window fluttering with curtains and evening sun. She switched on her telly and we sat on her sofa, tucking into popadams and cracking open our beers. We talked and talked, losing ourselves in long and winding conversations I cannot recall; the memories seem off-limits, as if they belong only to those two young versions of ourselves, right then and right there in that room. As the match went on, we found ourselves cheering in celebration, or holding our heads in frustration, though neither of us liked football.

With every passing minute, the gap between us on that sagging sofa diminished, until we found our knees touching, and then our hands, and then our lips, and by the time those penalties played out we were rolling together, one before becoming an after, and we watched England's hopes fall, naked in each other's arms, from the joy and safety of her bed.

I slammed the album shut and looked down upon the girl. She had produced her photograph again, and others with it, all torn and yellowed and held up for me to see as if they were the only truth she knew. Carefully, she pointed first at them, and then at my album. Her finger hung quivering in the air, willing me to understand.

*You have those in there*, she seemed to say. *And I have these.*

We watched each other with Lineker between us, and the three of us remained still and silent until, finally, I took a breath. "You cannot stay here," I said. "You may sleep here tonight, but you must go in the morning. You can sleep on the sofa."

She made no reply, so I left and went to bed.

I lay awake for some time, clutching the album to my chest and wondering in that cold, dark room what on earth I was supposed to do.

I know what she would have said. "Protect her, Reginald. Look after her and take her where she needs to go. She's just a child; she needs your care."

That's what she would have said.

But what does that matter? She is dead.

# CONSEQUENCES

## REGINALD HARDY'S JOURNAL
### DECEMBER 10, 2021

THE SUN WAS ALREADY up when I woke. I dressed and went to the living room, groggy with sleep but glad of it.

"Now," I said. "I shall pack you some food—light stuff so you can carry it—and water. I shall also provide you with a map marked with a route so you can find your way to the base. You can do it in stages, but you should be able to make it in a day or two if…"

I looked around the flat. Lineker lay on the sofa, thumping his tail, but the girl was nowhere to be seen. The door of the flat was open.

"Where'd she go?" I said. Lineker responded with a yawning growl.

I ran to the window and pressed my face and hands against it, looking down. Lineker sprang up and joined me.

"There," I said. "There she is. What the devil is she…?"

She was halfway up the street, standing a few feet from the body of the boy that had been shot. She looked at it sideways, hands raised from her sides as if the sight of him had caught her unawares.

"Hey!" I shouted. "What are you doing?"

I banged on the glass. The sound of it must have reached her because her head twitched and she turned back to the road. She continued on, picking her way over the rubble and creepers with her hands still out.

"Silly girl."

I pulled on the balcony door, but the handle was jammed. I shook it, Lineker now on full alert, barking encouragement up at me. Eventually it gave way and I burst out into the cold air of the overgrown balcony. Lineker bolted past and jumped up against the ledge, launching into a whinnying howl that echoed along the street.

I leaned over the edge and cupped my hands. "Where are you going?" I shouted. "You have no map, or food, or…"

The girl stumbled on a rock, kept her balance, and kept on walking.

"Can you hear me?" I yelled. "Oh, hell's bells…"

I ran downstairs with Lineker at my heels. She was almost at the corner when we burst out onto the street.

"Hey!" I shouted and walked after her. I glanced at the body of the boy, and Lineker gave it a sniff. He had swollen in the few days he'd been lying there.

The girl was at the junction looking left and right, trying to decide which way to go. I stopped behind her.

"Look," I said. "Come back inside. You can have some more food, water. I shall give you a map and…" I sighed. "Maybe I could…maybe could even get you as far as…"

The girl made a wary grunting sound.

"What is it? What's wrong now?"

She was pointing north up the main road. I joined her at the junction and followed the line of her finger. On the road, next to a bank of shops, was a purple truck. A door banged and the engine started. Lineker growled.

"Come with me," I said. "Now. Come on."

She was rooted to the spot.

"Whatever is the matter with you? Come on!"

She gave a furious shake of her head. Lineker growled again, louder this time. The truck pulled out and started slowly toward us. Instinctively I reached to pull her away, but my fingers shriveled into a terrified claw before they could make contact.

"For heaven's sake," I said instead. "Come on or you'll get us both killed! Shut up, Lineker!"

Lineker's growl had risen into a full-on, head-down bark, with his snout pointed directly at the approaching truck. I did not know if they could see us from that distance, but I was sure they could hear him.

"Please," I said to the girl. "Please, come with me. Those ones, they are the bad ones, do you understand? *Bad* ones. Because they are Purple, yes? Understand? Purple means bad, so you have to come with me, please, now."

I held out my hand. It was still curled and shaking as if it had been crushed in a vice, not simply moved in the direction of a young girl's shoulder. I stared at it, grimacing, willing it to do its job. Lineker's barks filled the air and the truck's speed picked up. I could see the windshield now, and the face of the driver set on the road.

"Please...please..."

I shook my hand, clenched my fist, closed my eyes and...

The space I had grabbed was empty. She had already turned and was running down the street. With some relief, I followed her. I called Lineker, but he seemed deaf to my voice, intent instead on standing his ground. As the truck reached the junction, the girl ducked into a side street and I jumped in beside her. We lay shaking against the wall.

A door opened and slammed. Lineker's bark fell to an undulating growl and boots crunched in the dirt. Then the growl was cut short, followed by silence. There were a few scuffles, sharp thuds and yelps, another door slamming and more footsteps ending in two smart heel scrapes. Whoever it was said a single word I could not make out—sharp and direct, female—and then there was a series of quick thwacks, each one punctuated by a man's cry.

I edged to the corner and looked around. To my surprise, Lineker was sitting with his eyes turned up to a tall, raven-haired woman in the unmistakable Purple uniform of the BU. I tried to get a closer look. There was something about her I could not place. She was wearing an extremely large amount of makeup: pitch-black mascara, dull blusher, and brutally red lipstick, but beneath it all...a face I swore I knew. She appeared to be quite high up in rank, so perhaps I had seen her on the television, or in those propaganda rags they had handed out. Something told me otherwise, though.

In one hand she carried a cane. At her side was another dog. A man limped away from her.

She said another word that caused Lineker to cock his head. Then she bent down and ruffled him on the head. The girl made a noise and I held a finger to my lips. She blinked in understanding.

I looked back and saw that the woman had returned to the truck. The door slammed, the engine roared, and they rolled away down the main road.

When it was quiet, I jumped up and ran for Lineker.

"Lineker!" I shouted. I found him next to the wall, licking his paw. When he saw me, he gave a kind of shocked snuffle. His fangs were red with his own blood. "What did they do to you, eh?"

I gave his ribs a once-over. He flinched a little, but there did not appear to be any breaks. Eventually he stood up and plodded around for a bit, then found my side and leaned against my shin. He was trembling.

I turned and saw the girl standing behind me, holding the cuffs of her coat in her fists. She walked over and stood close, looking down at her feet. She was shaking too.

Decision swayed beneath me.

I am not a hero. Altruism does not exist. There are the things a man wants to do and there are the things he must do, and the things he must do must be done, because if he does not, then the consequences linger. That is really all there is to altruism: the avoidance of bad feeling.

There I stood on that empty, rubble-strewn street with an injured dog at my side and a lost, mute girl before me, my shadow drawn thin by the midwinter sun, and my being torn between the want and the must.

It was unfair, but I had no choice.

"I shall take you as far as the river, young lady," I said. "But I am not crossing it. After that, you are on your own."

# PART 2

# HER

**LINEKER**

Well, that was weird.

Proper. Fucking. Weird.

One minute I feel like I'm me, doing my job and giving those Purple twats what for, hackles up, snout out, teeth bared, and full of righteous indignation—I tell you, there's nothing like a bit of righteous indignation to get your hackles up; they were after the girl, I knew they were, and I just couldn't let that happen—and the next, I'm...I'm...

I don't know what I am.

That cunt came out, I remember that. Him with the long arms and shiny, dumb face who smelled of sour lamb and shaving foam— he came out first and suddenly all that righteous indignation turned to pure rage. I was still in control, I knew what I was doing, and there was no way I was letting him past me. He wasn't going to get the girl, no matter how much he towered over me, or eclipsed the sun with that thick head of his, or cocked it to the side as he raised back his shiny, black boot with a childlike thrill on his face, as though this was going to be fun, this was, to...

To kick me. Yes, *Lambchops* got one in first, all right? He gave me a lazy thump in the ribs, but so what? Maybe I'm a little rusty—it's not as if I've had a lot of combat experience recently—but I would have got him back. All I needed was a second or two to get my head together, shake off the shock, and jump back in the fray. I would have been ready for action, ready to pounce on him, ready to tear him to pieces. I would have fucking had him, I would.

But then She came out. She and that husky bitch of Hers.

I already knew She was there. Not consciously, but on some level. I couldn't see Her because the windows of the truck were blacked out, and I couldn't hear Her because the only sound in my ears was that of my own blood raging and the mumbles of that imbecile as he waited for my next move. But I knew She was there. Somewhere beneath all the fury of that moment, beneath the red mist and tang of blood, there was this other scent, like fresh snow in a place with no people, colossal pines, and icicles dripping in low sun. And there was something else too, something deeper, more pungent and familiar. It ran beneath everything like a deep river, and it had done since we'd first seen that truck three days ago. It was calling me.

As I regrouped, I suddenly felt my hackles fall and my tail go limp, as if some great power had swept all the anger from my guts and carried it away on a polar wind. Feelings and thoughts disintegrated, and I drifted with them, but the sound of a sharp slap brought me back from my stupor. I looked up and I saw Her.

She was beating him. Wordlessly, She was clobbering my adversary around the head with a single gloved hand, not in a fist, but straight out like a blade. He cowered and yelped as She delivered his punishment.

Her blows were measured and well timed, each one landing with the same force as the last. I counted them—seven, eight, nine—and my eyes drifted to the source of that other, deeper scent: the husky bitch sitting patiently by her side. She was the first dog I'd seen in three years.

Our eyes locked—mine still trembling as the fury left my body; hers unwavering, a brilliant, treacherous blue. Her coat was a landscape of blacks and browns and whites, like tundra sweeping down two lean flanks into a coiled tail and four slender legs with full, white paws. Her ears were folded in soft points toward me, and her snout was marbled black with freckles. She lowered it an inch and I saw something in her, a ripple that seemed to say, *Well, hello.*

The lady, her mistress—*She*—was finishing up, arriving at the twelfth blow with a neat thwack against the nose of Lambchops who, by now, was whimpering and for whom I was starting to feel a kind of disgusted pity. She stepped away, placed Her hands on Her hips, and said a single word: *truck*. And what do you know? Off to the truck he scampered, leaving Her, the Husky, and me alone.

She removed Her cap and brushed it off, revealing a glistening, black sweep of hair. Her skin was arctic white, and Her lips were painted a fierce orchid red. She smiled. Two green eyes gazed down upon me, squeezing out whatever remnants of fury still quivered within my gut.

*Fucking weird*, I thought in some far-off region of my mind.

Her chest rose and fell with each breath, a single strand of loose hair undulated in the breeze, and Her head slowly tilted. I got lost in the rhythm of it all, calm and empty as a shell. I blinked, feeling my own breathing match Hers and drinking in that scent as if it were an elixir, filling every cell in my body with its memory. And once again my eyes wandered to the bitch who, with the slightest inclination of the head, said, *It's all right, just go with it.*

It was magic. Not the kind with flashes, lights, or tricks, but the kind that makes you feel what's underneath everything. It was The Howl, that's what it was; a direct mainline hit from The Howl. For a second I forgot that I was me.

I try to do my best by Reg. I try to do what he asks me: to come when he calls, to stay when he wants, and to sit when he asks me. But it takes concentration and I don't always get it right. Sometimes I get distracted.

But this, this thing She was doing, there was no getting distracted from that. This *was* the distraction. So when She filled Her lungs, raised Her chin, and said "Sit," that's exactly what I did.

She looked between the husky and me.

"Veronica seems to like you," She said. "How unusual."

I don't know what would have happened if that radio hadn't crackled. When the truck's engine started and the plonker driving it shouted something at Her, the moment just buzzed away, and I was back, standing in the rubble without Reg—albeit now looking at a pretty tasty-looking husky who, if I'm not very much mistaken, had the hots for old Lineker too. Before I knew it, She had replaced her cap and returned to the truck, with the bitch hopping in behind her, and the doors had slammed, and they were away down the road in a cloud of dust.

As I got my bearings and the world fully returned, Reg was next to me on his knees, checking me over and looking all worried—bless his fat-packed heart—and the girl was there too, stroking my head and making me feel like the bravest dog on Earth.

But not the last, clearly. Like I said: fucking weird.

But none of that matters now! Forget it, done, in the past, *weird bit* definitely but time to move on. And moving on we most fucking well are, because it looks as though we're going on a little adventure! Reg—the man I love and trust more than anything in the world— the girl, of whom I'm growing fonder and fonder by the hour, and little old me, we're heading—wait for it—north! North toward all those wonderful buildings where my dream birds land, the impossible places I visit when I fall into a nap at my window.

Reg has packed supplies, so I can tell that this is one serious fucking walkies. It's a fresh new day, all wintry and bright, and the world is ours alone. The sights, the sounds, the smells… I can't wait for them, and apart from the strange memory of that moment, the scent of Her still lingering in my hairy nostrils, and the dull ache in my side from that twat's boot, I haven't felt this good in ages. I feel hopeful and alive. I feel free.

# THE GIFT OF NOT CARING

**REGINALD HARDY'S JOURNAL**
DECEMBER 10, 2021

So there is this Duchess, you see. Only you should understand that she is not really a duchess, more of a princess or a queen. It is rather complicated to explain because it all happens in a different time and an imaginary place. But she is called The Duchess. That is her name.

The story takes place in a mighty kingdom called Karafall, and The Duchess has just led her people bravely in a ten-year war against a horde of fierce warriors from across the sea called The Skellt Droves. But now the war is over and Karafall lies defeated, so The Duchess must flee from her mountaintop tower, abandoning her crown and all her riches for the greedy Skellt to plunder.

She walks among her people, but without her fine clothes and jewels nobody believes who she is. She stands in a market square declaring her title and imploring her people to follow her once again, but they jeer and throw rotten fruit at her as if she is a lunatic. The more she insists, the less people believe her and the more fruit they throw. And then this beggar arrives...

Twenty years I have been writing this story and I still cannot get to the end of it. I have written it so many times in so many ways, but each time, just when I think I am going to crack it, I hit this wall.

I get stuck, and I cannot move on.

How can I save The Duchess, and what will she do when she is saved?

I would not normally have been thinking about my book during daylight; I save my writing for the morning and the evening. But today I needed a distraction.

She is small and still a little weak from her time in the stairwell—*when you refused to help her, Reginald; yes, thank you for the reminder*—so we were moving rather more slowly than I would have liked. Lineker ran ahead and she walked behind, scurrying every now and again to keep up. She does not complain, though. In fact, she does not say a word, just keeps her head down and follows. So I suppose that is a blessing of sorts.

My plan was to head for Vauxhall Bridge, taking Peckham High Road (well within my map) until Denmark Hill, then northwest up Camberwell New Road (a little outside the boundaries) until we hit the water (which is completely off the page). The whole route was just under five miles which, at the pace we had been keeping, would have taken us about three hours. I had a map for her with a route marked upon it and a small bag with food and water for her journey. After Vauxhall, I would send her on her way and be back in Peckham in time for tea.

The problem with my little scheme was that I had not ventured north of Peckham High Road for the best part of three years, and so I had no idea what was there.

The cold mist clung to everything as we made our way along the middle of the road. Three-story shopfronts lined the street on either side: curry houses, barbershops, cafés, and bookies, all with their windows either shuttered, boarded up, or smashed in like everywhere else. Every surface—every wall, lamppost, phone box, and door—was plastered with posters and flyers from top to bottom, each layer bearing evidence of its era like the rings of a tree trunk. Poking through at the bottom were advertisements for events—music festivals, concerts, plays, and comedy nights. The names of the acts and celebrities seemed so distant it was as if they came from a book or a film, a different story that no longer belonged in reality. I can barely remember the sounds that used to blare from radios and sizzle from headphones.

On top of these were election campaign posters. Primary yellows, reds, and blues, each with a happy, caring face advertising the candidates' charm and suitability for the job. And nestled among these, in lesser number, were the purple sheets. There were no faces on these, just Union Jacks adorned with words like "change" and "unite."

The next layer was overwhelmingly taken over by something called *The Manifesto*. These had been scratched, defiled, and muddled with handwritten notes, most of which appealed for help finding family members. Others were scrawled with times and places or stamped with a small emblem: an open palm and a star.

The second-to-last layer was made up of single sheets with the heading *POSITIVE STEPS FOR A POSITIVE FUTURE*. Underneath was a list: *Study your neighbor, Respect your curfew, Encourage vetting*, that kind of thing, and over them all were stuck red squares emblazoned with the starred palm. These were either torn, scratched, smeared with spit, or graffitied with suggestions of activities the supporters of this symbol might like to engage in with their mothers, or fathers, or certain animals. The insults were set off with the occasional swastika for good measure.

I glanced over this little history lesson, affording it the same interest I had when it unfolded in the first place. Caring, you see, that is what it comes down to. The quality of your peace upon this godless rock is, I believe, a function of how much you decide to care. Caring leads to nothing but disappointment, confusion, and pain.

Not caring, however, does not mean not watching. I was fully aware of the seismic shifts that were occurring in the political landscape back when the glue on these flyers was still wet. I saw how people reacted. I remember once getting stuck in traffic on the Old Kent Road. I was waiting next to a bus full to the brim with passengers all facing down as they swiped screens, turned pages, and shook their heads. Nothing unusual about that, I thought. But then, two panes of glass and three feet of smog-filled air away, I saw a man in his thirties. He looked like he'd done all right for himself, had a pricey-looking suit and watch (I immediately marked him as a handshaker). Suddenly, he dropped his phone on his lap and turned his face up to the sky, contorted in a bizarre and sudden spasm of anguish. He stared into the sun with mournful eyes and a drooping mouth, looking for all the world like a stained-glass saint beholding the crucifixion. Then, ever so slowly, as if pulled there by some unseen force of despair, his gaze trickled down the grubby window toward me.

And do you know what he did? He started bawling, that's what he did. He cried his eyes out at me. I hardly knew where to look, so I kept my eyes front and willed the truck ahead to move. To my relief, it eventually did, and I used the space to swap lanes and whirl away home.

"It's the end of the world," a young mother in East Dulwich lamented another time. I was fixing a socket in her kitchen as she leaned against the sink, cigarette trembling in her hand. She sucked and puffed at it like a child pretending, avoiding all the smoke. "Don't you think?"

I tightened the screws on her socket and told her that the end of the world was not something I knew much about, being an electrician.

"I'm being emotional, sorry," she twittered, extinguishing the cigarette under the tap, "but that's what I think. It's the end, I can feel it."

I had finished, so I packed my tools and stood to leave. She bit her nails and shot me nervous glances as her children's tablet computers beeped and bubbled from the back room. Without quite knowing why, I found myself speaking again.

"The world ends every day, madam, and it always has done," I said. "Inside every third set of eyes, you will find a little apocalypse raging. You don't need bombs for that."

She had stopped fidgeting and I had run out of words. We faced each other in a silence that went on far longer than was comfortable.

"My apologies," I said at last, but her expression changed as I turned to leave. With a single glance in the direction of her distracted offspring, she flopped her shoulders in surrender and sprang into my path, arms outstretched and mouth agape. I barely had time to snatch my laminate sheet before she was upon me.

"Madam, please!" I announced, holding it up like a flaming cross in the face of the devil himself. She froze as I shook it at her. "Please! Control yourself!"

"I'm sorry," she said, reading it and deflating. "I'm so, so sorry."

Then she curled up on the floor and cried. I marched straight out; no charge. The sound of her sobbing over the digital beeps and bubbles of her children's computer games stayed with me as I strode down the street.

I remember the night marches too. Every evening another mob would stream through the streets. These were not young hoodlums, vested baboons, or flag-waving terrorists, but what appeared to be normal people: families, couples, youngsters helping the old folks, all singing cheerful songs and swaying their torches with a thousand grins. *Reclaiming what was theirs*, they called it, and that is what they did, every single night. There were always bodies in the morning.

Then there were beatings in broad daylight. I once saw a girl on the pavement outside the Overground station being kicked by three men. The crowd of commuters flowed around them with not a flicker on their faces. It is not unheard of in London to see violence being ignored by passersby, but this was different. The reason for their lack of engagement was not fear; it was that this had become normal now—a girl like her should not have been in that place.

I saw all this happening. I watched people filling with anger, fear, hope, and glee, and the more that storm of feelings grew, the calmer I grew as I became detached from it.

Do you know what a gift it is not to care? It is a choice you can make. Take it from me—I know what I am talking about.

As we continued along the road, a curious feeling overcame me. Engrossed as I had been in the papery relics of that time before the bombs, a small part of my brain had still been marking our progress against the map. I came to a halt at a crossroads, immediately aware that I was standing on the upper-left vertex of my boundary. I had not ventured this far north or this far west for many a year.

I hovered there, staring down at the invisible line before me. Lineker gave me a cursory glance and scurried ahead. The girl stopped next to me and peered down at my feet, no doubt wondering what on earth I was looking at.

*Perilous*, I thought, my toes flexing in their boots. *Perilous to embark upon that which you are about to embark, Reginald Hardy.* I shuddered and felt a nauseous swell. Then, with a short breath, I stepped across.

I walked like an astronaut on the moon, enduring—enjoying is not the correct word—such a surge of adrenaline that it made my vision swim. I kept walking, trying to ignore the shifting patterns of this unfamiliar new world. The girl followed without a sound.

As the rush subsided, I allowed my eyes to wander the shopfronts on either side. Something caught my eye. It was a pawnshop or its modern-day equivalent, branded to assert that the items on sale were anything but the artifacts of misery and desperation that they clearly were, and in its window was a pair of binoculars. Huge things they were, with gleaming green metal and thick rubber handgrips. I fairly salivated and took a step closer to peer through the mesh at the specifications.

Carbon fiber, powered focus, image stabilizer…24× magnification…

Twenty-four times. Good gracious me. I checked the door, running an exploratory finger around it for a way in, when I heard Lineker making a peculiar whine. I looked back along the street and saw him standing next to the girl. She was peering up a side street.

"Come on," I called back. My voice bounced eerily between the papered walls of the street. "You need to leave yourself plenty of time for your journey. What are you looking at?"

I stole another look at the binoculars, as if they might get snapped up. *Twenty-four times...*

"Heavens to Murgatroyd." I sighed and trudged back. "What on earth have you found?"

What she had found was a thin street empty of cars. Faded bunting hung between the houses, and down the middle of the road was a long trestle table covered with a tattered linoleum tablecloth, cups, saucers, and plates. A light breeze ruffled the sodden, long-popped streamers hanging from a chair.

"A street party," I said. "Must have been from after the election."

The girl walked toward it.

"Wait."

She looked up and down the table, then ran her hand along the red-and-white plastic until her fingers found a teacup still sitting in its saucer. She picked it up and peered inside at the layers of dirt.

"We had a street party once," I said, picking up a small teddy bear in a party hat, "for the royal wedding. Charles and Diana."

I remember that day. It was 1981 and I had just turned twelve. It was hot, and I had to help my mum make hundreds of cucumber sandwiches. "Reg," she'd told me as she spread margarine on thin white bread. She'd been flushed with excitement and sherry. "Always remember that these are the things that hold us together. Days like this are the knots that tie our communities tight."

She'd nodded up to the commemorative plate she had saved up for.

"Just like that lovely couple, God bless 'em, and the wonderful marriage they're about to enjoy. They'll be your king and queen one day, Reg, they will. And a fine king and queen they shall be. Oh, bloody hell, Pete!"

Her boyfriend had chosen that moment to swoop in and goose her, landing me a wink as he swirled her outside in giggles and whoops, leaving me in a room full of bread and vegetables. He would be long gone a few weeks after.

"Do you think she fancies him?" said Neil later. We were sitting on the step and watching the party with bottles of Fanta, counting the ten-pence pieces the adults had flipped us as they danced past.

"Who, Mum?" I said.

"No," said my brother, jabbing me in the arm. "Fucking Diana. Do you think she fancies Prince Charles?"

"Oh, I don't know. I suppose she must if she's marrying him."

"But he's got massive ears."

"There's more to marriage than ears, Neil," I said with a shrug.

My brother gave me a look, screwed up his face, and jabbed me again.

"Wanker."

Neil called me when it all happened. He had moved his wife and kids to Essex after Mum died in '99, opened a printing shop with some money he'd squirrelled away. He wanted me to come out to him, to help him and his boys "sort out the country," in his words. I told him no, I was staying put, and I didn't want any part in battle plans spread out in the back rooms of pubs.

"Right," he replied, voice crackling. "Then we're coming to get you."

That was the last I heard of him—the same day as the M25 disaster.

The girl cradled the teacup for a bit before placing it back on its saucer. Then she eyed the bear I was still holding.

"Do you want this?"

I held it out and she took a step back.

"Go on, take it."

She looked past me at a lamppost. There, as if it had only just been pasted yesterday, was a picture of that man. I remembered it: the victory shot. The purple of his tie was bright, a gleaming river running down the line of his suit. His arm was held out to the camera and his white-toothed sideways beam seemed to say that he and he alone held the key to life itself, if only you'd just take his hand and follow him.

She stared at the picture, swaying in the mist.

"Do you remember him?" I asked.

Lineker barked from the main road, and she ran off. I took one last look at him, that man still beckoning me to join him, and left.

I found Lineker and the girl near the wide crossroads with Camberwell Road. She was kneeling by him, ruffling the fur around his neck as he looked ahead. A crane had fallen onto the rooftops beside us, crushing the slates and balancing there with its hook dangling through a window. More worrying, however, was what greeted us over the road. A tall fence ran north to south as far as I could see in either direction, blocking our path.

"That does not help us," I said.

I looked left and right. The fence ran into and out of the thick mist.

"We need to find out how far this thing stretches."

But as I took a step toward it, Lineker growled.

"What?"

I followed his upward stare to a spot above the fence. There was movement in the mist, and up in the tower of what had once been a doctor's stood a sentry guard.

"I see," I murmured, motioning for the girl to follow me back behind a nearby dumpster. I crouched down and she sat next to me, dangerously close.

"You stay where you are, please!" I demanded, a little more tremulously than I would have hoped, to be honest, and moved along so that I could get a peek at the tower.

*Why did they have a fence?*

I pulled out my binoculars, suddenly disappointed by their plastic grip and the dial you had to turn yourself, and held them up. The guard was a Purple: round-faced, bald, wearing a bandana of all things, and carrying a firearm. It was a rifle of some sort, though I know nothing about guns. I tracked him as he walked the length of a short scaffold and back, scanning the crossroads.

I was wondering what he'd look like at 24× magnification instead of my measly 12× when we heard the growl of an engine. Before we knew it, two motorbikes had sped from the south on the other side of the fence, BU flags flying from posts stuck into their seats, and disappeared north as quickly as they had come.

The girl gasped and grabbed Lineker, who responded with a comforting lick.

I retrieved my map and found our position, tracing the line of the fence north along Camberwell Road. How far did it go? If I wanted to find out, we would have to skirt through the side streets, keeping clear of the fence and any other sentries who might be manning it.

I did not much fancy that, especially with them being so close. The only other option was to backtrack into familiar territory and head north instead, meeting the river farther east. I had wanted to avoid that bank, given how close it had been to the bombs. But unfortunately, it looked like we had no choice.

I checked the guard through my shoddy binoculars, waiting for him to reach the farthest point on his scaffold before we left the protection of our dumpster. Just as he turned, the sun chose its moment to make an appearance, breaking through the heavy sheet of cloud that had hitherto kept it hidden. A blinding flash hit my second-rate lenses and the resulting glint must have reached the guard on his scaffold, because suddenly he was looking straight at me. I could see the alarm that gripped his face, despite the fact that it was a mere twelve times its normal size. He pulled a radio from his belt and spoke into it, keeping his eyes on us. Then he shouted down.

"You down there, come out where I can see you! State your names!"

I did not consider this such a good idea.

"Run," I said, and we did.

Well, *I* did, and Lineker darted ahead until we were on the other side of the street, out of the guard's sight. But the girl stayed right where she was, crouched behind the dumpster with her fingers plugged in her ears. The guard renewed his shouting, adding warnings and threats to his commands that involved shooting bullets at us with that gun of his.

I beckoned to the girl, but she would not move. Lineker barked across at her, his message clear as day: *Get over here!* But she just shook her head, eyes wide.

*Now would be the time,* said a voice in my head. *Now would be the time to turn and run, to get back home in one piece and forget about all this. This is what happens, is it not, Reginald? This is what happens when you get involved. So why don't you get yourself uninvolved right now and return to what you know? Now is the time.*

A peculiar little voice, that, and not unfamiliar either. I had a feeling it might have been with me longer than I thought.

Lineker stopped barking and began worrying me with his nose, making little whines and whimpers and scampering about the pavement. I pushed him away, but he kept coming back, nagging at me to *do something.*

The guard had stopped shouting orders and was, I imagined, either training his gun on us or descending the steps.

I looked at the street behind us, curving perfectly out of sight with plenty of places to hide. I could be up it and out of the way in no time.

That nose again, insistent and wet, trying to push me into action.

*Now would be the time.*

I let my gaze drift away down the street and back to my boundary. I thought of Freddie Mercury and the boy with his arm outstretched, and I wondered: How much can a mind deal with? How much weight can a conscience bear?

But some part of me had already made its decision. I scrabbled up the wall, turned, and ran.

I heard the first shot before I was properly on my feet, by which time my heart was already galloping with all the grace of a crippled mare. The bullet, or shell, or whatever it was, hit something close behind, which for all I knew could have been flesh or brickwork—I had no idea.

The second shot hit the ground near my feet, sending up a spray of dust and rubble. I felt a nick in my knee and instant wetness. The words *YOU HAVE JUST BEEN SHOT* ticker-taped somewhere in my mind.

I was dimly aware of squeals and urgent barks behind me, but I refused to look back. My eyes were locked on the crossroads and the invisible boundary that ran across them. The only time they strayed from their target was when I allowed myself one last wistful glance at those glorious binoculars in the shop window.

Then I quickened my pace, unaware of whether child or dog were following me.

*Did he care at all?* I imagine you are wondering. *This coward, this useless husk of a man—did he feel no shame?*

Of course I felt shame. I shivered with the stuff. It coursed through me like a swollen river, poisoned with all my misdeeds and mistakes, everything I had and had not done. Shame made my spine buckle at the sad and dismal reality of being me. Shame made me want to tear a hole in the street, bury my head in the dirt, and let the worms devour me.

But then that was a feeling I had grown used to over the years. Because I couldn't save her, you see? Nothing I did could save her.

As it happens, both child and dog did follow.

When my legs and lungs could stand no more, I staggered to a halt by an old pub. Once I had recovered, I looked up and saw them standing side by side some distance from me. The girl glared at me. Even Lineker's usual glee was spiked with a nervous suspicion I had not seen before.

"Well, we can't just stand here," I said at last. "They might be following us."

The pub was boarded up, but an alleyway led to a back door that was less secure. With a shove and a jostle, I managed to break in.

"Come on," I called up the alleyway. They were still standing in the street. "Before they find us."

Time drew out and still they did not move. Each second of inactivity seemed to be another mark of their mistrust, another opportunity for my cowardice to be examined.

And how could I blame them? I had abandoned them.

Eventually, and with considerable hesitation, they followed me inside.

Most of the place had been gutted, but I found some bottles of juice and crisps in the storeroom, and a half-empty bottle of vodka which I drank liberally. After a few drafts I worked up the courage to inspect my knee. There was no sign of a bullet, but something had taken off a sizeable chunk of flesh. I poured some vodka over it—an excruciating experience—and bandaged it with what appeared to be a clean bar towel. Then finally I sat back.

The girl crouched in the opposite corner, sharing her crisps with Lineker. I kept my eyes on the window for signs of trouble, but I could tell they were watching me—she with that glare of hers, and he with that fresh and terrible mistrust that made my insides squirm. At last I could take it no longer.

"What?" I snapped. The girl froze in mid-munch and Lineker's head ducked. Still their eyes were upon me. "Why are you looking at me like that? We're safe, aren't we? You are both unhurt." I pointed at my knee. "It's me who's flipping well injured!"

A moment passed in silence. Then, as if by some pact, Lineker raised his head and the girl resumed her munching. I looked away and took more ruthless swigs of the vodka. I have never been a particularly accomplished drinker—the place alcohol takes me to is full of quicksand and tall cliffs—but I am afraid to say I drained that small bottle dry with little effort. When I was done, I tossed it on the floor where it spun in three shameful circles and stopped, pointing back at me.

I noticed that the girl had spread out her photographs on the floor before her. This, emboldened by the vodka's toxic fire, infuriated me beyond reason. I snapped at her.

"I don't know why you keep those things with you, young lady. They're useless, whatever they are. Memories or fantasies, it doesn't matter—they do you no good. You should get rid of them."

Of course, as I realized sometime later, it was not *her* photographs I was referring to.

She looked up at me, impenetrably calm. I made a noise of exasperation and dragged myself from the floor.

"Come on," I said. "There's nobody out there. We should get going."

I hobbled through the door and looked back, but they did not move.

"Lineker," I called. "Come."

His ears pricked, but he stayed where he was. This more than anything overwhelmed me with grief.

"Suit yourself," I muttered and turned to leave. Only then did he spring up and chase me out. The girl got to her feet and followed.

We pressed on. The girl kept close to Lineker's side and the sun that had given our game away followed like an unwanted friend, yellowing the cold, wet streets. We were even slower now that I had developed a limp, and I staggered along in a haze of alcohol, pain, and indignity. It was almost 4:00 p.m. before I realized I had taken a wrong turn.

I stopped. The road we were on was bland and unfamiliar—just another dull strip of shops with flats above them—but something about it screamed at me. I could see no sign and it was definitely nowhere I had been before, but, somehow, I recognized it. I looked up and down its length, seeing a squat church at one end and three blocks of flats at the other, and something clicked.

With creeping dread, I pulled the map from my pack. There was the church and there were the blocks, right where I thought they would be. And there, right in the middle, a circled dot with a name against it...

"Good afternoon!" said a voice from above. "Blessings upon you and many welcomes. Lovely day, isn't it?"

I looked up to see a bare-breasted Indian woman sunning herself on the flat roof above a betting shop. She let the foil cardboard she had been holding beneath her chin drop and called through the open window.

"Mother! We have guests!"

"What kind of guests?" croaked an ancient voice from inside. "Do I need to arm myself?"

The woman got up from the chair, her full, brown belly drooping over the waistband of her yellow bikini bottoms.

"No," she said. "I don't think so."

She dropped her sunglasses.

"What's wrong?" she said. "You look like you've never seen a woman's body before."

I wanted to say that I had not seen *any* body for three years, but apparently my mouth had stopped working.

So this, I realized, was Shilton. Light number three.

# CONNECTION

## LINEKER

THERE'S SOMETHING ABOUT THIS girl. It's strange, but I already feel like we're a part of each other, like we're connected somehow. Is that possible?

It must be. Take Reg and me, for example—now that's connection, right? Proper deal, same wavelength, totally tuned in and locked on. No doubts there, none whatsoever.

It took time, though, and those first few weeks together weren't exactly a honeymoon. Unless your idea of a honeymoon involves lots of pissing and shitting, of course, which maybe it does. Who am I to judge?

I was so happy to be out of that place, finally free from my cage and away from those dickheads yowling all day. Everything was bright and different. There was the journey home for a start, that rowdy-engined van bumping me about in my box, all those colored streaks everywhere, and Reg's voice, the radio, the smell of oil, hot metal, Polo mints, sandwich crumbs, and a thousand layers of dead skin streaming up from his exquisitely filthy floor mats.

And then came the flat itself, an enormous kingdom of odors, nooks, and adventure. I couldn't believe it; I actually lived there now, with this man, this hero, this king of the dom.

But yeah, lots of wee wee, lots of poo.

Reg corrected me, of course, gently. I had to learn. Couldn't very well turn his house into a toilet, now, could I? It pulls at you, though, doesn't it, learning not to do the thing your body's telling you to do? You'll have experienced it when you were a nipper too. One day that nappy came off and never went on again, and all of a sudden you were free! Free as the wind! So your bum said, *There! Do it there now!* And then your mum said, *No!*

Your bum and your mum. Two opposing voices—one small and fierce from long ago and deep within, and the other from outside, still growing, getting itself together, looming. The first shoves you on and screams what you need; the second pulls you in and tells you how it has to be done. This is how you change. This is how all things change—under the direction of two conflicting forces. Odd that. And it never stops, does it? Funny.

Those first few weeks were hard. I got scared, and I admit that sometimes I wondered if I might not be better off back in my cage, where things were shitty but at least they made sense. And I hadn't even been outside yet.

Then, one afternoon, about three weeks after I'd been set free, I woke from a fretful slumber on the floor near a fresh puddle, looked up, and saw Reg asleep on the sofa. It was autumn and a low blade of orange sun grazed his cheek. I watched him dream and grunt as the fridge buzzed in the background and doors slammed safely in the distance. I stayed there for an hour at least, finding myself twitching whenever he did, or cocking my head when his eyebrows lifted. I was following the map of his dreams, and somehow I knew they were going places nobody should have to go alone. That's when I first caught wind of Reg's deep smell, that frozen bone sack abandoned on a moor.

I couldn't fathom how I knew this at the time. The Howl was only just making itself known, like leaves rustling before a tornado.

All of a sudden, I found I could no longer lie still, so I skittered over and sprang onto the sofa. It took me a few goes, but I managed to clamber up with my claws and found my way into the crook of his arm, all warm and soft and smelly, and I put my tiny pink snout right into his face and licked him back from those nightmares until he was fully awake, bearings found and laughing at my antics. We stayed that way, chuckling and snuffling in that beam of sun, until we settled back down and both fell into a sleep of excellent new dreams.

That's when we found our connection, Reg and I, and now we're solid as a rock. But it took us the best part of a month.

This girl, though, it was instant. She doesn't speak (apart from a few sounds I'm fairly sure Reg doesn't hear, little grunts like something's trying to escape from her), but oh, the conversations we have together. She gives me fresh smells by the second, each one a new story from her life. Her base scent is of foal hair, woodsmoke, and cream, but there are other ones stuck in her clothes. Coarse soap, concrete, wet paper, onions, worms, tomato soup, salt water, vomit, a powdery thing I can't quite place, and slate. And voles, a thousand voles from a thousand holes.

But buried within all that there's this other smell too that I've never really smelled before. It's only a glimmer, but it's something like pebbles laid out on cotton, cut grass, glacial water, and peanut butter. Something like that. I'm searching for it all the time. I know that it's a power smell, which means it represents an emotion that can either drive you or hold you back, like Reg's sack of bones. The strongest I've smelled it yet was during all that business at the crossroads, when Reg…well, I mean, there's no two ways of saying it—when Reg ran off.

Ha! Honestly, it sounds so stupid when I say it out loud. *When Reg ran off.* As if he would! Reg, solid as a rock, heart of gold, straight as a die, trust him with your life—Reg. Running off. Ridiculous!

But he did. He ran off. Didn't he?

No. No, it's too stupid to think about. He wouldn't. He was probably just confused and thought we were right behind him. He was leading us to safety, creating a distraction—that's it! Charging off down the road and drawing fire like a ruddy great hero. He even took a bullet for us—fucking legend.

It was probably my fault. Stupid cunt, I should've used his clever diversionary tactics to get Aisha back over quicker, fucking idiot I am sometimes. But it all happened so fast.

I remember crossing the road and hearing something zip by my ear. Most unusual smell, it was—glee, quarries, and cobwebs. By the time I'd skidded to a halt by the girl, Reg was already powering down the road and putting his life on the line so that I had a chance to get the girl. Blimey, to think—such nerve, such valor—gives me the proper shivers it does. Anyway, there's me on the other side of the road (daft mug) and all I could think to do was bark.

"Get up! Come on, you silly twat, get up and run! I said get up and *run!*"

And she did. She jumped up and followed me down the road,

bullets flying all around, and all I was thinking was: *I would die for this girl. I know I would. No question.*

Do you ever get that? That feeling that you'd die for someone you've only just met?

I know, it's probably more complicated than that. There's way more stuff going on in those clockwork noggins of yours than my dumb dog brain can assimilate. It's not as simple as just dying for someone, is it? You probably need a cause or something. Tons of people die for causes, *tons*. Although, not as many as kill for them. Right?

Can you tell me, though, what is a *cause*? Because I've been racking my brains about this one and I can't...

Fuck, I'm rambling, sorry. It's just that ever since we started out on this little adventure, my mind's been whirling. All those posters and smells along that street, the ghosts of what happened. Human beings fired up about a cause, enough to kill, but not to die. I don't get it. I don't know what a *cause* is.

Forget it. These aren't issues for a dog to ponder. All I know is that this girl and me, we're connected somehow, and I'm not imagining it either. Me and this little human have got a thing going on. True love, I reckon.

So there I was trotting along, following Reg up even more new roads and getting extremely used to having this little human around, and what happens? Another one comes along. And this one had her tits out.

# MIRA'S PLACE

**REGINALD HARDY'S JOURNAL**

DECEMBER 10, 2021

"So, TELL ME YOUR names," said the lady, landing heavily on a long, claret sofa.

I had not wanted to stop, but I was in somewhat of a daze. The vodka, the sight of this great being beaming down upon us, topless in the winter sun, and the realization that I had unwittingly stumbled upon the border of the lights, had rendered me senseless.

Before I knew it, she had arrived on the pavement, imploring us to come in. I had backed away from her great hands—and the rest of her of course, swaying about in monstrous tides—but she had ushered Aisha inside and Lineker zipped in after them, hungry for the exotic smells emanating from within.

The front room was long and painted white, with a dark-wood floor and rich decorations, completely at odds with the drab exterior. There were rugs on the walls, neatly hung and woven with bright reds, blues, and golds. Some bore triptychs of Indian villages with men in tall hats and long trumpets and women with baskets on their heads. Between them were paintings in thick, gilded frames.

Dark portraits of ancient strangers, rugged landscapes, and blue-skied deserts mingled with more modern pieces, flashes and swirls of abstract color. Beneath them, lining the walls, were dark-wood cabinets ornately carved and adorned with gleaming ornaments of elephants, monkeys, and trees. Everything had been arranged with care.

I loitered at the doorway. The girl stood next to me, although not for my sake; her mistrust was still evident in the distance she maintained. Something was stopping her from crossing the threshold, though, and I noticed that the lady's voice—which caused the ornaments to rattle—made her flinch.

"Well?" said our host.

"Reginald," I croaked. "Reginald Hardy."

Unless you count my exchange with the soldier outside our flat, this was my first conversation with another human being in three years. She beamed at me.

"Welcome, Mr. Hardy," she said, inclining her head. "My name is Mira Dhaji."

Mira was not an unattractive lady. She had glistening brown eyes, a cascade of long black hair that fell around her bare shoulders, and a wide-lipped mouth. This was pulled into a permanent quizzical smile, revealing bright-white teeth that were just a little too big for their surroundings.

There was a hoot and a coarse chuckle from a room at the back which, judging by the spicy smells, sizzles, and clattering emanating from it, was a kitchen. Lineker had already made a beeline for it.

"My, you're a hungry boy, aren't you!" came the voice again. "There you go."

I peered through the gap in the door and saw another lady, white-haired and hunched with age, feeding Lineker a sliver of something from her stove.

Mira turned and sighed.

"You'll have to excuse my mother," she said, waving a hand. "She is always cooking."

"Not always," her mother called back.

"Always!" insisted Mira. She rolled her eyes. "She cannot go outside, you see, so I have to do everything else."

"Why can't she go outside?" I was intrigued.

"Because she's allergic to sunlight." Mira leaned toward me, one eyebrow raised in derision. "Can you believe that? Sunlight! Of all the things to be allergic to!"

"I have sensitive skin," protested her mother from the kitchen. She leaned down with another morsel for Lineker and patted his head.

"Sensitive skin," said Mira. She smiled and fluttered a hand down her curves. "Not such a problem for yours truly."

"It is very cold out there," I said as my eyes dropped.

I have neither sought out nor indulged in sexual activity for some time now, apart from the occasional bout of onanism whenever the pressure dials start twitching, but I am afraid I may have looked a little longer than I had intended at what Mira had on display.

Mira cleared her throat, and I pulled my eyes away from their enormous distractions. She had one eyebrow cocked like a pistol.

"Art should be admired, Mr. Hardy, not stared at."

"My apologies, madam. And it's Reginald."

"Besides," she said, brightening again, "cold air is good for the skin."

"Not mine," said her mother from the kitchen.

"Shut up!"

"I wish you'd put those terrible things away. Just once."

Mira rolled her eyes and grabbed a huge green-and-silver throw from the arm of the sofa.

"All right, all right! But bring us some tea, would you?"

There was more clattering from the kitchen. Mira pulled the throw around her, tying it in a knot, fluffing, picking, and smoothing it down around her. When she was happy, she sighed and smiled. "Aren't you going to come inside, Mr. Hardy?"

My feet did a strange shuffle of their own accord. My knee was throbbing with pain and I could think of nothing I would rather do than have a nice sit down, but it had been some time since I had been invited into somebody else's home, least of all by a half-naked woman. And I had neglected to bring my laminate.

Getting no reply, Mira looked down at the girl beside me. "And what about you, Chicken? Won't you come in? What is your name?"

The girl's fingernails nibbled the edge of the doorframe.

"Your daughter?" Mira asked me in a gentle tone.

I flinched. "No."

"Oh. Then who?"

The door opened, and the old lady wobbled in with a tray, upon which clattered a tea set of intricate patterns in black and gold. Steam rose from the pot, smelling nothing like tea. She laid it down on the table, gave me a shiny-eyed smile, and hobbled back to her stove, where she recommenced her cooking and Lineker's bliss.

Mira was still looking at me, awaiting an answer.

"Her name is Aisha," I said. "I found her in the stair of my block. I think she was being evacuated, but she was separated."

Mira turned to the girl again. "Do you know where you were going?" she said with a cautious smile.

Aisha blinked.

"Hmm," said Mira, looking around. "Let's see… Aha."

She stood and went to a corner table, from which she plucked a stuffed bear.

"Here," she said, kneeling down before the girl. "You can have this. It was mine once—his name is William. Take it, go on."

The girl took the bear. As she examined it, Mira noticed the tag around her neck.

"Wembley," she said. "Is that where you were heading, my sweet? Do you know?"

"It's no use," I said. "I've tried talking to her, but she won't respond. I don't think she speaks English."

The girl shot me a look as if I had spoken out of turn. Mira laughed.

"I believe that says it all, Mr. Hardy." She laughed.

"Reginald," I corrected.

"She does speak English; she just finds it hard right now. Right, Chicken?" She looked deep into the girl's eyes. "You've been through too much for your years already, haven't you?"

The girl ignored her and continued her examination of the bear.

"So she's mute?" I suggested.

Mira sighed and rested on her haunches. "We used to see a lot of children like Aisha back in the beginning, either rescued during a BU raid or freed from one of the sorting camps. They would come through here on their way to the evacuation centers. I thought that was all done with now. Where are you supposed to be, Aisha? Do you know? Where's your family?"

I neglected to ask exactly what "here" meant, or "back in the beginning."

"She is an orphan," I said. "It says so on her tag."

"Not necessarily. Many of them had just been separated from their parents. You remember what a mess it was back then. We were just starting up and the army was on its knees. More often than not, they would mark children as orphans simply because they had no idea where their families had been taken."

"What do you mean? What about identification records, passports, national insurance numbers, that sort of thing?"

Mira laughed. "Yes, not particularly useful when there is nothing to check them against, Mr. Hardy."

I frowned. Her look of amusement wilted.

"We lost everything—internet, communications, records—don't you remember? Everything that tied our society together was destroyed."

After a moment's thought, I considered this a plausible scenario, and I was about to explain to Mira that my focus on basic security and sustenance, not to mention the location of a suitable power supply, had perhaps preoccupied me to such an extent in those days that I had neglected to keep abreast of developments farther afield, when suddenly the girl dropped the bear and pulled something from her coat pocket. It was an envelope, and from inside she produced the photograph she had shown me the previous afternoon. She held it out for Mira to see.

"What's this, Chicken?" said Mira. "Can I see?"

She reached for the photograph, but the girl gasped and snatched it to her chest. Mira held up her hands in surrender.

"It's OK. I won't steal it. Can I see? Show me, please. Show Mira."

After some deliberation the girl held the photograph up once again, this time keeping it a safe distance from the potential thief.

"A lovely photograph," said Mira. "Beautiful hills, a river, trees, very pretty. Is that a farm? What is this place? And who's this? Who is that, Aisha? Your mother? Your aunt? Grandmother?"

I heard a faint breath from the girl's lips, and she hastily replaced the photograph in its envelope. In doing so, she gave us a glimpse of others inside.

"And what about these ones?" said Mira. "Can we see these too?"

She reached for the envelope, but the girl flinched and squealed. Then, without warning, she grabbed my wrist.

The touch was like an electric shock. My arm shot through with pain—*real* pain—deep within the flesh at the point of contact, followed by a torrent of volts up to my shoulder and down my spine. My lungs filled, my eyes popped, my heart lurched, my gut churned. I found I could not move.

The reaction must have been obvious because, to my horror, Mira held out a hand to steady me. I watched it creep toward my other arm, my paralysis rendering me unable to recoil from the growing heat of her flesh. Her touch brought a fresh shock of pain that stiffened my body even more so that I stood rigid, suspended between the two of them like a human guinea pig strung between the contacts of some mad scientist's crude and terrible machine.

The twin points of contact throbbed with a sick, urgent pulse. It was nothing short of a nightmare. I shut my eyes and screamed like a little boy.

That is what I mean by *the heebie-jeebies*.

I do not know what happened next. A brief blackout. Either I broke free or my reaction caused such a surprise that they released me, but somehow I found myself cowering against the doorframe. The girl blinked, confused, and ran inside. Mira staggered back with her hand to her chest.

"Mr. Hardy, whatever is wrong?"

"My..." I stammered, patting my coat uselessly. "My laminate. I have neglected to bring my laminate. *Blast!* It explains everything, you see, but I don't carry it with me anymore because, well, I have not needed it for such a long time now. Three years, in fact. *Three years!* Lineker!"

I stood up and craned my neck, foot tapping. Mira's mouth hung open.

"Come on, Lineker, we have to go. Chop chop!"

"What?" said Mira. "Why? Where are you going?"

"Lineker!"

"Mr. Hardy, you've only just arrived. Come in, sit down, please calm—"

"It's Reginald, for crying out loud. Lineker!" I screamed, eyes bulging. It was dark in the stairwell and twilight outside, but I wanted to be out in it, anywhere but here, out and away from those two hands of hers hovering there, waiting to...

"Lineker, will you get your bloody arse in here *now!*"

Lineker appeared in the doorway, tail between his legs, ears down.

"Come on, we're going."

I turned, but my knee, which had been still for too long, twisted and shot through with pain. I cried out and fell upon the floor.

"Your leg," said Mira. "It is covered in blood. Let me help you."

I watched as those two mountainous arms descended upon me, preparing to engulf me within their hot, fleshy valleys.

"No," I gasped, holding up a hand and pushing back with my good leg. "Please, do not touch me. I cannot have you touching me."

"Why not?"

"I just can't. It's like, it's like your mum with sunlight. I can't have it, do you understand? Please, don't."

She backed away, clutching her hands to her breast.

"OK," she said at last, the word turning in a slow circle of calm. "But that leg requires attention."

"I'm all right."

"I believe that is a little far from the truth, Mr. Hardy."

My back found the wall and I rested there, panting. My knee felt like a Catherine wheel spitting with excruciating sparks. Mira tapped her lips for a moment, thinking.

"How about if I wear gloves?" she said.

I was made to sit on a sofa with one trouser leg rolled up while Mira saw to my knee. Her proximity was nothing short of torturous, but she wore a pair of blue surgical gloves from the kitchen that prevented any flesh-touching, and her hands worked deftly, dabbing at the wound and picking out dirt with tweezers.

"Ouch."

"It's filthy. Hold still."

The girl was sitting in an armchair with her legs dangling, watching me.

Her demeanor had changed after my little outburst at the door. Although her eyes were still filled with scrutiny, they had lost a little of their frost. I do not believe it was pity she was feeling, but neither was it judgment. I believe she wanted to understand me.

I caught her eye and she looked away, gazing around the room instead. Mira glanced at her as she worked.

"Do you like the pictures, Chicken?" she said.

The girl ignored her and looked at me, then back at the walls. Mira smiled and went back to work.

"She looks to you," she whispered. "She knows you're looking after her."

"I wouldn't be so sure about that," I mumbled.

"Pardon?"

I shook my head. "Nothing."

"Hmm. Either way, she looks to you."

"I'm just getting her to the river, that's all."

Mira frowned. "The river? And then what?"

"I have no idea. I suppose I will attempt to get her onto a bridge, after which she can make her own way to Wembley. I drew her a map."

Mira stopped and sat back on her heels, her mouth turned down in a great black crescent of disgust.

"A map?" she said. "You're going to leave a little girl at the river with nothing but a map?"

"Some water too, and some food, crackers, and what have you."

Mira released a cry of horror and the girl jumped in fright. Her hands sprang to her ears.

"Too loud," I muttered.

"Crackers?" bellowed Mira.

From the corner of my eye, I saw Lineker's ears prick up.

The girl and I had locked eyes. Unbeknownst to Mira, she was performing a series of twitches as if the words she wanted to say were bouncing around inside her head, unable to escape. She was trying to speak to me.

"Your voice, Mira," I said. "It's—"

Mira did not hear me. Her face blazed with scorn. "Nothing but crackers?"

The girl squealed.

"Mira," I exclaimed, mustering as much authority as I could. "Please, do try to speak more softly."

I nodded to the chair behind.

Mira turned and, seeing the girl's discomfort, shrank. "Oh…" she breathed.

"I don't think she likes loud noises," I said.

"Forgive me, Chicken," said Mira.

She turned back to me, and her apologetic expression quickly regrouped into disdain. "Have you even been to the river lately?" she said.

Her voice quietened as she went back to work on my knee, although her bedside manner now left a little to be desired. The girl's face was aflutter with a dozen half-built coping mechanisms, but there was relief in there somewhere too.

"No," I said. "I never venture north."

"Clearly. Well, you should know that the South Bank is no longer full of galleries, museums, and restaurants. There are no bridges, and it is certainly no place to abandon a child."

I absorbed this information, feeling glum. "I never asked for this," I said.

"What?"

"I never asked to look after a child."

She turned those moonlike eyes up at me.

"No? Well, she never asked to lose her family or have that tag strung around her neck, and I never asked to look after an old lady who shits in her bed every other night. But these are the cards we are dealt, Mr. Hardy—get used to them."

She opened a bottle and dampened some cotton wool with whatever was inside, regarding me coolly like a nurse loading up a syringe with something that might kill or cure me. I felt distinctly uncomfortable.

"I am sorry," she said, "but this will hurt."

She pressed the cotton wool to the wound, flooding it with an acidic sting. I braced against the pain, trying to ignore the glimmer of satisfaction in my nurse's eyes, and searched the room for some distraction.

"Suppose you, er, looted all this then, did you?" I struggled out, referring to the artwork.

Mira removed the cotton wool and disposed of it neatly in the basin beside her.

"Looted? No. I liberated it."

"That's just a fancy word for looting."

The furrows in her frown deepened, and she trained those two brown marbles upon me with a tight whistle in her throat.

"And what have you been living on?" She nodded at my chest. "Nectar points?"

I looked down at my binoculars, lifting them sadly. "I only take what's necessary, and I make a note of everything." I patted my top pocket where my logbook lived. "All accounted for."

"Art *is* necessary and can never be accounted for."

Her smile returned as she rummaged in the box of first aid supplies beside her.

"Where did you get it all?" I ventured.

She measured the wound and scissored some bandage and strips of surgical tape.

"Untold treasures lie beneath this ground, Mr. Hardy, wrapped up in plastic and covered in cloth. Explosions of human expression locked away in darkness. You have no idea what people keep hidden in their cellars. Beauty, life…"

She glanced up at me. "Pain," she said.

All at once I felt raw and exposed, as if a section of my skin had been torn away. Mira's eyes flicked between mine; she was looking for a way in, I could tell.

"What happened?" she said, almost a whisper.

My muscles tensed. "That is none of your business."

She screwed up her brow. "What? I mean, how did this happen? Your knee?"

"Oh," I said.

The sound of Lineker's appreciation and the old woman's delight continued in the kitchen.

"The fence at Camberwell Road," I went on. "They shot at us."

"You were fired upon?" Her voice boomed, and I saw the child startle again. "How close did you get? Did they come after you?"

Those frightened eyes trembling behind her, head shaking, asking me, *imploring* me to put a stop to the noise.

"It was fine," I said in my calmest voice. "We weren't followed."

"Why was she in your stairwell? How did she get separated?"

"They were ambushed. They were having a bathroom break when those Purples—"

Mira straightened. "The BU?"

"Yes, the BU attacked the truck she was riding in. Those army boys, I'd not seen them for years. I thought they were all dead and gone. The last time I saw anyone in green was when it all happened."

"You mean the bombs?"

"Yes, the bombs, and the panic and everyone leaving and what have you."

She nodded and gave me a curious frown as she fastened the last piece of tape—I shuddered as she brushed my shin. Then she stood up, pulling off her gloves. "So you saw the BU this side of Camberwell Road?"

"The Purples, yes."

I tried my knee, bending it. It was still sore and stiff, but I thought I could stand.

"They must have extended the zone," she said to herself, eyes darting about. "Taken more of the south, blocked the routes…"

I stood up, glad to feel the knee take my weight.

"Where exactly did this happen?" said Mira.

"Outside my flat in Peckham. Here…"

I took out my map and showed her. She squinted at the spot I had tapped. "But that can't be right," she said.

"It can and it is. I should know, I've lived there for thirty years. Anyway, it's starting to get dark, so we really should be getting on our way. Lineker!"

I glanced at the girl, who seemed unwilling to leave her chair. Mira was still peering at my map.

"You mean to say you live here, on this street, in this tower?" she said.

"Correct."

"So you're not from Collective 18?"

"What? No, Seton Bayley, I told you. It's written right there, see? Lineker, come on!"

"And why is there a circle around *my* flat?" she asked.

"Because you're one of the lights. Lineker!"

"Lights?"

"Yes, the others. The stay-behinds. I spotted you through my binoculars, ten of you. Well, nine now that Beardsley's gone, of course." I held out my hand. "Could I have my map back, please?"

Lineker padded through from the kitchen and sat at my heel. Upon his arrival, the girl slid from her chair.

"We need to go," I said. "We really do."

Mira looked between us, rubbing the map's edges between her fingers. She appeared to be reaching a decision. "I believe that Aisha will be far safer with us, Mr. Hardy," she declared at last.

I paused. "Really?"

"Yes. We have contacts at the river and farther north. She has a much greater chance of safe passage with us than with you."

You can float through most moments. Others you have to wade through. Mira's words brought me a wave of relief but, beneath it, an unexpected undercurrent: loss. Deep, surprising loss.

I looked down at the girl. I wanted to get home and yet—there she was.

It did not even occur to me at the time to question why on Earth a little girl would be safer in the hands of a middle-aged woman and her incontinent mother than with a middle-aged man and his dog, such was the muddle of doubt in which I found myself. This push and pull must have played out on my face somehow, because Mira, turning her head a little to the left, said, "So long as that is all right with you, Mr. Hardy?"

I straightened my neck. Cleared my throat. "Of course it is. Yes, you're quite right."

One middle-aged woman and her incontinent mother.

"Right," I said, patting my pockets uselessly. "Right, well...are you sure?"

"Yes, I am quite sure. But where will you go?"

"Us? We'll go home, of course. Where else?"

Her face looked as if I had just declared myself king of England.

"We'll be on our way then, Lineker," I said. "Be home before midnight, I expect. Thank you, Mrs. Dhaji."

I looked down at the girl again, enduring another surge of that same loss as if I were standing too close to a precipice and fumbling for the appropriate words to say at such a juncture. In the end, I just said "Right" and turned to leave.

But I froze before I reached the door. "Mrs. Dhaji," I said, turning back.

"Yes?"

"Who are Collective 18?"

She smiled. "Those are nice binoculars, Mr. Hardy," she said, nodding at the pair around my neck. "But I have something a little more powerful upstairs. Would you like to see it before you leave?"

# STARS

## LINEKER

I FUCKING LOVE THAT old woman. *Love* her. She'd be by new best friend if I didn't already have one, or an old best friend, of course. No change there. Nope. Reg, my master, till death us do part and all that.

Although he's not been his old self, our Reg, has he?

You can't blame the poor bloke; it's been a right busy few days. But that moor-sack smell of his, it's there all the time now, swelling and shrinking, never disappearing. And he's nervous too. He jitters and jumps like his skin's full of frogs, biting his nails and mumbling things to himself wherever we go. I can't watch him too much in case I get it too, whatever he has, that fucking twitch of his. Can't stand it. And the *shouting*. I've never seen him shout like that before, and certainly not in my direction. "Bloody arse!" he said to me. Fucking charming! Made me drop my tail like a dead snake that did, especially after I'd been so happy with all the…phwoar, fuck me, yeah, so this old bird. She's fucking lovely. A proper queen.

Firstly, there's the smell of her. Unbelievable! Lemons, pickles, mothballs, eggs (*rrripe*), charred lamb, and a whole cellar of spice caking her flappy, old skin and setting every single one of her bodily aromas aglow with the warm winds of Delhi. And that's just the start; that's just the tip of her. *Her past reeks.* I can smell one hundred thousand shadows of moments passed, some in the sands of far-off shores, others in market squares, empty halls, and lusty hovels. Beautiful.

You might think your years are behind you, but they're not. They follow you around, those ghosts.

Then came...food.

An endless supply of *food.* Morsels, chunks, and titbits rained down on me one after the other like the droppings of heaven. Each time she gave me another bit of chicken or potato or that other sticky thing—no fucking clue what it was, never touched the sides—I thought: *Got to be the last one that, got to be, you can't be that lucky, but not to worry you've had a good innings here, Lineker, mustn't grumble, holy shit, here comes another!*

And then do you know what she did? She poured three ladlefuls into a huge bowl and laid it down on the floor for me, all steaming and glorious. I had to look at it for a while, just to make sure it was real. *Pour moi?* I thought, gawking. She winked and scratched my head.

"Go on," she said. So I did, I went on. I stuck my snout in her grub.

Terrific, lovely, smashing, stinking grub. Thank you, thank you a thousand times, Your Majesty.

I admit, I completely missed the scent of her cooking at first. Normally I would have picked it up from miles away, but even as we stopped outside and Big Tits stood up, I was oblivious to all that heaven sizzling away upstairs. The problem was that I was so engrossed in the girl's smell ghosts and all their stories that it passed me by. I was lost in The Howl. It's all part of the connection, I think, this bond that's growing. I feel like I'm being drawn somewhere, pulled along almost, like I'm a raft that's come loose on a raging river, getting faster and faster.

If so, why? Is it The Howl? Where is it taking me?

Great questions to ponder when you're looking up at the stars. Which I am, my friends, I am.

Reg is sticking out of the attic window with Thundertits, peering through her telescope and being all scientific and stuff. Fuck knows what's going on in that noggin of his. *Amazing* things, though, I shouldn't wonder. Equations, measurements, projections and quantifications, assessments and examinations of all kinds. God only knows.

Does God only know? Or can we know too? Are we supposed to know? What would we do if we did?

Blaaahdy 'ell, what the fuck has gotten into me? Proper unusual feeling, this, *proper* unusual.

Anyway, so Reg is up there doing his crazy scientific shit (although his angle looks all wrong—he wants to slew that tripod around and tilt up to get the full show, otherwise he's just clocking buildings), and I'm down here on the flat roof watching the sky and getting my head rubbed by the girl, nice and full, with my mouth still drooling from the feed.

Ahh, lovely.

It's busy up there in the sky with all those stars and planets and galaxies twirling about. They're like partners in a billion interstellar reels, dancing away the eons. Then deep in the shadows, out of sight, you've got your weirdos—the gas giants and black holes, suns gone mad that devour the darkness till there's nothing left but pinpoints of insanity. Photons stream into them like ships in a maelstrom, and as they do, fresh nebulae boom and thunder with showers of nuclear sparks that erupt for a million years. From this, new suns are born. They pull in cold rocks and warm them, breathe life upon them, then kill them and eat them and die like all the rest.

It's all ever so pretty. Twinkly.

Here's something I know about those stars. If you were able to stand on one of them with a telescope like the one Reg is looking through now—maybe one with a teeny bit more magnification—and looked down on us, you wouldn't see us at all. Depending on which particular pinprick of light you chose and how far away it was, you might see me as a pup having a bash on my old mum's tits, or you as a baby kicking your legs. Or you might see the blitzkrieg raging, or great ships drowning in a North Atlantic fire, or a man talking softly to a crowd about how simple life is, or the first stone of the great pyramids crashing into place amid the silent roar of slaves. Go a bit farther out, deeper into the night and onto the stars that you can't see, and you might see dogs creeping down the hillside with fires flickering in their eyes.

That's because light takes time to travel and everything's far apart, so what you see is never the truth, just a shadow of it. And that's not just true of stars. It's everything. The falling leaf has already fallen, the sun has already set, your lover's laugh has already waned. All we see are shadows and reflections.

Gravity too, that's a funny one. What makes that thing over there want to come over here when there's nothing in between it but space? Answer: because space is twisted and warped by the things themselves.

Fuck me. Can you believe that?

*Space is twisted.*

Not only that, but the things themselves *are only* just twists and warps in space. And all things are in constant motion. Nothing is still. There's no such thing as the speed of now, and there's no such thing as perfect rest. Everything is moving and unaware of reality.

We're all slipping and sliding together in this impossible, crumpled blanket of time and space with no control, so to say there is nothing between us makes no sense, because there is no us at all, just this thing, this blanket trying to form a shape. You and I, we're connected. Like me and this girl wrapped up beside me who's rubbing my fur and making me all sleepy. There is no "her," and there is no "me." There is no "we" at all.

Christ on a bike. What the fuck am I going on about? Amazing what a good feed will do, isn't it? You should try it sometime. Next time you're down or weary, or the world makes no sense—have a nice curry and look up at the stars.

Fucking magic.

# FIXING BEARDSLEY

THREE HUNDRED TIMES MAGNIFICATION. Three hundred. I can barely look *at* my binoculars now, let alone through them.

"Did you, er, liberate this too?" I asked, as I stood at Mira's attic window, marveling at her beautiful telescope as she adjusted the dials. Its chrome-rimmed barrel gleamed in the starlight.

"No," replied Mira, stepping back. "This was my father's. Take a look. Go on, put your eye to it."

I bent down to the eyepiece and my vision immediately filled with dark brickwork, iron railings, and glass.

"What am I looking at?" I said.

"Home, Mr. Hardy. That is your flat."

"No, that's not…"

But it was. Sure enough, buried in the twilight between the peaks of tenements, parking garages, and bare trees, was our block. On the balcony, I spotted the empty plant pot that had always been there, the brush, and the old rusted seat. Through the window I could just make out Lineker's chair and, barely visible, I saw the ink circles I had made, one of which I was now standing in, looking back.

"So it is," I said, standing up. "You saw me too, then, did you?"

"I suppose we must have."

"Suppose?"

"Well, it's not like you're the only one out there."

I nodded.

"I saw them too. Did you ever meet them? They must be that way…" I craned my neck to look east along the street. "A bit tricky to see from this angle, though."

She gave me one of her strange looks again. "Not those ones."

I frowned as she checked her watch. Then she gestured toward home again. "Look."

The sky had darkened, and the buildings were now in shadow.

"I don't see anything."

"Any second."

I waited while nothing happened. But then, over the shoulder of Seton Bayley, I saw a glimmer. A light had come on. I pushed my head out of the window and watched in disbelief as it grew.

"Who's that? Who *is* that?"

I reached for the telescope and swung it right, searching. Dark shapes swept by in muddles, but within them I saw a bright streak. I stopped and swung back. The view shuddered as the scope steadied.

"How do I focus?"

Mira reached for a dial. "This one."

Gradually the light sharpened. It was another window—a dormer set into a rooftop about half a mile behind our block.

"I didn't know about that one," I said.

"Watch," said Mira.

Another one appeared beyond the first. Then another, and another. My neck prickled as, slowly, the dark, muffled rooftops illuminated with a scatter of light. I edged away from the telescope.

"There must be twenty...thirty other lights out there," I said.

"Roughly, yes. You really didn't know about them?"

I shook my head, befuddled. "They're all behind us. I wouldn't have seen."

"What about from the roof? Haven't you ever been out there?"

"The door to the roof was locked and I always keep locked doors *shut.*"

She paused. "What about from the other flats in your block?"

"I only went in them once, the open ones, for food. I only ever looked this way. I never...never thought to look behind me."

"So you never made contact?"

"With whom?"

"Collective 18, of course."

"What? What do you mean, 'Collective'?"

She frowned. "Mother!" she yelled.

A muffled voice came back from downstairs. "Yes?"

"It's dark, so find your coat. We're going out." She made for the door. "Come, Mr. Hardy."

I took one last look at the array of twinkling lights surrounding Seton Bayley, feeling my nerves jangle, picking my fingernails. Then I followed her.

"But what about on the streets?" she said, picking her way down the steep, narrow staircase from the attic. "Surely you must have seen them?"

"No…no, I keep to the same streets, the same area, only open doors. Routine and territory, you see, that's what it's all about. Routine and territory, keep to your own."

I stopped at the bottom of the steps. The front room was lit by two kerosene lamps, their burned amber halos crossing in a pinched oval on the ceiling.

"So you saw me?" I said.

"Mother!"

"Yes, yes, I'm coming."

Mira's mother was lifting a heavy parka from a hook near the door.

"And the others: Pearce, Gascoigne, Butcher…"

She screwed up her face. "What the devil are you talking about?"

I shook my head. "The other lights, the other ones in this area. You know them?"

"Know them?"

Mira helped her mother with the huge coat. I noticed that there was another light in the corner; a small bedside lamp struggling to power its dim bulb.

"Where do you get your power?" I said.

Mira ignored me, too busy struggling with the old lady. "Come on, Mother, you old vampire."

I stuck my head out of the window, where Lineker was lying fast asleep with the girl in the corner of the balcony roof. His eyes opened, and he jumped up, padding across the bitumen sheet to meet me. The girl, roused, sat up and rubbed her eyes.

"Come on," I said, and she followed us in.

"Mother, seriously! Push your hand through!"

"All right, all right, no need to shout, so angry with me."

I looked at the table lamp, buzzing. "I don't hear a generator," I said.

"There," breathed Mira, plonking her hands on her hips. "Finally."

Her mother zipped her coat up to her chin with a shrug and a childish smile. Mira turned to me.

"Now, what were you saying?"

"Power," I said, pointing at the lamp. "Where's it coming from?"

"The generators are all rigged up in number 26, but there's a problem with them. There's no power at all going to the east of the street, and the fridges in the storeroom aren't working either. Nobody's found the problem yet."

"Generators…" I said. "And, er, how long has your power been out?"

"About a week. It's getting cold, but that meat still won't last long if we can't fix the power supply. We could really use an electrician."

The girl had buttoned her coat and gave a groggy yawn, while Lineker sat patiently by her side. I smiled, thinking how nice it would be not to have to red-card Beardsley after all.

"Do you have any tools?" I asked.


"Rats," I said.

Mira had taken one of the kerosene lamps and led us through a door at the back of their flat, which wasn't really a door at all, but an oblong hole torn in the wall. I had fingered the tattered plasterwork as I ducked through.

"You do know this is a load-bearing wall, don't you?" I had said.

She had ignored me, striding down a dark, creaking corridor that I imagined had once been the landing of the next-door flat.

"Good evening, Emily," she had said to a small girl in a long dress who was lighting candles with a thin taper.

"Hello," the girl had replied, catching my eye and smiling at Aisha. I had flinched as she passed.

Soon we had passed through another makeshift door with planks hammered over its corners. Candles were already burning along the soot-stained walls.

"We decided it was easier and safer to knock all the flats through," Mira had said, striding ahead. "That way we can get to where we want to be without having to go outside. It's a much more natural way of living, don't you think? Sharing space like this. Better for the children too."

She had winked at two boys playing with fire engines.

"I don't know about natural," I had murmured. The idea seemed like hell. "And I'm surprised these joists haven't buckled."

After a few more similar corridors, we had found ourselves in an open room with stripped floorboards covered with a mess of wires and cables. Along one wall were three generators, all off. I had set down Mira's toolbox and regarded the chaos. It hadn't taken me long to find the problem.

"Definitely rats."

I looked at the ragged cable covering and the frayed wires within. Lineker's snout addressed the cable and he sat back, licking his chops as if in agreement.

"They'll chew through absolutely anything. The one that did this must have lost half his face in the shock. Probably knocked him senseless for a bit, then he crawled off to die somewhere. Not far, either, judging by the smell. Pass me those pliers will you, Mira?"

I heard rummaging and, from the corner of my eye, saw the pliers thrust at me as I inspected the cable.

"On the floor is fine," I said. She laid them next to me and stood back.

"I'm not surprised, in all honesty," I continued. "You've opened up all these walls after all, got all this movement between the buildings, dirt, food, people, children. How many of you are there, anyway? Rats will have been streaming in here in droves. If you'd only sealed the holes...screwdriver, please, flathead."

After another search, a screwdriver appeared neatly on the floor.

"Thank you. If you'd sealed the holes, done a proper job of the plastering, then you might have stood a chance. And this cabling..."

I looked around at the black spaghetti knotted around the room and stuck through walls. "Did you even think about how this was going to work? Duct tape, please."

An inky black roll landed on the floorboard. I picked it up and tore off some pieces.

"You haven't even insulated the main cables. The whole thing's a farce. It wouldn't surprise me in the slightest if at least two of those machines had shorted. Do you even have a fuse box? You can't just rig these things up and pray for the best, you know. Another driver, Phillips this time. And that yellow voltage tester."

More rummaging, and the clatter of tools at my feet.

"No." I sighed. "I'm afraid people don't do proper jobs anymore. They simply don't put the time or effort in; it's all careless, slapdash, lick-and-a-promise rubbish that gets done these days. Not what this country used to be built on. I mean, the Poles are hard workers, but nobody does a decent *finish* anymore. And if a job's worth doing, it's worth—hammer, please—you know you could have a serious accident? One spark and the whole street could be wiped out. You've already created a wind tunnel by knocking those walls through, a blaze would tear through this like a herd of ruddy wildebeest…there."

I sat back with a sniff. "That should hold. Let's give her a whirl."

I held the lamp over the first generator and made a few adjustments to the choke. Lineker sat by my heel, tail wagging on the floor.

"Ready?" I said. I tried the starter, and after a few spluttering yanks, the beast roared into life. The bulb hanging from the ceiling glimmered and glowed bright, and Lineker jumped, spinning and barking for joy. "There!" I said, grinning. "It's just a patch, mind you, but it should—"

I turned at the sound of a clang. Standing by the toolbox, where I thought Mira had been, was the girl. The tools she had been holding now clattered at her feet as she threw her hands to her ears, her face creased in fright. Mira was nowhere to be seen.

I switched off the generator and it spluttered to a stop. The bulb faded, and the room returned to its dim, amber state, the roar of the engines replaced by the putting hiss of the kerosene lamp.

"Were you…?" I said, looking in disbelief at the array of tools around her. "Where's Mira?"

Cautiously, the girl took her hands from her ears and pointed at the door, through which I could hear voices murmuring. I followed the sound out onto the landing and found Mira in conversation with someone a little way down the corridor. Their voices were hushed and serious. Mira's mother sat reading a book to three children.

As I drew nearer, I saw that Mira was talking to a man, thickset with a bald patch. He looked up as I approached.

"Rats," I said. "You have rats."

He blinked and unfolded his arms. "We heard the generators," he said. "So you were able to fix it?"

"Just a patch. The entire setup needs rebuilding from scratch."

"Reg Hardy, this is Benjamin," said Mira. "He's the duty officer this week; we take it in turns."

"Ben. Welcome, Reg," said the man, offering his hand.

I stepped away with both of mine held up. "Reginald," I corrected. "Nothing personal."

Mira explained. After a moment's consideration, Benjamin nodded and let his hand fall to his hip.

"Thank you, Reg. Thank you for your help."

"Not a problem." I said.

The girl arrived next to us. Ben looked at her, then back at me.

"So where are you from, Reg? Collective 18? I don't recognize you. 16?"

"It's Reginald, and I'm not really—"

"He's not part of a Collective," said Mira, giving him some encoded look.

"I see," said Ben, glancing at the girl again. "Well, no offense, Reg, but we don't tend to get many visitors from outside the Collectives. Do you have any papers? A contact?"

"He was taking this young lady to safety. She was separated from an evacuation party heading north through Peckham. It was an ambush."

"In Peckham? But that means—"

"I know, Ben," said Mira, placing a hand on his arm. "I know."

Ben rubbed his chin, exhaled, and looked down at the girl.

"And who is this, then?" he said, forcing a smile. "Do you have a name?" He bent down, and she gasped, springing back. Ben looked up at me. "All right," he said, standing. "All right."

"I said that we would take the girl from here," said Mira.

"Right." Ben nodded. "Much safer. She can travel with one of the data runs. They're heavily guarded. If that's all right with you, Reg?"

"Reginald, and yes, there's no reason why I—"

He had already turned to Mira. "This changes things," he said. "I'll need to meet with the council. We'll send out scouts, contact the other Collectives. Reg, it would be safer if you stayed with us tonight."

"I would rather be on my way."

"I insist." He put out his hand. "Thank you again."

I looked down at his hand. With a nervous huff, he withdrew it, nodded, and walked away.

"Mira," I said. "I should greatly appreciate it if you would explain where I am."

She smiled. "Follow me, Mr. Hardy."

"Reginald," I muttered, as she led us back down the corridor.

# COLLECTIVE 17

**REGINALD HARDY'S JOURNAL**

**DECEMBER 10, 2021**

WE ARRIVED AT A back door. Light and movement glimmered through its dusty pane, and when she opened it I almost fell back upon the stair in shock. There were people—a whole street of them, lit up with gas lamps, torches, and candles, sitting on steps, chatting in huddles or standing around blazing trash cans.

People. Terrifying amounts of them in knotted streams and mingling clumps, all writhing about with wanton disregard for personal space. Touching, bumping, brushing—they did not care. I shrank, mouselike, into the doorway.

The road was clean, strewn with sawdust, and where you would usually see cars, there were tables laid out neatly with food and supplies. Figures sat behind them and others walked between the stalls, inspecting their wares. I heard music and my eyes were drawn to a band of guitars and violins playing a dithering folk song to a cluster of onlookers. Next to it was a bar of some sort, surrounded by a looming crowd holding drinks in jam jars and mugs. I smelled warm bread and meat cooking, and followed a trail of smoke and steam to a barbecue and what looked like a stone oven. More people there, gobbling the food and nudging together. There was space, ample space, but would they use it? No, they mashed together in their fleshy tangles, untroubled by the contact, *seeking it*.

I felt dizzy. The place had a strange, dense light and a walled-in hush as if we were somehow enclosed. I realized that at either end of the straight terrace there stood high fences and towers, upon which I saw figures moving. There was no way out.

I wanted to run, to about-face and hurtle back through the building and out into the quiet, empty night beyond where things were cool and calm and made sense.

But I found I could not. To my surprise, the girl had shuffled closer to me. Could she be seeking my comfort? The threat of contact burgeoned at my hip, but I stood my ground.

"Welcome to Collective 17, Mr. Hardy," boomed Mira with a smile of pride. The girl flinched.

"Collective?" I said, voice warbling.

"You're telling me you don't know about the Collectives?"

"No," I replied. "I do not."

Lineker suddenly sped off through my legs. I called him back.

"Let him go," said Mira. "There's nowhere he can escape. Besides, we haven't had a dog around here for ages. People will enjoy talking to him."

I watched him skitter down the street, wagging his tail as people stopped to pet him, eyes and mouths wide with delight.

The band had finished playing their song to a gentle ripple of applause. They started up another number, this one louder, with brash trombones and a rhythm marked by a gentleman beating a bass drum strapped to his chest. The crowd gave a little cheer as the musicians marched them down the street toward us. The girl looked up in fright, moving ever closer.

The music was like some New Orleans funeral I'd seen once on the television, streamers flying, tambourines jangling, clarinets whooping. Everyone had their drinks raised and danced along with them up the street, then back down the other side. Lineker barked at the bass drum player, running in and out of his feet and almost tripping him up, causing further hilarity from the crowd. Mira and her mother, oblivious to our terror, cheered the approaching band.

As the crowd reached us and their wave of noise and proximity crescendoed, the girl and I froze in unison. For a few long moments we stood as twin icicles of dread—me rigid and aghast, she with her fingers plugged in both ears.

Finally they passed. The space opened up, the music drifted away, and our panic melted. The girl removed the fingers from her ears and looked up at me with a trembling breath. Relief. I felt every ounce of it.

"Come on," said Mira. We both jumped at the sound. "Let's get some bloody food. I'm absolutely famished."

The barbecue was far from the band and its crowd had, mercifully, diminished. I felt a little calmer in this quiet oasis, and hungry too. We sat at a rickety table beneath the flame of a torch, with paper plates of blackened lamb, steaming potatoes, and flatbread. There was water and warm beer. The girl wolfed the food with her arms forming a protective cocoon around the meal. People glanced at us from other tables, their faces friendly and curious.

Mira leaned back in her chair with a jar of something hot and pungent from which she drank regularly with loud, satisfied sniffs and exhalations. Her mother sat with her chair facing the street, watching the scene like a girl at a fireworks show.

"The Collectives are strongholds," said Mira. "The Rising Star's idea."

"Rising Star?" I said.

She gave a quick roll of her eyes and waited. When my face remained blank, she sat forward and fixed me with her gigantic eyes. "The Rising Star," she said, enunciating each word as if to a child. "You know?"

She pointed at a lamppost behind us, upon which three posters were pasted. There were none beneath it and none above, and there was no graffiti either; they had been placed there with care, not slapped on in the middle of the night like the others we had seen.

"Oh," I said, popping the last chunk of lamb in my mouth—lovely, it was—and wiping the grease from my hands. "That's what they called themselves."

"No, that's what they *call* themselves."

After a long silence, during which I could tell she was coming to some decision or another about me, she spoke again, the incredulity in her voice now replaced with curiosity.

"What do you remember, Mr. Hardy?"

"It's Reginald." I pointed to my empty plate. "Any chance of, er, some more of this?"

Mira caught the eye of one of the chefs, who nodded and began to load up another plate.

"What do you remember in the time after the attacks?"

I shrugged and wiped my mouth with a napkin. "I don't know. I like to keep abreast of things, you know, read the papers when I can, watch the news and what have you. But it was a very busy time for me. Lots of callouts, lots of work. I was out in the van most days. Why?"

"So you remember the swabs?"

"Yes," I said, mimicking her slow, cautious tone.

"And the first evacuations?"

"That was soon after. As I recall, Seton Bayley emptied quite quickly. I am not an idiot, you know."

"What about the appeals?"

I paused, sniffed, and threw my balled-up napkin on the plate. "What appeals?"

Mira sat back with a deep breath, obviously having found the missing link she was searching for. "The Rising Star…" She paused. "The people who resisted the BU."

"Mm-hmm," I said, turning to check the chef's progress with my plate.

"They called for support, kind of a last stand for London. They wanted people to stay in those areas of the city the BU hadn't yet taken over. With everyone gone, it would be easy for them to spread out, so they asked for volunteers to stay behind to show that we weren't yet beaten."

"Right." My eyes were still watching the barbecue.

"The BU had already taken over most of the affected zones north of the river, but the south wasn't quite as beholden."

The chef arrived with my freshly loaded plate, and I responded in the same way I always had whenever I was served with anything—a wavering cringe manifested by those two conflicting urges to meet the food and yet recoil at the approaching human. I averted my eyes as he slid the plate before me, hesitated, and left, a little nonplussed by my demeanor, no doubt.

"We became the Collectives," Mira continued, "fenced and gated fortresses populated by communities trained and armed by the Rising Star to protect the roads around them."

At the other end of the street, the band had started up again with another rowdy number. The girl's jaw tightened in midchew as the bass drum thumped and the crowd made its way toward us. She turned to me, terrified once again.

"Mr. Hardy?"

I looked from the girl. "Reginald. Yes?"

"You really don't remember any of what I am relaying?"

"Like I said, it was a very busy time."

I returned to my food, only now I was distracted, keenly aware of the fresh panic growing between the girl and me as the band threatened its approach. The bass drum boomed, and the crowd cheered behind them, drunk now. Mira shook her head, her frustration having found its way back to the surface.

"But these were global events. Everyone knew—"

The girl jumped as a snare drum joined in, machine-gunning. She flashed me a look.

"So this Rising Star," I said, trying to distract myself from the hammering in my chest. "Couldn't they man these fortresses? These Collectives, didn't they have troops or something? What about the army?"

"They left some, yes. To train us and maintain contact."

"Left some? Why did they leave in the first place?"

"They were needed elsewhere."

"Where?"

Mira frowned and leaned forward. "Everywhere," she said.

The band had reached our end of the street. The walls seemed to close in as they turned toward us, and I saw the girl's fingers travelling to her ears.

Mira's look had softened. "The point is, Reg, you are not alone. There are Collectives everywhere. One hundred and nineteen of us in the south from Greenwich down to Bromley, and more in the north as well. We've guarded the east for three years without attack. I'm astounded you never knew."

"What difference does it make?" I said. I prodded at my meat, but my restless heart would not have allowed another mouthful.

"Don't you see? You don't have to live on your own anymore. You can be part of a community again."

"I happen to like living on my own," I said, dropping my shaking fork.

"For three years?"

"I have my dog. Where is he anyway? Lineker?"

"A dog isn't the same as human company," she snorted.

"It's better. Lineker?"

"What about friends, family? A wife?"

"No interest in that." I hurried the words.

"Then what about your city? Your country? The people around you, those who occupy the same space as you? Don't you want to look after them?"

Her words swarmed into distant nonsense as the band turned and jigged past. A trumpet player swung his instrument out at us, raising one eyebrow as he blew a rude blast. The girl's knees hit the table in fright.

"Don't you care, Mr. Hardy?"

"No," I said. "No, I'm afraid I don't."

Mira looked down at my hand. "I don't think that's true," she said, one eyebrow raised.

The girl blinked up at me. With horror, I realized that I was gripping her arm. I snatched my hand away and stood, dizzy and wayward.

"Mr. Hardy!" called Mira. "Where are you going?"

"It's Reginald!" I bellowed, stumbling away. "Reginald is my name, and I need to be on my own."

# LOOKING BACK

**REGINALD HARDY'S JOURNAL**

**DECEMBER 10, 2021**

I MADE MY WAY back through the corridors of Collective 17 and up into Mira's attic. The moon was a bright pearl suspended over the southern skyline, illuminating Seton Bayley and everything else still visible through the fog in an unnatural, spectral white. I fiddled with the telescope until our flat took up the whole view, marveling at this strange new picture of home.

You get used to seeing things from a certain perspective, I suppose.

The nature of grief is that you are always looking back. You might say it is a telescope—a monstrous one with unlimited magnification that shows you everything, whether you like it or not. Mistakes, misdeeds, and missed moments—it lays them all out for you and says: "Look what you did, and what you did not do." Even the most forgivable offenses become grievous crimes for which you will never be allowed to atone.

I believe I was a good husband. I worked, I never stayed out, I never drank, I never strayed. But that is also the nature of grief; it will always find something to make you wonder.

Our early marriage was a time of intense bliss and activity. We lived together in her flat—a squeeze which we enjoyed—and I set myself to the task of learning my trade. My world became a whirlwind of fuses, switches, circuits, and zones. At night, once Sandra was asleep, I would stay up and read books way beyond the scope of my boss, Trevor, and every day I would be out before dawn in the quiet hiss of the pre-rush-hour streets to ready the van for our rounds.

Trevor would always arrive with a paper under his arm, slurping his tea and firing up his first Marlboro. He would look at the van and shake his head. "Fuck me, Reg," he would say (his language was deplorable). "You don't have to make it so fucking perfect every fucking day, you know."

But I liked things clean and tidy. One morning I was a little late getting out of the door. Sandra was already up as I hurried to pack my things.

"Do you have to go to work?" she said, stretching in her sleep-warm pajamas.

"What?" I said. "Of course I have to go to work, it's not flipping university you know."

"Oh. I just thought maybe we could do something. Mum's away visiting my sister and, you know, it's just me on my own."

I was fiddling with the buckle on my tool belt. "Stupid thing, come on… What are you talking about, Sandra? I'm late enough already. There, got it. Right." I gave her a peck on the cheek. "I've got to go. I'll see you later."

"I love you," she said as I raced for the door. I turned and saw her standing despondently at the table. She gave me a watery smile.

"Love you too," I said and left.

I was at the van just before Trevor. He raised his eyebrows at the clutter in the back.

"Not to your usual standard, Reg," he said with a wink. "Mind you, wasn't expecting you, to be honest."

*What is wrong with everyone today?* I thought. It was midafternoon before the penny dropped.

"Where are you going then?" said Trevor as we pulled away from a job on Dunstan's Road.

"What do you mean?" I replied.

"Where are you taking her?"

"Who?"

"For her birthday. Twenty-first isn't it? Aren't you taking her out?"

An hour later, I burst through the flat door with a bunch of cheap flowers to find her sitting at the table with a magazine and cigarettes. She beamed as I showered her with apologies and kisses, and I took her out to an Italian place I would not have been able to afford had it not been for the twenty-pound note Trevor had slipped me as he dropped me off. I spent the rest of the evening making it up to her.

Objectively this is a cheerful story, but is it the flowers on the table I remember? Or Trevor's calls of encouragement as I scrambled from the van? Or the wine we drank, or the food we ate, or her blushes as I told her over and over how much I loved her, or her moans of happiness much later in the warmth of our little bed? No, grief has no interest in those things. Grief wants me to remember the downturned face, the hand resting on the table, the sigh as I left the flat, and all the unknown thoughts she had that day.

Grief's light is harsh and never goes out.

I heard a floorboard's creak and turned to see the girl standing in the doorway, picking the cuff of her sleeve. There was a jingle behind her and Lineker nipped through her legs, leaping onto the bed that was tucked away in one corner of the small attic room.

"Where's Mira?" I asked.

She blinked at me, looked back down the hall, and made for the bed, where she curled up next to Lineker. I watched her close her eyes and drift away, and I wondered how my moment of cowardice at the fence might appear when illuminated in the past's light. Would that same light of grief be present? How would it be in some dark future, as I remembered my fleeing and her unknown thoughts as she watched another person fail her? How would it feel not knowing her fate?

Not good, I decided. Not good at all.

# FIRE

**LINEKER**

The machine goes on...machine goes on and...bosh. Bosh.

Bosh bosh bosh. Bosh?

Where's the machine? This isn't our flat, this is...

Ooohhh, *this* place! I remember now. This place is fucking *amazing!*

I slap my chops, scratch an ear, get my bearings. I'm in the attic, funny place, on a bed (a bed!) with the girl (the girl!) curled up next to me. She's warm and streaming with the smells of heavenly sleep. I watch her face lit up in a slender shaft of moon, feeling her heart and lungs flutter and pulse to the rhythm of her dreams. And I know what they are. She's running on a warm day with mountains and snow above her, and she calls for someone, her rapturous voice echoing from pines and boulders wet with glacial water. I'm lost in it; I want to be there too, if only I could just fall in beside her. If only.

Then I remember last night. All those people, all those friendly faces pleased to see me and not minding a good old lick. All those hands stretching down to pat and scratch me, each one pungent with its own palette of emotions. All that music—didn't like that big drum much, or those tin whistles, but otherwise, yeah, good band, good party. And the food, fuck me the food. Everywhere I looked there was more of it coming my way; scraps of meat and bread and leftover bones, and that's after my tum's still bulging from Her Majesty's curry!

You have to remember, it's just been me and Reg for a good while now, so a party like that was a bit of an eye-opener. Not that I mind it being me and Reg, not that I'm complaining or nothing; if there was one human being I would want to be trapped with for all eternity, it would be the big guy, after all.

And maybe the girl.

Why *are* we on our own, exactly?

Bit early for questions, Lineker. Not even had breakfast yet. I take my eyes from the sleeping waif and see Reg in the corner, slumbering in the armchair. He snores like a boar with its face stuck in a mud hole and great clouds of frost billow from his open mouth. I have no idea what he's dreaming. But I remember that I love him.

Last night…all that movement, all that music, all that torchlight.

You unlocked it, didn't you? Fire. It took you no time. Zip, straight in there, no messing, chink, chink, *whoomph*, lovely. Almost as soon as you'd scampered down from the trees and shaken off that useless fur—*drags you down, that stuff, cramps your style, you need to be bald and lean, right?*—the flames sprang up all over the place. You bent your nimble fingers around that flint and gave it all you had, until your camps were filled with sparks, then flickers, then roars. And you leaped and cheered and gave yourselves a great big opposable thumbs-up. Fuck you, Nature. Fuck you very much.

We watched from the shadows, flames and sapiens dancing in union, unsure whether this was the end of the world or the beginning of it. Turns out it was a bit of both.

Now you stayed awake at night eating cooked flesh and making noises. Freed from the chill, you started chattering, and you got just as much warmth from the stories and the songs as you did from the flames.

We watched and listened, and we crept ever closer.

It's still dark outside and the street is suspended in a silent, predawn chill. I wonder how we'll get up without the machine? I'm thinking this idle thought, wondering whether it matters, when suddenly I get that buzz and I'm up. Neck straight, eyes open, snout to the air. Something's up, I can feel it. Something's out there in the street. There's no sound, no shadow, no smell, but something is different. It's like the future is pressing against the present, two moments bulging, squeezing, straining for space. And then…

Something's definitely up. *I'm* up, off the bed, paws at the window knocking over that telescope and barking my fucking lungs out. Reg jumps awake, throws off his blanket, and screams at me. The girl's squealing now and I'm still barking—nothing I can do about that I'm afraid, just got to let it out—and Reg pulls me down from the window.

"Lineker!" he shouts. "For Pete's sake, what are you barking at, you idiot dog?"

Huh. Right charmer, this one. I might not be fire-making material, but I'm no idiot. I know when something's up, and something definitely is, but this is no time to be offended. I fidget, pad, growl, whine at him.

Reg looks back at me, eyes wild like dandelions. A door slams somewhere far away.

"There's nothing there!" he hisses.

And then the moment bursts through. From somewhere outside, there's a resounding thump and Reg's face changes color from moonlight to buttercup. It stains lemon, canary, orange, and then, with a whizz and a whistle, the world catches fire.

The room gives a shudder as flames ignite outside and plumes of smoke unfurl like terrible, black flowers. Reg falls to the floor with a cry that's lost in the rumbling air, and I spin around to check on the girl. She's curled in a ball at the end of her bed with dust shaking down on her from the ceiling. I leap across the twisted sheets and bark at her—*Get up!*—but she just shrinks farther away.

From somewhere in the distance I hear cries of alarm, doors slamming, and boots stampeding on old wood. Outside are other voices, clipped and taut over rapid gunfire. The peace of the night has been torn through and ripped apart with fear and fury. Reg is still sprawled on the floor, struggling to pull himself up the chair, and the girl is motionless, resigned to her fate like a pebble on the tide. There's another thump, closer this time, and the floorboards bounce. It's all too much and I dive beneath the bed.

It's darker down here. My left ear is whistling and in the other one a siren screams like a drill bit boring into my skull. I whimper and I whine, feeling my courage drain like piss down a lamppost, and all at once I'm cold and shivering, and I don't know what to do, or who's where, or what's up or down, or…

I hear another sound, a windward wail rising up like a distant storm, calling me on, calling me out. And I realize that it's me; I'm howling. Howling like I've never howled before, with my snout pressed against the cold springs of the bed. And all at once it stops, and the siren stops too, and for a few moments, there is quiet apart from the noise of people scurrying about downstairs.

I open my eyes and see feet moving beneath the bed, making for the door. Two little shoes and torn stockinged calves turn to face me, and large boots shuffle behind them. The door opens and the feet depart, and in the relative quiet my senses return. This is my only chance; I have to go. So I do; I spring forward and scatter down the staircase behind them.

They're already through Mira's living room, and the smells of last night's glorious curry are now ruined by ash, wet stone, and panic. There's urine too, and as I fly past Her Majesty, struggling with her coat again, I realize it's coming from her.

Out in the corridor it's lighter somehow, and I see faces and bodies running everywhere in various states of undress. Men and women in pajamas, pulling on robes and shepherding children with bears and bunnies clamped to their faces, others pulling on black jackets and helmets, ushering the rest down flights of stairs. I see a bleeding woman in a nightdress stumble from the pack, hands out, lost, before a man, just a youngster in black fatigues, puts her right and she rejoins the downward exodus.

Crowds are now gathering at the stairs on each landing. Reg makes for the nearest one and the girl follows close behind, but before I can join them, I get caught in a fresh stampede. I jump this way and that, dodging feet, ignoring the clips to my chin and the whistling in my ear, trying to find them. This is a bad bit, a bad bit, a bad bad bad bad— What's that? Reg's trouser leg, there, get it, *go*.

I make a dive for him. I need to be in front, ahead of them, leading them, not behind.

There's another sickening thump and a wall comes down. Amid the shrieks and rumbles the sky opens, and for a second I get a glimpse of the bright moon spinning above in a white halo. It is impossibly distant and full of quiet, like an eye peering down upon all of our mess. Then the sky closes in again, and I feel weight pounding against my hind quarters. The whistling in my ear becomes a scream that takes over all thought until, finally, there's nothing left.

I'm gone. For a second I'm lost, just like when I'm lost in the long grass of The Rye. There's no whistle, no panic, no movement, nothing.

But it returns, and when I open my eyes, I'm outside. At least, the inside I was in is now outside. The roof is gone and all that's left are triangles of brickwork, scorched and torn, with that big old moon looking on, whitewashing the world and making sharp shadows out of the broken walls and torn girders.

It's quiet here and the air is cold. My arse is stuck beneath the edge of a pile of rubble. I wriggle and squirm my way out, giving a yelp as my hip catches on something sharp. When I'm free, I turn to inspect the wound, where a dark well of blood has sprouted. I lick it clean, then do my paws and give the old arsehole a once-over, before limping away from the rubble.

Just me and the old moon now, and the whistle now joined by a strange, angry buzzing. I try to get my bearings, work out which end is up, and after a few sniffs I realize where I am. I'm in the generator room—the place where Reg did his magic the night before— only now it's chaos. The wall to my left has collapsed in a landslide of brick and mortar, and the three generators are now black and smoking, with little flames flickering here and there. The tangled cables are raised up in a net, and one has come loose and split, its naked end sparking and twitching. Water pours from somewhere, flooding the floor.

Not a safe place to be.

I look for an escape route, but I'm blocked by the pile of rubble, and to my left is a drop I would not survive. Ahead is another staircase, but it's on the other side of a gap. I pick my way over to it and look down into a pit of stone and sharp, twisted iron. I assess the jump; it's a little more than I'm comfortable with.

Another distant thump shakes the walls and the room drops, sending me sliding toward the drop on my left. I skitter back to safety, but the jolt has disturbed the broken cable, and it's now thrashing about on the wet floor like a python spitting sparks. In one rotation it whips out at me, and I slide back again. My eyes turn to the gap, which, I am somewhat pissed off to notice, has widened. There's no way I can make it. So I'm left with a choice: succumb to this electric beast, fail to leap an impossible distance and impale myself upon a metal skewer, or let myself fall and shatter my tiny skull upon a thousand bricks below.

*I'm done*, I think. *This is how it feels to be done.*

I let my paws go loose, and I feel myself sliding back, and I think, *This is how it* might *feel to be done, if there wasn't this other feeling too, the feeling that, maybe it's not quite as simple as that, that something else has a say in this decision too, or someone…*

Sliding, sliding, sliding, thinking, thinking, thinking, and then— whoops!—I'm off my feet. But I'm not falling, I'm flying. There's an arm about my tummy, holding me tightly—*Reg! My hero!* I'm straining to see him, trying to claw my way around to get a view of that lovely mug of his, tell him that he saved my life, and that I'd do the same for him, anytime he wanted, *just say the word, my old fella,* and suddenly we leap and we're flying, weightless, with the moon gazing down upon us, and it's a happy old satellite because this right here, *this* is the shit, not all that noise behind us, not all that shouting and blood and fear, it's this, a dog being saved from certain death by his best friend, this diamond geezer, this beautiful man, this…this…

In midair I look up. Soaring across the night and lit up in amber and bone is a pale face streaming with black hair. Her eyes are bright and fierce, and I feel the familiar poetry of that heart fluttering beneath her coat. As we free fall, I hear the echoes of her dreams again, and I swell with the aromas of deep pine, warm grass, and ancient rock. We land with no stumble, and she pulls me to her chest, letting me bury my snout in her warm neck as she scampers down the staircase, through corridors and doors until I smell fresh air.

She puts me down, and I sneeze the dust and soot from my nose. Outside, things make more sense. My ear's still whistling and there's smoke billowing in the dark, but the ground is straight, and the sound of guns is farther away. Reg is there too, talking with Mira in urgent voices. I hear words like *north* and *safe* and the number nine repeated again and again.

There's another bang from up the street that rocks the watch tower, and two men fall, one after the other in slow arcs. Mira shouts—*Go now! Go on!*—and pushes us to a door on the other side of the street. She hugs the girl, and we're away, back into a dark corridor and out the other side, away from the fray and running down dark, empty streets into the night. I try to find Reg's side, but all I can think of is this fucking whistling in my ear, and all I want to ask him is, *Where were you? When they attacked and Aisha saved me? Where were you when I needed you?*

# WHERE THE DAY BEGINS

AFTER AN HOUR OF stumbling through dark streets, chasing the fading beam of the flashlight Mira had thrust in my hand as she pushed us away, we found ourselves on a green and misty common, and the din of the ambush far behind. I fell down by a worn tree and closed my eyes, gasping. The frost crackled as the girl joined me on the grass, her own breaths short and tight. She raised a hand to Lineker as he limped from the mist and dropped down beside her.

Dawn was breaking, and I switched off the struggling flashlight. Dim orange pulses of whatever we had just fled from played out against the southern sky, and daylight seeped across the common. Soon the outline of a building appeared ahead. Turrets and towers grew from the mist as if some hidden quill was scratching them from the murky ink. The shapes darkened with red brickwork, and at one end an enormous, onion-shaped bulb materialized.

"The Royal Observatory," I said, still gulping for breath. "This is it."

According to Mira, my warning had primed Collective 17 for an attack, but they were not expecting one so soon. In the confusion and noise of the street, she had shoved a small bag in my hands and told us to go north, aiming for Greenwich Common where another Collective, 9, had assembled in the observatory. They were smaller but also more mobile and well armed. Perhaps they could get the girl to safety, and Mira would try to get word to them before we arrived.

Lineker gave a shuddering sigh. The girl ran her finger along the thin ridge of bone in the middle of his head, and he responded with two dull whacks of his tail. It was hard to piece together what had happened in there, but I know we lost Lineker, and I know that she had found him. I don't know how, but she had.

I had called her name when that wall came down, and the crowd had screamed in the fresh tide of rubble pushing itself down the staircase.

"Aisha!"

I had been carried down with them backward, struggling to get back up, but she was out of sight. All I could see was the sky breaking through the crumbling brickwork. I believe I had mentioned those load-bearing walls to Mira.

Before I had known it, I was outside in a heap of dust with the interior street lit up in orange from the flames. My head was still pounding from the shock of the first impact, and I staggered about in the smoke, trying to find her, calling her name as faces streamed around me in all directions. And then, there she was at my side again with Lineker at her feet and her fingers plugged in her ears.

*What now?* she seemed to be saying to me, and I thought, *Maybe you're the one who should be telling me that, young lady.*

I opened the bag that Mira had given us and found some water. The girl's expression leaped, and I handed her the open bottle, finding another for myself. She immediately poured the water in Lineker's mouth, but I reached across to stop her.

"No," I said. "You first."

She gave me an uncertain look and, with a slight shake of her head, continued to fill the dog's throat until half the water was gone. Only then did she take some for herself.

"You have to look after yourself," I went on. "That is how you survive."

With one last gulp, she turned and fixed me with a frigid glare. I do not believe she could have made herself any clearer. Eyes still flat with disdain, she rose and marched away up the hill with Lineker bouncing beside her.

"Aisha!" I called.

I got creakily to my feet and followed.

"Aisha, wait!"

As I climbed the steep bank, the sounds of distant gunfire and explosive thumps ceased behind me. I might have wondered what state Mira's little Collective was now in, but right then I was more concerned with matters closer to hand.

As we reached the top of the hill, I could sense something wasn't quite right. A tall fence had been erected around the observatory, run around with barbed wire and plastered with Rising Star emblems, but the gate to it was open, creaking on its hinges. It was far too quiet, and where were the guards?

But again, I had more pressing concerns. "Aisha, please," I said as I entered the gate.

She was standing in the middle of a wide concourse outside the main building. Lineker scurried along the base of a wall.

"So you do understand me," I said, stopping before her.

She raised her chin ever so slightly and, as if she had called it into being, a low breeze blew from the west and scratched the cobbled ground with dead leaves. I took a step nearer and worked up the will for what I was about to say.

"I am sorry, Aisha," I said. "For…what happened at the fence. I behaved with great cowardice, and I shall be forever ashamed of myself, truly I will."

Another breath of wind blew a lock of hair across her face. Within the protective blink, I witnessed her expression soften. Wincing, I knelt at her feet.

"But I shall not fail you again, young lady. On that you have my word. I will make sure you get to Wembley, somehow. I promise you, and they will look after you there. You shall be safe."

A glimmer of a frown, a tremble in her mouth. Sensing her retreat, I searched for the words to pull her back, my fingers all aflutter.

"I…I…I have certain neuroses, you see. It's hard to explain…"

I stopped as she took out her envelope and presented it to me. I cradled it, unopened, like a long-awaited letter. Reaching inside with the tip of her finger, she pulled out the photograph of the woman at the gate by the farm and held it up for me.

"Your family," I said, taking care with my words. "You still believe they're alive, don't you?"

She turned the photograph and tapped the words on the back twice.

*Gorndale, Bistlethorpe, Yorks.*

MAGDA. X

Something occurred to me, curious and chilling.

"You...you did not get separated from that van, did you? You escaped."

She said nothing, just stood there swaying.

"You escaped to find your family? In Yorkshire? That's where you want to go?"

She gave me a slow blink, which I took to mean yes, and waited, as if she had asked me for nothing more than a pony ride.

Yorkshire. A galaxy away. I sighed.

"I had a family once," I said. The words seemed normal, though they had not been uttered for a long time. I was still kneeling at this point, and the pain in my knee was wretched. With great difficulty I rose to my feet, one leg at a time, and looked around the cobbled square. Beyond the wall, fog-smothered parkland stretched out beneath us, and suddenly I realized something and laughed.

"Of all the places," I said. "We came here once, Sandra and I. We used to like coming into town on Saturdays and sitting in parks with ice creams, making fun of the tourists. That was one of our favorite pastimes, if you can believe that."

I turned to her with a smile. "Do you like ice cream?"

Her gaze took on a gloomy shade. Perhaps it was not so kind to remind lost refugees of sugary treats.

"Yes, well, never mind. This Saturday was in—now, let's see—1996, if I remember correctly. That's right. Summer. A hot day, *sweltering*, in fact. There was an election coming up, campaign posters and such all over the place. One of them had our future prime minis-ter's face on it, but a strip had been pulled away to reveal demonic eyes. Nasty tactic, I thought. Anyway, we sat with our ice… I mean, we sat on our bench and Sandra asked me if I thought he would get elected, this man on the poster. I told her my brother—his name is Neil—said it would be the death of the country if he did.

"I remember, all of a sudden she seemed to shrink, and I wondered what on earth I had said. Then she turned to me. 'But what do you think?' she said.

"'Me?' I replied.

"'Yes, Reginald, *you.'*

"I could tell I had frustrated her, but quite how I did not know. So I thought about it for a moment and said: 'I suppose I don't trust anyone who smiles that much when they're close to being put in power.'

"'That means anyone who's ever been elected' was her response. Then she stared into the distance and heaved a sigh. I honestly had no idea what was going on."

I turned to the girl. Seeing that I still had her attention, I hobbled to the wall and leaned on it, trying to decipher London's broken skyline through the murk.

"I used to enjoy watching her, Aisha. I could watch her for hours—the way her eyebrows wiggled during a daydream, or the way her jaw worked when she was concentrating. Sometimes I swore I could even read her mind, but for the life of me, I could not tell what she was thinking that day on the bench."

I straightened up and slapped the wall with my palms. "'Let's get out of here, Reginald,' she said at last. 'Let's get out of London, get away from all these noises, all these streets. Let's find somewhere quiet to live.'

"Well, this floored me. 'But this *is* where we live,' I told her. 'This is where we grew up, it's where we're from. Why would you want to leave?'

"I remember the muscles of her face suddenly tightening at that. Then she said a word I shall not repeat and crossed her arms.

"'Nothing ever changes with you, does it?' she spat. 'Nothing *touches* you.'

"'What on earth has gotten into you?' I said, and she just replied, 'Nothing.'"

I turned back to the girl.

"But something had, Aisha. Something *had* got into her. And it grew and it grew until there was a big bump and then, nine months later, right around the time that man with the devil eyes stood grinning on the doorstep of Downing Street, it popped out. So yes, I did have a family once. And I understand what it means to miss them."

I looked at the envelope still in my hands and offered it back to her. She pocketed it, and her eyes dropped to the ground between us. At our feet was a metal groove that split the concourse.

"Oh," I said, my interest sparked. "Now that, young lady, would be the prime meridian."

She gave me a blank look.

"The dateline," I went on. "You know, where the day begins and ends."

I shuffled around so our feet were flush against the line.

Then I stepped over it.

"Look, here I am in Yesterday. Hello, Tomorrow." She gave a

startled look as I waved, then hopped back again on my good leg. "Now I am in Today."

She wobbled and, with a little thrill she jumped, landing neatly on the other side.

"Today…" I repeated and jumped after her. "Yesterday."

She jumped again.

"Yesterday…" Another jump. "Today. Today…Yesterday."

We jumped from side to side five more times, quicker and quicker until she caught up with me and we both landed firmly on the right.

"Now we are both in Today," I said.

She giggled.

And that was something I was not prepared for. I felt something drop inside like a great sail collapsing from its mast, and I stared at her, grinning with those fierce eyes and one gold incisor caught in the gleam of the rising sun.

I went to speak but gulped instead. When I tried again, her head had already whipped toward the building, and the open door through which Lineker had just darted beneath a volley of barks. She ran after him.

"Come back," I yelled, jumping through Yesterday and into the building.

It was dark inside, and she was waiting for me at the bottom of a winding staircase, halfway up which I saw Lineker, pausing with one paw raised. Next to the corridor was a room lined with windows, and I could see that a huddle of old desks had been brought together in the center. Unplugged cables lay everywhere, chairs toppled and papers strewn across the floor, as if whoever had been working in here had left in a hurry. There was a whiteboard on one wall dotted with photographs, map fragments, and yellow squares of paper. A network of different-colored string connected them all in some complex arrangement. Rising Star posters covered the space around them.

"Hello?" I called down the empty corridor. "Does anyone here know Mira? Mira from…from Collective…"

There was no answer, only the wind banging doors, so I followed the girl upstairs.

Lineker led us into a room full of clocks. There were great shining discs hanging from the walls, ornate grandfathers towering in the corners, and squat table clocks and pocket watches arranged in rows upon shelves. Lineker began sniffing at the skirting boards.

"Probably a rat," I said.

Low sunlight streamed through a curved window and filled the room, brightening the clock faces. The girl walked between them, running her hand over their wood as she passed. Each one was set at a different time, each one stuck in their own moments. The chamber led into a second and, as we entered it, my feet, heart, and lungs drew to a united halt. The entire room was filled with telescopes.

Now, Mira's had been impressive, but these…these were something else. They were old, I could tell that much by their ivory barrels and polished brass fittings. But the size—breathtaking. And taking pride of place upon the central plinth was a monster, black and gold and half the height of the room. It was pointing directly at another window, this one facing west. I looked at the girl, whose face seemed to be suggesting the same idea as me. We found a chair in the corner and positioned it at the lens.

It took a little practice, but I worked those dials and levers until

I knew what each one did. The parts were well greased and had a heavy quality about them. *Marvelous* did not do this beauty justice—and I wondered how much effort it might be to lug it three miles south. But if I could do it with a generator...

Finally the picture focused, and I trained the lens on a tree across the common. I zoomed in close until a squirrel's face filled my vision, and it sat there, motionless, staring at nothing.

Perhaps I could set this up on The Rye. Or the balcony! Just imagine those parakeets at this magnification.

I became aware of the girl beside me, and I took my eye from the viewfinder. She looked hungrily up at the telescope.

"Do you want a go?" I asked.

She nodded eagerly.

"Come on up then."

I stepped down, and she pulled herself up on the chair, wobbling. At arm's length, I showed her where to look, and she squashed her eye against it.

"Do you see him?" I said.

She nodded, eye still down, and then began to turn its wheels.

"Oh, I wouldn't do that if I were you..."

The barrel dropped and swept in a slow arc around the room.

"No, now don't touch that, it's very sensitive..."

The barrel stopped, and she gasped, standing erect.

"What is it? Give it here."

She jumped from the chair and jabbed her finger at the window, hopping from foot to foot.

"I don't see...hold on..."

Taking her place, I turned the magnifying dial until a wide stretch of grass came into view. Still there was nothing, but then from one corner I saw movement: a set of legs running down a slope. I pulled back and zoomed in on the head of a young woman with spiky peroxide hair and an untold number of piercings. Her face was contorted in fear and her arms cartwheeled as she sprinted down the slope. Behind her was a chubby male in his twenties with black, scruffy hair, a khaki jacket, and a pair of thick glasses hanging from his sparsely whiskered face. He was carrying what appeared to be a battered laptop under one arm, covered with stickers—one of them, I saw, was a palm-covered star. They ran tumbling down the hill toward us, looking back over their shoulders with every few steps.

I jumped down and called for Lineker, beckoning the girl to follow.

We were outside next to the meridian line before they reached the fence, and they didn't spot us as they swung through the gate, wheezing and panting. The young man tore left, aiming straight for the main building.

"Where the fuck are you going?" screamed the girl—an Australian accent, I thought. She was short and skinny, with black cargo pants and a leather jacket pulled tight to her chin. "They're right on top of us!"

Aisha covered her ears at the sudden din.

"I have to grab the codes!" yelled the boy as he disappeared down the corridor.

"Fuck sake, Travis!"

Lineker growled. In a split second, the girl had whipped around to face us, pulled a knife from her belt, and drawn it back across her shoulder. Her eyes widened as she saw the girl, freezing her instinct to let the blade fly.

"Who the fuck are you?" she bellowed. "Step back. I'm faster than any gun, you know."

I held up my hands. "Mira…" I muttered.

"Who? What are you saying, old man? Come on, speak up before I put this through your fat belly."

The girl hid behind me, hands still on her ears.

"It's all right," I whispered.

"What? Talk to me not her, you fat bastard."

Rather rude, she was. She glanced behind her, through the open gate, then turned back. "Hey! You put your hands up."

"They are up," I replied.

"All the way up. Come on, that's it. What are you doing here? Who's she? And call your fucking dog off before I split him in two."

Lineker's throat shuddered with another growl.

"Mira," I repeated. "Mira sent us here from Collective 17. I fixed their generators."

"Mira?" said the girl.

"Yes, a sizable lady. She's—"

"I know who fucking Mira is. What do you mean you fixed their generators?"

"I am an electrician. They had a terrible setup, accident waiting to happen if you ask me. I told her, I said—"

"Stop talking. Why did they send you?"

"We had to leave. They were attacked last night."

The girl relaxed her grip on the blade for a second, thinking. Then she tightened again and called back to the building. "Travis, get your arse out here now, we have to go!"

"I'm coming!"

The boy tumbled out, now carrying a stack of papers under his other arm. He skidded to a halt when he saw us.

"Who the fuck...?"

"Mira sent them," said the girl, knife still trained on me. I didn't think it would take much for her to flick it.

"Mira?" said the boy, struggling to hold the papers together.

"Why did she send you here?" said the girl.

"This is, er, Collective 9, isn't it?"

"It was," she replied. She turned on the boy, barking, "Until lard arse here fucked up the codes."

"I didn't fuck them up, Trudi!" I sensed a lilt in his accent, somewhere north of the border, I thought. "We were hacked!"

"You fucked them up!"

"It wasn't my fault!"

"Look," I broke in. "I am sorry, I can see you're busy, I just need to find Collective 9. Mira said they could help me get this young lady to safety."

The knife relaxed again as she looked Aisha up and down. Then she shook her head. "No, not a chance, sorry. Not after today. Are you serious? Collective 17 was attacked?"

There was a noise from the common and the boy looked back. Lineker's ears pricked up and he launched into a full-throttle bark.

"Trudi," said the boy, Travis, jumping between his feet. "We should really get going."

"Who are you running from?"

"Who do you fucking think?" said Trudi. "And shut that dog up!"

She resheathed the knife and marched to a low gate in the far wall. The sound of voices grew louder.

"But you can't leave us here," I said, walking after her. Aisha followed, but Lineker maintained his sentry, barking into the mist beyond the fence.

"I don't have a choice, and you should never have come this far north."

The boy gave me a shrug of apology as he ducked through the gate. I hastened after them. On the other side was an old blue Audi with an open trunk, into which Travis was throwing his kit. The girl was already in the front seat, trying to start the engine.

"Is that an '80?" I asked, admiring the car's boxy lines. The boy turned as he slammed the boot.

"Aye." He stopped and put his hands on his hips. "Nineteen eighty-nine, two liter."

"V8?"

"Too right."

"You don't see straight lines like that on motor cars anymore," I said, running my hand along the sill. The starter motor wheezed and coughed from the front, and Lineker's bark reached its crescendo beyond the wall. "Lovely."

"I know, mate," he said with a wince of regret. "That's just the way the design process has gone, evolutionary algorithms running through everything, and—"

"Travis, get in you sack of shit!"

The boy sprang around and scampered to the passenger side, throwing himself in. I leaned through the open window.

"You might want to try your choke," I said to the girl, who was yanking the key back and forth as the engine failed to start. "Before you flood the engine."

"There is no choke!" she yelled, face straining.

"Automatic," said the boy.

"Really? I thought that was only on the later ones."

"No, they brought them in—"

"Will you two shut the *fuck* up! And, you, call that stupid fucking dog off; it's leading them right to us!"

I stood up and gave a sharp whistle. "Lineker!"

No luck; he was lost in it. I returned to the window. "Can you just give us a lift out of here? Oh, there you go, there's that V8."

The engine purred into life, and I exchanged a look with the boy. "Lovely."

"Get your hands off the car," said the girl. "We're leaving."

"Please," I said. "There's room in the back."

"Come on," said the boy. "Let them in."

She rolled her eyes. "All right, but call off your damn dog!"

"Thank you."

I opened the back door and called Aisha, but she was standing facing the building. Through the open gate, I could just make out Lineker's silhouette, head raised in a furious howl.

"We need to get in, Aisha, come on. Lineker, get here now!"

Aisha was staring into the mist, working her mouth. A fragile murmur arrived at her lips.

"What? Linekeeer!"

Another peep from Aisha.

"We're going," warned Trudi, revving the engine. "Ten seconds."

I looked between her resolute face, the girl's nervous shuffle, and the outline of Lineker in the mist. No time...not enough to get to him and back.

"Aisha, please, come on. Lin-iii-kaaaaaaar!"

Deep engines rumbled beyond the Audi's anxious thrum. Then Aisha squeezed her fists and took a breath. "Linnka! Linnka!"

Her voice was like a rusty piccolo. I froze in astonishment.

"Five seconds, I mean it," warned Trudi.

There was no time, no time at all. I had to get Aisha inside, but she had taken another breath—deeper this time—and her voice found its strength.

"Linn-kaaa! Linn-kaaa! Linn-kaaa!"

"That's it," said Trudi. She wrenched the handbrake. "Time's up."

I had to make a decision.

It was not my fault.

There was no time.

I leaped for the girl and pulled her back, squealing from the wall. Whatever queasy reel of contact I may have felt was lost in the panic of the moment.

Before I knew it, we were rolling back into the seat and the Audi's tires were spitting gravel. I pulled the door shut, with my dog's cries still echoing from the redbrick walls and down the prime meridian, and Aisha screaming through the open window—*Linn-kaaa! Linn-kaaa! Linn-kaaa!*—as the four of us sped away north.

# ALONE

## LINEKER

IT'S LIKE, YOU THINK you know someone, and then…

Fair enough, I *was* a little distracted. My world was split into four slices, if you can imagine that. You probably can't, so let me explain.

There were four layers of urgency—alarm bells, you might say—all going off at the same time and quickly finding their position in the pecking order of my attention. My attention, I might add, is superlatively fucking sharp, *superlatively*, but also only capable of being pointed in one direction at a time. It is a quantum, my attention, a unique and unsplittable force. Once I'm locked on, that's me, there's no tearing me away from it. Not good multitaskers, us dogs, not like you with your keys and your fridge magnets and earphones and plastic bags and all that, whatever. So these four alarm bells…

The first was Reg, who had swung way into the background and was occupying a shimmering space somewhere on the fringes of my focus—still there but doing his own thing and not a priority. What was a major fucking priority was the second alarm, which consisted of a whole cascade of threatening noises and smells rolling down from the mist toward us.

Now, it is my fucking duty to bark at that kind of threat, and like I say, once I get started on something…

What's more, there was a nuance to this threat that made ignoring it even less possible, a familiar smell that I realized, with a curious mixture of shame and delight, I liked. I couldn't place it at the time, but I would soon enough.

Then there were the other two alarms. The first was the whistling in my ear. That first explosion back at the place of meat and people had planted it there and now it was growing. I couldn't shake it; it was like a parasite, feeding on my torment.

And the final one, as if the other three weren't enough—as if this was at all fucking necessary given the state of play—was that I had just realized the entire park was riddled with squirrels.

Reg, threat, pain, squirrels. What chance did I have against all that? What hope did I have to do the right thing? (The right thing which, as I am only too aware now, was to shut the fuck up and go and find Reg. Duh.)

Answer: None. Zip, zero, nada.

So I stood there in that misty, wet courtyard doing the only thing I could: bark.

And then, breaking apart all of this chaos, came an olfactory pile driver, a primary scent, strong and indivisible, that felt as if it was written in my very bones. Her. She was near.

I knew She meant danger—even then, I did—but something stronger than fear was drawing me to Her. I had never felt it before and could not fathom it. I was losing control again. I was losing… myself.

But all of a sudden the alarm bells shuffled about. I was back.

Priorities were rearranged. Whistle pain? Yes, still there. Squirrels? Yes, very *much* so. Her? Yes. But threat? Not threat anymore. Now it was peril, which meant fear, which meant tail down, ears back, and—whoopsie!—a quick widdle on the cobbles before scarpering back into the observatory. And as I darted up the stairs, I just had time to ponder the silence left by that first alarm bell.

Where the fuck was Reg?

I found my way into that room full of clocks, jumped behind a curtain, and made myself small. Outside I heard engines and voices, one of which gave me that same quiver of interest I'd had before. I pushed myself farther down as the sound of boots filled the corridor downstairs.

Hardly breathing, listening to doors opening, chairs scraping, and words murmured, I spotted something move through the window. Outside was a branch and on that branch? A squirrel. And he was looking right back at me.

My hackles shot up like porcupine quills.

*Calm yourself*, I thought as I swallowed a growl. *Just ignore him.*

Then he gave his bum a little shake. The twat.

But before I could react, something drew my attention away. Footsteps were approaching the room, sharp and measured, followed by soft, quick pads, a jingle, and a pant. They stopped at the door. I squeezed my eyes shut and hunkered down.

I knew it was Her now; I could smell Her calm power drifting over to me in a hypnotic cloud. I could smell Her husky bitch too, hot like steaming straw and apricots swollen in the sun. They made a slow sweep of the room, stopping between the clocks, and I heard that bitch's snout sniffing me out along the floorboards. As they reached the window I saw black boots and white paws stop through the gap beneath the curtain.

*Done for*, I thought.

And then, through the window—I kid you not—that squirrel began to dance.

*Oh, you bastard. You vindictive little bastard.*

Up and down that branch he ran, back and forth before them, virtually pointing me out with one cretinous right claw as the other gripped his precious, cunting nut.

The husky bitch growled. She'd found me. *Run for it*, I thought. Perhaps I could dart between them and lose myself in the mist outside before I was caught. I sensed Her moving but, as I prepared my muscles and readied myself to spring, She did nothing more than reach forward and knock on the window. *Rap-a-tap-tap*, She went, and the squirrel jumped away in fright. With a satisfied little huff, She turned to leave, but that husky was having none of it. She was locked on to me.

"Veronica, come. It's just a squirrel."

She tugged the leash and the Husky whined, paws scrabbling as she was led from the room. When they had gone, I stared out at the squirrel quivering on the end of his branch, nursing his terrified heart. A cunt, yes. But this one might just have saved my life.

Once they had all cleared off and I was sure I was alone, I crept back outside and through the gate. The mist on the common had thickened into fog, and I could barely see two feet in front of me through the swirling gray. I sat down on the cold grass to think. The last few minutes soon caught up with me.

He had left me. I was alone. I began to whimper.

Solitude—it's just not for me. I need other life around me: humans, dogs, anything to bounce around with. Otherwise, what am I? Nothing but a bundle of thoughts with nowhere to go. We're nothing on our own.

I had a hard time as a pup when Reg started leaving me in the flat. Hours and hours stretched by with me scratching and whining, trying to find anything of his—socks, pillows, toenails—to cuddle up next to and feel that otherness he gave me. But whatever I found was never enough to calm me because it was never what I needed, which was him, and I'd end up making a mess on the floor and shivering in the corner until he came home.

The relief! Oh, fuck me, that flood of warmth when he stepped in and I flopped at his mercy. *Oh please, oh please, oh please don't be angry, I'm not a bad dog, I just miss you, I miss you I do, so much, so much it hurts me, please don't leave me again.*

But he would leave. Every single time.

Eventually I toughened up. I remember the day it happened. I was crawling about the flat in my usual woeful agony, yowling and gnashing my chops and thinking, *Why does this happen? Why does he leave me? Every day it's the same, he goes and then he comes back and then he goes and comes back, again, and again, and… Hold up. There's a pattern here.*

I realized—yes, a little slow, I know—I was never really alone. There was always a time when I would see him again, so all I had to do was fill that time with useful activity. And that, my friend, was when I discovered the delights of the eternal nap time, and the watching of distant birds. A sea change, you might call it.

No matter how much I napped, or how many different flocks I clocked, he would always, always come back to me.

But this time, would he come back? This wasn't normal life, and it wasn't our flat. All my lines were chopped and knotted, and maybe the normal rules no longer applied. *Maybe*, I thought with growing dread, *there are no more rules at all.* My blood ran cold as I stared into the mist, trying to imagine how my life would be now. Could I survive on my own? Would I even want to? What kind of existence would this be without Reg? And the girl! Oh, how I missed the girl, my little hero, my lifesaver.

Woe was me. All the woe, every kind of it, even kinds of woe you had never imagined, rained down upon my poor, wet, lonesome hide, and—oh, now it's started to rain too, how appropriate, how fitting it should precipitate *now*.

I lifted my snout and howled.

Oh me, oh my, let this miserable tide of rain wash me away with it. Let this pitiful, loveless hound drown in oblivion. Goodbye to the sky, and goodbye to The Rye, and farewell to all my dead friends and plundered maidens. May you all find something other than this gloom, this anguish, this sorrow, this odious, heart-flattening—

*Whoosh.*

What was that?

Ears pricked, neck stiffened, air crackling in my ears and snout.

See what I mean? A few moments on your own and your brain turns to horse shit.

*WHOOSH.*

Once again…

What.

Was.

That?

I raised myself off the ground, keeping my head low. Mist whipped around my right flank—*fuck*. I spun around, sniffing the air. That smell. Strange. Nothing I'd smelled before, and yet familiar... so familiar I couldn't even match it to a mixture of other smells. It was base, primary, raw.

*Whish.*

Another swirl of mist. I turned, heart racing, and attempted a growl.

Then there was silence. An unnatural stillness gripped the air as if space and time themselves were being throttled by this new presence. I peered into the gloom. A shape appeared, seeping like black ink on a tide.

"ZOUNDS," said the wolf. "WHAT HAVE YOU BECOME?"

# THE DOME

THE AUDI BUMPED DOWN a wide slope, hit the road, and sped north. Travis was still struggling with his seat belt.

"Buckle up!" he yelled as Trudi weaved the car from curb to curb. Fantastic handling, given the circumstances.

I felt wayward, on a brink, ready to slide away. In some dim reality, I could hear Aisha's fractured cries over the growls of the V8.

So, The Duchess. These jewels of hers, they're special. For starters they're incredibly valuable, made from the rarest metals and all the shiniest stones of the kingdom cut by the finest—

"Linn-kaaa! Linn-kaaa!"

She was kneeling, screaming through the back window. I pushed myself into the corner to avoid her flailing arms. Trudi's eyes were ablaze in the rearview.

"Can you see them yet? Get her head down!"

But they're magical too, these jewels. When the true Duchess of the kingdom is near them, they glow and make music so beautiful that everybody around falls into an ecstatic trance.

Trudi swung right, and the car bumped over a curb. We rattled down another steep verge, hitting dirt crests and sunken potholes until we landed on a boulevard.

"Christ!" Travis squealed. "Will you take it easy!"

But above all that, they're precious to her—sentimental—so she has to find them. That's her quest. The problem is that nobody believes who she is, and the only way she can prove her identity is by getting her hands on them and making the magical music. So, you know, it's one of those catch-22 situations.

"Just keep your eyes on them! And get the girl's fucking head down!"

I read *Catch-22* once. It was rather good.

"Fuck me, will you get her down!"

"Linn-kaaa! Linn-kaaa!"

Aisha reached for the rear window, but I looked straight ahead. Was he running after us, scampering with good intentions, trying to keep up? Or was he sitting with his head cocked on a hill, watching us leave him there alone. I didn't want to look in case I saw him.

"Linn-kaaa!"

"Get her down!"

So, anyway, she befriends a beggar in a flea market who sells her a map for a strip of fine silk from her dress. Then she wanders through an enchanted valley and comes across a forest filled with light and creatures who whisper truths about the world. After almost starving to death, The Duchess encounters five great battles, and a siege... I don't know. The words are all there but somehow I can't find where they're taking me... Oh my God, oh my God, oh my God, oh my dog.

My mouth was bone dry when I opened it. "We...we have to go back."

My mumbles were lost in Aisha's screaming.

"Brace yourselves!" yelled Travis.

The Audi hit a small bridge and, for a few seconds, we were airborne. I felt myself departing from the seat, with just enough time to share a brief look with Aisha, floating too—eyes and mouth seeming to drift apart in the momentary loss of gravity.

"My dog. My dog. Please…"

Screams—screams from all around me. I wished they would stop.

"Hold on… Chriiist, Trudi!"

The Audi landed with an axle-bending crunch, and Trudi threw the car into a hard left, skidding across a wide, paved area and coming to a halt beside a series of tall columns.

The engine cut out, but the screaming continued, piercing, shrill… No, lower now, a kind of drone, familiar…

My scream. Just me screaming. I opened my eyes and stopped. The rest stared at me in silence.

"Get out," said Trudi.

"Where are we?" I said.

"Shut up and get out," she repeated, already through the driver's door and slamming it behind her.

"HQ," said Travis, gathering his papers and laptop.

I unbuckled and got out, and Aisha jumped after me.

"Linnka, Linnka," she breathed, tugging urgently at my coat.

"All right," I said. "It's all right."

We were in a gigantic, empty pedestrian square surrounded by buildings—chain restaurants and bars with dead neon signs smashed in, covered with dirt and crawling with plant life. In the middle of them all was a tall spire wrapped in thick tendrils. Treelike limbs sprouted from the broken concrete and clawed for the sharp point. At the far end was a huge circular building topped with a canvas roof, cut in half and studded with what appeared to be the broken masts of a gigantic ship.

"Is this the Millennium Dome?" I asked, following them across the windswept concourse.

Trudi ignored me, striding for the entrance.

"O2 Arena, to be precise," Travis shouted back.

Aisha gave my coat a final yank and let out an exasperated grunt. I stopped and looked down. Her face was streaked with tears.

"Lin-e-ker," she said, screwing up her mouth with effort.

"I know," I replied with a biting at my chest. "I know."

We followed them inside and walked beneath two gigantic banners hanging from the ceiling—black with a silver-and-red stamp of palm and star. Birds flew between them and their roosts in the roof's metal girders.

"This way," said Travis, leading us through some doors. Trudi was way ahead, ranting to some bullish-looking man about codes and incompetence. It was then that I felt an energy looming, a dreadful density ahead that quickened my heart with every step. Aisha hurried behind.

"Linn-kaaa," she whispered.

"I know. I know, I know, I…"

But as we reached the auditorium, I froze.

Inside was a cacophonous bedlam. The roof was torn in two, so that half was ragged sky spilling with mist and water. The floor beneath was flooded, and the seats were crawling with weeds. They ran up from the ground in shallow flights circling the stage—a narrow, raised platform in the center, illuminated by dazzling flood-lights that made eerie shadows in the mist.

The great hall swarmed with countless troops in black fatigues running training drills, marching the stairs, unloading pallets, and eating in long tents filled with smoke and steam. In one corner, a squadron stood at ease watching a stocky woman shout at them through a megaphone and tap a pointer around an enormous map of London. Upon the stage two blood-streaked men stood boxing. A crowd jeered as they circled one another with murderous eyes and swung fierce blows.

A thunderous crack echoed from one corner, where someone had rigged up a clay pigeon catapult for target practice. Aisha cowered, hands leaping to her ears as a second disc shot up into the mist. A tall gunner followed its arc, and with another sharp crack, the disk exploded into dust.

I gaped at the cave-like arena and the havoc within. My pulse thumped. Sick gulps of blood. I felt myself drifting away.

Travis glanced back. "Keep up," he said.

"No."

He stopped and turned. "It's this way."

I shook my head. After a pause, he returned to where we lingered on the threshold of the arena.

"You need to follow me, mate," he said in that kind tone reserved for children and invalids in shock (which, I suppose, was what we were). "We can help you, get you fixed up, maybe…"

"I cannot," I said, still transfixed by the mayhem within the dome. "*We* cannot. Not here."

Travis followed my gaze. "Oh," he said. Seeming to understand, he tried a nervous smile. "I know it looks a wee bit chaotic, but it's really not so bad. You're safe here. We can take care of you. We can take care of her."

I looked down at Aisha. She mouthed that word, the only word she had.

"No," I said. "We are not staying here. It is not safe. What about those Purples back there? They could be here any moment."

"The BU? Aye," replied Travis, raising his arms. "And look around. This is a Rising Star military compound, so if those bastards do turn up, they'll have a fight on their hands."

"Well, I don't want to hang around here for a war to break out. Besides…" A vision floated before me: Lineker alone on a hill with his head cocked, waiting. "Besides, I happen to have lost my dog."

"Linn-kaaa."

I straightened up and cleared my throat. "Thank you for your help, but we must be on our way."

The young man looked between us. "Where exactly are you going?"

"North. Across the river."

"North? Nobody's going north. It's way too dangerous. The BU will be flanking east, and the M25 corridor is impassable, which means you'd need to cross the river somehow. It's an impenetrable swamp. And even if you can make it across… Look, you just have to believe me; right now, this is the safest place for you to be."

"It is not safe," I said, trembling, "and I need to find my dog."

"Listen, mate…" He gave me a smile of pity and reached for my shoulder, but I stepped back sharply. He frowned. "I'm only trying to help you."

"Travis!" bawled Trudi from inside the arena. "Get in here, you stupid fucker!"

The young man's face gave a twitch of annoyance. He shuffled uncomfortably.

"Young man," I said, "if you want to help me, then tell me the safest way to the South Bank."

His jaw dropped. "South Bank?" he said. "Mate, if you think this is bad..."

"Please."

He stared at me, dumbstruck. "You're insane," he said.

I hesitated. "Do not believe that I have not considered that possibility on a number of occasions."

He gave a puff and shook his head. Finally, he rolled his eyes and leaned in. "Fine. You can leave through the back. Take the corridor right and you'll come out at the loading bays. Head north and follow the river west. Listen, mate, this is no guarantee, you understand? But some people were still operating ferries the last time I was at the South Bank. Some might even offer safe passage through London. Ask for Charlie Jenkins."

"Jenkins," I repeated.

"But..." He brought himself close. "It is *not* safe there. Keep your wits about you and be careful who you trust."

"Thank you," I said.

"Travis!" Trudi cried again.

His face glowed crimson. "All right!" he screamed back.

There was no response. As he stood there, fuming, I took one last look inside the arena.

"I do appreciate your help. It is just that...this is not my world. And I have things to attend to."

The rage slowly drained from his face. "Aye, mate," he said with a fragile smile. "I can see that."

He looked down at my hand. It was tight around Aisha's shoulder.

Following Travis's directions, we soon found ourselves outside beneath a colorless sky. We were on the bank of the Thames, and what had once been a wide stretch of water separating the south from the gleaming towers of the north was now a bog strewn with metal objects in mid-sink—cars, buses, cargo crates, boats. Beneath the devastation, I could make out two lines of rubble in the mist: the broken roofs of the Blackwall Tunnel, now surely filled with sludge and decay.

Peering hard into the mist, I could just about make out the north bank, and the Isle of Dogs farther west, which had been swept into the bog. Its towers had toppled and were scattered like a child's bricks, now committed to their own long sink beneath the mire.

The wind picked up as I turned south. I let my gaze travel past the dome and its bleak neighboring towers, back toward home. Somewhere out there was Lineker, hungry, scared, possibly injured. It was afternoon now, and it would soon be dark. With a pang of misery, I realized that I had never spent a night apart from him since I took him in.

I turned west and traced with my eyes the mud-caked track around the bank. In the distant fog were gray shapes and dim lights.

I nodded, heavy with sadness, the terrible decision made. "We should be on our way," I muttered.

Aisha was bent over a squat, spiky shrub growing from the bank side. She scrabbled about and pulled something from the lifeless branches. I limped over.

"What is that?"

In her hands she held a stuffed toy—one of those Japanese creatures with wide, open grins and huge eyes. It was yellow, or had been once, and it looked up at her, its expression a parody of uncontrollable delight. She squeezed its tummy, watching it bend and bow at her will.

"Linn-kaaa," she said, breathlessly.

I sighed and knelt before her. "I am afraid we cannot search for Lineker today. It is too dangerous, and I do not want to risk your safety again."

"Linn-*kaaa*," she repeated with an urgent fury.

"I know, Aisha. It is all I can think about too. But if that young man in there is correct, then this whole area will soon be crawling with people who want to... Well, who are not at all pleasant. But listen..."

"Linn-kaaa."

"Listen, I know my dog. He is brave and hardy, and blessed with a superlative nose. I have absolutely no doubt that he will find his way back to us."

I looked up at her, trying to find her gaze. "Do you understand? He will be all right, Aisha. Trust me."

I was even starting to believe the words myself. Aisha sniffed and rubbed the filthy, tattered fur of the toy in her hands.

"Do you want to keep that?" I ventured. "Do you want to look after it?"

She looked up at me and a gust of wind whipped her hair back in an inky spray. Still squeezing the toy, she turned and looked out at the endless bog before us. With a flinch and a grunt, she drew back her hand and launched the thing from the bank side, screaming as it sailed in a spinning arc and landed with a splat in the mud. She turned and fixed me with a look of grim resolve.

"I don't. Like. Teddies," she said, clear as day, and marched past me.

I watched dumbly as she followed the track toward the lights in the west, then hurried behind until I was walking alongside her. My hand brushed her arm. I felt no shock.

# THE BIT WITH
# THE WOLF

LINEKER

MY BACK LEGS FALTERED, and I staggered back.

"WELL? DID THEY CUT OUT YOUR THROAT AS WELL AS YOUR BALLS?
SPEAK, HOUND!"

"Now then, I don't want any trouble, mate…"

"TROUBLE? THE WORLD IS TROUBLE. EXISTENCE IS TROUBLE. ME—I
AM TROUBLE. BUT YOU…"

He prowled before me, snarling, eyes shaking with hunger. "YOU
ARE NOTHING."

Charming.

"Where are you from?" I asked, and if you've ever tried to make
small talk with a wolf, then you'll know how ridiculous I felt. Still,
he did stop.

"FROM? FROM. I AM FROM THE FOREST OF ETERNITY, FROM THE
VULVA OF THE ANCIENT HOLY MOTHER…"

*Christ on a bike.*

"FROM THE—"

"Are you from the zoo?"

"YES, FROM THE ZOO, AND FROM THE WAYWARD STARLIT BRACKEN

OF FLESH, THE NEBULOUS GODS OF BLOOD THAT STILL RUN THROUGH MINE AND WILL BLEED BACK INTO THE EARTH WHEN MY BODY DIES. THAT IS WHERE I AM FROM, *HOUND*."

I told you. *Way* too serious. "But from the zoo, really."

He panted, hot breaths pumping into the fog. "CRUEL INCARCERATION. THEY KEPT ME, MY PEOPLE AND I. WE WERE CHAINED BEHIND WALLS OF ICE MADE WARM BY THEIR TREACHEROUS WIZARDRY."

"Glass."

"YES, GLASS, AND WEAK GRASSLAND UNFIT FOR EVEN A MOUSE AND DOTTED WITH PITIFUL TREES THAT KEPT US AWAKE WITH THEIR WEEPING. AND THEY CAME AND WATCHED US WITH EVERY SUN, AND SMILED AT US, KNOWING NOT THE POWER THEY BEHELD, KNOWING NOT THE DEATH THAT WALKED BEFORE THEM, KNOWING NOT THAT THE FLESH IS THE LIFE. THEY KEPT US THERE UNTIL THE DAY OF RECKONING, THE DAY WE FREED OURSELVES."

"How did you get out?"

"SOMEBODY LEFT THE DOOR OPEN."

The wolf scowled at me as I scanned the shapeless mist behind him.

"And, er, how many of you are there, exactly?"

He dropped his head and pawed the dirt. "ALAS, MY PEOPLE ARE NO MORE. DWINDLED. DEAD. TAKEN BY THE WORLD. I HAD TO EAT MY LAST SON NOT BUT TWO DAYS PAST."

I paused. "You what?"

The wolf narrowed the dark hoods of his eyes until two fierce points of light shone out from between them, like coals crushed into diamonds. "THE FLESH IS THE *LIFE*," he hissed.

"Yeah right," I muttered. "So long as the flesh isn't yours, eh, bruv?"

He deepened his already subsonic frown. "BRUV? WHAT IS 'BRUV'?"

He searched the ground.

"Oh, nothing. It just means—"

"PERHAPS YOU REFER TO ONE OF THE FALLEN GODDESSES OF MITHRACHTULL?"

"No, no—"

"OR THE VALES THAT RUN ALONG THE WHITE HAVENS OF EMECHZDAHL?"

"No, not them—"

"WHAT, THEN, HOUND? EXPLAIN YOUR TWISTED WORDS!"

"It means 'brother.' You know, bruv? Brother? Just a turn of phrase, really."

His mouth flickered, and he began a slow pad toward me, shoulders rolling. "SO YOU STILL RECOGNIZE THE BROTHERHOOD?"

I backed away. "Brotherhood? Nah, nah, it's not that. Like I say, just—"

"THAT IS ENCOURAGING. PERHAPS YOU ARE NOT FORGOTTEN AFTER ALL. PERHAPS THE HOWL CRADLES YOU YET. BRUV."

I felt my ears flatten and my tail droop. *Not now*, I thought. *Show some balls on your way out at least, you little tart.*

The wolf bore down on me with a disgusted look. "WHAT HAVE THEY DONE TO YOU?"

"They haven't done anything to me, all right? Just back off."

"YOU TREMBLE AT THE SIGHT OF ME."

"I don't. I've just had a bad day, that's all."

"YOU SHAKE BEFORE THE IMAGE OF YOUR PAST."

"I am *not* shaking."

"YOUR BLOOD CHILLS TO WITNESS THE MAJESTY OF WHAT YOU ONCE WERE."

"No. I was never you."

"WHAT YOU COULD HAVE BEEN."

"You and I, we're nothing alike. We evolved separately."

"WHAT YOU LOST. WHAT YOU... WHAT?"

"We evolved separately."

"EVOLVE? IS THIS ANOTHER FALLEN GODDESS?"

"No, just basic science. Look, you and I, we're different strands of the same rope. But we're not the same. So back off, will you?"

The wolf stopped. His haunches rocked forward, then backward. Then he sat down. "YOU MAKE NO SENSE, HOUND."

"It makes perfect sense, actually. See, the thing about us canids—"

The wolf stood. "CANID? IS THIS ANOTHER—"

"No, it's not a god. Sit down, sit down."

And what do you know? He sat. Good boy.

"Yeah, so us canids, that means member of the *Canidae*..."

"A SPIRIT TRIBE?"

"Kind of, I suppose, more of a family really. Anyway, the thing about us canids is that we're adaptable. That's our thing. We just fit in where we need to fit in."

"FIT IN."

"That's right, good lad. So one day long ago, there was a canid running about the place that probably doesn't even exist now, and some of them found a way of fitting in deep within the forests, and some of them found a way of fitting in on the fringes, and *those* ones ended up spending a bit of time with humans—"

"MONKEYS OF *LIES*."

"Not monkeys, no. *Apes*. And we kind of ended up fitting in with them. See? So they became us, the dogs, and the others became you, wolves. Simple."

He sat quite still, breath seeping from his nostrils. "MONKEYS…"

"So," I went on, "you and I, we're no more the same than a human and a baboon."

He stared straight at me—through me, it seemed—as a low wind skulked about his paws. Then he stood and commenced his approach. "YOUR MIND HAS BECOME TWISTED. THE HUMANS HAVE MADE YOU DERANGED."

Fuck.

"I'm telling you, it's the truth."

"YOU HAVE ABANDONED THE HOWL, AS DID THEY, JUST AS THE ELDERS FORETOLD."

"Now, now, I can assure you I have most certainly not abandoned The Howl, thank you very much. The Howl and I happen to be very much connected. As it happens—"

"YOU HAVE DEBASED THE PURITY OF THE CREED. YOU HAVE MURDERED THE MOON."

He snapped and snarled, only a few feet from me now. I could smell his gullet, and his gut, and all the terrible things inside of it.

"YOU HAVE SQUANDERED YOUR VERY *SOUL*."

I was done. No chance of outrunning him, no chance of talking him out of whatever he had planned next. Death was coming, and all I could do was stick two fingers up at it. That's what you'd do, right?

"All right," I said, planting my feet, back leg still quivering. "I'm getting tired of your bullshit. Back off."

"THE EXCREMENT OF A BULL IS STILL PURER THAN YOUR DECEPTION."

"Back off, I mean it."

"BUT DO NOT FEAR, *BROTHER*. I AM HERE TO SAVE YOU."

"I'm not your brother, and I don't need saving. Now *back off*."

"I AM HERE TO BRING YOU BACK. TO CLEANSE YOU OF YOUR DELUSIONS."

"You're the one who's deluded, you scraggy, murderous—"

"THE AGE OF MAN IS OVER, BROTHER! IT IS TIME TO TEAR THAT RING OF SHAME FROM YOUR NECK AND RETURN TO THE FOLD!"

"Return? Return where? The only place I want to return to is home, to my cushion and a nice chew stick."

"TO THE FORESTS!"

He closed his eyes and sniffed the air. "CAN'T YOU SMELL THEM? THE TREES, CAN'T YOU FEEL THEIR LONGING TO RETURN? THE ROOTS ARE MOVING, BROTHER, THE SOIL IS SHIFTING, AND SOON THE TRUNKS WILL BREAK THROUGH AND TEAR DOWN THESE TOWERS OF DECEIT YOU SEE AROUND YOU. THE LAND WILL BE COVERED BY CANOPIES ONCE AGAIN, AND THE WOLF WILL RULE THE BRACKEN AS THEY DID BEFORE THOSE HAIRLESS MONKEYS DROPPED FROM ABOVE AND SET FIRE TO THE WORLD."

"They're *not* monkeys. And what would you know about forests? You're from the fucking zoo!"

"COME," he said. "IT IS TIME."

"What, you want me to come with you? Come and help you start your little tribe again? No fucking way. I'd rather snuggle in with those squirrels than help you out."

Probably a lie.

"No," he said, and his eyes gave a feverish flash. "I DO NOT NEED YOUR COMPANY. IT IS MUCH SIMPLER THAN THAT."

I felt a terrible dread as his little scheme made itself apparent.

"THE FLESH IS THE *LIFE*."

He snarled and snapped, but as his fangs bared and that foul maw pried open, I felt a thundering in the ground. The noise grew as the wolf coiled to pounce, and then, as he finally lunged and I turned my face away, I just caught sight of a black shape shooting from the mist like a cannonball, straight into his side.

I watched in disbelief as the wolf fell and the black missile bouldered him over and over. Then, as he came to rest with his legs still reeling and the boulder that had sent him there took a few solid paces back, my jaw fell open—at least it would have done if that's what dogs' jaws did when they saw old friends long thought dead.

"Wally?"

"All right, Lineker," Wally said, with a quick glance over his shoulder and two wags of that sausage-like tail. He returned to his quarry. "You stay down! You hear me, wolf? Don't you touch my friend."

Wally. A cocktail of emotions—equal measure love, fear, relief, and disbelief—rushed through me. A fleeting reel of bright memories—grass, sun, hot flanks, sweaty tussles, the warmth of my pack—flashed before me. He was alive.

"What the fuck… How did you…?"

But the wolf was already up on his feet, hackles raised like burned scrub and eyes glowing with fury.

"WHAT IS THIS MONSTROSITY?" he shrieked. "THIS ABOMINATION? THIS *WHORE* OF AN ANIMAL! TO WHAT LENGTHS HAVE YOU GONE TO DEMEAN YOUR CREED THIS TIME?"

"Now that's not very polite," said Wally from the deepest regions of his throat. They circled each other, the wolf's shoulders rolling and Wally's thick as rocks. "That's not very polite at all."

"Enough," I said to the wolf. "This is over, done. Now why don't we just walk away and put this down to experience, yeah? We'll go our separate ways—you go back to your home and I'll go back to mine and we won't say anything more about it. I told you I didn't want any trouble."

The wolf turned those flaming embers of eyeballs upon me. "AND I TOLD YOU, THE WORLD IS TROUBLE. WE ARE BORN INTO TROUBLE!"

And with that he jumped again, straight at Wally. Wally dug in, but the impact knocked him from his feet and rolled him in the grass. Before he could set himself straight, the wolf had pinned him on his back and attached his jaws to his throat. Wally let out a gargling yelp.

"Wally!" I cried and leaped upon the wolf's matted back. He bucked, fangs still clamped on Wally's throat, but I dug in my claws, bared my teeth, and sunk them into the neck of that terrible beast. With every ounce of my strength, I chewed into his loathsome flesh until the sour tang of blood filled my mouth, and though he kicked and struggled, I didn't let go.

Wally was putting everything into his claws, which he was using to scrabble desperately at the wolf's underbelly. I saw sprays of red hit the grass on either side, unsure of which of us they were coming from, and as the wolf's blood pumped into my mouth and shreds of his muscle and fur slithered over my tongue, I became aware of a strange sensation deep within. It was like a memory unfolding, a door opening into a room you had never entered but always knew existed, a room that was just for you, that kept all the secrets of what you really were. My eyes became crystals and the world gained supernatural clarity in their new gaze.

*The blood is the way*, I heard a voice say from untold depths. *The flesh is the life.*

And I realized—I had never before tasted the blood of a living animal.

*No*, I thought. The shock shook me from the trance, and I pulled my teeth from the wound. Looking down, I saw Wally's face creased in pain as the wolf renewed its pressure on his neck, and the wolf's own neck open beneath the ears where I had bitten in. Wally's efforts beneath were slowing, and I could feel us sink down as he flagged, so I pulled out my claws and began to scratch with everything I had. I dug away at that wolf's neck as if it were a flower bed of sinew and muscle. I dug and dug and—what was that? A hoarse yelp from his chops as I hit a nerve. I went farther, pulling at fibers and feeling the wound mash into pulp. He bucked and kicked but I would not stop and, as his own grip weakened, Wally renewed his efforts until we were both scrabbling in unison on either side of the wolf.

Finally the wolf buckled, just enough for Wally to escape its jaws and smash his huge head against his attacker's snout. The wolf threw me from its back and, in doing so, lost its footing, and in that split second, with a howl of rage and pain, Wally spun from his back and snapped his enormous jaws around the dazed animal's front leg. The bone gave a sickening snap and the wolf rolled away, yelping and whimpering, as Wally and I got to our feet.

"Enough!" I screamed, still shaking from the impact and my recent brush with bloodlust. "Stop!"

The wolf tried to pounce again, but his broken leg wouldn't hold, and he yowled. "This is how you want it?" he wheezed. "I give

YOU A CHANCE OF FREEDOM AND YOU CHASE ME AWAY WITH THIS FAT BALL OF IDIOCY?"

"That is also," said Wally, gulping, "extremely impolite."

"You were going to eat me, you cunt."

"THE FLESH IS THE—"

"Yeah, yeah, the flesh is the life. I heard you the first fifty times. But not *my* life, all right? Not *my* life."

"YOU FOOL. EXISTENCE IS NOT A SINGLE LIFE. YOU DO NOT UNDERSTAND THE MYSTERIES OF THE HOWL."

"Maybe not, but I understand enough to know when someone's lost their way. You do not eat your kids; that's a no-no, wherever you think you come from."

"You're a very bad dog," croaked Wally.

We faced each other in a triangle, our breath crackling with spit and blood.

"FINE," said the wolf at last. "LIVE AS SLAVES. I CARE NOT."

And he limped away, dissolving into the rising mist. When he was gone, Wally collapsed.

"Wally!" I said, running to him, nuzzling his head and whimpering for him to get up. "How did you find me? What are you doing here? Where have you been?"

He rolled over, and I saw the wound on his neck—a tattered gash from which dark blood oozed, staining his fur and the grass beneath him.

"I've been tracking you for…two days now," he said, laboring. "I caught your scent all the way from the other side of the river. Don't take this the wrong way, but I can smell your balls from three miles away."

I gave a shivery kind of laugh. "I bet you can, mate, I bet you can. Now come on, we've got to get you up, get you some water…"

He winced and wheezed. "Too late for that, I think, Linny. Too late for that."

A fresh gush of blood flowed out from the wound, and I bent down to lick at it. Beneath my desperate urge to help my friend, that ancient feeling once again took hold, and I wonder, if Wally hadn't nudged me away, would I have been able to stop?

"Nah," he grunted. "Get off. Don't do that."

"I've got to help you."

"I told you, it's too late." He lay back, panting at the sky.

"What happened, Wally? Where did you go after the bombs?"

"I don't remember," he said. "I lost him, my two-plates, and I wandered about for a bit."

"What about the others? Scapa, Jez, Wonky, Pebble?"

He shook his head. "Dead," he said. "I thought you were too."

I hung my head. As I did, I noticed something around his neck, a tattered purple collar with a brass emblem coated with blood.

"What's that, Wally? What's that collar?"

"It's what they put on me," he gasped. "It's what they made me wear in that fucking place. It was horrible, Lin, horrible. But I escaped. I got out, got away."

"Away from where?"

"Them, those *fuckers* in the north."

"Who? What are you talking about?"

"Lineker, promise me…"

"What?"

"Promise me you won't go north."

"Why? What are you talking about?"

"Stay south, get farther away. They make you do things. They're not like other humans, Linny. They're not... They..." He gulped and gargled as another red fountain splashed from his chops.

"Wally, I don't understand."

"Don't go north," he said, straining.

"But I have to. That's where Reg is going."

"Well, he shouldn't be. It's not safe...telling you...not safe for man nor dog. Promise me, stay south. Don't...go..."

A dense, hot cloud puffed from his mouth and his chest deflated.

"Wally?" I nuzzled him. "Wally, for fuck's sake talk to me! Wally!"

But he was gone.

There was nothing to be done. I heaved a sigh and lay down by his side, pushing my snout into the folds of his still-warm neck flesh. And I whined, and I wept, and I must have fallen asleep, because when I opened my eyes again, the mist had melted away, and Wally's still body was steaming in the winter sun.

# SOUTH BANK

**REGINALD HARDY'S JOURNAL**

DECEMBER 11, 2021

IT BEGAN TO RAIN about an hour after we started our walk along the dead river. By the time we reached the beginnings of the South Bank, a messy north wind was at play, sending cold sprays up and down the track. Mud appeared where dry dirt had been, and beads of water clung to our clothes, hair, and skin like spiders' eggs. The farther we went, the wetter the mud became, and rivulets appeared like the veins of a great leaf, running into pools. Before long the mud was covered in shallow water that occasionally found the shore and lapped it in tiny waves.

The fog was still thick, so I heard the noise before I saw its source—murmurings and shouts, things being dragged along concrete, music, hoarse laughter, thuds and cracks in the distance. When our toes found concrete, I saw people moving ahead. Some were stacking wooden pallets along a wall, while others were coiling ropes and running buckets to and from the water's edge. As the fog cleared I saw that some of the ropes were attached to tall men in wetsuits, masks, and waders, who were staggering out in the shallows, knee-deep in the mud. Those on the bank side kept the ropes taut, bracing themselves against the lip of stone left by the broken wall and yanking back if their man got stuck or fell over. I passed three men struggling with one rope, trying to pull out a man who was down to his chest and sinking fast. He waved his hands, screaming at them to exert themselves, but the ordeal was clearly too much for them, and they rolled about, helpless with mirth at the sight of their friend in such peril.

We walked on, and I wondered what it could be that was making them take such risks. Then I saw one emerge.

*Heave!* bellowed his little team as they pulled him out, and with an enormous squelch he hit the concrete spluttering like a landed fish. The stench was foul, and Aisha squeezed her nose shut. Even the rope hands held rags to their faces as they gathered him up, and as they did, he held out a sack, which one of them—a young woman in baggy jeans and a flapping, orange jacket—took and poured into a bucket. I heard the clatter of shells and saw mussels, oysters, and cockles in a dribble of silt.

The woman worked quickly, scrubbing the creatures one by one and transferring them into a clean bucket. There was an iron pot boiling behind her. She glanced at us as we passed.

"Shells?" she asked with a brisk smile. "Hot shells?"

I shook my head. "No thank you. I'm looking for somebody. Do you—"

The woman looked at a couple wandering behind us. "Shells?" she said again, ignoring me. "Hot shells?"

"Keep moving!" shouted one of the rope hands, bustling by with a clean sack and a bottle of something brown for the man he had just helped pull from the mud. "Dredging work!"

The man in the wetsuit took the sack, grabbed the bottle, and took a long drink. He handed it back and, after a pause, during which he hung his head and the rope hands waited, he nodded and beat his chest twice. The rope hands cheered and readied themselves with the rope, as the dredger slapped his way back to the shore for another try.

This procession of hot pots, ropes, and men hauling other men from the mud lasted for about half a mile along the shoreline. The air was thick with the smell of sewage, mud, and steaming shellfish, and all about were cries of alarm, cheers of praise, laughter, and the occasional scream. At one point I saw a huddle of rope hands trying to comfort their dredger, who sat on the wall, sobbing with his head in his hands. A young boy in an oversized puffer jacket sat at the pot he was scrubbing, shaking his head.

As we walked farther, I saw what I supposed had caused the dredger's upset. Sticking from the watery mud were sharp and tattered objects that I realized were human skeletons. The Thames had always had a reputation as a busy graveyard—plagues, fires, and suicides feeding it fresh cadavers every week, year, and century. I wondered how many more had been emptied into it by those bombs that had dammed it, dried it, and robbed it of its ancient bridges; bridges that I now realized had been reduced to huge stubs of brick-work and dangling cables.

As we left the dredgers, we came upon a stretch of market stalls lined up against the back wall. One such stall was stacked with an odd assortment of vessels—plastic, metal, and glass—filled with water. Aisha looked up as we neared. I nodded.

"I'm thirsty too," I said. "How much for, er…" I began, pointing at the rough collection.

The lady sitting behind the stall looked between us and smiled. Without a word she gestured to one of the bottles near the front.

"I don't have any money," I said. "I haven't had any for…"

She frowned and waved my offer away, nodding for me to take the bottle.

"Thank you," I said, handing it to Aisha, who drank from it in greedy gulps. The woman gave her a hard smile as she came up for air. Aisha stopped and blinked at the woman, with water dripping from her open mouth. Then, cautiously, she offered the bottle to her. The woman's face opened like a flower in an unexpected beam of sunlight, and with a cry, she threw up her hands, jumped from her seat, and wobbled around the stall to envelop Aisha in a tearful hug. Aisha, rooted to the spot and still holding the water aloft, looked up at me in astonishment until the woman finally released her, wiped her eyes, and blubbered happy words in a language I did not recognize.

Aisha kept her eyebrows raised in surprise, and as we continued through the market, she took my hand. Again, I felt no shock.

We passed stalls of shriveled fruit, stacked packets, and bent tins. Some even sported supermarket signs, the sellers clothed in shabby versions of the matching uniforms. At each I stopped and said the name "Jenkins?" but everyone we passed shook their heads and waved us on.

Eventually the stalls petered out and the bank widened. In the larger space, still skirted with mist, were small tables and chairs at which folk sat in hats, coats, and mittens nursing steaming drinks and talking in low voices. Between them were flickering fire barrels, jugglers, buskers, and dancers all performing for their own crowds.

All were wrapped up against the cold, which was noticeable now that we were exposed to the wind. I felt Aisha tighten against my arm, whether it was against the drop in temperature or the growth in the crowd, I did not know, but the fact that I was able to endure her touch had not escaped me. It was not that my condition had simply vanished—I still took great steps to avoid the rushing limbs of the crowd through which we now walked—it was just that, somehow, her touch had become bearable. More than bearable, in fact. I found that I sought it out as comfort.

One of the performers, a long-haired, bearded guitarist in a neckerchief and overalls, seemed to have drawn a larger crowd than the rest, and we skirted around the edge of them as he hollered and plucked out a simple, dirty kind of song with slaps of his guitar strings and stomps of his feet. The crowd clapped along, their drawn, dirty faces pulled into grins.

I was beginning to wonder why the river had been described to me in such warning tones by Mira and Travis; so far I had only seen hard workers looking after each other, good-natured market tenders, and lively music. My discomfort at being so far from home—the shape of my little safe street map still burned in my brain, yearning for me to return—and so close to water, and all these people, was tempered by the strange, familial warmth from the music, and the fires, and the people. Even my abandonment of Lineker felt like a necessary and temporary state of affairs that could be fixed in due course.

Things, I thought, might just work out for the best. So long as I kept away from the crowd, and far from that murky water, and—it was still a surprise to note—continued to hold on to Aisha's hand, I would finally find this Jenkins fellow and get the girl to safety. But

I did not have long to enjoy this fantasy because, in the distance, lights moved slowly up into the sky. At first I thought they might be towers, but as we walked on I saw that they formed a huge circle: the London Eye.

As I wondered why and how that overgrown Ferris wheel might still be turning, or why the lights on each pod were fiercely bright and sweeping the fog in slow arcs, I noticed heads swinging in its direction. Then, as if by some hidden agreement, the crowd contracted until soon Aisha and I were standing quite apart from everyone else. The guitarist stopped abruptly, with his long hair swaying over his instrument, and my relief at the extra space we had been allowed by the crowd was overtaken by a creeping concern for what might have made them move.

I peered ahead to see what could be happening. There were flurries in the mist and voices raised in alarm. Three or four of them were shouting at each other, and they seemed to be moving in our direction.

"Aisha," I said, and she gripped my hand tight at the sound of my voice. I had never before seen crowds as safe places, but right now this one seemed like the right place to be. "Hold on to me."

One of the pod lights suddenly swung violently to the bank and, after a furious sweep of the ground, shuddered to a halt. It then began a steady track toward us. As it moved, the voices grew louder and more urgent. I heard the clatter of metal, feet hitting concrete, and thundering footsteps.

At this, the crowd lost their new shape and began to disperse with cries and shouts. Suddenly the space filled with people again. The searchlight crept ever faster toward us, and six figures emerged from the fog, running wildly. As the first one drew near, my insides turned. A boy, I thought at first, but no, she was female.

A young woman. A terrible sight from a different time.

She was stick thin with a shaven head and striped pajamas flapping around her flailing arms. She was running—on what energy I could not begin to fathom, but running she was, as fast as her brittle limbs allowed her. Her breaths came in short, tight gasps, audible even above the growing murmurs of concern from the retreating crowd. She searched madly about and finally looked directly at me, dark eyes widening as if, somehow, I was now her goal—if she could just make those final meters, she would…

There was a deep crack from the pod and a green flare shot from it, rising in a slow arc and then floating down above us. With a crackling fizz, the fog and the bank side became illuminated in a marshy light and the woman looked up in terror. She stumbled to a halt, arms out, searching the sky. Her eyes shone in the glare.

The crowd were on the move now, like a hunted herd finding their pace. In the green light, five more figures emerged and stopped in the clearing. The woman's face slackened, her shoulders slumped, and she turned to me again. All panic had left her, replaced by something numb. Slowly, she lifted her arms.

There was a moment of silence, when even the crowd hushed and all we could hear was the spluttering flare descending. Clouds drifted from the woman's mouth, slower and smaller with every breath, until finally she blinked and looked down at Aisha.

A businesslike rattle reported from the pod, and a flower of red appeared on the front of the woman's shirt. Her eyes widened as she fell. The pod shot five more bursts and, one by one, the figures dropped.

The crowd erupted and scattered.

Someone grabbed my shoulder and yanked me from shock. Suddenly, everywhere I looked was a terrified face or a hand swinging inches from me. Someone brushed my back, then again my neck, and I shivered. My grip on Aisha's hand weakened, and before I knew it, she was gone.

"Aisha!"

I peered through the swarm of limbs moving in the mist, looking for a pale face and black hair, then spun on my heels, looking around and losing my bearings in the process.

"Aisha!"

Panic now. I ducked beneath arms, protecting my head, buffeted between bodies and cowering from the shock of every impact.

*Don't touch me, don't touch me, don't touch me, please don't touch me.*

But it was no good; I couldn't escape them. Closing my eyes and taking a breath, I plunged in and ran through them all, calling for Aisha as I endured the hell of a thousand hands, limbs, and torsos.

Everywhere I turned there were angry faces, cries, hands that pushed and shoved and threatened to pull me farther within the dense human forest. But no Aisha.

Push back, push back, push back, and push through—and suddenly I was out. The crowd retreated, and I was stumbling over cracked paving slabs, my arms freewheeling. Somehow I had found my way down a side alley, away from the fleeing crowd. Steam rose from vents along the wall.

And there she was, standing alone with her hands clasped together. There was a man with her, kneeling down. She saw me and ran to my side, jaw set.

"Aisha!" I gasped. "It's all right. You're all right."

"Thank goodness!" called the man, standing up. His face was flushed with relief. "I thought she was lost!"

"No," I said, swallowing. "She's with me."

The man ambled over. He was young, early thirties and fine-featured with kind, intelligent eyes. He wore scuffed brogues, corduroys, and a gray woolen overcoat, with a scarf wrapped loosely around his long neck.

"It's easy to get lost in this crowd, eh, little one?" he said with a gentle ruffle of Aisha's hair. She blinked as a strand hit her eye.

"I haven't, er, seen you around here before," he ventured with a careful smile.

"No," I replied. "I live farther south."

He raised his chin and opened his mouth in understanding. Then a look of concern crossed his face, and he nodded behind me at the riverbank, now abandoned and empty. "You just saw all that?" he said quietly.

"Yes, what happened?"

He shook his head. "Another failed escape," he said. "I just don't know what makes them think they can outrun those things."

I coughed and reached for my bad knee, now roaring in pain after my exertion. The man bent down and found my eyes. "If you don't mind me saying so," he said, "you look like you could use a drink."

I shook my head. "I don't have time for a drink. I'm looking for someone."

"Who? Perhaps I can help?"

"A man named Jenkins. Someone told me he could get this girl to safety."

He paused as a pattern of thoughts danced across his face. Then he smiled. "Well, in that case, we can kill two birds with one stone."

I frowned. "You know him?"

He bowed his head. "I do indeed, and I can take you to him."

Something drew his attention to the alleyway behind me. I turned and saw a hooded figure jump from sight.

"We should go," he said. "It's not always safe once the crowds depart."

He held out his hand. "John Farmer," he said.

I hesitated at the human hand held out before me, but somehow, perhaps after my immersion in the crowd, it seemed less monstrous than it normally would have done. "Reginald," I replied. "Reginald Hardy."

His grip was warm and firm.

# DEATH

**LINEKER**

DEATH. IT'S A...

(Come on, Lineker, sort yourself out, Chief. *Get it together.*)

Haaa. Hooo. Ahem. Yes. Death. Funny one.

Did Wally know he was going to die? Did I? Were we both aware, as we lay there bedraggled in that bloody heap, that we were on a precipice from which one of us would soon fall and—with one last gasp—move no more? Did we even know that happened?

I bet *you* did, you clever bastard. The moment that brute sunk its fangs into Wally's jugular, you knew his clock was ticking. *Uh-oh,* you thought. *That's not so good for old Wally. That might be game over.* He was on that dreadful downward slope, and all you could do was watch until fate either dragged him back up or let him slide, disappearing into the void; bye-bye, Wally.

Because you know all about death. You've learned about the straight line of life and its fuzzy, frayed ends. *"Once you weren't here!"* you tell your young, and then, later, when the time is right, when the family goldfish or octogenarian or, gulp, DOG, pops its clogs in full view of the rest of the clan, you hold them close around the gurgling corpse of Jaws, Grandpa, or Fido and say, *"And one day you won't be, I'm afraid, little loves."*

You carry that with you all through your life; the fact that at any given moment all this—the sky, the sea, and the beautiful Earth with all its cheeseburgers, ladybirds, underpants, and submarines—will vanish in a puff of unknowable dust. You carry that with you.

It jars a little, this burden. It jars so much in fact that you pretend it simply isn't the case, that life goes on, even though it doesn't. You spend so much time pretending this that you build huge buildings to pretend it in, and read pretend books in, and sing songs and hold hands and smile and pretend together. And sometimes the pretending gets so real that you start to shout and scream about it. And the stories overtake the life they're pretending to sustain, so that this extension to life becomes the actual life, and you blow yourselves up to get there quicker, and you take others with you, just for fun.

If only you knew how simple it was. This Howl. There are no trumpets or tall gates, no silver swords, no waking again as donkeys or hummingbirds, no waiting to see, no other side. There is no veil to lift; it's *already fucking happening.*

It's hard for you to grasp, I know. You deal in straight lines and your one ends, so that's the truth you heave around with you.

Or do you?

Because it's funny: us dogs don't know about death, and yet, by your own reckoning, we live each day as if we're moments away from it. But you, who live in death's shadow, spend most of your days as if it's nothing but a passing cloud. You'll laugh about it, joke about it, even use it as an excuse to behave worse—"May as well, eh, might die tomorrow!" you'll say as you pop open another bottle—but the moments when you honor that one dark certainty, that you must *live* today, are few and far between.

I know Reg has had them. He keeps memories of them somewhere I can't see.

Now I'm no fool; I know they probably don't involve me and that's OK. I'm not jealous. I'm not going to start tearing his shirts and underpants to shreds with my teeth (would *love* to, though). I just wish I knew what they were. Sometimes I catch glimpses of them in the lines of his face, lingering like smells, I suppose, telling him it's all right, that whatever other bollocks this big bad world throws him he'll always have those moments.

So why doesn't he live a little more?

Maybe we don't understand what death means. Or maybe we do, and you're the ones in the dark.

Either way, I'm not afraid of it. Which is why I've left Wally's body to the worms of Greenwich Park and, against his advice, I'm heading north. I'm flying into the fray with this fucking whistle still bansheeing in my ear, my paws barely touching earth, and my snout filled with all the smells of hope and life.

I need to find Reg.

I need to warn him.

# JENKINS

THE PUB WAS WARM and dry, with wood panels and floorboards. The sky had darkened with the onset of evening, and candles lit the long tables at which drinkers sat on benches, murmuring in conversation and ignoring the soft sounds of fiddle, pipe, and banjo drifting from the corner band.

Aisha and I sat at the end of one of these tables while John Farmer ordered us drinks at the bar. Our presence drew a few glances and murmurs; there were no other children in the place.

I saw John and the barman in close conversation. The barman looked over at us before disappearing through a side door, and John walked back to our table carrying two pints of dark-amber beer and a mug of steaming milk.

"I've asked for word to be sent out," said John, licking milk from his thumb.

"For Jenkins?"

"Yes, that's right." He smiled. "Shouldn't be too long."

I looked around the bar. "Everyone seems nervous," I said.

"Yes, well, understandable after what happened earlier. That's the third one this week." He hung his long fingers over the rim of his glass. "They rarely get as far as the fence."

"What fence?" I replied.

"The camp fence. It was only supposed to be a temporary holding area while they set up better installations outside the city. But I suppose…well, there's been some resistance there, of course, so maybe that held things up. Either way, it's become a little more permanent than I think everyone had hoped."

"What camp?"

This time the frown went all the way. "Exactly how far south do you live?" Almost immediately, his face broke into an apologetic smile. "Please forgive me," he said. "I forget that we're somewhat in the middle of things up here. Perhaps news doesn't always propagate the way it once did. It's not as if we have Facebook or Twitter anymore to tell us what may or may not be happening, do we?"

"I was never on Facebook," I replied. "If I must communicate with other people, then I prefer it to be face-to-face."

He gave a laugh of surprise. "Good for you!" he said and took a drink. His smile retreated a little, and he gave me a thoughtful wink. "Perhaps if we'd all been like you, Reg, we wouldn't have found ourselves in this mess, eh?"

Aisha was cradling her drink and kicking her legs under the table.

"Reginald," I corrected as I watched the milk spin circles in her mug.

John looked around the room. "People are a little upset today, but things aren't really so bad around here. Actually, they're a little *easier* if you want my opinion."

"How so?"

"Well, there was so much to think about before, wasn't there? Everything now feels…I don't know." He shrugged, and the candlelight shimmered in his eyes. "More normal."

The band had finished their tune and in the silence that followed, the door behind me creaked open and a woman entered, dressed in layers of sweaters and coats and wearing a shawl around her head. John eyed her as she made for the bar, ordered a drink, and took a single seat in the far corner. She kept her face hidden as she drank.

"But out there," I said, leaning across the table.

John turned from his distraction. "What?"

"What happened this afternoon. That's not normal."

His expression became pained. "I'm not saying I agree with it, but what are we? Politicians? How the hell do we know what's good and bad for a country? Are we all supposed to be experts at running things?"

"No, but…they killed them."

He turned back to his glass. "We just do what we need to do now, Reg. No need to worry about things outside of our control."

"Reginald," I said, but he had turned to the door behind me. It opened, bringing in an icy chill and two sets of boots that stopped behind us. The music and murmurs stumbled to an early finish, and Aisha froze over her milk. John looked back at me with a sudden cheerlessness.

"I am sorry, Reg," he said.

I stood abruptly and spun around. There before me was a woman and, behind her, a man. Both wore purple jackets. The man was unremarkable, just another well-built, well-trained BU guard. But she—she was instantly recognizable. Her face was inches from mine;

a brutal geometry of sharp mascara and thick, red lipstick, framed by hair like raven feathers in an oil slick. It was her I had seen outside my flat, only—I realized with shock that a mere day had passed—the previous morning. But that was not where I had seen her first.

"Well, I never," she said with a ghastly smirk. "Hello, little Reggie H."

"Angela," I said. "Angela Hastings."

She tapped a gold emblem on her lapel. "*Captain* Angela Hastings," she said with a wink. She looked around the quiet room. "As you were," she said.

The music started up again and conversation resumed.

"You know each other?" said John Farmer, slouching somewhere to my right.

"Oh, yes," replied Angela, her eyes still on me. "Reggie and I go way back, don't we, Reggie? Grew up together, in fact. Funny place to bump into an old friend, eh, Reg?"

Her voice still carried the same unnerving mischief it always had done, only now there was a curious clipped quality to her accent. It was that self-conscious over-pronunciation you sometimes hear when certain people catch a whiff of a life beyond their own, like minor windfalls or cruise ship holidays won in puzzle magazines. That desperate attempt to sound more refined than you are.

It did not make Angela Hastings sound more refined. It made her sound terrifying.

She cocked her head. "When was the last time we saw each other?"

"Peckham Rye," I said. "Years ago. You were handing out pamphlets."

"Of course!" She tutted and shook her head, as if at some forgotten embarrassment. "That's when I'd just joined up. How things change, eh? Time does move us on, doesn't it, Reggie?"

Her eyes flashed. I tried a smile and she nodded, biting her lip and—it was obvious now—refusing to acknowledge the girl at my hip. I could not help but notice the swabber hanging in her belt, inches from her fingertips.

John Farmer made a noise, and she turned. Her face fell. "You can go now, Farmer," she said.

He cleared his throat, looking for all the world like a groveling bellboy.

"Oh," said Angela, with a trace of disgust. She glanced at the guard behind her, who fished out a thin envelope and tossed it at Farmer. He fumbled with his prize and gave me a miserable look.

"I'm sorry, Reg," he said. "We just do what we need to do." And with a last nod at Angela, he left.

"Sorry about that," said Angela when the door had closed. "I hope you don't mind. We have to have eyes all over the place these days; this whole stretch is absolutely crawling with undesirables."

She chose that moment to look down at Aisha. "And who do we have here?" she said, beaming. Her forefinger idly tapped the swabber. Aisha flinched and pressed herself to my side. I wondered at how familiar the warmth of her touch had become in so short a time. I felt no heebies and no jeebies—just comfort and the raw, untethered instinct to protect.

"Daughter," I blurted out. "This is my daughter."

Slowly and robotically, Angela cocked her head and turned her frozen grin to me. "Daughter?" she said. "But I thought..."

I put an arm around Aisha. "Like you say. Time moves us on."

She blinked. "Captain," she corrected. She let her smile fall. "Was so sorry when I heard."

"Yes, well, all in the past now. I—"

"Where's Mother?" she interrupted.

"Pardon?"

"Where is the girl's mother?"

I noticed the guard straighten at this change of tone. My back was against the bench. I eyed the entrance, the swab on her belt.

"I...er..."

Angela's eyes traveled to Aisha again. It was the same look she had given Lineker all those years ago—cold, withering repugnance.

"She's not here right now," I faltered. "We were, er, separated in the incident outside. The escape attempt, you know."

As I fumbled for words, Angela pulled the swabber from her belt. I froze and gripped the bench behind.

"Have you ever seen one of these, sweetheart?" said Angela, giving Aisha a sugary smile.

"No," I said. "I mean, she doesn't need to be, you know... You don't need to..."

She held up the device and made a great display of examining it. "Oh," she said, "what's this switch?"

She flicked it and made an O with her mouth, wide-eyed as the charging whistle rose. Aisha released a gasp of panic.

"Oh, there's no need to be afraid!" said Angela. "It's just a little thing. I'm sure you've had one before. Haven't you?"

The swabber's charging whistle reached its zenith and held.

Aisha stared up at it, jaw tight, trembling.

"What's the matter?" said Angela. "Cat got your tongue?"

At that moment, the swabber gave an unhappy beep. Angela frowned at it. She pressed the charging button again, but it responded with the same disconsolate noise.

"Bloody thing," muttered Angela. She turned to her companion. "Give me yours."

"I-I don't have one, ma'am" was his reply.

Angela gave a rasp of frustration and turned back to her swabber, shaking it and banging the side with her palm.

"It's the battery," I said, remembering my afternoon investigating the ones I had stumbled upon in the dumpster. "Substandard. They leak. Or it could be the contacts. Either way, shoddy work, in my opinion."

Angela ceased in her punishment of the device and looked back at me with what I now accepted was her natural expression of malice. I sensed movement nearby, and she shot a look to my right.

"Reginald! There you are!"

A figure had bustled to my side. It was the woman in the shawl, which she had now dropped to her neck. She was in her fifties, face weathered by age but still showing the young woman she had once been. Her white hair was pulled into a long ponytail.

"Darling!" she said, flashing me a conspiratorial look and holding her hands out for Aisha. Aisha hesitated but, sensing the deception, allowed herself to be lifted into the woman's arms.

"I thought I'd lost you for good!" said the woman. She shot me another glance. I was supposed to say something.

"Yes," I said, doing my best to feign relief. "Thank goodness. Angela. I mean, Captain Hastings. This is my, er, wife, and, er…"

"Come on, dear, we should be on our way," said the woman,

edging toward the door and pulling at me to follow. Still holding the faulty swabber aloft, Angela watched us stumble away with a curious frown.

"Have to get going…" said the woman as we pushed between benches and tables. "Must be off."

"Sorry," I said, fumbling with a glass I had toppled.

The guard moved to pursue us but stopped as Angela raised a finger. We reached the door and pushed it open, and I just had time to see her incredulous stare follow us out into the freezing, dark fog.

"Follow me," muttered the woman, picking up pace. "Before she changes her mind."

"Who are you?" I said, stumbling down the steps.

"Charlotte Jenkins. Call me Charlie. Now come with me. Run!"

# LONDON'S FUCKFEST OF SMELLS

## LINEKER

I SAY *FLYING*. ACTUALLY, it took a while for me to leave Wally's body. It was like I was stuck in his gravity, and I had to pad around him a few times before I could break the orbit.

But once free I picked up the pace and locked onto the fresh scent of Reg and the girl. It felt good to be running again, dashing through hedgerows and scampering up strange new streets. Odd feeling, though, not being by Reg's side, not on that invisible leash that might be yanked back at any second with the call of my name. I was, I realized, untethered for the first time in...

Could it have been my entire life? Had I not tasted freedom until now? Had I been...?

No time to think about that. I had a purpose, a cause, a quest! That's right. Fucking knight of old, me—road for a steed, snout for a sword.

The scent. I had it. I had it almost all the way. Ten and twelve miles by my reckoning. Reg's smell, and the girl's by now, were branded upon me. There was no possible way I could ever rid myself of them. I felt sure of that.

The first place I stopped was a huge dome—full of distractions, that place, fucking *rammed* with humans in various states of excitement, anger, fear, hope, sharp arrows of determination trained upon some target I couldn't fathom, far less care for. I kept myself hidden, tracked the scent, and followed it out.

Then came the river, bursting with all those glorious temptations made of mud, grime, and fish scales, but raise the banners and blow those fucking bugles—this knight remained true to his quest. Nothing could stop me, *nothing*, because I was on the right path. I was doing the right thing.

Feels good that, doesn't it?

I left the river and found myself in a maze of streets, and that's when I was properly tested. I mean, have you smelled London on a good day? It's nose porn, a fuckfest of smells. History, in case you were unaware, is having an orgy right beneath your very nose. It's an endless replay of worlds colliding, centuries mashing together, and millions of souls sharing their secrets and hopes. Every alleyway I passed held the ghost of some ancient murder or the lingering jizz of a long-concluded dalliance. Every gutter held the tears of a wartime widow clutching a letter, or the drizzle from a dead queen newspaper headline dissolved in chip fat. It's a lot to ignore for a dog like me.

As it happens, I did find myself straying from time to time, whether due to jizz, chip fat, rat, cat, squirrel, or whatever other bellend happened to have minced across my path. But it was never for long. Occasionally, I'd lose the scent altogether and find myself floundering in fresh air, but then I'd catch a whiff in the old peripherals and I'd be off again, face to the floor. It never left me, not once. Not for all those miles.

I tracked that scent like I'd never tracked anything before. I got a surge of it through a jungle-covered parking garage and ran so fast I barely noticed the fence. Got myself stuck, didn't I? Two hours I struggled there, barking, whining, thrashing with my paws in a thorn bush. Eventually I gave up and slunk down, wondering how long it would take for me to become a skeleton and for my bones to slip down into the earth.

It was getting dark by then. Right proper mope I had, grumping about everything that had happened to me that day—the fire, Reg leaving me, Wally—and I was about to let that mope turn into despair when suddenly I thought, *Have a word Lineker, old son, why don't you try the other way?*

So I did, and pop! Out I came like a runt from his mum. Daft cunt, I am; two hours of pulling and all I needed to do was push. Fucking hilarious. Anyway, I was free again! Eyes shut, nose to the wind… Wait for it, there was Reg, and—mercy me, be still my fluttering bowels—there was the girl too.

Little widdle, smack of the chops, and that was me on my merry old way again! *It can't be far*, I thought, as I trotted up the tracks toward the dangling shreds of London Bridge station, *I can virtually taste them.* The sun had long made its excuses by then, so the streets were dark, but it didn't matter; I followed that scent like a taut rope, up onto a platform, across the abandoned concourse, and out into the night.

And that's where I lost them.

# CHARLIE'S BARGE

"What were you thinking? That pub is not a safe place for a child."

Charlie whirled around the long, squat room, whisking curtains shut and bolting hatches.

"Certainly not one dressed like that."

She gave Aisha's hair a passing stroke as she hurried to a mount above the door, from which she pulled a shotgun and broke open its barrel.

"You knew that woman?" she asked.

"Yes," I said. "At least I used to."

"Then you were lucky. It made her think twice."

"What did she want with Aisha? What do you mean *dressed like that*?"

"Isn't it obvious? She's a Straggler!"

"Straggler?"

"Yes! An undesirable"—she touched Aisha's cheek as she passed—"sorry, sweetheart, you're really not—who fell through the net. You can tell it a mile off."

She pulled two red cartridges from the box and fed them into the gun's chambers. "Whatever's the matter with you?" she said, glancing up at me. "Have you never been on a boat before? Sit down, man."

I was standing, clammy, with my hands pressed against the ceiling. The floor rocked beneath me. Aisha looked up at me from the galley table wearing what I could have sworn was a look of amusement.

Our escape from the pub had seemed like only minutes before, Charlie leading us into the murk and dropping Aisha so that she ran between us holding our hands with her hair flying as if she were being wheeled through a fairground.

We had ducked left and right down countless alleys, through gaps in fences and doors that seemed too small for humans, beneath bushes and away from the flames that lit the bankside until, at last, we had slowed and stopped. For a moment Charlie had stood still until, satisfied with the silence, she had led us along a wall and down some steep steps. A flashlight, produced from some deep pocket, picked out rough, misshapen steps and walls of dripping wet rock. Before long we had reached a wooden door that had taken us out onto a narrow strip of dirt, against which I could hear water lapping. Charlie had bolted the door behind us, and it was then that I had found myself suddenly frozen to the spot, for there beneath an overhang and moored at the water's edge was a barge, rocking gently on shallow water.

"What's wrong?" Charlie had already boarded with Aisha. "Why have you stopped?"

I had found I could not speak but, eventually, with much persuasion and a great many sickening rolls of my stomach, I had made it onto the deck and down the hatch.

Charlie snapped the barrel shut. "Sit down, for goodness' sake," she said. "You're making me nervous."

I peeled my hands from the ceiling and edged to the table.

Charlie checked through a curtain. "They don't know this place exists," she murmured. "At least, I don't think so."

"Where are we?" I asked.

"London Bridge," she replied, letting the curtain drop. "The ruin created a deep well, which is why you can see water and dents beneath the bankside. They're not all safe, but this one seems to be holding."

She peered cautiously above her. "Not like the last," she added.

She took a breath and looked around the barge with worried eyes, still checking. There wasn't much inside—a few books stacked on a shelf, some pictures, pots, and a well-worn cushion. A solitary plant grew on the shelf above the stove, next to a framed letter in spindly writing.

Finally she lowered the gun and her eyes turned to me. "Why are you here?"

"Because," I began, still reeling at the sensation of floating. "Because you brought us…"

"No, Mr. Hardy, why are you *here*, on the river?"

"How do you know my name?"

She rolled her eyes. "I've been following you since you bumbled into the market this afternoon. Haven't you heard of caution? A little bit of stealth? You may as well have carried a target around your neck. In fact…"

She frowned, then strode over to Aisha. The girl flinched as Charlie reached for her neck and pulled out her tag.

"I don't believe it," wailed Charlie. "You even kept this on her? What were you thinking?"

"I wasn't... I-I thought it might help get her where she needed to be."

"Help those bastards identify her and pick her up, more like."

She tapped it. "'Target.' It says 'target.' Do you know what that means?"

"I suppose...I suppose I do now, yes."

She released a frustrated rasp and tucked the tag back, catching Aisha's eye as she did. "I'm sorry, poppet," she said, folding a hand around her cheek. "Sorry."

She fell into the last seat at the table and took a pouch of tobacco from one of her many pockets, from which she began to roll a thin cigarette. "So tell me, please," she repeated. "Why are you here?"

I told her. When I was finished, she watched me, motionless, leaning back in her chair with her legs crossed and a straight, blue line rising from the glowing tip of her cigarette like a chimney on a still night. Eventually she took one last drag and stubbed it out. She looked sideways at Aisha, blowing smoke from the corner of her mouth.

"I expect you're hungry, poppet, yes?"

She got up and began to move pots around the stove.

Aisha looked at me, holding her nose with her eyebrows raised.

Charlie served us bowls of beans and sausages, which we ate in silence as she smoked. I saw Aisha glancing at her, nose twitching between mouthfuls.

"I haven't operated since spring," said Charlie. "It's been too dangerous since they stepped up operations, and since that *camp*." She made a face as if she'd tasted something sour, and put out her cigarette. "To be honest with you, I've been spending the last few weeks planning my escape."

"Escape?" I said.

"Yes. From London. It's funny, I'd always wanted to leave before but it never seemed like the right time. Some places have a way of keeping you, don't they?" She pulled a loose strand of tobacco from her tongue. "It's extremely dangerous, Mr. Hardy, crossing that river. And there are dangers on the other side too. It's not safe."

"Where is?" I meant it—a real question—but I got the feeling she thought I was just being clever. "Listen," I said, "I can't pay you. I don't have any money."

"I don't want money," she spat, turning away. Her look of disgust softened when she saw Aisha rubbing her eyes and giving an enormous yawn. "You're tired, sweet girl."

Aisha nodded, bleary, with a fuzz of loose hair dangling over her face.

"Come with me," said Charlie, holding out her hand. "You can sleep in my bed tonight."

Aisha followed her through to a poky room at the back of the barge, the entire floor area of which was dedicated to a bed. After some ruffling of covers and whispers, Charlie returned, pulling the door closed.

"A drink, Mr. Hardy?" she said.

I nodded, although she had already swept a bottle and two tumblers from the galley shelf.

"It's Reginald, by the way."

She stopped and turned. "Reginald," she said and returned to her pouring.

So that's something.

"Do you live alone?" I asked.

She paused, with a half turn and cocked eyebrow over her shoulder. I cringed. I meant nothing by it; I mean nothing by *anything*. I was certainly not…you know… It's a young man's game, all that nonsense.

But it was out now, too late to take it back. I fumbled with my fingers as she finished pouring, and brought the two glasses back to the table. She set mine before me, fixing me with a look that made me feel like a naughty boy being humored.

"My husband hightailed it out of the city as soon as it all kicked off," she said, sitting down. "I might have gone with him, but, well… what was the point?" She folded her arms and made a mute, wide-eyed face. "How do you like that? Twenty-five years of marriage and he pisses off at the first sign of trouble."

"Where did he go?" I asked.

"No idea. His sister's in Nottingham probably. They were always close."

"Maybe he's still there," I said hopefully.

She shrugged. "Good luck to him, I say. Me, I couldn't give a shit. Cheers." She lifted her glass.

"Cheers," I said hesitantly, raising mine. The liquor was sweet and strong, and I winced as it hit my throat.

"The problem was we were never tested," she said, gazing into the glass. "Things have to be tested to survive, don't they? Things have to be put under pressure in order to strengthen, and our marriage was not. We had our own careers, our own lives. We weren't rich by anyone's standards, but we never struggled. We had no children, no health worries, stable jobs."

"What did you do?"

She cocked her head and frowned. "What do you mean? You think I haven't always been a ferry-woman?"

She stayed that way for a moment, frozen in deadpan, before finally she let out a deep, fruity laugh. "I was a social worker," she went on. "Young offenders mostly. My husband, wherever he might be, was a journalist. I suppose if there's one thing we shared it was that we both wanted justice." She shrugged again and gave me a thin smile. "Waste of time now, though, eh?"

"You helped other people," I replied. "That's not wasted time. That's good, that's noble."

She puffed through her nose. "Noble. Perhaps." She rolled her eyes around the squat walls of her boat and let them fall in a dark corner. Something seemed to lift her expression. "I tried for a while after it all happened. I thought if I could help people get to where they needed to go, keep them safe, it might make things better. But now with the camps…" She shook her head. "Truth is I'm tired of it all. I've run out of fight."

"So you can't help us?" I said.

"I didn't say that," she said.

After a pause, she took a breath. "I know a team on the other side of the river," she continued. "They run contraband along the disused Tube lines. They're good people and I trust them. I can hook up with them at Charing Cross and they can transport her north. They'll look after her."

"What about me?"

"What about you?"

"Can they take me as well?"

"I doubt it. It's risky enough with a child."

"But I promised her I would get her to safety."

"Then this is the best chance you have."

She was right, of course. I had already lost Lineker, and had barely made it to the river without losing Aisha too. How could I hope to navigate whatever path lay on the other side? There would not always be a Charlie Jenkins to help.

"She's not your burden, Reginald," said Charlie.

"No," I replied. "That is not the word I would use at all." My words felt hollow and clumsy. Embarrassed, I drained my glass. Charlie refilled it.

"I'll need to cross early, though," she said. "It's too dangerous in daylight."

"Thank you," I said.

"Don't mention it."

We drank and talked some more, mostly about her life, her childhood, and the places she'd traveled. I took care to direct the conversation away from my own life, for no other reason than that I found talking about it distinctly uncomfortable. Charlie kept a close watch on the windows, but there was no sign of our pursuers, and as the night wore on, her checks became more infrequent. She kept our glasses full, and I became somewhat tipsy, as did she. Occasionally I made her laugh. I had no idea why, but then I freely admit that the mechanisms of the feminine mind are quite lost on me.

As the night wore on, my thoughts—as they tend to when bottles drain—began to darken. The night was cold, and I wondered where Lineker was and whether he had found a place to shelter.

Charlie must have noticed my change of mood because she filled the glasses and corked the bottle. "One last drink," she said. She knocked hers back, motioning for me to do the same, which I did. When I had finished, she leaned over to replace the bottle on its shelf, placing her hand on my shoulder to help. But it lingered too long and, as her neck and bosom pushed close to my face, she squeezed.

When she sat down her face was different. Her eyelids were low, her lips softer. Her breast swelled. I was terrified.

"Now," she said, smoothing her dress and letting her eyes perform a little dart around the table. "Sleeping arrangements." She caught my eye and smiled innocently. "Hmm. The seat behind you pulls out so you can sleep there, and I'm more than happy to sleep with our little cargo. However…"

Another deep breath.

"If you'd prefer…"

She let the words hang like a baited hook. I failed to bite.

"There's someone else?" she said. "You're married?"

"Yes," I replied, cradling my glass. "I was."

She paused, her sexual armory dismantling before me. "Were you tested?"

It was my turn to hesitate. "Yes," I said at last. "Yes, I would say we were tested."

Like I said, I do not understand how women work or how they do these things. But somehow, Charlie knew the exact question to ask.

"Reginald," she said as if she were unwrapping a bandage, "why were you so afraid of my barge?"

So I told her. I thought I wouldn't, but I did.

# NORFOLK

**REGINALD HARDY'S JOURNAL**

**DECEMBER 11, 2021**

PROVIDENCE SEEMED TO GUIDE us out of London that day. Every traffic light was green, every junction clear, the traffic on every motorway moving like a well-oiled machine. We reached the Norfolk coast as the sun dipped in its cloudless sky and Isla, my daughter, lay half-asleep in her mother's arms. As I walked to the door of the first cheapish-looking bed-and-breakfast, the ground was still warm and the hedge buzzed with evening insects.

It was September 2001, and we had just moved into Seton Bayley tower. We were supposed to be unpacking, but the heatwave had turned Sandra mad with the idea that we should enjoy the weather and take an impromptu holiday instead.

"They've got canals there on the Broads, Reginald," she had said, jumping up and down. "We can hire some bikes, go on a little ride, stop at a few pubs, enjoy the countryside. It'll be nice!"

I had not been quite so enthusiastic.

"Please? It'll be good for Isla too."

Two feet thumped through from the other room.

"What good for me?" Isla gasped as she caught sight of the view. "I can see Londin!"

Sandra's eyebrows lifted in a silent plea. I found her impossible to refuse.

So we left, leaving our new flat littered with unopened boxes.

They only had one room left at the bed-and-breakfast—a posh one which we could not afford—but when the landlady saw Isla's sleepy face lift from Sandra's neck, she clutched her bosom and said we could have it at the normal rate. Sandra squealed at the four-poster and posed on the balcony that overlooked the sea. They had a table for us in the restaurant where we ate steaks and fat chips, and Isla was allowed a baked bean sandwich. I tried some wine—something French, I was told—which I was surprised to say I enjoyed, and then we all had ice creams that were too big for us, and I had to finish off both the girls' as well as my own. Tipsy and full, we made our way upstairs, brushed Isla's teeth, and laid her down to sleep. Then we sat out on the balcony, holding hands, and Sandra smoked as we watched the sun set and the stars come out over the roaring surf, and there was no need to say a single word.

The next day, after a sleep so deep I forgot who I was or where we were, we got up, had breakfast, and went in search of bicycles. The man in the shop was a friendly chap with a lazy eye who fitted a child's seat on the back of my saddle. He gave us a map of good routes along the canals and told us not to worry too much about when to bring the bikes back—tomorrow was fine, or the next day.

"You seem like nice folk," he said. "Life's too short and it's far too nice a day to be rushing anywhere."

We drove to a parking garage with the bikes rattling in the back of the van, then started out on a long, straight track by the water. It was hard at first, but we soon settled into a rhythm, and I grew used to the bumps and the regular stops to let others pass. We waved at barges and dog walkers, and gave fellow cyclists nods as if we were part of some secret club. Isla shouted at the ducks and waved big hellooos to the tractors in the fields.

We stopped at a pub for food and I had a ploughman's lunch, which—to Sandra's great delight—confused and upset Isla because she thought the ploughman might go hungry without it. I had a ginger beer and Sandra had a lager top, because we were on holiday.

Then we rode a little more. By midafternoon we were ready to head back to the B and B.

"I don't like the look of those clouds," I said, looking up and adjusting my collar.

"Swap," said Sandra. "Let me take Isla on the way back."

"Are you sure? The weight takes a bit of getting used to."

"We'll be fine. Right, Isla?"

We set off slow, but she soon got the hang of it. About half an hour later it started to rain.

"Told you!" I said. "Yuck, we're going to get soaked."

"Stop complaining!" yelled Sandra. "It's only water! Besides, it feels nice!"

She may have been right for all I know, and if I try, I can sometimes remember still feeling happy in those moments—the warm spatter of rain on my face, the click and whizz of my back wheel, and the peace of the fields stretching out across the earth like some heavenly dream. But those things don't stay long.

A couple of miles from home, we saw two boats ahead. Sandra seemed to be flagging.

"Do you want to swap back?" I said.

"No!" she cried. "I'll be fine. It's not far. What do you think's wrong with them?"

"They look like they're stuck."

The two boats were wedged against the bank as if their bows were locked. Two men were arguing on their respective decks about the best course of action.

"Mummy?"

"What's wrong, sweetheart?"

"Need a wee."

"OK, let's stop ahead. Maybe Daddy can help these two men."

We came to a halt, and I laid my bike against the hedge.

"Whoops!" said Sandra as Isla's weight almost made her topple. "Oh, bollocks, I'm stuck."

"Everything all right?" I said to the two men.

"Getting there!" laughed one. "Bit of bother with our lines getting tangled in the water. Do you think you could pass us that rope? It's tied up in the other one, do you see?"

"No problem," I said, picking up the two ropes and examining them. The men busied themselves with a knot of their own.

"Oh, shit," said Sandra from the bike.

"Mummy, I need a wee."

"I know, sweetheart. Mummy's got her shorts stuck on the handlebars, that's all."

I glanced around and saw her leaning over the bars, balancing on one toe.

"Reginald, can you help?"

"Yeah, just a second. I'm just untying this."

"Reginald, please, I'm stuck!" She laughed.

"Almost done."

I heard a *plop*.

"There," I said, freeing the ropes.

"There," sighed Sandra. "I'm free."

I handed the ropes back and turned around. Sandra did the same.

"Isla?"

She was not in her seat. We looked to the hedgerow, thinking she'd hopped off to sort herself out, but she was not there either.

I locked eyes with Sandra as our panic rose. We had forgotten to strap her in.

"Good God!" shouted one of the men from the deck. "She's in the water!"

We looked down and Sandra shrieked. There in the triangle of black canal between the two boats was a trail of bubbles rising from an expanding swell of circular ripples. I jumped in as a coil of ropes slipped from one of the boats.

"Get her!" screamed Sandra. "Reginald, get her!"

I dived down, floundering in the growing snake of rope and weed, feeling about for a hand or a leg or piece of her dress, but there was nothing. I resurfaced to the sound of Sandra's hysterical cries and the splashes of the two men jumping in to help, then I dived down a second time, kicking deeper. This time I found her, a little hand in mine. I pulled and it gripped back.

"Got you," I bubbled and made for the surface.

But she wouldn't come. I pulled again. She was caught on something.

I stared down into the murk, feeling the men's legs hitting my back and seeing Isla's face lit in the gray light above. Her eyes were wide, panicking like me. One of the men found me, and I placed her hand in his while I went down to free her leg. It was caught in a knot of rope, which was itself tied in a thick clump of weed. I tugged and tugged, feeling my lungs burning, my mind pondering the terrible choice of trading vital seconds at the surface for a better chance of saving her. Just when I thought I could stay down no more, I pulled off her shoe and pushed her foot through the knot, feeling a small snap, then I kicked up and grabbed her hand, pulling her to the surface and dragging her out onto the towpath, where she lay, facedown and still as I spluttered and vomited in the dirt.

Later, I found myself in the hospital consultation room, half listening to words of sympathy from a doctor whose face I never saw as Sandra howled in the corner. I felt incalculably numb. The moments passed like flecks of ash on an upward breeze, safely carried away from the agony below. I wished to be with them—to dissolve into time and be no more. But the moments abandoned me. Still I remained.

Outside in the waiting room, a crowd of patients watched the television in dumb horror as two great towers fell into dust. I was barely even aware of them.

I stopped talking and let the barge creak on. It had been some time since I had told anyone what had happened, and never had I done so in such detail. Perhaps it was the alcohol, or the strains of the past few days, or losing Lineker, or the bond I was feeling with Aisha. Either way, it all now hung between us, naked and vulnerable as the dying flame.

Charlie stared at the table. She had not made a sound or moved a muscle since I had begun.

"That's what that woman meant when she said she was sorry when she heard," she said. "And now I see why Aisha's safety is so important to you. I am sorry."

"You don't have to…"

"I'm sorry if I was improper."

She smoothed down her skirts and stood, avoiding my gaze. "We have an early start tomorrow."

She picked up the gun and wandered to the bedroom door, turning when she reached it.

"Good night, Reginald," she said and closed the door behind her.

# THE WRONG PATH

**LINEKER**

I STOOD STONE-STILL IN that empty street. The problem was not that the smell of Reg and the girl had disappeared. The problem was that another one had burst into my consciousness and flattened them to smithereens.

It was Her again. She was close.

I lost myself. All thoughts of finding my master drifted from me and, struck dumb, I followed the sour perfume into the darkness. To this day I could not tell you what streets I took or the stories they cradled. They were of no consequence, background noise beneath the siren toward which I was helplessly being pulled. Eventually I found myself sitting, fragile and out of sorts, by some steps and a door, through which I could hear the clanks, shouts, and sizzles of a working kitchen. There were smells too, I imagine, though they must have dissolved like everything else. She was in there, somewhere, and I knew it.

A voice grew near, and the door opened. At the top of the steps stood an enormous-bellied man wearing a stained white apron and carrying a tied black bag. He was laughing at something, but he stopped when he saw me.

"Hello there, little fella," he said. He waddled down the steps and held out his hand. "Where did you come from then, eh?"

I growled. He was in my way.

"What's wrong? Don't be like that. Come 'ere."

I snapped—a proper bite that caught him on two fingers with my fangs. He yelped and sprang back, shielding his hand. I slunk back to a growl, teeth still bared. His wounded look quickly turned to anger.

"You little bastard!" he yelled, hurling the bag of rubbish at me and retreating inside. The bag hit me square in the head and tore open. I picked through it, dazed, and gnawed half-heartedly on a chicken bone. But before I knew it, I had dropped it and was off again, around the side of the building.

It was clearer than usual, freezing cold, and above the silhouetted skyline, the cloud was hooked on a talon of the moon. The place was a pub, still open. Its windows glimmered with candlelight and the raucous sound of slurred words, and an aimless fiddle warbled from within. A barrel stood beneath one of the windows, and I jumped on top to peer in. Dark shapes, shadows, flickering faces, filthy leers, and sweat-drenched cheeks heaved over the tables. Scum, thieves, scoundrels, villains, whores, and…

In the corner, huddled in some furtive discussion with three others I could not see, there She was. All sound muffled, all light blurred until Her face was the only thing I could see, brightly focused in the surrounding blur. I watched it—the movement of Her bright-red lips, the glancing of Her rookish eyes between Her cohorts—I watched until, suddenly, as if She had known I was there all along, She looked right at me.

My heart machine-gunned—*fuckity fuckity fuckity fuckity fuck*—
and I jumped down behind the barrel, breathing fast. Soon the door
opened, and She stepped out, hands on hips, scanning the empty
street. Her scent roared like a flame in the frozen air. I cowered,
heart still pounding. I wanted to run to Her, *yearned* to close those
final few feet and be by Her side. Every muscle twitched to do so,
and I think I would have gone had it not been for that last glimmer
of reason that told me: *She's still dangerous. You do not want to follow
this bliss.*

Hardest thing I ever did. But I did it. And after a few moments
more, She returned inside.

As the door swung shut, I sank into the dirt. Whatever spell had
entranced me was now gone, like a snatched blanket, leaving me
cold and troubled.

All my lines were blurred. Who was I? That certainty I had felt
as I followed Reg's scent, that feeling of truth that I was on the *right
path*—if all that could be destroyed by the mere whiff of a stranger,
then who the fuck was I? Just some dumb, fur-covered machine. And
who was Reg? He was supposed to be my master, he was supposed
to look after me like I looked after him. But he had left me to save
the girl.

I knew I should understand why, but the truth was I just didn't.
I didn't understand anything anymore. I was in a strange street,
surrounded by strange buildings and strange people, but nothing
was stranger than this new place inside my head. I was adrift on
strange tides.

Eventually the distant sound of breaking glass roused me, and I
got wearily to my feet. I had no scent to follow and no energy to

follow it, so instead I slunk off in search of a place to sleep. I found an overturned, rusted dumpster and crawled inside. The rats scattered as I turned three circles and lay down, whimpering myself to sleep, confused as hell.

# THE DOOR

## REGINALD HARDY'S JOURNAL
### DECEMBER 12, 2021

WHEN I WOKE UP, the barge had stretched. I looked down an impossible corridor of galleys, benches, shelves, and cupboards all accelerating into a vanishing point at the far end—a minuscule space that streamed with amber daylight, a bed, and curtains wafting in ethereal flames of sun. The rest of the barge was dark and still, stuck inside the cold, stubborn night.

"Come here, Reginald," called a distant voice. "Come on, come back to bed."

I saw miles-away shadows moving in the light, a hand outstretched, and hair falling down across a pillow.

"Sandra?" I said, my breath freezing.

"Come *on*." The voice giggled.

"I have to go," I said to the body I knew was lying beside me with its back turned. I pushed off the blanket and walked out into the dream.

The boat creaked as I walked its length. Floorboards seemed to wobble with each step, pots and pans quaking when I passed as if my body had some new and dangerous magnetism. I steadied myself on the ceiling, which felt feathery and light against my fingers, bulging at my touch. Halfway there. The bed was clearer now, and I saw that it was hers, the one in which we had shared each other's joy on that July afternoon all those years ago. She lay there, naked and tangled in its covers, warm in the sun that filled her cluttered, dusty bedroom.

I walked faster but my feet were splashing in something. I heard a trickling sound from my left and saw a hole in the boat's side. River water was spilling in, forming a rapidly growing pool on the floor.

"Reginald," whispered Sandra.

"Wait," I said. "I have to fix it."

"Leave it."

"No, we'll sink. Just, just let me…"

I fumbled in a drawer full of shotgun shells, all stuck together by a treacly substance. I pulled one from the mess and plugged it into the hole. It fit and the water stopped, and I continued on my way. As I drew near, Sandra's face became clear, and she smiled and lifted the sheet, flooding me with arousal at the sight of her young, brown body.

"But how…?" I asked.

"It doesn't matter. Come in. It's cold out there."

I reached the bed, feeling lighter somehow, and as I bent down I caught sight of myself in the cracked mirror on the wall above. Hair black and all intact, face clear, body slim—I was me from before as well.

"How…?"

"I told you, it doesn't matter. Shut up and kiss me."

I let myself fall onto her, drowning in the smell of almonds in her hair, and the warmth rising from beneath the covers, and the salt skin of her neck.

"Oh, Reginald," she moaned, between long mouth kisses. Her legs wrapped around me. "Oh, Reginald, I've missed you."

"I didn't know this was possible."

"*Help me.*"

"What's wrong?"

"Nothing," she said breathlessly. Her toe caught in the elastic of my underwear, pulling them down.

"You said *help me.*"

"No, I didn't. Reginald, fuck me, please."

"*No. Help me.*"

I looked over my shoulder as she kissed my neck and rubbed herself, wet, against my thigh.

"Oh, Christ, Reginald, my Reginald."

There, at the other end of the corridor, was a different bed. Not the bed I had left, but one from another time, another place. No sunlight in this room, just a cold, gray dawn spilling through drab hospital curtains.

"*Help me. I can't breathe.*"

"Wait," I said.

"What's wrong?" said Sandra, beneath me. "Come back, where are you going?"

"*Help me.*"

I followed the voice back along the corridor. Now I seemed to be climbing uphill. Pots, pans, and bottles slid down shelves, and water from the leak was streaming over my feet. The shell had popped out and the hole had grown worse. Water was gushing in, flooding the barge.

Halfway back and I saw her in the bed, dark circles under her eyes where freckles should have been. Her hair was in straggles.

I stopped at the leak, wondering what I could use to block it.

"Help me," she croaked. "I can't breathe."

"There's a leak. We'll sink."

"You can't fix it."

"But we'll drown."

"You can't fix it. Help me."

"But..."

I woke up again. Frost clung to the air like the dream to my thoughts, and Aisha stood at my bed.

"You were dreaming," she said.

I faltered, thinking that perhaps I still was, for her voice was as clear and unbroken as the moonlight that bathed her.

"You can speak," I said, sitting up.

"Were they bad dreams?"

I shook my head. "Yes. Yes, Aisha, they were."

Her eyes dropped. "I have them too." She was holding a photograph in her hands. "But I have good ones sometimes," she said.

I rolled my stiff legs out of the narrow cot. "Listen," I said, searching for the words to explain. "The nice lady, Charlie, she—"

"Where will you go?"

Her eyes were still on the photograph. I was astonished by the sound of her voice, the color, croak, and inflections that had been hiding behind her silence.

"Pardon me?"

"After you've found Linn-kaaa, where will you go?"

I hesitated. "Home," I replied. "Home is where I will go."

She rubbed the edges of the photograph, then held it proudly out before me. "I have a better home," she said. "You should come and see it."

As I sat there, paralyzed with awe, the door opened and Charlie entered. She looked between us.

"It's time to go," she said.

# THE CROSSING

## LINEKER

NEVER UNDERESTIMATE THE POWER of sleep. Even when it occurs in a piss-drenched, burned-out dumpster, it has the power to restore, reset, and reignite. I woke up nothing like the dog I had been. The confusion of the previous night had disappeared like a fever, drowned in a distant dream of a sinking barge.

My eyes sprang open, twin diamonds in the dawn, and I jumped to my feet. I had the scent. Reg and girl were center stage once again.

Sound the bugles!

Off I went, running, running, running through the early morning streets, past leafless shrubs and wooden shacks. I hurdled the legs of slumbering drunks, dodged buckets of slop thrown from doorways, and cleared fences, weightless and dizzy in the liquor of my own volition. I saw a horse. A horse! It was tethered to a barn, still asleep and steaming in the morning frost. The sight made me spin like a top, but I did not slow, I had no time, I had to get on. Somehow I knew where they were, and what's more, I knew how to get there.

Sleep! Sleep and a new day—wondrous things, priceless gifts, and

I was taking both of them. I ran, ran, ran, down to that stinking river and the skyline beyond, stooped and broken like an army of wounded giants rising from the murk of a battlefield—the buildings full of birds that had once filled my dreams.

And you know what? As the sun crept over the water, I looked up at those crumbling towers and wondered at how bleak they seemed in comparison to my life. I wanted to be far from them, back home in the safety of my chair and looking out, not up. They could keep their shit-stained rafters; I was a dog, after all, not a bird.

The scent was strong now, almost eye-watering. Soon I would find him, we would be reunited, and all we would have to accomplish was our journey home.

I saw them from a brickwork jaw jutting from the bank that had once been a bridge. The three figures were dim in the mist but unmistakable. His slight stoop, his cautious movements, I could even tell what he was thinking by the shape of his profile. Reg.

I ran toward him, filled with love.

They were on a barge moored to a jetty, talking in whispers, arranging coats and bags in the narrow space below the hatch. I was still some way off when I saw them stop. I stopped too, because I was hit by the most almighty smell from Reg's pores, like nothing I'd ever smelled from him before. I almost fell to my belly. What *was* this? The blood tang of hope, the aching wet wood of despair, and relief's seaweed all gushing out of him at once, spiraling into something I knew even he couldn't put into words. He wiped a tear from his eye and placed a shaking hand upon the girl's shoulder. Then he turned and climbed the ladder back up to the jetty.

I continued on, and as I drew near I got a similar scent from the girl, only it was quivering and less developed, like raw jelly trembling in her heart.

The woman pushed away with the pole, and the barge swung silently out onto the water. The girl stood with her hands on the stern, looking back at Reg like some radiant angel sent to watch over him. She gave him a slow wave that didn't stop, and Reg waved back with a smile that tore at my heart. I watched him, swirling with wonder and pride and sadness, and his smells began to change yet again. All those voles of fear began to scatter, freed at last and flowing over his cliff tops like lemmings. Whatever mysteries were inside of him were shifting now, making room for other things, good things.

I had to be near him, so I picked up the pace.

The boat had almost disappeared into the mist when he dropped his hand. It was time to leave. I barked, and he turned in surprise.

"Lineker?" he said, a beautiful beam spreading across his face like a sunrise. "Lineker, you found me!"

He held out his arms, and I broke into a gallop.

Home. I knew it wouldn't be easy, not after what we'd been through to get here, but we'd make it somehow. We had each other, and at least we weren't going north.

North.

*Hang on*, I thought, my eyes drifting to the barge. *We're not going north, but are they?*

My thoughts began to fuzz around the edges. I got a sense of something and looked back at Reg. He was no longer opening his arms but standing upright, staring out at the water. And those voles of his…they weren't falling anymore. They were climbing back up.

My ears twitched, paws jolted.

Focus.

I was close now, almost there.

Reg was no longer smiling. His eyes and mouth were wide open. Fear was returning to him in droves. I followed his line of sight and saw what he saw—a halo of sickly green light hanging over the boat. The woman looked up and pulled the girl to her waist with her free hand.

Reg was calling to them—*Come back!*—but the woman was frozen, head shaking, still scanning the sky above them. From out of the mist came two birds, buzzing like enormous bees. They hovered there, two cameras tilting down at the boat. Not birds, not bees—drones.

My hackles were up, my mouth was full of froth, my senses were on fire. In a split second I had lurched across the full spectrum of my physiology, from one extreme to another. Green to red. Danger.

A voice crackled from the opposite shore.

"*Continue to the north bank. State your names and identification numbers.*"

The woman shook her head and pulled the girl close. Reg was running up and down the jetty, hands to his head. I was almost upon him, now riding the thermals of *his* panic as well as my own.

"*Names and identification numbers,*" insisted the voice. On the north bank stood a line of purple figures, two trucks on either side.

Reg seemed to come to a decision and stopped, looking down beneath the jetty. Tied to it was a small, square raft. He turned to me, eyes wild. "Stay," he said. "Lineker, *stay.*"

I came to a halt. Just a few strides separated us.

*Stay? Are you fucking serious?*

He clambered down the ladder and untethered the raft, shaking as he uncoiled the rope.

*Stay? What the fuck?*

Then he knelt down and paddled away from the shore. Leaving.

"Stay!" he called up to me, voice as high as a warbling nightingale. "Good boy."

*Good boy, is it? I'll show you good fucking boy, you piece of... STAY?* No fucking way, sunshine, not this time. I'm coming with.

I scampered up and down the jetty, snapping and snarling at the water, muscles coiled, ready to spring. My senses were on full alert now, *overload*, information from all angles buffering and bouncing around my brain with a rotating red alarm screaming *JUMP!*

On the other bank, the monotone repeated its demands.

On the boat, the woman crouched on the deck with the child in the protective cocoon of her arms.

In the air, the drones hovered lower, closing in.

On the raft, Reg paddled, almost at the boat.

And on my side of the water, some trucks had pulled up.

People were standing next to it. Purples.

And out of the passenger side came...

*JUMP!*

I jumped. And for a second or so, I swooped through the air, and I thought, *So this is what it feels like to fly, just like those beautiful birds. Except, of course, for the fact that...no wings...*

I landed with a graceless plop and the cold water hit me like a slab of iron. I thought I was dead for a second, could feel the thoughts splinter and my eyeballs freeze. My muscles hardened to stone, and I felt myself sink, down, down, soon to be silt on the riverbed, into the mud, back to The Howl, back to… No, no, you're a dog, Lineker, you can *swim*, for fuck's sake! My paw twitched and the other one replied, harder. Soon they were twitching together. My back legs joined in, clawing the water beneath me, until finally my nose broke the putrid surface and I was out, spluttering, looking wildly about for signs of Reg.

I saw him. He'd reached the boat. If I could just get there with him, maybe…

But the drones were upon them, and above them a larger bird had appeared. A dark-purple helicopter, ladder extended, and a uniformed meat monkey ran down toward them, gun swinging.

If I could just…just… My legs slowed. Whatever fumes of energy they had found were now nothing but black smoke. I had nothing left. Nothing. I drifted down, just catching sight of Reg being lifted from the water, and the woman and the girl kicking and screaming with him, up into the sky.

And I drifted down, dragged by those strange tides again, thinking, *This time, this time I'm going, I'm definitely going.*

Something yanked my collar and the river fell beneath me. I hung there from that hook, limp and dazed, watching the gray world spin below until I was deposited upon the concrete like a wet fish. I lay there on my belly, shivering and dripping with the sound of Reg's cries echoing somewhere behind me. And with my last dribble of energy, with all my lines blurred beyond recognition, I opened my eyes and looked up. And I saw Her.

# PART 3

# CHILDREN

**THREE MONTHS LATER**

REGINALD

A JAB IN MY ribs. Not hard, just enough to wake me. I opened my eyes and, as I did every morning, saw Aisha. In one hand she held a bottle of water, and in the other a crust of bread, which she held out for me, saying nothing. She had stopped talking again, and those bewildering words she had spoken in Charlie's barge seemed like they had never happened now. She was within her barricades once more, and I do not blame her.

I sat up on our mattress—a festering, springless slab filled with unimaginable human residue—and took a breath of heavy air. Charlie was already awake and cleaning her face with the hem of her outermost skirt. Aisha shoved my breakfast impatiently toward me, and I took it, leaving her to continue on her way. She had business to attend to.

Children—they are not the flimsy waifs we imagine them to be. While us adults sat in that place, fretting, pacing the walls, making useless speculations and half-baked plans, the children set to work in silence. They did not cry for toys or television or books or entertainment. Instead, they did what they had to in order to survive—which was to find something to occupy their time.

Our nearest neighbors, by which I mean the people on the mattress next to Charlie, Aisha, and me, were a Nigerian man named David and his son, a quiet boy of six named Clifford.

Clifford collected rocks. Chunks of masonry mostly, but stones and pebbles from the yard too. He kept them in neat piles, ordered and reordered countless times by size, shape, pigment, and a dozen other categorizations he alone knew in the depths of his mind to which he retreated during the waking hours. We took it upon ourselves to help him, and it was always a delight when one of us found a new treasure for his collection. The cherry-shaped obsidian pebble with gray contours that I had presented to him had kept him smiling for hours.

Other children carved endless patterns and imaginary animals into the soft, crumbling brickwork, or played elaborate games with plastic bottles and the paper bags in which our bread arrived.

Aisha's distraction—the ongoing duty she took upon herself to fulfil every day, without fail—was to ensure the even distribution of rations. Bread, water, porridge, that foul and feeble fluid that passed for soup; it was all to be shared out equally.

I had soon come to realize that the thing Aisha cared about most was care itself. The weak were not to be treated unfairly. No one was to be left behind—a rule of which I was reminded every night by the soft, cruel calls of Lineker's name in her sleep.

Perhaps she had seen so little care that it seemed a treasure in itself, some precious commodity the world lacked, but of which she discovered in herself an unlimited store. If it was a product of what she had been through—and her experience still remained a mystery—it could easily have had an opposite effect, had she been made of different stuff. I am sure that history has no end of examples of how mistreatment causes equal amounts apathy as empathy. Such times show us our mettle, I suppose, and Aisha's mettle was strong; on her watch, nobody would go hungry.

At least, no one in our small corner behind the fallen pillar. For there were thousands more beyond.

In near darkness we huddled in warrens of rubble spilling from walls that had once withstood the ravages of three centuries. Some of the brickwork shone with traces of gold trim, and you could still make out the splintered chessboard of the floor, but otherwise all was a gloomy brown covered in dust and mold.

We kept our voices low on account of the guards, who wandered the great hall constantly. Our whispers carried up into the heavens—the tourist gallery that now provided a lookout—where they met wet mist and bleary sunlight straining through the gash in the gilded dome.

At night they dangled gas lamps from the gallery, with flames so dim they barely lit an inch of space around them. We slept beneath a haze of orange spots, hissing like the breaths of dying angels, and the flicker of makeshift candles scraped from ancient wax drippings and lit secretly from the guards' flicked cigarettes.

St. Paul's Cathedral, though now in ruins, had survived the bombs.

Charlie, Aisha, and I had found a space in one corner of the northern aisle, which had been divided by a fallen pillar. The effect was that we were separated from the rest by a natural wall with a rough, rubble-strewn door where the pillar had split in half. We had blankets and a thin mattress like most others, although it had taken us a few days to acquire them. Others lined the walls on either side of us. There was no segregation—individuals, couples, and families of all ages, colors, and accents claimed their own space in the makeshift prison. Those of us who had been there long enough knew not to take more than our fair share, not to cause a scene, and not to complain about anything to the guards.

Duncan, on the other hand, had only just arrived. "Why am I here?"

He was in his forties and wore a suit that had probably been expensive once, but was now creased and baggy. He paced a short section of broken wall, running his hand through his flop of crow-black hair.

"Anyone? Can anyone tell me why the hell I'm in here? Because I just don't get it." He paused at the end of a section of pillar and gave a trembling huff. Then he resumed his urgent pacing. "I'm not black. I'm not Indian. I'm not Muslim. I was born in Wiltshire, went to fucking Oxford…"

David cupped his hands over his son's ears at our new guest's language. At this, Duncan rolled his eyes and scuffed the concrete with his once-gleaming brogues.

"I'm not gay, I'm not a commie, I read the *Financial Times*, I even pay my taxes, for Christ's sake! At least I did when there were taxes to pay." He smacked a palm against the wall. "I've never claimed benefits. I had an excellent job…" He scanned the walls. "One which I managed to keep through all this, I might add." He nodded, jabbing a finger at us all. "Oh yes, which is more than I could probably say for all of you, eh? Isn't it? I kept my fucking job!"

"Please," David said to Duncan. "Keep your language civil for the benefit of our children."

"Pffft, sorry," spat Duncan. He kicked the ground like a moping teenager. "But I did. Three years I spent trying to keep that bank going; no mean feat when there's no electricity or internet."

He gazed dreamily away.

"There was a time when I watched seven-figure deals coming in before I was halfway down my first latte. And I've just spent the last six months transferring a database onto fucking graph paper using car batteries and a dot matrix printer. Not exactly the life of a City boy, is it? But I did it, I put my fucking oar in, I did my fucking bit."

"Sir, please," David insisted, getting to his feet.

"Oh, fuck off!" said Duncan, spittle flying over his shoulder.

David stood as tall as his five-foot-seven-inch frame would allow. "This is not making anything easier on us," he said. "And if you won't adjust your behavior for the children, then do it for your own safety, I implore you. The guards do not like—"

"My behavior?" Duncan turned, hands on hips. "I was on my third data run between Manchester and London when they picked me up. I had all my credentials ready as always—ID, passport, company visa, right to travel, everything, and nothing to hide. What do I get? A sack over the fucking head and no explanation. Nothing. So, excuse me if my behavior is a little irate, but I do so very much want to know: Why the fuck am I here?" He opened his arms. "Why are any of us here?" he babbled, his voice jumping an octave.

"Hey," said a girl sitting on her own who I had not heard speak before. She was in her early twenties and wore tight black jeans with a gray tank top and a red, checked shirt. Dark roots showed in her straggly bleached hair. Her accent was from somewhere across the Atlantic. "Will you keep your voice down?"

"Shut up," said Duncan, without taking his eyes off David. He took a step toward him. "You. At least you know why you're here. What are you, West Indian, Jamaican, or something?"

"My family was from Nigeria," David replied.

"Well, there you go," he said. "Foreigner, probably had one of those phone shops, or"—he gave a hideous grin—"what, were you…were you one of those idiots who sent me fake emails telling me I'd won a fucking yacht?" He looked around, delighted with himself, but his grin shriveled in the silence.

"He's a British citizen," said the girl. "And he was an IT support technician."

"Oh yeah? And how would you know?"

"Because I listen to people." She looked at him coolly, raising one black eyebrow. "You ever try that, fuck nugget?"

Duncan stormed toward her but found David in his way. I went to stand too, but my bad knee, having not moved for some time, shot through with pain.

The corners of Duncan's mouth pulled down. "Fine," he said. "Fine."

Duncan straightened his suit and turned to the girl. "What about you?" he said, unable to control the tremble in his voice. "What's your name?"

"Dana."

"Canadian?"

"Full marks," she replied, unimpressed.

Duncan raised his chin. "I used to go to Vancouver with work every other month," he said. "I know the accent. What were you, a student? Activist, is that it?"

"I am a nurse. And yeah, I was an activist. So what?"

"Well, that explains you." He bit his nail and scanned the dark walls.

"Foreigners, benefit cheats, layabouts, lefties, and Arabs…"

There was a scuffle of boots and half the room was on its feet, either holding him against the wall or trying to prevent others from doing so. Charlie and I shared a look and turned from the argument. We had no desire to get caught up in a quarrel that would draw attention; we had only one priority, and she was currently feeding moldy bread to a four-year-old girl.

I have no idea how I made it to Charlie's barge. When I look back, it feels like a dream, untying that raft and paddling across the hellish water. All I remember after reaching the boat's stern is the deafening whack and slice of helicopter blades and a blinding light as I was dragged from the raft. Then I felt sackcloth pulled tight around my face. *Lineker*, I thought. *Not again*. Then everything went dark.

When I woke I was still in the sack and bound by the wrists, lying in the back of a truck. I could hear Aisha's breaths nearby.

"It's all right," I said uselessly, because clearly it was not. Only the most innocent child would have believed me in that situation, and I honestly don't know how much child she had left in her by that stage, let alone innocence.

It is hard to piece it all together, the next few days; time and location became muddled by endless journeys in tight spaces. But, somehow in those tight spaces, something happened between Charlie and me.

People have certain expectations about relationships. Love must carry them through their life. It must keep them happy, fulfilled, and interested. You need to be "compatible" to succeed in love.

But these expectations are just a function of the time you believe you have left, and Charlie and I did not believe we had much. So in those dark and claustrophobic days, our expectations became dense and fertile, vivid with desperation. All we wanted was comfort, all we needed was a familiar smell and a source of hope. And we found that in each other. When everything else is stripped away, a human relationship is simple and requires no effort. You don't need to be compatible. You don't need long walks, a shared sense of humor, or common interests; sometimes all it takes is the warmth of a finger looped in your own.

Although touching others was now a daily torture I had to endure, unless I wanted to attract the attention of the guards, Charlie's touch—like Aisha's—brought no torment, only comfort. I suppose you could say my heebie-jeebies were showing signs of weakness.

At one point, we found ourselves in a huge, crowded space full of murmurs and rain. I peered through the gauze of my sack, but all I could make out was light and dark separated by jagged line. We remained there for one night. Sleep was impossible, so I busied myself by chewing a small hole in my sack so that I might see out. As I ground my teeth against the tough fabric, I became aware of a man muttering to himself. I spat out the cloth.

"Who's there?" I whispered. There were guards nearby; I could sense their flashlights roaming over us. The man stopped his twittering and his sack rustled as he turned in my direction.

"Nobody!" he wheezed with a giggle.

"Do you know what's happening? Why are we being moved about so much?"

He stopped laughing and made a grave warning note in his throat.

"Being moved about is good," he said. "It's when you stop that you need to worry. That's when they test you, stick those things in your gobs and see what's what. They've got their rules, see; they like to stick to the rules. Beep, beep!" He chuckled.

"Why don't they just test us all now?"

"Ha! Because they don't have enough, that's why. They're all breaking, cheap foreign shit!" He gave a shriek of laughter and a flashlight swung in his direction.

"Quiet!" shouted a guard, and the man gasped. I heard nothing more from him.

The next day I felt a prodding in my ribs. "Up," said a voice.

Keeping close to the sounds of Charlie and Aisha, I allowed myself to be shepherded in another trudging line. The air chilled as we were led outside, and I found that I had chewed enough of my sack to give me a dim view of the world. We were walking across a clearing in which a large wooden structure had been erected. I shook the sack to gain a clearer view and, with a dreadful turn of my stomach, I saw what it was: a long line of gallows with twenty or thirty people standing before nooses.

Now, hanging is a rather fascinating business. It used to be a respectable trade, as it happens, and to execute a person correctly using a noose required a high degree of care and expertise. Everybody is built differently, and a person's height and weight had to be taken into consideration when the noose was prepared, if the job was to be done properly and the drop ended with a clean break of the neck. Too short a rope could end with a long and painful strangulation; too long and the head could come clean off. It was, I believe, a matter of professional pride to ensure a swift and painless death.

I watched the trapdoors swing open and the ropes snap, lamenting once again the fact that nobody does a proper job anymore.

We were pushed onto another truck. I called for Aisha and Charlie but my distraction at the gallows had caused us to become separated. I hung my head and cursed myself; not only had I lost Lineker again, but now Aisha and Charlie too. The engine growled and, as we pulled away in that dark, stifling box, I called their names in vain.

Among the whimpers and sniffs I heard a faint voice from the opposite corner.

"Reginald? Reginald, are you here?"

"Charlie?"

"Yes!"

"Do you have Aisha?"

"Yes, she's here. Where are you?"

"Wait, I'm coming across."

I stood, much to the annoyance of my fellow passengers, and attempted to balance on the truck's rocking floor. With my hands still tied behind me, every jolt or turn would send me crashing into another crowd of people, and I stood on countless limbs and probably a few heads as I followed the sound of Charlie's voice. Eventually I reached the corner and fell down in a heap beside them.

"Don't let go again," said Charlie, feeling for my finger.

I did not.


Aisha, oblivious to or uninterested in the tense atmosphere that remained in the wake of Duncan's protests, completed her morning rounds and returned to sit beside me on the mattress. From her bag she produced what little remained of the rations and ate it, slowly and deliberately. Charlie coughed and winced in pain, holding a hand to her chest.

"What's wrong?" I asked.

"I'm fine," she replied, but it was far from the truth. She was ill, and had been growing steadily worse for the past two days. She was not the only one either. Many of the others, including the children, had begun to cough as well.

"What about you?" came a voice from the opposite wall. It was Duncan again. In spite of all advice to the contrary, he had refused to sit still or be quiet, intent only on understanding the reasons for his incarceration. His question was aimed at me. "Well?" he went on. "I see you sitting there all day long scribbling in that book of yours, but you don't say or do anything. What are you? Some kind of writer? A journalist, is that it? Did you write for the *Guardian* or something?"

I let my book drop to my knee. "I am an electrician," I said.

After a pause, he gave a dry huff. Then he turned his head to the ceiling. "I shouldn't be here," he whispered restlessly. Then, "Well, to hell with this. Guards!" He got to his feet and strode for the pillar.

We all held out our hands for him to stop.

"Sit down!" someone hissed. "You'll get us killed."

"Guards!" he yelled. "Guards!"

David leaped, but before he could reach him, a slack-postured Jamaican man appeared at the opening. He wore a denim vest over a dirty white tank top, black combats, and a battered cap, and the skin of his bare, muscled arms glistened in the low light. A squat, powerful-looking gun was slung across his torso. We knew this man as Jag.

"Great," said Dana, burying herself into one corner. "Thanks a lot, asshole."

Mr. Jag was not a pleasant gentleman, and it had become quite apparent that he was taking advantage of his position to coerce certain prisoners—namely the younger women—into sexual congress. Thankfully he did not appear to have pedophilic tendencies, but he had been giving Dana more attention than any one of us was comfortable with.

Behind Mr. Jag stood two other guards. One was unremarkable, but the other...the other gave me grave concerns. He was tall with huge arms, a thick chest, and an enormous belly, and he had that look of trouble about him—the buzz cut and squint eyes you would try your best to avoid if you passed him in the street. But it was not his appearance that gave me concerns. No, it was the way he looked at me. I found it most unsettling.

"What do you want?" he drawled.

"Yes, hello," said Duncan, slapping his hands together. "Thank you for coming so quickly. I have something to... I mean, I..."

Jag looked him up and down. With a curl of his lip he slouched toward him. "What do you want?"

Duncan tapped his fingers together. "I want..." He gulped. "I want to know why I'm here."

Jag paused, cocked his head. "Same reason everyone's here. Sorting. Right ones, wrong ones, useful"—he flashed a grin—"not useful."

"But...I am right," said Duncan. "Everything about me is right. Right religion, right background, right business, right—"

"Color?" said Jag. He tutted and ran a finger up the lapel of Duncan's threadbare suit. "It's not as simple as your skin, Mr. Businessman. Or where you're from, or what you do or believe."

"I don't understand. How did someone like..."

"Someone like me?" Jag yelled, and in the hush that followed, he gave Duncan's cheek a gentle slap. Then he spoke more softly. "How did someone like me get this job, Mr. Businessman? Walking around with a big gun, keeping you in line?" He tapped his skull. "I used my head, Mr. Businessman. Made myself useful. Used my vote!"

Duncan frowned. "I don't understand."

"You were on the wrong side," David piped up from across the room.

Jag looked down at him and beamed. "Wrong side," he repeated, nodding.

"What do you mean, the wrong side?"

"You didn't vote for them, did you?" said David.

Duncan hesitated, thinking. "What difference does that make? They got in, didn't they? And I accepted that. That's democracy. I didn't protest, didn't go on any of those stupid marches or join those idiots, the Rising Fist or whatever the fuck they were."

"But you did not vote for them, and that is why you are here," said David.

"This man speaks the truth," announced Jag with glee.

"Impossible," said Duncan. "Voting is anonymous."

Jag turned to David, still grinning. "Go on," he said, nodding in encouragement.

"That it may be," said David hesitantly. "But all the information was already there."

Jag clapped his hands. "Yes!" he cried. "Yes, yes, yes!"

David went on. "Social media, CCTV, credit cards, loyalty cards—everything you did built a picture of the person you are. They just needed the right algorithms to process it."

Duncan frowned. "You're telling me that I'm in here because of my Twitter feed?"

Nobody spoke.

"Right," Duncan continued. "In that case, I, er…" He smiled. "I would like to hereby pledge my allegiance to the BU."

Jag's grin lost its sparkle.

"Yes," said Duncan. "That's right, and I, er, want to offer my services as an, er, experienced economist and a talented mathematician, and if I can help in any way, then please consider me your slave—I *mean*, I mean—sorry—I mean, servant. Your servant."

He clasped his hands together and closed his mouth, breathing long breaths through his nose. Then, ever so slowly, he bowed his head.

Jag looked around the room. "Is he for real?"

When nobody responded, Jag bent to look up at Duncan's downturned face. He put two fingers to the terrified banker's chin and raised it. "Look up," he said. "There. That's better."

Duncan smiled and released a shaky laugh. "Right," he said. "I'm glad you—"

Jag caught Duncan in the jaw with the butt of his gun, then landed a boot in his stomach. Duncan fell to the floor, clutching his side.

"Anyone else want to pledge allegiance?" said Jag, all his mirth now disappeared.

Nobody answered.

"Good."

He turned to leave but stopped at Dana's mattress. She looked up, instinctively drawing her knees to her chest.

"What?" she whispered.

Jag knelt down, looking her over. He gave the air around her a few sniffs.

"You know what, turtledove."

The room was silent, apart from a few uncomfortable shuffles as Dana looked for support. I felt Aisha's discomfort next to me, twitching and picking at the mattress. I knew what she wanted to do, so I laid a quelling hand upon her shoulder.

"Easy," I whispered. "You will get in trouble."

"Jag," said a voice from outside the pillar. "Come on, man."

Jag slumped his head and sucked his teeth. He glanced up at Dana with a cheeky smirk.

"Bad timing," he said. Then he blew her a kiss, stood, and left.

As his companions turned to follow, my buzz-cut friend let his dull gaze land once again on me, and he gave me that curious look of his. I did not like it. Not one bit.

Duncan crawled back to his mattress, where he lay clutching his jaw. After a minute of silence, I felt Aisha stir beside me.

"Where are you going?" I said. "Aisha, no, sit down."

But she was already on her feet and picking her way across the rubble to Duncan's mattress, where she knelt and produced a water bottle from her coat. This she held to his lips, allowing him grateful sips.

David nudged my elbow. "Some child," he said, watching her in awe.

"I know," I replied.

# ROUTINE

## LINEKER

THE MACHINE GOES ON.

The machine goes on and I'm awake. At the slam and whir of the generator, my eyes snap open, and I watch each fluorescent strip light buzz on, one by one, along the length of our kennels.

Some cages still rattle at this false dawn. They're either home to the new recruits who have spent the night whimpering and howling and who'll soon learn the hard way that's not how things are done around here. Or else they're the ones containing dogs who just have not learned, will not learn, and will soon no longer be a problem.

I am not one of those dogs.

I stand and face the door. Seconds later it opens. Again, some dogs—those new fish or hopeless cases—will bolt at the sight of their imagined freedom, so the rest of us endure the familiar sound of paws skittering on concrete followed by thumps, boots, and yelps as they're reminded of the protocol.

Stay inside until you're told otherwise.

Boots clomp and shuffle to a stop, one set in front of each cage. I see my pair, bulbous and steel-capped, gleaming in the strip light, topped with a towering set of sturdy legs and a black tank top stretched across a brutally hard midriff. Two hands curl by my handler's side. The right one clicks its fingers twice, and I am up and out.

Our handlers lead us around the rim of the kennels and out into a covered paddock. The problem dogs, still trembling at their little reminder, are clipped onto chain leashes to prevent any further nonsense, and with a blast of a whistle, we start our trot. My handler and I are usually near the front or occasionally at the rear, but never in that messy middle of panicking dogs straining and tripping over each other. I have responded well to training, a fine example to my pack.

After another whistle blast, we stop dead. At least, most of us do. I have to suppress whines of frustration when I see those idiots who continue to run or cower at the sharp sound, or who gnaw at their leash, or give long, nervous yawns. Some more reminding occurs until every dog is still and silent. Then the whistle blasts again and we trot on our way.

It's not rocket science. Do that and you won't get hit. Get it?

After an hour of this, we're led into the feeding yard. There are two troughs, one along each wall. The first contains high-protein kibble and, if we did well the day before, scraps from the handlers' dinners. The second contains water. There are no bowls or allotted spaces at the troughs so it's a free-for-all, and it can get nasty. It's no use trying to edge your way in or find a quiet spot at the corner to avoid the fray; the only way to get your fill is to shove your way in and claim it. If someone tries to take your share, you get in their face and show them what for. Sometimes things can get out of hand, and I've seen dogs try to settle their dispute away from the trough with a full-on fight. But if you've got a fucking brain—which, luckily for those of us who do, many do not—you soon realize that fighting over food does not get you fed. First, you lose your space at the trough. Second, you waste all your energy fighting. Third, if you fail to win you've got fuck-all chance of getting a place at the trough the next day. No cunt will let a loser in.

And fourth, you might get shot.

Just claim your spot, stand your ground, and eat.

When breakfast's done, it's time for a proper training run out in the yard. This is my favorite place. It's set up with logs, tunnels, sheds, and these scarecrow things on sticks. Now it's just me and my handler with his stick and a whistle, and I have to follow him and do what he says, which means respond to his whistle blows by jumping, crawling, retrieving, stopping, flattening, returning, growling at or attacking a scarecrow. And I get reminders from that stick of his if I don't get it right.

These days I always get it right. Not so much before.

The other good thing about the training area is rats. They're fat and fast, mostly keeping to the perimeter and the crumbling ruins of the houses in which we practice sniffing out trouble. If you get a chance, you can snatch one for a bonus breakfast top-up. You don't get the stick for this; killing of any form is encouraged.

After the training session we get more water and sometimes my trainer will throw me something from the scrap box, like liver tubes or heart or a string of fat. This gives me a surge of a feeling I have no name for. You couldn't call it pleasure; it's like pride or a snap of purpose, I suppose, but then what's the use in describing feelings? You just have them sometimes. It's a waste of time to reflect.

We're led out to the prep area and the energy changes. The handlers suit up and buckle our harnesses. We try not to get restless, but it's hard because we're excited, and there are a fair few sticks in action to keep us in check. Once we're ready we march out onto the square and stand in our places, facing the front, waiting, waiting, waiting…

That mangy old wolf was right about one thing. My life was squandered before. I'm supposed to have a purpose, and this right here is it. It's my calling. It's my life.

There are no good or bad bits, not anymore. Just existence.

Pure and deadly existence fueled by the will to kill.

I feel like…I feel…

Nothing feels the same anymore. I have been liberated from the dog I once was. My days were once filled with fruitless questions and aimless walks that left me lost in long grass, drifting on thoughts with no beginnings or endings. Wasted days.

Now my questions are asked and answered, my decisions posed and made. Hunger—eat. Fatigue—sleep. Alarm—wake. Whistle—run. Straight lines, straight edges, sharp as blades. Even smell now serves a purpose. Scent belongs to creatures I am told to hunt.

It is true, I do sometimes wake at night and lift my head in the dark, searching for something: a human shape shifting in the moonlight, the urgent smell of rook bones and sackcloth, and the sound of two hearts beating. But these are just ghosts that evaporate in the darkness, until the only smell is of the fretful dreams of sleeping hounds, and the only sound is the rattling of a flag in the wind outside.

We are there in the yard. Waiting, waiting, waiting…

Then at last the door opens and a unit of troops marches out before us, resplendent in their purple jackets. And up onto the podium for our morning address steps a shining light showering us with warmth and the closest thing to pleasure we ever have. It is *Her*. And She is here to give us our orders.

The last dog on earth? What a fool I used to be. There are thousands of us here, all with one job: to chase down the ones who need chasing down.

It was hard at first. A raging storm of pain, despair, and confusion. I howled through it all, with no idea where I was and no idea what I was supposed to be doing. My lines were torn apart and burned until nothing made sense, and my mind became a whirlwind of untethered thoughts and feelings. Sticks, boots, and fists were my constants—the only things I could rely on.

I howled and I howled and I howled.

And then, one morning, I woke feeling different. I was hard, focused, uncarved. The storm in my mind had finally been swept away, and now all was calm, all was simple. I knew what I had to do, and nothing else mattered.

And what's more, I finally knew what made you tick.

# PROTECTION

## REGINALD

OUR FRIEND, MR. JAG, was quite correct; we were in a sorting prison. And my old chuckling friend in the other place was right too; the sorting was to be done by swabbing alone. This was the one rule to which the guards kept. I don't know why—perhaps it was a way of keeping order in the ranks, or perhaps it was merely something concrete, however brittle—passed down by the superiors to keep their troops engaged in whatever twisted societal ideals they were using to fuel their campaign.

As I have said, to this day I have no idea what insanities that man or his generals wreaked upon the world and I never will, but, whatever this rule was, it was not to be broken. Our fate relied on those flimsy plastic devices.

One morning the guards woke us early and ordered us to stand. We formed ragged lines and traipsed through the broken hall until we found ourselves outside in blinding, fog-smeared sunlight. We were in a space that had once comprised the western aisle of the cathedral, the paved entrance and a crescent of tall buildings leading to Ludgate Hill, but which now resembled a wide training yard bordered by enormous barbed wire fences and the blackened remains of the Georgian facades beyond. In the center of this yard stood two towers flanking the cathedral's steps, now separated from the main building by empty space. The soot-stained statue of Queen Anne stood between them, looking dismally away.

The air was close and eerily quiet as we wandered the yard with Aisha held tightly between us. My eyes were drawn to the walls where I saw low timber stacks covered with tarpaulin. Charlie saw them too.

"What are they building?" whispered Charlie.

"Just keep Aisha close," I replied.

We were herded into long queues, each of which ended at a trestle table. I peered ahead from our place near the back and realized, with dread, the reason why. At each table was a guard brandishing a swabber.

Suddenly we felt like drug mules at airport security.

"Don't draw attention," I said. "Try to keep calm."

"Keep calm?" hissed Charlie. "You know she won't—"

Charlie stopped as she noticed Aisha looking up at her, and placed a trembling hand on her head. I lay mine next to it.

"I won't let them," I whispered. "I won't."

But whatever heroics I may have been planning on bungling were not necessary that day. We had barely shuffled forward five spaces before we heard voices raised ahead. Our guard was banging his swabber against the table and, finally, he hurled it to the floor and thrust his hands upon his hips.

"Faulty swabber," I murmured. "Like the one in the pub."

He barked for our queue to merge in with the one to our right, but it appeared that a similar situation had occurred there too. Soon, all of the guards at the tables were standing up, either engrossed in a frustrated examination of their malfunctioning equipment or having long since abandoned it. We stood for a moment, the guards wavering on a decision. Then they corralled us back inside, pushing us more roughly than they had on the way out.

"Surely they must have more?" said Charlie.

They did have more. Lots more. Every day we repeated the same journey outside, joined the same queues and waited for our fate to finally be dealt. And every time Charlie and I performed the same dance. We watched the flow of people and positioned ourselves so that we joined a queue as far back as possible. Then we endured the half hour or so of barely concealed panic, and I prepared myself for the red light I was sure would come when it was Aisha's turn, and for whatever pointless theatrics I would perform when it did—tipped tables, flailing punches, doomed runs at the barbed wire with her in my arms.

We would watch our queue shortening to the sound of beeps or chirps and the ones ahead were led one way or the other, and then there would come a time at which the swabbers would fail, and finally we would be led back inside, hearts thundering.

Occasionally a guard patrolling the halls would pick out an individual for a random test. Sometimes they would fail like the ones outside, but on more than one occasion we saw a family or a couple or a mother and child divided, and the shrieks would echo like hawks in the shattered dome above.

They chipped away at us. The queues shortened and, gradually, the population of St. Paul's slowly diminished.

And through this torturous period, Charlie and I performed our dance. Our life became a well-rehearsed routine of hope and calculation. We put everything into keeping Aisha hidden as much as possible, in case a guard caught sight of her and fancied his chances with a fresh swabber. We negotiated our ways to the backs of the queues and, if we saw a guard approaching our corner, shuffled around so that Aisha was hidden from view. Our every waking moment was dedicated to keeping her invisible.

But we knew it was only a matter of time.

The nights were never good, but one was particularly bad.

In the echo chamber of the cathedral's split dome, no sound was forgiven. Whispers, groans, sobs, and footsteps cast ripples in the air like sand in a pool, and the tide of a thousand murmurs moved restlessly through our dreams. But on this night, the familiar background wash was punctuated by loud yelps, screams, and wails, which we recognized as the agonies of yet more pairings broken apart. As well as the disturbances inside the cathedral, we heard them farther afield: faraway cries of dissent, shouts from the guards, boots stumbling on gravel, and several deep, concussive thuds. Something was happening.

There were dogs too, snapping, growling, barking. At one point in the early dawn, Aisha raised her head.

"Linn-kaaa," she said, looking through me, still in a dream.

I lay awake, thinking of my dog.

It had taken me a while to think of a name for him. In the end the answer came to me in a dream. I had fallen asleep on the sofa one afternoon in autumn, exhausted after another night of him whining and scratching at my door. In the dream I was Paul Gascoigne in the closing stages of the England vs. West Germany Semifinal of the 1990 World Cup—the only football match I ever knew. At this point in the game he begins to cry, because of a yellow card that would prohibit him from playing in the next match. It is a somewhat iconic moment in English football history, I believe, primarily because of how Gary Lineker, the English striker, reacts. Within the emotional hubbub of the scene, he is caught on camera, making protective circles of his teammate while mouthing to his manager, Bobby Robson, on the sidelines. "Have a word," he seems to say. "You need to have a word."

He cares for his teammate. He cares for his team. It's the moment I always watch out for.

In the dream I was crying, only not for the same reasons as poor Paul. I could hear the crowd's roars and whistles, see the press cameras flash, and smell the sweat of a ninety-minute match in the jersey I was weeping into.

"Have a word," I heard and looked up. It was Gary Lineker, standing right in front of me. He smiled, put his hand on my shoulder. "You need to have a word, Reginald. Have a word, all right?"

Then Gary Lineker started to lick my face. This somehow brought me happiness, and a roar from the crowd. When I opened my eyes, of course, it was my dog, wagging his tail and lapping at my chops. I laughed and said his name out loud.

There in that dark cathedral I tried to focus on this happy memory and ignore the other miserable ones grief was already stockpiling for me: the lost face on the riverside, the lonely figure howling in the mist at the observatory, even the shameful tail-flittering cower he had made as a pup whenever he'd made a mess in the flat. I gripped Aisha's hand to remind myself of the reason why I had left him behind, and clung to the notion that, somewhere in that alien canine mind, there might have been some glimmer of understanding.

At some deep hour after midnight I woke to rearrange myself on the mattress—the twin huddle of Charlie and Aisha having conspired to push me to its farthest edge. As I crawled back, I heard rowdy shouts from beyond the pillar. Some of the guards were drunk and stumbling about the cathedral, laughing and hollering as they went. There were yelps and groans from the slumbering bodies over which they were clearly trampling.

"What's happening?" murmured Charlie, sitting up. The disturbance quickly woke the rest behind the pillar, and we waited in anxious silence, sharing looks of consternation over what this might mean for us. Only Aisha seemed unafraid, looking up into the darkness with her usual stolid expression. I wished I had a fraction of whatever she had, because I was shaking like a leaf.

"Cooee," crooned one of the guards. His voice was deep and fat; produced by what was obviously an enormous larynx that made him sound like a slowed-down cassette tape, his attempt at falsetto created a truly horrifying effect, like an excitable troll.

"Wakey, wakey."

There were chuckles and a few clumsy crashes.

"Who wants to play a game, eh?"

The noise grew near, echoing terribly from the walls above us, and beneath it was a click, click, click. At first I could not place it, but then came a dreadfully familiar sound: the unmistakable chirp of a swabber.

"Anybody want to play a game?"

Charlie and I gripped Aisha between us, pushing her down as if to squash her from existence. David did the same with Clifford, as did a man named Pete who had a large brood. I saw Duncan's swollen face caught in moonlight, eyes wide and trembling.

"How about you, eh?"

His voice drew near.

"You? How about you? Or how about…"

There was a scrape and a shuffle, and a face sprang out of the darkness, pale and clammy and lit up in the upward beam of a flashlight.

"In here?"

We shrank against the walls as he pushed his way in, and his two cohorts stumbled after him. Both were young. One had ginger hair and a cock-eyed, drunken leer pasted over his sparsely whiskered face. The other was a young woman who seemed nervous and unsure of herself, preferring to hang in the shadows behind.

"Ooh," said their captain, looking around. "Nice little place you've got here. Very cozy."

He was as big as his voice had suggested, with the dense bulk of a man who had spent his life a slave to his own chromosomes. "Have you seen this?" he said, eyelids flapping in independent blinks. He held the swabber aloft. "A swabber, this." He regarded it in the low light, swaying and struggling with some slow-moving thought.

"Now I know you all might think we're not very nice in here—*nasty* p'raps—but I can assure you, we are not what you think. We're not…not fucking *barbarians*."

He swung to his underlings behind. "Isn't that right?"

The ginger one murmured something in agreement. His captain nodded appreciatively and turned back.

"For example, these things, these swabbers here, they're what we use to, you know, check you all out. See what's what, wheat from the chaff and all that." He curled his lip and gave that great, noisy sigh of the drunkard. "Processing, you understand? Science, see? These things tell us who's right and who's wrong. We're not allowed to decide for ourselves. We're not allowed to process anyone unless they fail a swab test. That's the rules. Whether we like them or not."

His face darkened, and he stood there looking glumly around the walls. "Problem is, most of them are fucked."

For a moment, I thought he may have forgotten what he had been intent on doing, but suddenly he grinned and held the swabber up again.

"This one's not, though. It's on its way out, but I reckon it's got one more bite in it. I thought shame to waste it. Right? So I decided we'd play a game."

He jabbed a thumb at his chest. "You see, I know," he whispered, nodding. "I know who's right and wrong; I don't need these things to tell me, and I bet you"—he swung his finger around the room— "I can get this swabber's light to turn red by choosing the right one of you to try it on. If I lose, you can all go back to beddy-byes, night-night, but if I *win*…well, if I win, then we get to do a little processing right here, right now."

He looked around, head wobbling. "Sound like fun? Course it does." A sudden guttural announcement brought a fist to his chest. "Pardon me. Now, only question is"—he narrowed his eyes—"who to pick?"

He prowled the walls, clicking the button of his swabber with every step. "You? Nah… You? Nah…"

Pete stood up. "Me," he said. He was a little rough around the edges, bald, and thickset. He'd already been in a couple of tussles with the guard. His wife was a skinny, greasy-haired woman named Anna, who I sometimes watched. Although she spent much of her time in a state of nervous exhaustion, she had a particular smile which she only displayed when talking to one of her children. It looked like it had sprung from another, happier life. She flinched at her husband's words and buried her children's heads into her breast.

The guard met Pete eye to eye. "I don't think so, mate. Sit down."

But the big man stood his ground. "Do it on me."

"I said sit down!" The guard dealt Pete a splintering headbutt that sent him staggering against the wall. Covering his nose, he slid down to his mattress, where Anna pulled him close.

The young female guard stepped from the shadows. "Sir, please."

"What?" snapped her superior, still fuming red.

"Please, we shouldn't. This is—"

"Shouldn't?"

The captain marched unsteadily to the door until he was glaring down at the girl. She was barely in her twenties. "I decide who should and shouldn't, understand?" said the captain.

There was silence.

"*Understand?*" the captain screamed, and she nodded, trembling.

"Yes."

"Now, fuck off back to the mess if you don't want to be here."

She looked around at us, turned tail, and ran, leaving her ginger comrade grinning with delight.

"Now," said the captain, turning back with a fresh grimace. "Who's it going to be?"

He walked around, shining his torch in each face, closing in on us.

"Not you...or you...or you..."

As the beam swung toward Aisha, I sprang to my feet, ignoring the pain bursting in my knee.

"Me," I yelled, a little louder than I had expected. "Try it on me. Go on."

He swung the beam in my face.

"I dare you," I said a little quieter.

"What?" he said. "Why?"

Why indeed.

"I, er, because I believe I have a rich family heritage, all sorts of interesting alliances in there down the line, proper melting pot, I am, Italian, Russian, French. Why, I believe an Indian gentleman once..."

"So why would you want to be swabbed?"

I hesitated as he scanned me with his flashlight.

"Eh?" he said.

"I—"

"Unless, of course..."

His beam crept down to our mattress, landing on Aisha. She sat ablaze in the light, exposed to the world. My heart lurched.

"Aha," he said. "Now, that's more like it."

"No," I said, reaching for her. "Please."

With a lazy shove, he sent me flying backward, tripping over David and Clifford's mattress and landing in a heap on the stone floor. Charlie screamed, and as I scrabbled to my feet, I saw her being pulled away by the ginger guard and reaching for Aisha as the captain crouched before her. The room was full of nervous shuffles and moans of despair.

"This won't hurt, little girl," said the captain, waiting for the swabber to charge. The light came on, and the guard gripped Aisha's mouth to open it. She stared back in terror.

"No!" I cried, but just as I was struggling back, I saw a shadow flit before me. Duncan was on his feet, and in a flash he had snatched the swabber from the captain's hand.

"What...?" said the captain, jumping to his feet. He pulled out his gun. "Give that back."

But Duncan, with his back against the wall, had already plunged the swabber in his mouth and pressed the button. He stood there, waiting, staring defiantly back at the captain.

The captain roared and launched himself at Duncan, but just as he was upon him, there was a beep. He froze, hand out in a claw, and Duncan's eyes widened. He pulled the swabber slowly from his mouth. It was red.

"What?" said Duncan. "It can't possibly be..."

"Oh dear," said the captain, with a grin stretching. "Oh dear, oh dear, oh dear."

"Wait, no. There has to be some mistake." Duncan shook the swabber as the captain reached for him. He replaced it in his mouth, sucked at it, pressed the button, removed it. Still red. The light faded until it had extinguished completely. "No!"

The captain grabbed Duncan by the arm.

"Hawkins?" he said. "Would you be so kind as to make the arrangements?"

"Yes, sir!"

The ginger guard released Charlie and ran off, chuckling, through the doorway. We heard him clattering through the hall, a door banging, and boots echoing in a distant stairwell. Charlie crawled back to the mattress and huddled close to Aisha.

"Where is he going?" I said.

"Never you mind," said the captain. "Thanks for the game, now. Nighty-night!"

He led Duncan, protesting, away. "No, you can't do this. That was a faulty swabber. *Clearly* it was. I mean, look at me, for Christ's sake. Look at me!"

The captain laughed as their voices disappeared into the great hall. We heard a zipping sound and looked up at the gallery, where a stark silhouette of the ginger guard stood in the moonlight, feeding a long rope down to the floor below. There were sounds of a struggle—grunts and puffs from the captain and a gargled cry from Duncan—then "Haul him up!" The young guard above braced himself against the wall and heaved.

Nobody made a sound. I crawled to the mattress, where Charlie lay sobbing, and lay my head close to Aisha's, trying to conjure some reality in which only the peace of her face existed.

We heard spluttering and choking, caught the shadows of legs cartwheeling above us and then, once the guard had lashed the rope to the railing, we saw Duncan swinging, legs still going, hands at his throat. Distant peals of laughter disappeared away into the hall.

Later, as the rope creaked and Duncan's still body swung in and out of a shaft of gray dawn light, I heard footsteps on the gallery above and looked up to see another figure. It was the young woman, the guard who had tried to step in, working at the rope with a knife. After a minute of furious cutting, it snapped, and Duncan's body fell with a thump. The guard stood and looked down. For a few moments she did nothing. Then she folded her knife, replaced it in her belt, and left.

# SEX

## LINEKER

YOU KNOW WHAT MAKES the world go round? Not love, not money: sex. Sex is why the world howls.

They put me in with bitches sometimes. It's for breeding, I expect, not that I care either way. It's all good. I go in, we sniff about each other, and if I take to her then we do our business. There are no blissful cuddles afterward. I am sated, and I sleep.

We're slaves, you and me. This urge that drives us, this code snaking through our chemicals that forces us to strut, preen, and fight over each other, to sell our souls for the chance of a quick fuck— it is our master, and we follow it blindly. There is a reason dogs snarl when they see one of their own who's been freshly neutered: jealousy. That dog is liberated, free from the chains of lust.

Lust. Greasy, dark lust. It lurks within every thought and under every deed. Don't fool yourself; that piece of art you're crafting, that higher thought you're pursuing, that scientific expedition upon which you embark to lift you from the mire and swing you up to the angels? It takes you to no such place. You end up where you began. The fruits of your labor—the sculpture, the book, the mathematical equation—it's peacockery, something for you to present to the world and say, "Look. Look what I did. Now, don't you want some of this?"

Einstein? He was just trying to get laid.

There are a trillion, trillion steps between you and the sludge that once hauled itself across this planet, each one some version of a fuck. Fucking is what we're made of. Fucking is the meaning of life.

Last night they put me in with that husky. It was a reward of some kind, perhaps, or maybe they just did it to see what would happen. Makes no difference to me. I went in as usual, she smiled as our eyes locked, and my world slipped into fierce cobalt as the door slammed behind.

And I'm not going to say what we did in there, but I can tell you this: she was a very, very bad dog.

# WORK

### REGINALD

Sleep seemed impossible, but somehow it snuck up on me, and I woke to find everyone else already awake. Nobody spoke. The body was gone. Fog had crept in during the night, and now hung in a loose halo far above the ground.

Charlie was combing Aisha's hair with her hands, a ritual of theirs that I could not help but watch, no matter how much it hurt. Charlie's face was paler than usual, and a dry crust had formed around her lips.

"You're sick," I said, rubbing my neck.

She shook her head. "I'm fine. I'm certainly not the worst in here."

She glanced at the opposite wall, where Dana was kneeling by two pale-faced children, inspecting their eyes and mouths in the low light.

Boots approached, a sound to which we each performed our own Pavlovian response—flinches, stoops, jumps, and shuffles—before Mr. Jag sauntered in holding a foil-wrapped sandwich. Aisha raised her nose to the cruel scent of hot meat, and I saw the other children do the same.

"Good morning," he boomed, mouth full and grinning. "Breakfast is served."

A dark-eyed, skinny man in striped overalls scurried in carrying a tray of bread and something that looked like porridge, which he laid on the floor. He gave us nervous glances as he left.

"Enjoy," said Jag, and he turned to leave.

"Wait," said Dana from the far wall, where she was standing, rubbing her palms. We all froze. A breath left her body as Jag stopped and turned.

"What do you want, turtledove?" he said with a smile.

"The children," she said with gritted teeth and clenched fists, fighting her fear like an animal caught in a snare. "They're sick. I think they might have the flu...and...and..." She drew a sharp breath as Jag approached.

"Slow down," he said through the last mouthful of his sandwich. He screwed up the empty foil and licked his fingers, one by one. "Tell Jag how he can help."

Dana seemed to falter, perhaps rethinking her plan, but just then Aisha, who had been watching from the mattress, stood up.

Jag turned at the movement.

"Aisha," I said, reaching for her.

"Ah-ah," he said, showing me the barrel of his gun. "Get back."

I shrank to the wall.

Jag relaxed his pose and regarded Aisha, nonplussed. He lifted a hand as if to say *Well, go ahead*, and to our horror, she walked to Dana's side and took her trembling hand. Not once did she take her eyes off Jag.

At Aisha's touch, Dana seemed to calm.

"They need medical attention," she said, her voice having re-plumbed the depths of its natural register. "Painkillers, antibiotics, antiseptic, bandages, and blankets."

Jag stared back at her with a look of bland amusement, then turned his gaze to Aisha. I fought the urge to leap to her side.

"You, little girl," he said. "You feel sick?"

Aisha shook her head slowly. Jag then cast his eyes around the walls, landing on Clifford, who was sitting on his own with his rocks.

"You, boy?" he said, walking over and taking a rock from his hands. "Sick?"

Clifford shook his head.

"Huh," said Jag. "Nobody's sick. Nobody."

Spotting the neat piles of rocks next to him, Jag spilled them with a careless kick of his boot. Clifford gasped and fumbled for them, desperately trying to reform their complex piles. Jag laughed, and, feeling a spear of rage rise inside me, I got to my feet.

"We are," I announced. Jag snapped his attention to me, his laughter silenced. "You can, quite clearly, see we are. And if you don't give us medical attention, then…then it's against the Geneva Convention."

David got to his feet and stood shoulder to shoulder with me.

"We just need some medicine," he said, shaking.

"And more food," said someone else. "Our children are hungry."

The roofless room, having found its voice, suddenly erupted with demands from every corner.

"Quiet!" yelled Jag, spinning around with his gun raised.

The voices hushed. After scanning the walls to make sure everyone was back in their place, he returned to Dana. Aisha renewed her grip.

"Wait here," Jag said, then left. A minute later, he returned carrying a zipped white case.

"No more food," he exclaimed. He cocked his head at me. "And Geneva fell, so sit down."

Reluctantly, I took my seat.

Jag held out the case for Dana, but when she reached for it, he snatched it back.

"You," he said to Aisha. "Get back."

Aisha stayed where she was. Jag's brow squashed into furious, deep furrows. "I said get back!"

Dana took back her hand.

"Go on," she whispered, pushing her away. "Please, go."

Aisha finally backed toward us, still holding Jag's glare.

Charlie and I pulled her down to the mattress.

A leer crept onto Jag's face as he turned back to Dana. "What is this worth?" he cooed.

Dana swallowed and shook her head. "I don't…"

"You can give Jag something nice too?"

She released a breath. Then, with a dip of her eyes, she nodded.

"I'll go with you," she said. "You give me the medicine, and I'll go with you."

Jag beamed, but as Dana bowed her head and went to take his hand, the air filled with a sharp, deafening blast.

We all looked around, including Jag.

"Outside," he said. "Everybody outside, now."

There were no swabbing tables in the yard this time. This, and the fact that the piles of timber had been uncovered and were now being sorted through by men in boilersuits, made everyone even more unsettled than usual. Even the guards had formed huddles and were glancing about, eyes full of questions.

Charlie and I kept Aisha even closer than usual, and David joined us with Clifford. The young boy clutched a rock to his chest.

"What's wrong with them?" whispered David, nodding at the guards.

Charlie coughed. "They're worried," she said. "Something's troubling them."

"Those noises last night," I said. "What was going on out here?"

David shook his head. "Something bad. Or good?"

Pete, Anna, and their children joined us, closing the circle. "We have to do something," said Pete, nodding at the mass of prisoners. "Look, there's hundreds of us. We outnumber the guards, what, five to one? Six? We're not chained; we're not cuffed. We could take them."

"Don't be ridiculous," said Charlie. "They're armed."

"Yeah, Petey, calm down," said Anna. "You jump on one and the other'll shoot you. Think about it, yeah?"

I could see the muscles in his jaw work. "But if we all go together? Yeah?"

He looked around, trying to rally us, as if were a squadron of trained killers, rather than a rabble of sick, exhausted prisoners.

Charlie coughed again and pulled her cardigan tight.

"You're not well," I said.

"I'm fine."

A metallic whistle sounded from the far corner, and we turned to face it.

"*Your attention please,*" came a voice over a loudspeaker. We gathered the children and formed a huddle under the guards' close scrutiny.

"*We are seeking skilled workers to help us restore and improve the structural integrity of the unit, ensuring the safety and well-being of yourselves and your fellow detainees.*"

"'Structural integrity'?" said David. "That suggests problems to me."

"*We ask that every able-bodied adult inform us of any practical skills in which they once had a trade. In particular, we are looking for carpenters, bricklayers, plumbers, and electricians.*"

Charlie shot me a hopeful glance.

"*Those and the families of those selected to work will be rewarded with more substantial living quarters and greater rations. They will also be granted immunity from vetting procedures.*"

"Reginald," said Charlie.

So that's what Jag meant by being "useful."

It seemed a rotten way of doing things, but I had no choice. As far as they knew, we were a family, and if families were protected too, then this was our only hope of saving Aisha. I joined the line and informed them of my skills. Then we were led back inside.

Two days passed without a word. Then, early one morning I woke to find a guard kneeling next to me, rocking my shoulder. Everyone else was still asleep.

"Reginald Hardy?" she said, looking at her clipboard. It was the guard who had cut Duncan's body down.

"Yes."

"You're an electrician?"

"Yes."

"Come with me," she said, standing sharply.

I went to wake Charlie and Aisha, but she stopped me.

"Leave them," she said.

"But they're my family."

"They'll be sent for. Follow me, please."

"But…"

"Now."

After a moment's hesitation, I stood and followed her through the mass of sleeping bodies to a door near the back of the cathedral. She nodded at the guard beside it and led me down some stairs into a long corridor lined with further doors. Halfway along, she opened a door and led me inside. It was a small room with a single bed with starched sheets, a sink, a bucket, and a desk beneath a high, barred window through which gray dawn light seeped.

"This is you," she said with a friendly smile. "You'll receive your work duties later this morning."

"My family," I reminded her. She looked away.

"They'll be sent for," she said and left, locking the door behind her. I stood in the chill silence, staring down at the small bed and wondering what I had just done.

# HUMAN

## LINEKER

IN HERE I HAVE a different name. The name of a dog.

Out there I had the name of a human. I was treated like a human, told to behave like one.

Why do you do that—humanize us? Is it because you failed with yourselves?

What did you see when we crept from the safety of the trees?

Company? Protection?

Or a mirror?

Perhaps you had already caught a glimpse of the monsters you would become, sensed the havoc you could wreak with those reckless minds, those busy fingers, and those two transcendent thumbs. You already knew that, no matter how far you reached for the light, something much deeper and older than you would always pull you back to the dark.

Then you saw us and thought we might convince you otherwise. Our furry faces—kind, reflective surfaces in which to drown your failings, the same way you drown ours.

But you mistake us like you mistake yourselves. For we are

savages: killers, murderous hearts. Love slips from us at the first scent of blood.

So here is the truth: You and me? We're animals. And animals kill to survive. There's nothing more to it than that.

Roach-enslaving wasps, assassin bugs with paralytic skewers, sharks with teeth like subterranean drills, and lumbering lizards with filthy mouths. Nature—it's one big suicide pact. Beautiful? Maybe, but drawn beside the blueprint for the antelope's heart is another for a claw to shred it.

Worms, maggots, parasites, viruses, hornets, rattlesnakes, tarantulas, crocodiles, hawks, jellyfish, wolves, bears, lions.

Dogs.

Killers.

And then there's you. And we have nothing on you.

You slaughter the forests with giant saws. You throttle the sea with plastic. You drown the sky with soot. You kill everything in your path. And why? Not to survive—you've already nailed that one—oh no, you kill to give yourselves little luxuries like skin scrubs, painkillers, and boxes to chatter on. You—you kill for no other reason than comfort and curiosity. You kill so your eyes don't sting when you wash your hair.

Bravo, you fucking maniacs, you murderous hearts. I mean it, I'm impressed.

But even that's just the start of it. Because, not content with killing us, you kill each other too. And *this* is where you truly surpass yourselves.

From the cruelest nightmares of a sexual predator in his homemade dungeon to the trained torturer trembling over the car battery, your thirst for the blood of your own species knows no bounds. Then there are the drone operators, the generals pushing figures across tables in windowless rooms, the sweatshop account managers. You would rather children died than pay a few quid more for your underpants.

Death by proxy. Beautiful.

You crowd around women as they shriek in flames because somebody invented the word *witch*, and if you think that was an embarrassment consigned to history, then look east to the back alleys of Saudi and south to the Kenyan hills. You'll still see the fires burning bright.

You place men, women, and children in chains and tell them to work until they die. Another phase you grew out of? Take a peep in through the window of that house you thought was condemned. You'll see families inside shackled by broken promises and one-way tickets.

Bravo, bravo, you murderous hearts.

Your greatest accomplishment—and the natural evolution of that wondrous discovery, fire—was to delve so deeply into the fabric of the universe that you tore it open. You bled out the very thing that held it together. And what was the first thing you did with this enlightenment? You vaporized a city. Because you needed to. That's what you told yourselves—*collateral*.

You take killing to the next level, you really do.

And afterward, once the smoke has cleared and you've wiped your knives clean and buried the dead, this is what you do: you write little poems and books about how terrible it all is, and about how sad it makes you.

Boo-hoo.

*The next level,* I'm telling you.

But you know this already. You've seen the cracks darkening in the mirror, and the thing that's lurking behind it, you don't need a dog to remind you of that. Oh no, you need a dog to convince you otherwise.

Well, I'm done with all that. It's time you came clean and owned up. Accept who you are. We have.

What's holding you back? I'll tell you: love, and the illusion that you're in any way capable of it.

Or is it God you're searching for?

Well, my murderous hearts, I'm afraid I can't help you there. You see, I've found my God. She feeds me, shelters me, draws me lines, and gives me purpose. She has long fingernails and gleaming skin and smells of aluminum, cream, and sour apples.

# BLISS

**REGINALD**

I SPENT THAT FIRST morning sitting on the bed, just listening.
Sometimes I would hear footsteps outside in the corridor, and I
would turn to the door, hoping for it to open and for Charlie and
Aisha to stumble through in joyful tears and embraces. But each time
another door would open and close, and the footsteps would disappear the way they had come.

Finally, sometime in the early afternoon there came a rattle of
keys at the door. I stood as it opened, but my shoulders fell as the
young female guard entered, alone. I saw her fully in the light now.
She was slight and dark-skinned, and her purple jacket hung loosely
over a grimy white shirt. She faced me with a haunted expression,
as if she endured the constant chill of a knife upon her throat, and
presented me with the box.

"You're to fix these," she murmured. "There are some tools in
there, and...a soldering iron, I think."

"My family is supposed to be here," I said.

She paused, then looked at the desk. "You can find a power

socket beneath the desk, but the supply is intermittent. You'll have to be patient."

I took a step toward her. "Please," I said. "I was told they would be sent for."

She lowered her eyes. "I don't know anything about your family."

"What's your name?"

She hesitated. "Megan," she said, her eyes drifting away.

"Megan," I repeated. "Please…"

Her attention snapped back. "Lieutenant Hughes to you, prisoner. Now take the box."

She thrust the box into my arms, turned, and left, locking the door behind her.

Within the disappearing tail of her footsteps and the echo of the slam, I felt my fate drawing in. A closed door, a full set of tools, and a project with no distractions. Once this would have been bliss, but now it was torture. They were out there and I was in here. Aisha was exposed. How could I ever protect her now? Would Charlie manage alone?

The silence stretched out, agonizingly thin, and in that cold and empty room, I began to tremble. I dropped the box and released a single loud sob. Another joined it, dry and heavy, and another, and another, until I pulled at my hair and fell to my knees and wept. I wept for the walls and the bolted door. I wept for Aisha, and Charlie, alone. I wept for my dog—my dog, my dog, my dog, who was *alive*—and I wept for my wife and for my little girl, and for grief, grief, grief, which is the end of all worlds. But most of all I wept for me—God knew, if that cruel bastard knew anything, that I wept for me—Reginald Hardy, the man who had locked himself away from the world and watched it end without a tear in his eye, the man who could not bear the touch of others, the man who left his dog at the riverside, the man who I was now *sick* of, who I wanted to tear myself away from, who I wanted to…

I felt an energy growing, a nervous breed of fury I had rarely felt before. With a howl of rage I jumped up, kicked the box into the corner, and ran for the door.

"Open up!" I shouted, hammering it with my palms. "Open this door at once! I…I want a transfer. I want to leave! I want to go back! Send me back!"

I banged and shouted until my hands hurt and my voice cracked, and eventually I heard swift footsteps and a jangle of keys. I stood back from the door as it opened, expecting Megan again. But this time I found myself face-to-face with a tall and furious guard.

"What do you want?" he yelled.

"I want to go back," I said, breathing hard. "I've changed my mind. I can't do this. I want to go back to my family."

The guard straightened up and fixed me with a frown. For a moment I thought he was considering my request but then, in a flash, he strode over, gripped my shoulder and dealt three lightning-fast punches to my stomach. I fell to my knees, breathless with shock.

"Do your job," he ordered. "And do not fucking bang on that door again."

With that he left, and I was alone again. Winded and wheezing, I crawled to the corner and curled up in a ball, searching the tilted planes of floor, wall, and ceiling. My eyes traveled to the skirting board where, in the dusty murk, I picked out lines in the broken grain and turned them into shapes: the line of a child's brow lifted to the sun, a woman's arm in a protective cup, the brow of a hill with a dog leaping for its summit. And I wept again for all the things I had never wept for before.

I woke with a jolt to a darker room, cold air, and the sound of activity somewhere in the distance. I picked myself up from the floor, wincing as my stomach tensed.

The noise came from outside. The window was too high to see through, so I stepped—with great difficulty—onto the desk. It wobbled, but I found my balance and peered through the dull glass. I had a fair view of the yard, it seemed, and could see figures moving by the timber. The noise was of hammers and saws.

Just then, without warning, the single bulb hanging from the center of the room turned on. The surprise made my legs jerk, which unbalanced the desk and sent me tumbling backward onto the floor. I landed with a cry upon the box I had recently discarded, a dozen sharp plastic corners needling into my back. I rolled off the box, coughing, and saw a dozen swabbers scattered upon the threadbare carpet. I picked one up and inspected it in the harsh light. Substandard battery, shoddy soldering, thin wires. Mumbling something, I replaced them all in their box and lifted it onto the desk. And with nothing better to do, I went to work.

# SUNRISE

## LINEKER

ANOTHER DAY, ANOTHER GRAY sunrise. We're outside again, awaiting orders. With her bitch beside her, She stands before us, proud as ever, her coat fluttering in the March wind like the flags above us.

The microphone squeals, and She clears her throat, leafing through paper. She seems different today. There's a smell in the air I can't quite place.

"Some of us are moving on," She says. "We are needed elsewhere."

There's a rumble of feet and voices from the handlers, and I get that scent again, stronger now and amplified across the yard. I exchange a glance with the dog to my right, a German shepherd whom I know to be friendly, which means he won't snap if I go near him. The look in his eyes mirrors mine.

*What was that?*

"Squadrons 18 to 32, you are to join me for a temporary assignment at processing camp C5, St. Paul's."

There are more murmurs and huge wafts of that same scent.

"The rest are to remain, first priority being to investigate *possible breaches*"—the microphone whistles again, and she continues—"in the fence and suspicious activity in the northern sector. That will be all."

She collects her papers and leaves the podium. The yard is awash with nervous conversation, and then I realize what that smell is.

Fucking voles.

# WORK

### REGINALD

DAYS WENT BY AND I barely left the room. They brought me food. It was better than the slop they served in the cathedral, but the taste was never anything but sour. Aisha was still out there with only Charlie to protect her now. I wondered if the captain remembered her. I wondered if he had found another swabber that worked.

The hours were torturous, and the only way I could take my mind off Aisha's safety was to engross myself in the work I had been given. This may seem counterproductive, given that the work was to fix the swabbers that would seal her fate, but understand: fixing those swabbers was the last thing on my mind.

A child could have seen what made them faulty. Either their wires had come loose, the vial had emptied, or the battery had leaked. In each case I salvaged what I could and assembled as many fresh swabbers as I could, discarding the remaining parts. These swabbers were far better than the originals, with correct soldering, firm insulation, and added impact protection with the help of a few foam offcuts I found in the toolbox. They would not break so easily and would, as was my intention, give the user a long and reliable service.

But the main thing about them was that, after a little creative rewiring, they always turned green. It was the only thing I could do.

My bucket was emptied daily. On one occasion I was led to a makeshift shower block where I stood naked with nine other men and soaped myself nervously under the watchful eyes of the guards. The water was icy and weak, but it was heaven.

Returning from the showers, I waited while the door to my room was unlocked and felt fresh air on my still-damp skin. At the end of the corridor was an open fire door, outside which two guards were smoking. One turned to me and I shivered, but not from the chill. It was my friend with the buzz cut and squint eyes. He smiled through the smoke and—I could have sworn—winked at me. I moved the desk against the door that afternoon.

The sound of carpentry continued outside, and I tried to ignore thoughts about what they were building. Sometimes I heard voices and feet shuffling, which meant that the prisoners had been taken out. When this happened I leaped to the desk and peered out for as long as they were there, trying to catch a glimpse of Charlie and Aisha. I think I did once, walking a slow circle around the perimeter. My hand would not fit through the bars to knock on the glass, and in any case, they were too far away to hear.

Megan brought me a fresh box of swabbers each morning and took the previous box away. Each day I asked her about Aisha and Charlie. Did she know if they were still together? Was Aisha all right? Were they coming to me? She never responded.

I continued to create my new, counterfeit swabbers, my only hope being that, if I was not the only person tasked with this job, at least I might be the most productive. But each day that passed was another in which my hope dwindled, and another in which Aisha might be discovered.

One day I woke to find my hope had gone. As I worked at the desk, I heard the door open and Megan enter. I heard her breathing behind me.

"You're good at this," she said. I could sense an attempt at a smile in her voice. "It's a pleasure to see somebody doing a proper job for once. My dad used to say nobody does a proper—"

I dropped my soldering iron onto the desk and turned. "I am finished, Megan. I am not going to work anymore. Whatever you give me to fix shall be in the same state when you pick it up later. I don't care what punishment I receive."

It was then that I realized she was carrying no box.

"You're needed," she said. "Outside."

I was led outside by Megan and another guard, the ginger-haired youngster who had strung Duncan up that terrible night. He whistled as we walked across the dusty yard, where there had clearly been some activity in my absence. The stretch of fence where the timber had been piled was now a work area, sealed off by a huge partition of flapping tarps and scaffold poles. A steady stream of men and women in overalls—prisoners on work duty—walked between it and the main building carrying tools and planks. Next to the partition were two standing floodlights, and it was these to which I was marched.

"You need to fix that," mumbled Megan, pointing to a cable connector on the ground.

I knelt down and inspected its charred socket and hardened rubber insulation. "I don't think I can," I said.

Megan rubbed her arm and gave me one of her haunted looks. Then she left. As I watched her stumble back across the yard, the ginger guard dropped a canvas sack of tools beside me.

"Just fix it," he said and strolled over to the partition to smoke.

I sat down on the ground, glad at least of the fresh air, unplugged the power point, and began to scrape the blackened contacts with a screwdriver. As I worked, the smell of fresh pine hit my nose and I glanced up. From this angle I could see what was behind the partition: a long platform supported by a crude framework of uneven carcassing and misshaped joists that could not possibly, I thought idly, bear much weight without buckling. When I saw the high scaffolds above, and holes being cut in the boards, there was no question of what they were.

My guard was leaning lazily against the partition, still smoking his cigarette. He had had a shave since I had last seen him, his face now free of whiskers. A messy tuft of orange hair sprayed from beneath his cap. His gun was slung low behind his back—not easy for him to grab in an emergency.

My hands were shaking. I dropped the connector in the dust and got to my feet, unsteadily, folding the screwdriver into my palm. As I made my way toward him, my innards seemed to shift uncomfortably, as if they were only now getting wind of my intent. My heart began to thunder, and my lungs flapped and heaved like ragged bellows.

I kept my eyes on the young man and the last slow trail of smoke rising happily from his lips. As he flicked his butt to the ground, he spotted me approaching and frowned, reaching for his gun.

"What do you want?" he said as I stopped before him. His eyes were a clear and wayward blue.

I breathed hard, fingering the cool bulb of my screwdriver's handle and feeling that moment approach, the one I would not be able to take back. The before and the after. Just a neat drop, a sharp upward thrust and—

The guard's head swiveled to the steps where there was movement. I followed his gaze. First guards, then prisoners emerged from the dark recesses of the western aisle. Soon they had flooded the yard.

"Get back to work," mumbled the young man, and he wandered into the throng. The moment passed, and the screwdriver fell in the dust at my feet.

*Charlie? Aisha?*

The prisoners gravitated toward the partition, curious or terrified as to what lay behind, and soon I found myself engulfed in shuffling figures. I desperately scanned the faces, ignoring the shocks of endless bumps and nudges, but they were nowhere to be seen. I called their names, hoarse at first, then louder, but all I got in return were strange looks from wounded eyes.

"Hey."

I turned at the deep voice behind. Pete towered above me, fingers fidgeting, frowning at the partition.

"What are they doing behind there?" he said.

"I...I don't... Pete, where are Aisha and Charlie?"

He ignored me, concerned only with the tarpaulin. His face blustered with questions. "Fuck this," he said and stormed past me. In the space he left, I saw his wife, Anna, and their three children standing in front. Beside them stood Dana, looking groggy and distant.

"Dana," I said, running to her. "Where's Charlie? Where's..."

Her flinch made me stop.

"What is it?" I said. I gripped her shoulders. "What's wrong? Tell me!"

"She's sick, Reg. Charlie's sick. She's inside. I'm trying to take care of her, but—"

"But what?"

"She needs help. She needs a doctor."

"What about Aisha?"

Dana blinked and let her eyes drift to something behind me. I shook her.

"Dana! Where's Aisha?"

She looked back at me with a gasp. "There," she said, pointing to a corner of the yard.

Aisha was with Clifford and David. The children were playing something in the dust, cautious smiles flickering on their faces.

"Thank Christ," I breathed, staggering back. "Dana, please tell Charlie they lied to me, but I'll be back soon."

Her eyes had drifted again. "Reg…"

"Just tell her, will you?"

"Shit, Reg…"

"What?"

I turned to see what she was looking at. Pete was standing by the line of workers walking between the partition and the cathedral.

"Hey!" he shouted. A few of the guards had already turned their attention to him.

"You," he said to a middle-aged man carrying a plank on his shoulder. "What are you doing?"

The man ignored him, eyes white with fear.

"Oi! Can you hear me? I said what are you *doing* behind there?"

The guards edged toward him.

"Look at me!" he yelled.

Anna left her children and shuffled toward him, one hand outstretched.

"Petey, calm down, love," she pleaded.

But Pete continued his furious patrol of the rope, and each worker he approached ignored him, keeping their eyes on the ground.

"What the fuck is wrong with you all?"

Every guard in the area was now moving in.

"Pete," I hissed. "Stop it."

From high on the wall a speaker whistled, and a voice announced, "*Disarray will not be tolerated. Please stand away from the construction area.*"

Pete stomped to a halt, and the crowd around him retreated. There he stood in the sudden clearing, chest pumping like a bull's. Gingerly, I stepped in beside him.

"The guards, Pete," I said under my breath. "The guards."

But he stood tall, glaring over the sea of heads. "Somebody tell me what's going on!" he screamed.

A guard was upon him, gun raised. "Get down!" he ordered.

Pete looked down at him. "No," he yelled. "No I fucking won't!"

"Get down or I'll…"

I heard Anna moan from way behind. "*Petey.*"

She had seen this before. It was written on her face. He had already passed the point of no return.

Pete launched himself at the guard. The gun went off but fired over his shoulder, and the guard found himself lifted off his feet and slammed to the floor. Pete, now a mess of panic and fury, fled into the horrified crowd and, against my better judgment, I hobbled after him.

There was a whistle, followed by the double chink of two unhooked chains, yelps of freedom, and the scrabble of paws in the dirt. The unleashed hounds accelerated past me. The first was a German shepherd, its back pulled straight as an arrow as it darted for its quarry. The second skidded to a halt in a cloud of dust, facing me with its fangs bared in the first rush of pursuit.

The crowd parted, and I staggered back. Every one of the animal's muscles was a coiled spring of rage. I covered my head, remembering from some distant childhood book that my jugular was on the left side of my neck.

Seconds passed. The attack never came.

I peered through my arms. The dog's head was cocked to one side and its fangs were still bared, but only because its lips had caught on them in a dry, clumsy curl. Through the matted fur of its brow I saw two incredulous eyes, and I have never seen a dog perform a double take before, but that's what this one was doing—this mutt, this mongrel, this scabby, patchy, mishmash of breeds...

"Linn-kaaa!" screamed Aisha from somewhere behind me.

It was him all right: shabbier, dirtier, skinnier, and fiercer, but definitely him. Lineker was alive.

Ten years washed over me like a warm tide. For a moment I was no longer lying in the yard, but standing before a cage one spring afternoon, looking down upon a lonely pup. The dog I had pulled from that place, who I had failed to train but succeeded in making happy, who had failed to make a master of me but succeeded in making a friend. The dog I had fed, whose warm shit I had plucked countless times from the dew-drenched grass of The Rye, whose head I had cradled when he caught his first cold, whose neck folds were as familiar to me as the dales and valleys of an old shepherd, and whose paw prints I could pick out from a hundred paces. The dog whose mind I could not hope to fathom but whose heart I knew better than my own, the dog I had rescued and who had in turn rescued me, looked back, asking with the same dumbfounded gawp the very same questions I was asking myself.

*How?*

*What?*

*And what now?*

I went to say his name, but before I could speak, a guard stormed past me, wielding a stick. Lineker—it *was* him—looked up and cowered.

"No!" I cried out.

The guard dealt two sharp blows to his hide. I felt both, the pain as real and visceral as if they had been aimed at me.

Then came a real blow, this one to my head. Dazed, I saw Aisha reaching for me in a silent scream. Then rough hands hauled me up and dragged me through the dirt. The German shepherd growled and snapped in the distance, and Pete's strangled cries were silenced by a single shot. Consciousness fell away. The last thing I saw was Anna closing her eyes and bringing her children to her breast.

# CHOICE

## REGINALD

THE ROOM IS ROUGHLY eighteen feet by...

The room is eighteen feet by twenty-seven and...

It's eighteen feet by twenty-seven, with three windows, one...

One on...

One on each doorless wall and measuring approximately...

Approximately four feet square. The chair is...

The chair is in the center of the room and...

And I had once read that the average person's punch...

Registers a psi of somewhere between...

Between forty-five and fifty. This...

These are a little higher in my...

In my honest opinion. Probably somewhere over 100. And he's...

He's about six foot...

Six foot five is my best guess but...

But it's hard to tell a man's height when he's beating you senseless.

"Stop."

The voice was a thousand rooms away. My punisher did as it instructed.

I was befuddled. My hearing was mud. My vision slipped and slid as if the world had been sliced into neat strips.

Through this confusion I saw the plasticine-faced maniac who had inflicted the blows take three steps back with his fists still clenched. Another figure stepped forward. She was smaller, slimmer, neater. Five foot four inches, narrow waist, wide hips.

"That's enough for now," she said. She leaned in and her face gained focus. It was as pale as a china cup.

"Must stop meeting like this, eh, Little Reggie?"

I coughed, spluttered, retched. Whistles of different pitches grew and receded in my ears like an old radio finding a station.

"Angela," I croaked. "What...?"

"Captain Hastings, if you don't mind, Reggie. Speak up, can you?"

"What..."

"What am I doing here? Good question. What indeed."

The room gradually lost its wobble. In one corner I saw a husky licking its paw.

Hastings straightened up.

"Do you know, Reggie, I was doing my job. Coordinating the dogs. Cleaning the mess from the streets, a task I have been doing quite successfully for the past two years, but, unfortunately, it seems some people aren't quite as confident in the roles to which they have been assigned."

She gave a frustrated sigh and paced the floor in front of me.

"Bloody idiots, can't even run a simple processing camp."

"Wh—?"

"Hmm? Oh, boring stuff. Too many people, not enough staff,

escape attempts, technology problems. Simple to fix, if you have the balls. But I'm afraid the warden here does not."

She rolled her eyes as if we were executives sharing office gossip by the water cooler.

"Anyway, I'm here to fix things up, crack a few heads together, know what I mean? And who should I meet on the first day but my Little Reggie."

She beamed.

"What do you want?" I finally managed to say.

"What do I want?" She sighed again. "Another good question."

She paused, and the leather of her boots creaked as she squatted before me.

"You know, there was a time when I wanted you." She pulled an awkward face. "I know! It's true, though, I did. Way back when we were kids, remember? I had a proper soft spot for you, Little Reggie, the real deal."

"You..." I coughed. "You used to make fun of me."

She shrugged. "Kids don't know what to do with their feelings sometimes. They come out all jumbled up. What starts as love and yearning can end up..."

She made a fist and launched it slowly at my face, making a popping sound with her lips as it reached the point of contact. She held it for a moment, allowing the earthy perfume of her fingertips to creep up my nostrils. Then she let it fall.

"They never quite leave you, do they, those crushes? It hurt me, proper hurt me when you found a girlfriend."

She cocked her head and gave me her sweetest smile. "That bitch."

I spluttered and strained.

"So sorry when I heard."

"You said that last time."

She stood smartly, ignoring me. "Still," she said, brushing the hem of her jacket, "we must move on, mustn't we, Little Reggie? No use dwelling on the past. Oh, I found your dog."

She turned to the far corner. There in the shadows sat Lineker with his neck bowed.

"That is him, isn't it?"

"Lineker," I breathed.

His ears pricked at the sound of my voice.

"Very good learner," she went on matter-of-factly, "easy to train. I was surprised when his handler told me what happened."

She turned back to me. "He should have followed through, see? With his target, I mean. You. That's the order he received. But he didn't. Of course, it makes sense now that I know it's you." She gave a joyless smile. "Chances, eh?"

"What are you doing?"

"What do you mean?"

"Why are you here, now, doing this? You're hurting people. Killing people. What happened to you?"

She folded her arms. "A little late in the day to be talking politics, isn't it, Reggie?"

"This is not politics. This is murder."

Her expression, and the grinding of her jaw, suggested that I had crossed some line or other. She turned and whispered something to my tormentor, who took one last look at me and left. Now we were alone in the room, with Lineker and the husky sitting patiently in opposite corners.

"You said something to me once that I'll never forget," she said, doing her best to soften her tone. "That time when I was handing out leaflets, do you remember? You said that you preferred the company of dogs to people." She raised her chin as if the words were poetry. "I thought it was just your grief speaking. It hadn't been long, had it? But when I thought about it I realized: that's how I felt too."

She pulled a chair from the corner, placed it squarely in front of me, and sat down. "You know it was just me and my dad? Well, he always kept dogs, my dad. He'd get drunk and buy them off wankers in pubs or find strays on the way home and take them in. At any one time, we had at least one mutt kicking around our house, shitting everywhere or tearing up the carpet. He never looked after them—too drunk—so I would instead. I'd take them for walks, feed them, train them, just simple stuff like come, sit, stay, you know?"

"What does that have to do with anything?" I murmured.

She blinked. "People, Reggie. It has to do with people." Her face fell, and she looked away, remembering. "My dad was a racist," she said. "No two ways about it. *Fucking blacks* this, *fucking Pakis* that, *fucking ragheads, fucking Muslims. Fucking women, fucking kids, fucking northerners, fucking politicians, fucking Chelsea, fucking Spurs.* Fucking anyone but him, when it came down to it, know what I mean?"

She gave a sad smile. "'We're not born to live together,' he'd say. 'We're too different.' And I'd argue back, 'We're no different, Dad. We're all the same deep down,' and then he'd point at me and laugh with that big, red, whiskey-blossomed face of his. Like I was an idiot.

"I could only stand being in his company for so long, so I'd take whatever dog we had at the time and find some peace outside. One day I was out a bit later than usual. We had a bull terrier called

Winston who was a bit of a handful, and I was just crossing The Rye with him, almost home, when I came to a fork in the path. This big bloke in a tracksuit came toward me from one direction, riding a bike. From the other I saw a girl on foot. She was wearing a headdress, hijab, I think. I thought nothing of it, but Winston didn't like it one bit. Her head was covered, you see? Dogs sometimes don't like that, and it was getting dark, so it freaked him out. He started barking at her, right at her, slavering and licking his chops. I tried to calm him down, but he was locked on, so all I could do was hold the lead tight as she stood there, screaming.

"Then the bloke arrived on his bike—angry looking—and he stopped and stared at me. 'What's going on?' he says. He pointed at me. 'What the fuck are you making that thing do?' I said, 'What? I'm not making him do anything, mate; he's just scared.' And he laughed and said, 'Scared? Fuck off, and I'm not your mate. Call that fucking dog off, you fascist cunt.'

"'Fascist?' I said. I couldn't believe it. 'I'm not fascist.' 'Really?' he said. Then he got off his bike, pointed at the girl—still terrified—and said, 'What do you see? Eh? What do you see? Look at her.'

"'I don't know what you want me to say,' I said. But I did. I knew exactly what he wanted me to say. He wanted me to say I saw a Muslim, and he was implying that I had trained my dog to attack Muslims."

She shrugged, stood, and strolled over to her husky, running her glove through its thick coat.

"It's possible, of course; you can train a dog to hate anything. But I hadn't. It would never have occurred to me. But that didn't matter. He'd made up his mind: I was a fascist, as he said. So when that girl finally turned and ran, and we stood there alone in the dusk, he walked straight up to me. Winston was oblivious, still barking after the lady, but I backed into a tree and he kept coming at me until his face was right in mine. He didn't do anything. Could have done, I suppose; it was dark enough and there was nobody about. But he didn't. He just looked at me like I was dirt. Then he pushed me to the ground, kicked Winston in the head, got on his bike, and rode off."

She gave the husky three sharp pats and turned back to me. "Funny thing was, it wasn't being pushed or what he did to Winston, but the accusation I couldn't shake, that I was some kind of monster like my dad. Fascist. I wasn't like that, was I? I was a nice girl. I believed in togetherness." She pulled her lips into a smile that was anything but.

"Then one day it came to me, clear as a bell. I realized I didn't like it because it was the truth. Beneath all those half-hearted illusions I had entertained just to argue against my father, deep down I felt the same as him.

"He may have been a drunk, he may have been violent, and he may have hated the world because he couldn't find his place in it, but that didn't mean he was wrong about everything. Maybe, I began to think, maybe people really are too different to ever coexist."

"I don't understand," I said. "You had a bad experience. That doesn't mean you—"

"It was a good experience, Reggie. It taught me about other people, and about myself. And the more I thought about it, the more I realized the truth."

"What truth?"

She placed her hands on the back of my chair and leaned in

close. "No matter how you sugarcoat reality, no matter how many friendly lies you tell about unity and togetherness, there are lines, deep lines, natural borders—chemical, biological, and cultural—that are designed to keep us at a distance."

Her eyes were closer to my own than anyone's had been for some time. I fancied I could see glimmers in them, trails of swimming thoughts and secrets, clues to what the years had made of her. But it was just the flickering of the strip light's ugly glare.

"There are no lines," I said at last. "Only the ones inside your head."

The words barely registered with her, but they hit me like a jolt from a frayed live positive. She stood up, ignoring my drifting gaze of surprise.

"It was really quite enlightening, Reggie. Good for Winston too, as it happens. He never barked at a headdress again, and I knew exactly what to do if a dog stepped out of line. They're just wolves, after all; they need to know their place. I got a bit political after that. Started reading books, looked into all kinds of movements and ideas—it always seemed to come down to the same challenges: territories, resources, freedoms, who should go where and what should they be allowed to do. The same question, basically."

She raised her hands. "What do we do with all the people?"

She turned and walked to Lineker, who lifted his head in expectation.

"You know, it's a common belief that dogs are not like us, but I disagree. Humans need exactly the same things as dogs: shelter, warmth, food, a set of laws to keep them in check, fences to mark their territory, sex, I suppose." She made a lazy, acquiescent grimace. "Dogs don't need freedom; they need a purpose. They don't need education; they need training. Correcting." Her hand traveled to the cane that hung from her belt. Lineker's ears swiveled, ready to flatten.

"So really," she went on. "Dogs are just like people." For a moment she delicately fingered the cane's handle. Then she released it and turned back to me, hands on hips. Suddenly she seemed bored. "Anyway, I met this girl in a pub—pretty thing with a purple beret—who told me about these meetings. The rest, as they say…"

"Territory?" I said. "Where people belong? How does that translate into rounding people up and killing them?"

"The maintenance of territories has always involved certain… necessary measures."

"Necessary measures? So that's it? You just…you just get to decide who goes where and who's allowed to do what based on how they talk or what color their skin is?"

"Come on, Reggie," she scoffed. "You should know it's not as simple as skin color anymore. The lines between us are just as much social as they are genetic. We all want different things; it's as simple as that."

"But what about the swabbers?"

"Well, obviously, genetics is important; the racial order still needs to be adhered to, but a person's choices, the ways in which they lean on certain issues, how they feel about the way the world works—these are all just as important gauges in determining their usefulness in the status quo."

"Usefulness?"

*Jag*, I thought.

"Yes, we're trying to build a new world, Reggie. A better one. So what use are people who don't agree? In any case, the swabbers were never really anything but a PR exercise. Fear, you under-stand—a vital tool—but what use is a computer that tells you what you already know? It's plain to see who sits on what side of the line. You don't need a glorified Breathalyzer to tell you that"—her expression darkened—"or a tag around your neck."

She knelt before me and placed her palms upon my thighs. My nerves tingled nauseously at the touch, but beneath the discomfort was something else: a shrinking inside, a need to protect some raw and hidden part of myself.

"She's not your child, Reggie," she said.

My gut clenched.

She smiled and shook her head. "And that is not your wife."

My vision, still blurred from the beatings, became blurrier still.

"And none of this is your burden."

Wetness on my cheeks, my shoulders shaking. She tipped her head, rubbed my legs, her eyebrows lifted in a parody of pity.

"I know you want to help them, love, but you can't. Just like you couldn't before."

Tears now. Real tears, and no option but to surrender to them. I dropped my head and sobbed.

"So sad, Reggie. It really was. But it wasn't your fault, and neither is any of this, so why don't you put aside all that sadness, all that guilt, and do what's right for *you* for a change. You and that dog of yours."

She stood up and sighed. "I'm shutting this camp down, Reggie. It's useless and broken, just like those swabbers."

I looked up through my tears. "And what next? Another camp?"

She shook her head. "Nobody's going anywhere, Reggie."

"The gallows," I said.

"There are over a thousand people in this camp," she said, "and ammunition is somewhat scarce these days."

She folded her arms. "I'm giving you a chance, Reggie. Put all this behind you and move on. You're a clever man. You always were. I can find you a good job—you'll be safe, well fed, free. No need for any more tears."

"And why me?" I spluttered. "Why don't you help everyone else too?"

She frowned. A touch of hurt. "It's like I said, Reggie—I've always had a soft spot for you. What do you say?"

I had a vision of another life, a world in which I would wake every morning to a day just like the last and lose myself in its simple tasks. I would follow simple codes and rules, ask no questions, move only in the space I had been allotted. I would seek nothing but those twin blisses: solitude and industry. I would turn from the world, leave no imprint, forget the past. Disappear.

"Well?" she said.

But I had already tried that once before. If grief has any purpose, then it is to bore you so much with the past that you have no option but to turn from it. So I looked away from Hastings's face and found my dog's instead.

Hastings went to speak, but before she could, the room was suddenly filled with an urgent wail. Lineker was on his feet, hackles raised. His eyes were all over the place, seeking reassurance, orders, or both. But Hastings ignored him and clicked her fingers for her husky.

A distant thump shook the floor. Voices echoed in corridors far away.

"We're being attacked, aren't we?" I said. "They're coming."

She ignored me and made for the door, calling my six-foot-five, one-hundred-psi fist-hurler back in.

"Punish him," she said. Then she turned to Lineker. "And make him watch."

She left, slamming the door behind her.

It hurt, but it was not the worst pain I had endured. Not even close.

# STORY

**LINEKER**

WHAT MAKES YOU CHOOSE?

Is it fear or desire? The threat of pain, or the promise of pleasure?

What made him choose her over me?

What made him leave me, again, just to save a child he barely knew?

Was he scared that he would feel shame if he didn't, or was the joy of her alone enough to propel him?

And what does that say about me?

It says that some lives are worth more than others.

Maybe you don't make choices at all. Maybe that great mind of yours is nothing but a theatre, a stage on which your decisions are acted out, scripted in advance by reptilian clockwork. All that browbeating, fist-biting, soul-searching—it's just a game of catchup. Your life is already written.

If so, then Reg is not to blame; he was always going to leave me on the bank, because humans are worth more than dogs.

Some humans, anyway.

## REGINALD

I hit the ground. It was dark and cold.

"Reg?"

"David?"

I could see only ripples of light in the darkness, face-shaped smudges moving about.

"Christ, what did they do?"

I was back in our corner of the cathedral. David helped me down onto the mattress, and I felt a small body hit mine.

"Ow."

"Be careful, Aisha," said David. "Let him sit."

I blinked and tried to focus on the shadows and blurs. "Who's there?" I said. "Where's Charlie?"

"I'm here, Reginald," she replied. Her voice was weak and dry. I felt her moving close. "We're all here."

"Dana said you were sick."

"I'm all right." She coughed. "I'm glad you're here."

A dark mass grew in the left of my vision, and David's face swam into view. I saw his son behind him, craning his neck.

"You're safe," said David.

One by one, the rest of them appeared. Dana, Anna, her children, and all the rest.

Dana stepped forward with the medical pack Jag had given her. "Sit back. I need to look at that cut on your eye."

I laid my head against the wall and let her swab the wound.

"Look left," she said.

I did and saw Anna.

"Anna," I mumbled, remembering the yard. "I am so sorry."

Anna shook her head.

"It wasn't your fault, Reg. I knew as soon as I woke up that morning that he was going to do something. He'd had enough."

"He was trying to protect you."

"He lost control." She stroked the brow of her young daughter. Lily was her name. "Not that he had much in the first place, the stupid bastard. And now he's dead."

She tried a smile.

"I'm almost done," said Dana. "There."

She sat back and gave her handiwork a grim once-over. "At least it's clean. Best I can do."

"Thank you," I said, the world gradually making more sense.

"Nada," said Dana.

I felt Charlie's fingers reach for mine. "We thought you were dead too," she whispered.

"I'm sorry," I said. "I should never have signed up for the work. They lied to me."

"It's not your fault." She kissed my swollen cheek and rested her head on my shoulder, shivering. "It's not your fault."

As the noise of conflict dwindled and the night fell back to its usual hiss and murmur, I laid my head against the wall. I did not even consider sleep. There was no telling what those distant shots and explosions meant for us or how much time we had left. For all I knew we did not even have the night. Aisha was still buried in my side, and if she knew anything at all about what was going on, then she had already made the same choice as me, which was to endeavor to spend whatever hours we had left wisely.

For her that meant comfort and dream. For me…

I felt beneath the mattress, finding the stub of pencil and my book still there where I had left them. At least, I thought, I might finally finish my story.

## LINEKER

I did not enjoy watching him being punished. I felt every blow and winced at every cry. And when he stopped protesting and his head just lolled there, taking the punches, the impact of that brute's fists seemed to match the rhythm of my heart—thump, thump, thump— and the room disintegrated until all I could see was his purple face, swollen and bleeding.

His face.

In his face I still see love and all the bright memories of a life before: grass I could lose myself in, blue skies swarming with birds, and endless sun-filled days. But he abandoned me twice; I don't know what kind of love that is.

In Her face I see security, predictability, purpose, stability. No surprises, apart from the sharp sting of the stick.

I don't know how much longer I can keep dwelling on this. My thoughts used to be bright, like sunlight through river water flickering with the shapes of birds above. But now that river's murky and those birds—they're circling low, and I can see their wings are shadowed with the black feathers of carrion. They're coming for me; I can feel them.

## REGINALD

I read the words of my unfinished story, feeling like they belonged to somebody else. I could barely remember writing those neat and hopeful opening paragraphs describing the changes in the seasons of Karafall, or the scrawled and scratched-out verses detailing the Great Battle of the Schrugian Hills, or the love story up in the lakes, where the General finally finds the lost dwelling of his uncle, and he and The Duchess sleep beneath the light of their dying second sun. For the life of me, I did not know what I had been trying to write about. It all seemed alien and jumbled, like cargo washed up on a shore.

And then I realized: Of course. I had been trying to write about me. My grief. That is why I could not finish it, because grief has no ending, happy or otherwise.

I let the book drop to the mattress. It was hopeless. But as my gloom threatened to engulf me, I became aware of a presence. I looked up and saw a pale face in the moonlight. It was Aisha.

"What are you writing?" she said.

I held my breath. Her voice again. Those words—bright stars, diamonds, lighthouse sweeps from an unseen shore—they cut through the silence, the darkness, my despair. I fumbled for my book.

"Is it a diary?" she went on.

"No," I whispered. I spoke carefully, in case my words might somehow damage hers and force her back into silence. "It is a book. A story."

"What kind of story?" she said. Her eyes did not leave mine.

"It's complicated."

"What is it about?"

"Hard to explain."

She paused, thinking. "It should be a good story," she said at last. "All stories should be good."

"I don't. It's…"

"You should tell us the story." Then she sat down, crossed her legs, and looked up patiently.

I glanced around. There was movement up and down the pillar as people sat up, awake, and to my surprise more faces had appeared, lit by their makeshift candles.

Charlie crept to my side, shivering.

"She's right, Reginald," she said, with half a smile on her face. "It's not like any of us can sleep anyway, and it might help the children."

"But I can't," I said. "It's not finished."

"Then tell us what you got," said Dana. She looked around as the others made space on the mattresses for those at the doorway, until I found I was before a small audience of flickering, expectant faces, young and old. With a smirk, she added, "Just, make it good, like the girl said."

I looked down at Aisha, waiting with her chin on her hands. It seemed I had no choice.

So, in the dead of night, breath clouding in the bitter air, I began.

"Once upon a time, there was a kingdom called Karafall, and in the springtime, the valley floor was awash with honey blossom…"

## LINEKER

I think it's simple. You do have a choice: you follow either the certainty of fear or the fantasy of love.

Reg has already made his choice, and as I lie here in my cage, bruised, shivering, and listening to a hundred other dogs whimpering through the night, I know I've made my choice too.

Today I fucked up. But I will do better next time.

## REGINALD

I told them my story. It was not the one I had been writing, but it was the one I should have been. I made it as hopeful and exciting as I could. The Duchess—once tragic—was now an unstoppable optimist. It was no longer her jewels she was searching for but (of course, it had to be) her son who had been taken from her during a raid. She roamed the kingdom she had once ruled as boldly as when she had ruled it, never once giving up hope, and spreading that hope as widely as she could as she neared her goal.

I tried to tell a good story.

I pushed all sadness aside and hers with it. I even gave her a dog as a companion, because what better gift is there to give someone who has lost their life? And when, at the end, she finally found her son upon that sun-drenched hillside, I drew on every painful memory I had of my daughter, and I squeezed every ounce of joy I could from them to explain how it felt to have your child run into your arms.

When I was done, the children were asleep, and after a few moments of stillness, the adults retreated quietly to their mattresses with smiles and nods. Charlie kissed my cheek tenderly before settling down next to Aisha, and as the room organized itself into its various shapes of sleep, I stared up at the dim, yellow lanterns high above, thinking, *Every moment is a new world waiting to begin and be better than the last*, and as the idea drifted up with the restless whispers and I slowly surrendered to sleep, I found myself believing it.

# SHAPES

## LINEKER

I'M AWAKE. HEAD UP, eyes open, mind skittering in the shadows. It's been a while since I've been like this.

I'm back in the flat. I can see the outline of the kitchen worktop, a moonlit rhombus on the tiles, the toaster, kettle, coffee machine yet to switch on, the sofa, doorframe, pictures...

I feel a soft blanket beneath my belly and the dip of a chair's cushion. The room is warm, and I hear the snores of a man I know from the room next door.

The smell—that's what woke me. The bone bag abandoned on the moor, stronger than ever, pungent, making my eyes water. I have a strange feeling about it, as if it has been finally opened and those crows and ravens with their beady, black eyes are pecking at whatever's inside. I want to chase off those ragged scavengers, I want to tear their filthy beaks out of it, these unworthy retches picking through Reg's memories.

Reg's memories. I realize now that's what they are. The ghosts he carries with him.

My belly tightens and suddenly that blanket doesn't feel so soft. It's hard and cold. Concrete. And that toaster, it's just a box of syringes. That kettle is a water canteen. The pictures are fire drills; the tiles are the walls of the medical unit; the moonlight is the skewed outline of a single thin window high in the cinder-block walls. The snore is of the ragged vizsla in the cage beside me.

The bars of my cage close in, crushing me. But they don't crush me nearly as much as the lingering smell of Reg's memories, or the fact that I'll never know what they are. I'll never understand them, like I'll never understand him.

But a thought occurs to me, a thought that has no earthly business occurring in the middle of the night to a cold, caged, wounded animal.

Is this what love is?

Is love being able to accept someone, even when you know that you can never hope to truly understand them?

And is it that you let them accept you back, with all your flaws laid out for them to puzzle over, as you do yourself?

Is love just the sharing of riddles?

But it's too late. No more questions. The machines are on, and with a whir and a click, the long room is illuminated in stark-white light, showing me the world in all its harsh reality.

The dogs are awake. Howling, barking, snapping. It's early.


## REGINALD

I was dragged from sleep by scuffles and grunts. Then the sound of choking forced my eyes open, and I turned to see David's face in mine.

"What's happening?" I croaked, my swollen face protesting at the action of speech.

"Jag," he breathed. "Jag is dead."

His body was alive with nerves, and his eyes—already twin moons—seemed to be straining to escape their red-rimmed sockets.

"I killed him."

"What?" I sat up, fully alert. It was early and only the occasional sound of a guard's footstep broke the hush. "How?"

David stood and faced the far wall, where Dana was crouching over something.

"He was trying to... He was making a nuisance of himself with Dana. It woke me up. His back was turned, and he didn't see me and I just...I just jumped. I wasn't thinking, and I leaped on him and he wasn't ready... Christ..."

I stood. My battered body howled with the effort. Dana was checking Jag's pulse.

"I had my arm around his neck, and I pulled it tight and, and, before I knew it..."

David's face shone with exhilaration. "He dropped. I killed him."

Dana turned. "Yup, he's definitely dead."

The three of us looked at each other in silence.

"Well, I'll be a Dutchman," I said at last.

"What do we do?" said Dana.

"If they find him, they'll kill us," said David.

"We're dead anyway," I said.

"What do you mean?"

"I mean..." I hesitated. "I mean, they intend to execute us."

There was a pause but no sign of surprise.

"How do you know?" said Dana flatly.

"Is it not obvious? They haven't been building those bloody great gallows outside for nothing." My blood was up, and I began to pace. "We have to get out of here."

"But how?" said David. "There's no way out. Even if we get to the yard, there's no way we can get over the fence. We'll be dead before we clear the steps."

"Wait," I said. "The corridor where I was kept. There was a door at the end of it."

"Locked?" said David.

"No. It was a fire escape."

"Did you see what was outside? Was there another fence?"

I remembered the guard with the buzz cut smoking, the shiver as he gave me that look, and what I could have sworn was a wink. Then the brief flash of gray beyond.

"There was no fence. Just a few dead trees and empty streets."

"How do we get there?"

"There's a door in the eastern aisle that takes you down some steps."

"Guards?"

"One on the door. But…blast—it's locked."

"These might help."

We looked over at Dana. She had shouldered Jag's gun and was holding up a set of keys.

"Found them on fuckwad's belt. So, are we going to do this?"

Charlie stirred on our mattress and sat up. She looked at Jag's body, absorbed the situation, and turned to me.

"What's happening?"

"Do you think you can walk?" I said.

She nodded. "If I had to, I could run."

"Then wake the others," I said. "And tell them to keep quiet."

★

We crept from the protection of our pillar and into the open space of the cathedral's northern aisle. Charlie, Dana, and I led the way, and David and Anna brought up the rear, with the children between us. I kept my eye on Charlie, supporting her through every stifled cough, but she brushed me off impatiently.

"I'm fine, Reginald," she said. "Just keep your eyes on Aisha."

We counted five flashlight beams, two moving along the long western aisle and three motionless by the outer walls, their owners either sleeping or smoking. We picked our way through the sleeping bodies and found a wall along which we walked, crouching. Whenever a beam swung our way, we would stop and duck against the concrete until we were sure we were safe, then continue on our way.

It was freezing cold. Some gloomy version of dawn had broken through the roof's jagged scar. The light that came through was moving with slow shadows and, as we reached the rough crossroads beneath the dome, I felt a prickling in my hair and realized what they were. Snow was falling into the cavern and resting upon the sleeping prisoners.

Aisha gasped, and I looked down; she was caught in a shaft of gray light, holding her tongue out to catch a flake. I watched her eager face in that glum light, and I wondered how many more times my heart could break before it fell to pieces altogether.

David broke my daze. "Where is the door?" he whispered.

I scanned the eastern aisle. The choir seats that faced each other were now heaped with sleeping bodies and the pulpit was cleaved in two. I spotted the door set into the opposite wall and nodded at it. "There, between those pillars."

I saw a shadow lumber across the doorway.

"And that is the guard," said David. "How do we get past him?"

"I shoot him," said Dana, raising Jag's gun.

"Simple as that, is it?" I said.

She curled her lip. "I know how to shoot this thing," she said. She narrowed her eyes and leveled them at the guard. "Bet I could hit him from here too."

"Wonderful," I said. "Very comforting, but I tell you what, why don't I save you the bother and run up and down the aisle with my pants on my head shouting out our location for the other guards?"

"Fuck you, we'd be there before they got to us."

"With seven children? Through all these people? Honestly, you Americans with your guns, it beggars belief, it really—"

"I'm fucking Canadian!"

"Keep your voices down!" hissed Charlie. "Now, what are we going to do?"

We peered across at the door.

"We need to distract him," I said.

"How?" said Charlie.

Nobody spoke for a moment. Then Dana allowed the gun to slide down to her waist. "I'll do it," she said. "I know what he wants."

"No," said Charlie. "You can't do that. I won't let you."

"I won't let him either, but I might be able to distract him long enough for you to open the door."

"But what if—"

"I'll be fine."

"No," said Charlie. She straightened up, trembling. "I'll do it."

"Come on," said Dana. "No offense, but even if you weren't sick as a dog, I'm fairly sure you're not his type. Don't you think he's more likely to go for someone younger?"

"Not his type? Nonsense!" Charlie spluttered with indignation, glancing at me. "Plenty of men like an older woman."

As they argued in hushed voices, I saw the shadow stop. There was a chink, and his face lit up in the glow of a lighter. My heart sank a little as his features flickered in the orange light.

"I'll do it," I said.

Charlie and Dana stopped.

"Don't be ridiculous, Reginald," said Charlie.

"Trust me," I said. "I have a sneaking suspicion that neither of you are his type."

# TOUCH

## LINEKER

MY IDLE FANTASIES OF warmth and comfort disintegrate in the lurid light. The door of my cage buzzes open and every muscle in my body is on fire, every fiber twitching under the same furious will.

My handler leads me out, and we follow the line to the feeding yard, just like we always do. But this is anything but familiar. It's too early, for a start, dark outside, and the air is full of unusual smells compounded by the scent of a thousand dogs reacting to them. I keep a steady trot and squeeze down the urge to dart away. It's the same urge that's pulling on every other dog in the line, and some of them aren't quite so able to bury it.

Two beagles—their barks insane with fear—leap from their handler's side. This causes a chain reaction in the dogs around them, and one by one they stray from the line, yanked back by their handlers until those of us still in control have to pass ten, twenty, thirty dogs being beaten on the concrete outside of the yellow lines marking our route.

I keep my eyes ahead. I need food. Now. And I'm not taking my usual share.

I find the biggest dog at the troughs—a black mastiff who takes up two spaces and is already gulping huge mouthfuls of slurry. I growl, pounce, and land on his back, sinking my teeth into his shoulder. With a gullet-clogged yelp, the gluttonous cunt rears back on his hind legs and hurls me to the concrete. The pain of the impact only feeds my fury and I turn, head down, fangs bared. He plants his front paws before him, and a wet growl shudders from somewhere in his mass of matted black fur. Our handlers, seeing the stand-off, move in. But they're not quick enough. I leap again with my fangs screaming in the strip light, and clamp my jaws tight around his eye and ear. With a pathetic howl he heaves his body from the floor, but I sink my teeth in, trying to find bone and nerve, tugging at his flesh. And it's too much for him. He drops, legs splayed and scrabbling on the ground. I release him and away he crawls, whimpering and flopping like a clubbed seal.

My handler comes for me, but I snap at him. Blood drools from my chops, and he backs away.

Back at the trough, the dogs lower their tails and widen the space left by the mastiff. I lumber up, stick in my snout, and eat my fill.

## REGINALD

"Hello," I said. My voice quavered like a newborn fawn.

In a flurry of metal and canvas the guard flicked his cigarette to the floor and swung his gun in my direction.

"Who's that? Put your hands up!"

I did as he said. He fumbled in his belt for his flashlight and shone it in my face.

"Sorry," I said, squinting.

I sensed his grip on the gun loosen.

"Oh," he said, with dreadful familiarity. "It's you. What happened to your face?"

I ventured a smile and an awkward shrug. "Bit of bother," I said.

He gave a soft grunt and lowered the flashlight, then stepped out of the shadows. His great face loomed down at me, gray and chiseled in the dawn light.

"What do you want?" he said.

"I was... I got lost on the way back from the latrines. Glad I found you."

I tried a smile again and glanced behind him. The others had crept to the wall and were sneaking along to the door. The plan was for me to distract him long enough for them to open the door. Then Dana would use Jag's gun to either hold him back or finish him off. We needed to give ourselves as long as possible to dash for the fire door without attention from the guards.

My friend began to turn in the direction of my gaze.

"Er, are those cigarettes?" I asked, nodding at the pack in his chest pocket.

He looked back and frowned. I do not believe he was particularly intelligent, and I had no idea what bearing this would have upon proceedings.

"Could I...?"

Another frown. He reached for the cigarettes, picked one out, and held it before me, tip upward like a branchless white tree growing from the enormous thicket of his fingertips. He moved as if through water, like an astronaut bounding. Or perhaps my own sense of time was clogged.

"Thank you," I said, reaching for it. But he snatched it back.

"What's it worth?" he said, eyes flashing.

Something's always *worth* something else.

I swallowed, glanced at the shadows on the wall. They had not yet made it to the door.

*Hurry up.*

"Well?" he said, taking a step toward me.

"I…" I faltered. "Well, I suppose… I'm really not sure what you…"

His face darkened. "Get down on your knees."

The minutes that passed on the canal side were as short as atoms and wide as galaxies. It was as if they existed in a different realm, sealed like some rare exhibit in a vacuum of time and space. If I choose to, I can view them in perfect detail. Every word howled, every shake of her lifeless body, every pump of her chest, every denial screamed into the sky.

We tried everything we knew until the ambulance arrived, and although it had long since given up its grip, I kept hold of Isla's hand until we reached the hospital.

Sometime later, as tubes were removed and machines shut down and we fell into that long, cold silence, they finally persuaded me to let go. Her last touch left me like a long-held breath. A second later, somebody put their hand on my shoulder, and I flinched.

I have no idea what neurological mechanism was responsible for my repulsion to human touch, but I do know it grew from that moment. I felt it—a terrible seed taking root in the fingertip and pushing its tendrils through my body. Within a day, I could not stand to be within an inch of another soul.

So do not for a moment think that my recent improvements

"Hands above your head," said the guard at the front. "And drop that."

Dana placed Jag's useless gun on the floor, and we raised our hands. Boots hammered the stairs behind. We were done for.

Suddenly the air was filled with a cacophonous drone. A siren.

The guards looked around. More of them streamed from the eastern aisle, heading for the yard. Bodies shifted on the floor.

The guard nearest us took a breath. "Everybody outside!" he yelled.

# DAVID

## LINEKER

THERE'S NO TIME FOR training, not today. Instead, we're hurried into the yard. Snow drifts against the fence. The air is freezing and full of thick flakes.

As we find a space in the front row, I notice that my handler's hands are shaking, and it's not from the cold. The whole yard is a whirlwind of smells and sounds both familiar and unfamiliar. There are new things near us, voices we don't recognize, strange engines beyond the wall. These things intend to kill us, unless we kill them first.

Intruders.

## REGINALD

We shuffled down the western aisle, packed like cattle and bullied toward the entrance by the guards. With every step I swore I could hear the fluttering of a thousand heartbeats.

"Go, go, keep going, keep moving, get outside."

The guards were in disarray, their orders nervous and unrestrained, in voices that rose with the sound of our footsteps, the wails and the sobs of fear, entwining in an inseparable hiss and hum that filled the dome until all was a roar that could not be hushed.

I witnessed many moments in quick succession. A woman, a mother in her late thirties, absentmindedly flattening the hair of her young son with one shaking hand, a reflex learned, I imagined, in some bright kitchen filled with the familiarities of cornflakes, radio chatter, and schoolbags.

The crack of an old man's ribs as a guard brought him into line with his gun stock. His face crumpled in annoyance—as if he had merely stubbed his toe on a chair leg as he rose to get tea—then he fell to the ground beneath the slow stampede.

A shriek from above followed by a guard tumbling from the dome's balcony and hitting the concrete with a wet crack. I searched the roof for signs of who had pushed him—perhaps some rebellion that might spell freedom—but the balcony was empty and the doors shut. His fall was either through choice or misadventure.

Then the horror of Aisha's hand leaving mine.

I heard my voice and Charlie's voice. *Where is she? Where has she gone? Do you have her? Aisha!*

I searched the crowd, got down on my hands and knees, and crawled along, scanning the floor for her legs. Then I stood.

*Aisha!*

No sign.

Then the touch of her hand once again. Joy—even in that dark place shifting with shadows and all the smells of death and doom. Joy.

She had found a little girl, five perhaps. She had lost her parents. Her face was scrunched and serious, her lips pinched together between finger and thumb, a rough version of a coping mechanism that she would not be allowed to perfect. Her father stumbled in and took her without a word.

We reached the entrance and spilled outside into the yard, already awash with prisoners, guards, and dogs. Howls of alarm emerged with us like bats released. Their reason lay along the far wall: the scaffold was complete, twenty gallows with one rope hanging from each.

Chaos. Snow overwhelmed everything. The guards wanted to form us into lines but there was no chance of that. Nobody would go quietly. The prisoners ran, some together, some alone, screaming in terror or wide-eyed and mute, scrabbling for hiding places where there were none to be found, for some crack in reality through which they might crawl. Some made for the fence, managing to claw up only three or four shaky footholds before being dragged down by dogs.

Having been so far protected by the weight of the crowd, we now found ourselves out in the open and at the mercy of the guards, who were shoving, prodding, and dragging prisoners toward those terrible gallows. We instinctively dropped to our knees in an attempt to shrink from their attention.

"Where's Anna and her children?" I said.

David gripped his son. "I can't see them. They must have been separated."

"Dana?" said Charlie.

"Right here," said Dana, stumbling breathless to the ground. "What do we do? What do we fucking do?"

Charlie squinted, surveying the mayhem. "The guards—they're not in control, and they're not using their guns."

"No," I said, remembering what Hastings had said the day before. "They're low on ammunition."

"And it's needed elsewhere," said Dana. "Can you hear?"

# MAGIC

## LINEKER

WE LINE UP AND await our orders. As She marches out with Her husky at her side and takes the podium, I can already hear fighting in the distance.

"Insurgents are attacking the western fence…"

Electricity courses through my spine.

"Units one to five—through the northern gate to flank the attack."

I want to be out there, moving, running, no thought, no feeling.

"The rest, with me in the yard, to assist with processing."

No feeling, just the wind and the snow and the smell of blood and oil.

"Go!" She cries.

And we go.

## REGINALD

The two towers of the cathedral entrance were now makeshift gun turrets, from which two long barrels—cannons of some type—protruded, aiming west. Whatever was outside was aiming for the walls, the derelict buildings that bordered the fence. The structure on the southern edge whose fallen roof we were using for cover had already been pulverized and now bulged dangerously against the wire. With every impact we felt more rubble land above us.

"We can't stay here," said Dana as dust showered her hair. "This is going to collapse at any moment!"

Clifford had gone limp with shock. I peeled his arm from my shoulder and placed him next to Aisha, where he sat, wide-eyed and mute. Charlie crouched beside him, wan with the recent effort. She caught me looking, blinked, and nodded in reassurance.

Another thud resounded above us, and I peered out at the yard. "The statue," I said. "Part of it has fallen away. Perhaps we can—"

"Look out!" said Dana.

There came a deep crack and another groan, and we felt the concrete shift around us.

"Get out!" I yelled.

We leaped out, Aisha pulling Charlie behind her just as the wall finally broke through and crushed our makeshift shelter. Bricks, glass, and timber rolled behind us as we spilled into the open, and through the frozen haze of snow, the statue's outline beckoned. Just a few more steps and we would be there. Just keep running...

Something hit me square in the head. A blistering crack rang through my skull and I fell, taking Aisha with me and hitting the ground face first. Dazed, ears ringing, I scrabbled to my feet.

"Aisha, are you all right? Aisha? There you are. Come here."

She was standing, staring at something behind me. I searched for the others. Dana had made it to the statue with Clifford, and Charlie was lifting herself shakily from the ground.

"Charlie, let me help you…"

"Reginald." Her voice trembled. Old. Fragile. Broken.

"It's OK. The statue's close…"

"Reginald." She nodded in the direction of Aisha's gaze.

"What?"

I turned. Two guards stood before us, their guns pointing at our heads. One of them dropped his eyes to Aisha. Instinctively I stepped in front of her, and Charlie joined me at my side.

The guards approached.

Time seemed to slow. I turned to Charlie, her ashen skin dusted with soot and snow. We shared a look and the same thoughts ran between us. In unison, we turned our eyes to Aisha, and as the guards drew near, we dropped to a crouch and gathered her into our arms, surrounding her in our limbs, heads, and torsos, every muscle and bone we had to offer her. We gripped so tight that it felt like a type of magic was at work. I felt the warmth of Aisha beneath us, and the strange new comfort of Charlie's head against mine, and for that moment the three of us—different, bloodless strangers—were one. Nothing could hope to break this grip.

Such magic does not exist, of course, but still, when that hand gripped my shoulder I believe I put up more brawl than I had in me. I kicked, punched, and butted with my fists, elbows, head, knees, boots—every extremity I had. I gnashed my teeth. I made a machine of my limbs, a furious piston engine that battered the flesh of my adversary until, eventually, another pair of hands—the second guard—joined the first.

Their combined force soon quelled my fight, and they hauled me away. Dragged by the throat, gargling cries of dissent and still kicking my feet, I watched as Charlie and Aisha disappeared into the blizzard, but it was only when I saw Dana's outstretched hand beckoning them from the statue that I finally ceased my struggle.

# TIME

## REGINALD

TIME DOES NOT MOVE. Time is just a lake of moments through which we wade, picking out the ones that matter. The rest dissolve like ink in the water.

Sometimes there are whirlpools—dizzying eddies with such gravity that time almost seems to stop. Like black holes, nothing is spared. They suck in everything and you stand, detached, an observer of your own life.

This is how I stood at the gallows outside St. Paul's Cathedral on that frozen mid-March morning, with snow on my face and my hands bound to my feet before me.

To my left and right were others like me. They screamed, kicked, begged, and wet themselves, and yet I remained still. I wondered: Did this feeling come to everyone who faced execution? Perhaps I was screaming too. Who knew?

Everything below me was a haze of snow and smoke. People running for their lives. In some far-off part of my mind, I saw it all as if I were a crow circling above: an aimless stampede of tears and racing hearts.

I could not see Charlie or Aisha. This was good; they were hidden, and if they could stay that way, then maybe they stood a chance of rescue. The rope hair tickled my neck, and I felt awash with peace.

My bindings were loose. I studied my executioner as he adjusted them. He was just a young man. His face was creased in panic, his breathing fast and tremulous.

"You do not have to do this," I said.

He glanced at me. "Shut up," he hissed, renewing his efforts with the rope that tied my hands to my feet.

"You really don't," I went on. "You could stop. You have a choice to stop. You always have a choice."

He abandoned the rope and stepped away. "Shut *up!*"

"You could just walk away. You do not have to—"

"Shut up, shut up, shut—"

A shot rang out and something whistled past my ear. The young man's mouth and eyes snapped wide open. He did not speak. A trickle of blood appeared on the side of his head, quickly becoming a surge. I watched him topple back, straight as a plank, and land in brain-splattered dust. I blinked and looked into the crowd, searching for the source of the gunshot. Close by I saw Megan standing, revolver trembling in her outstretched hand. She gave me a shaky smile, dropped the gun, and fled.

I looked down at my still-loose bindings and waggled my arm. It was not enough to free me. I faced the sky, closed my eyes, and took long, deep breaths. Still this peace, still this quiet...

But then, into this peace and quiet, tearing through it like a saber, came an ear-splitting scream. It was the scream of something that had been afraid, but that would not be afraid anymore; of something that had been bound, but that would now be free; of something small that would no longer be held down.

The scream of a child.

My eyes shot open. My pulse exploded. I looked along the line of struggling figures to my right, and the chill air caught in my throat. There I saw a woman contorted in a hopeless escape attempt, and behind her two stockinged legs and a curl of black hair blowing on the breeze.

Charlie and Aisha, each in a noose. So that was why I couldn't see them in the crowd.

I called for them, my voice strangled with horror.

Aisha's mouth was wide open, raised to the sky in its relentless scream, but at the sound of my voice she stopped.

Charlie looked across. "Reginald," she wept. "Oh Christ, Reginald."

There is nothing you can say before or after death that makes any difference or sense. It is an event that repels words. Yet, still I clamored for them, still I struggled to find the right combination of sounds, some expression of comfort or warmth to combat the horror of our fate.

And as I was distracted in this hopeless task, Aisha, very slowly, began to move.

It was not a useless struggle like the rest, but a slow, concerted walk—one step forward, one step back, two steps forward, two steps back. The guards, embroiled in an argument at the far end of the gallows, seemed oblivious.

"Aisha," I heard Charlie say. "What are you doing?"

The floorboards creaked beneath our feet.

Aisha was now at the back of the gallows, her noose at its farthest extension, her eyes fixed ahead.

"No," said Charlie, realizing her intent. "No, Aisha, wait."

Aisha ran, jumped, and swung. The noose tightened, and the gallows groaned. I looked down at the boards. Those joists. I knew they would never hold.

On the backward swing, she hit the boards.

"Aisha!" shrieked Charlie, trying to catch her as she stumbled past, spluttering. The noose was now tight around her neck, but she regained her footing and retraced her steps to the back of the gallows. Again the floorboards creaked.

"Swing," I said as it dawned on me. "Yes, that's it, Aisha. Swing."

I tried my hand again. My bindings were loose enough that I could just reach my neck. Slipping two fingers beneath the noose, I followed Aisha's lead and stepped back.

"Swing," I said to the gentleman next to me.

"What?"

"Swing!" I cried to Charlie. "Swing, swing, swing!"

I ran forward, timing my approach with Aisha's second attempt. In a few steps, our feet had left the boards together, and for a second, we were airborne. As momentum took me, I swung wildly into the crowd. My eyes bulged as the noose tightened. Then my feet found wood again.

"Swing," I croaked, my throat now constricted by the rope and trapped fingers. "For heaven's sake, swing!" Finally my neighbor understood and copied. Charlie too. I tried again. There were four of us now, and one by one along the line the others followed suit until, led by Aisha, twenty human pendulums swung from the gallows, throttling themselves a little more each time. Inch by inch, the towering structure rocked forward, creaking as they went, the wood cracking, the blood swelling in my head, the world draining of focus, until, finally, the wood gave in to our weight and the ground rose up to meet us.

I shared a last look of horror with Charlie and Aisha as we swung beneath the falling gallows, the nooses tightening under our weight, but before we hit the dirt, the air erupted.

Darkness.

I opened my eyes. I was deaf, lying on my side. All around was tumbling brickwork, fire, and snow. The ground was a blackened mess. In a sudden volley of direct hits, the southern rim of buildings had finally collapsed and broken through into the yard. Over the resulting mountain of rubble, a hundred men or more in black uniforms now swarmed with gritted teeth and all manner of terrible weaponry—pistols, mortar cannons, grenades, and machine guns. And in the hands of one was a tattered black flag upon which flurried an open palm and a bright star.

I could not breathe, could not stand, could not break my wrists free. I was choking. My face bulged, my eyes popped, my chest burned. Somewhere in the distance I saw a small body lying still.

Flashes of things, just like they say.

As a boy, looking up at my mother's flour-dusted face, the world insanely bright and filled with her smile.

My brother driving me in his first car, rain running in endless patterns down the passenger window, my smiles as he talked and talked and talked.

One summer dawn on an empty street, readying the van, the sun arched over the trees, suddenly gripped by the stillness of it all.

Sandra, the warmth of her fingers and her eyes burrowing into my soul.

A baby girl in my arms.

A dog in a cage.

The sound of a bicycle's chain on a hot day and the ripple of water beside me.

Does time just slow to a stop when you die? Do all these moments roll into one? Is that the ever after?

I was not to find out just yet. Because as blackness engulfed me, so too a pair of hands engulfed my neck and, after a struggle, freed me from the noose. I burst out, coughing, spluttering, alive. Now my hands were free too.

I rolled over and gasped for breath. Dana's face blotted the sky.

"Get up, Reginald!" she cried.

The roar of thwacking blades filled the compound. Dana helped me to my feet and, grasping my throat, I beheld three black Chinook helicopters hovering in the center of the yard like great whales suspended in a maelstrom of dust and snow.

"Aisha!" I cried. "Charlie!" The words caught in my half-crushed throat, and I fell into a coughing fit.

"They're over there," yelled Dana over the din.

I searched the confusion of snow and limbs and saw them, dazed but now standing, supporting each other, holding their red-welted necks. I ran to them.

"Young lady," I croaked, pulling Aisha close, "that was the stupidest, bravest thing I have ever witnessed."

She held on tight with stuttering breaths.

"We're alive," said Charlie. "And they're here, Reginald. We're saved."

## LINEKER

A sharp whistle tears through the air from somewhere beyond the wall. We turn our heads to see but it's gone. Then, with a deafening crack, the wall explodes.

The world shudders and fills with dust and men's screams. I run for cover, but my leash pulls tight. My handler wants me to go a different way so I follow, but it pulls tight again. Where does he want me to go? I turn back to see but a stray boot catches me in the jaw. I get up, shaking the dizziness from my head, and hear that whistle again, louder than anything, skewering every thought.

I hear more distant thuds and shots. The turrets on the outer wall are lit with gunfire. Gradually the dust settles, and I see why I have not been able to follow my handler; he's lying crushed beneath a heap of rubble. The only thing I can see of him is his bloodied hand and wrist, around which my chain is tightly looped. I cannot break free.

I limp to his wrist and prepare to gnaw through it, but before I can another hand reaches down and unties the chain. She stands above me, one half of Her face caked with blood. Her husky sits beside Her, panting.

She grips the chain.

"Come."

## REGINALD

"What about Clifford and Anna?" I said, getting to my feet.

Dana pointed at the helicopters and the open doors from which ladders were dangling. A stream of soldiers in flak jackets had dropped to the yard and formed a perimeter around the huge machines, into which they corralled the fleeing prisoners. Anna was holding Clifford's hand, leading him and her children inside.

Shouts came from one of the towers and the gunners began to turn their barrels slowly inward. Seeing this, a squadron of black uniforms broke from the perimeter and fired up toward the new threat.

"We don't have much time," I said. "They won't be able to stay long if they get those guns turned. Let's go."

I turned to Charlie. "Ready?" I said. "Can you run?"

"Yes," she said. "But just in case."

She pulled my head close and gave me a rough kiss on the lips. Then, with Aisha between us, we ran from the scaffold to our freedom.

We kept our heads down, stumbling through the snow and dust whipped up by the whirling blades. Two of the helicopters had already taken off and the soldiers were closing the perimeter at the last. Dana was at its ladder, and I could just make out Anna's face peering from the window.

We were halfway across the yard when I heard dogs and a sharp report of gunfire from somewhere close. I kept running, but it was not until I felt Aisha laboring behind that I knew something was wrong.

I stumbled to a halt and turned, praying to a God I did not believe in not to see what I thought I would see.

"Reginald!" cried Charlie from somewhere ahead in the billowing cloud. "Hurry, they're leaving!"

I peered back through the dust. And there was Aisha. She was facing to her right.

"Aisha!" I yelled in relief. "Come on!"

I grabbed her hand, but she pulled it away.

"What is it?" said Charlie, finally finding me.

"I don't know. Aisha! We have to…"

But it was too late. The Chinook was rising, and I saw that the gun in the turret had finally turned—our rescuers could not risk another second on the ground. As the dust settled and the noise lifted with our disappearing freedom, I saw what Aisha was looking at.

"Linn-kaaa!"

# KILL

## LINEKER

THOSE BEASTS FLEW OFF like giant rooks leaving piles of bodies—canine and human—metallic wrecks, and everywhere dust and snow drifted down at its own pace, as if gravity were reminding us that all the chaos in the world could not bend its will.

And it was through that falling dust that I saw her: the girl.

And then him.

The husky growled, rattling her chain as she lurched for them. *She*, standing above, pulled her back.

"Steady," she warned.

The battle was now concentrated on the rubble of the busted wall, and I flinched as one of the turrets exploded beneath a burst of fire. We were losing, I knew that much. But it didn't matter. We still had a job to do.

On the opposite wall was another, smaller hole, and it was toward that hole that Reg, the girl, and the many-clothed woman now ran.

She unhooked our chains and issued our command. "Kill."

And with that clink of freedom and that cold, bloody word, we ran.

The feeling—I cannot describe to you the feeling. The blood of that mastiff was still on my tongue, flooding me with dreams of dank forests and the bulging eyes of fallen deer. I ran side by side with my bitch across the yard, both of us feeling the same rhythm pounding in our bones. We flew effortlessly, feet hardly touching the ground, the world rolling past in awestruck streaks of light.

With a glance at me, she ran ahead, powering her paws into the dirt. And the scent was strong in my snout—the scent of the one I had to kill.

They were up on the rubble and pulling their way through the fallen rock. The husky hit first, slipping on the lower bricks, and I scrabbled up behind her. The pile was unstable, but we pushed on, springing between the rocks, driven on by Her shrieks from the ground.

"Get them! Faster, you mongrels!"

Quicker we went, quicker went our pulse, quicker went our blood. I was next to her now, our haunches bristling against each other and the delicious, sour smell of her sex swirling around me. Up ahead I saw Reg struggle. His legs trembled with every step. His flesh was far weaker than ours.

Our hearts roared, our lungs screamed, and the whistling in my ear grew and grew until I thought my skull would burst. They were almost at the top and we were almost upon them, and with a final growl the husky leaped, and I leaped too so that we soared together through the air, weightless, flying. *Just like birds*, I thought, opening my jaws and ready for the taste of flesh.

Then something happened, something I shall never forget, and this is the only way I can describe it.

In midflight I saw Reg turn and cower, and time and space fell from beneath me. For one boundless moment, I found myself sailing through pure nothing, and in that moment, the sun took its cue to break through a cloud in glorious streams, and there, standing on the wall's lip, was the girl, lit up in amber and gold. The blizzard seemed to freeze, and all at once the only thing that existed was her face. My heart dazed. My thoughts exploded. She fixed me with a piercing gaze, opened her mouth, and cried out my name in a beautiful song, louder and closer than anything I could imagine, and the note tore through that ringing in my ear and drew it out until it was something else entirely—deeper, longer, rounder, my own howl joining hers, my hatred draining too and—ah, there it was, that love, the love I thought I had forgotten, and I kept my eyes upon her, that burning heart in the snowstorm, until finally my teeth sunk into the flesh of my prey. The sky spun, and my eyes rolled upward, to where a flock of real birds—geese—were flying in formation. Beautiful. I closed my eyes.

Blood. Muscle. Sinew.

And pure white fur.

The husky yelped and shook, and the pair of us rolled onto a flat section of rock. We faced each other, snarling. Her perfect coat was ragged, stained with a crimson spray, and her snout shook with shock-filled hate.

But love—love, sweet love—can be just as furious as hate.

The blizzard whirled around us. The Howl rained down. It questioned me, and I answered: *I've made my choice. I made it a long time ago. Love, not hate.*

I stood my ground, hackles raised, with three human beings cowering behind me, and I knew I would die for all of them.

She leaped first, and I rose up to meet her, attaching my jaws to her gullet. She continued in her arc, pulling me with her until we landed, her weight on mine and my skull against a rock.

Out.

Then, one by one, my senses returned, deadened. I was groggy and weak, but I forced myself to stand because she was prowling again, though her throat hung low and her eyes drooped.

This time I leaped first and caught her on the side of the head with my outstretched paws. She gave a growl of annoyance and stumbled to one side; it was a weak strike, not enough to knock her over.

But the rock I had pushed her onto wobbled and her balance shifted. Now she was at the edge with nothing behind her but a sheer drop. I lifted my head, sensing the calculations flit through her muscles to the rock beneath her. She whimpered as she tried to correct her footing, but her paws slipped and, as those calculations settled on her fate, she took one last look at me with those steel-blue eyes and was gone.

I let my head rest, and darkness quickly overtook me.

## REGINALD

"Lineker!"

He lay lifeless on the stone slab. Charlie sprawled behind me with Aisha, crying. The rubble we had climbed fell down in a slope on the other side. At the bottom was a clearing, a squashed wire fence and a path that led out into empty, snow-drifted streets.

"I'm going to get him," I said, picking my way to the slab, but as I stepped onto the first rock there were cries from the skirmish on the opposing wall. A row of black uniforms standing along the broken lip were beckoning the rest to pull back, to leave the open grave of purple-clad bodies upon the mountain of soot-blackened, snow-whitened stone.

"They're pulling out," I said, wobbling. I looked down to the yard as five more black-uniformed soldiers ran from within the building and joined the retreat, motioning for the rest to pick up the pace. "They're leaving us. Hey! Over here!"

But my words were lost in a tremendous explosion from the cathedral. The wall shook, and I fell back, clawing for an anchor as the ground shifted beneath me. When it had finally settled, I found myself farther down the slope, with Charlie and Aisha still clinging to the summit and the slab upon which Lineker lay now raised up on a precarious plinth.

I craned my neck to look back. The yard was a maelstrom of snow, smoke, and fire, but through the flickering haze I could just make out the last of the black uniforms retreating from the wall, their battle won, and the three Chinooks banking west.

Charlie called down to me. "Reginald, are you all right?"

"Yes. I think so."

"Can you climb back up? We can make it down the other side."

"Right," I said, and got to my feet, but as Charlie turned to descend the rubble, I saw spidery limbs clambering after them. It was Hastings; she had made it up the slope. Her face was caked with hair and streaked with sweat, and her uniform hung in tatters with one huge tear revealing a bloody wound in her side. She grimaced as she scaled the rock, brandishing her cane above her.

"Charlie!" I called. "Watch out!"

I made for the lip, jumping and stumbling between rocks, but she was nimble and the obstacles only seemed to propel her on.

Charlie and Aisha, oblivious to their silent pursuer, had just managed to edge down to the slope when the rock behind them slipped, knocking Hastings off balance. The impact made her grunt and Charlie turned at the noise, catching sight of the rabid face with a shout of horror, and picking up her pace.

Hastings's slip had allowed me to gain some ground, and I was only a meter or two from her when, with a wheezing cry, she sprang.

I pulled at the rocks, ignoring the sharp edges as they cut my legs, but as I reached the summit she was already upon them. Charlie had fallen, and Hastings had grabbed Aisha. She yanked her around and gripped her by the throat, holding the cane above her head. I stopped and faced her through the blizzard.

"Let her go!" I yelled.

"No," she replied with a curled lip.

I held a hand to my forehead to protect it against the whipping snow. Charlie was dazed upon a slab of concrete.

"What are you planning to do with her?"

"I'm *planning* on disposing of her. What else?"

The rock upon which I stood slid a few inches back, and I shifted my feet forward to restore balance.

"But you've lost, Angela. Look around you. What possible reason do you have to kill her now?"

She grimaced and stretched her spine.

"It's *Captain Hastings*, and the reason is that it is my *purpose*; something that an idiot like you would never understand."

She renewed her grip on Aisha's neck. I had to get to her; I had to make time.

"Purpose," I said. "Yes, er... Oh, you were wrong about dogs, by the way."

"What?" said Hastings, spittle flying from her mouth. I edged up the rock, looking for a safer one on which to step.

"Dogs. They're not the machines you think they are, and they're not wolves either, as it happens. Not the wolves you think, anyway."

"What are you fucking *wittering* about, you—"

"It's, ah…" I stepped onto a nearby boulder, which took my weight. "Oh, good—a fascinating subject, actually, and one that's benefited quite substantially from recent advances in modern DNA, reassessments of studies performed in captivity, that sort of thing. Anyway, the long and the short of it is that dogs may well benefit from a *purpose* as you so grandiosely put it."

I swallowed and inched up the boulder until I was only a few feet from her. "It is a reasonable assumption that certain breeds of domesticated canines are sometimes happier when they are put to work: farm dogs, police dogs, that kind of thing." The boulder wobbled, then settled. "However, when all is said and done, what your dog really needs from you—the only thing he needs from you, truth be told—is not your mastery or your dominance or your training, but"—I stood on the tip of the boulder, arms stretched out for balance—"your understanding."

The rivers of snow felt cool upon my face.

"Dogs need our understanding," I repeated, "no matter how strange or different their behavior might seem to us. And in that respect, *Captain Hastings*, I would tend to agree with you: humans and dogs are indeed most alike."

She regarded me for a while, standing like a scarecrow on that rock. "Understanding," she said with a nasty sneer. "You don't understand anything."

She shook Aisha roughly. "This *child* does not belong here. That *dog* should be put down."

"You're wrong."

"And what would you know? You're nothing. A fat, useless, loveless, pathetic excuse for a man. *Nothing.*"

I fixed her with as steady a glare as my precarious position allowed.

"I may be some of those things, Angela, but I am not nothing. I am still a father, still a husband, though my family is gone."

My gaze traveled to the rock behind her. "And what is more, I have known more love and forgiveness thanks to that fine creature lying behind you than you could ever know, and that child you are holding has shown more courage, grace, and kindness in her short years than you or any of your army ever will. So I would greatly appreciate it if you would let her go now."

"Or what?" she said.

"Or that fine creature behind you will be the end of you, Captain Hastings. Go, Lineker! Go now!"

Lineker, who had risen and stood silhouetted on his slab, leaped at my command and clamped his jaws onto Hastings' shoulder, just as Aisha turned and sunk her teeth into her wrist. With a howl of rage, Hastings flung the girl away and ripped Lineker, growling, from her punctured body. He landed on his back but before he could get up she had brought down her cane upon his head—once, twice, three times with a terrible crack.

"No!" I yelled, scrambling from my rock.

"Linn-kaaa!" screamed Aisha as she slipped away.

Four, five, six—Lineker's struggles and yelps weakened with every blow. With one last surge of effort, I jumped the final stone and snatched the cane from Hastings' hand. She spun around and as that insufferable face met mine, I screamed into it with all the rage I could muster in that freezing blizzard: "*You do not hurt my fucking dog!*"

And I brought the cane down, hard.

Her head whipped back without a cry, and when it returned, like some nightmarish, rubbery toy, a dark-red line had appeared on her cheek. Her eyes met mine again and I thought I saw the beginnings of a smile, but it flickered out before it could take shape, like a flame starved of oxygen. The lids of her left eye twitched twice, and she gave me a strange kind of pout, before she stumbled back a few steps and, with a tired gasp, fell from the wall.

I looked over. She lay in the red snow with her legs and arms in a perfect diagonal cross as if she were just a little girl making a snow angel. Not far from her, her broken dog lay on its side, back straight and paws together, still obedient in death.

"You do not hurt my dog," I muttered into the wind and turned away.

Charlie had found Aisha, who now clung to her like a koala.

Lineker's body lay still upon the rock.

"Lineker," I breathed, picking my way over to him.

His eyes were closed, and snow was settling around his snout, but I could see his chest rise and fall in short breaths. I lifted his limp body from the plinth and, carrying it gently in my arms, we made our way down the ruined wall and headed north.

London's empty streets echoed with the sound of shots and cries, and we navigated between skirmishes as best we could, ducking into alleys and hiding behind cars. We skirted the blast zone of the first bomb at Kings Cross, where weeds and bushes now grew from the debris. We ran down freezing side streets, sharing silent looks with others who were, like us, fleeing the fray. Finally, we joined a main road crammed with burned-out cars, passed Euston station ablaze, and reached Regent's Park. From there, we climbed Primrose Hill. I carried Lineker all the way and never felt his weight.

## LINEKER

It is peaceful on the hill as I lie on Reg's lap. Snow dots my whiskers and nose in cradles of ice so small and light that they hardly seem to make any impression in the world at all.

The view is strange, but I can see farther than I ever have before. London is burning. Black trails of smoke fill the sky in messy swarms through which helicopters roam, jets soar, and missiles fly. Something is happening down there. But it has nothing to do with what is happening up here.

Smoke is a curious smell, hard to categorize—it can represent the comfort of a pipe or a snooze beside a well-stacked hearth, or it can represent the danger of an inferno, and the desperate flee from its flames.

Comfort or danger, opposite poles, and the risk we accepted when we chose to follow those first trails to your camps.

Right now, although this particular smoke is rising from a battle-field, I feel no danger, no threat, just comfort, safety, and peace. I look up at the brightening sky and see birds descending in a slow circle. Are they real? Can anyone else see them but me? Can you see them, Reg?

Reg unfastens my purple collar, slips it from my neck, and tosses it on the ground before us. My throat opens, and the air comes easier, although still in short, slow breaths.

I study my master's face and all fear slips from me.

Maybe it's true that love is to accept without understanding, but that doesn't stop me wondering: Where is his pain? What carved those lines in his face? Who are those ghosts that roam his moor? I wish I had been there with him before they came. I wish I could have shared his burden.

But I'm still glad, so very glad, that I was there with him after, all the same. Because you can't operate alone. Nothing can—not the wolf, who still craves the warmth of her pack, nor the bear who rolls with his young in the forest, not even the spider, who allows himself to be devoured whole, just for the chance of a sixteen-strong knee-trembler on a drizzly branch.

You of all things should know this. You who cluster in cities and build houses with many rooms, who make space for each other and yet fill it anyway, just to be close. You who are not murderous hearts at all, but burning hearts of love that only fail because sometimes fear, worry, and ignorance get the better of you.

You who are, despite everything, nature's one and only hope.

They're coming down; those feathers are descending, and I can see now that they only seem black from below. The tops of their wings are gold and pearl, gleaming with the light of a thousand suns.

Reg—my master, my friend, my one true love—is weeping.

*Don't cry,* I want to say. But I can't, because the language we share doesn't have words, so I try with all my will to find a way of making him hear me, and if there is such a thing as telepathy or the simple power of light in a mammalian eye, then I'm using it now.

I'm using it to say *Don't cry, don't fear, don't fret, and don't fight. Love, only love.*

And as The Howl turns in great circles above me and those beating wings bear down, stealing the light from my eyes, I have time to take one last look at his tear-stained face and think: *Don't ever change, Reg. Don't you dare ever change.*

# ENGLAND

## REGINALD

THINGS GREW QUIETER AS we left the city, and after another two hours, we reached Wembley Stadium, Aisha's original destination. Even as we spotted it from the top of a narrow hill, I knew that we would find it abandoned. The city was finally emptying out, self-destructing as those Purples fled, and black-and-yellow flags were raised over the ruins—another glorious new dawn, another power shift. Round and round and round they go. It never stops.

Charlie was dead on her feet and burning up as we stumbled through the doors. I dragged her to an unmade bed in the dormitory and searched for supplies.

Although it was empty, the base was still equipped, and I found food, water, and a little gas stove in a supplies cupboard. It was not much—a few tins and packets—but I fed Charlie as much as I could and left Aisha with her as I searched for medicine. I found some painkillers and antibiotics in a red box. I had no idea whether they were the right ones, but I had no choice but to try.

That night I moved three mattresses into the storeroom and locked it, just in case. The city boomed and crashed through the night, but nobody came. I held Charlie close, slept like a dead man, and woke to a quieter, snowless dawn.

We stayed there for three days. Aisha and I took turns staying awake with Charlie, holding cold towels to her forehead, feeding her food, water, and pills. One day I awoke to find Aisha looking down at me.

"Aisha?"

I sat up. The towel was hanging in her hand.

"Charlie…" she said, the word as clear as water.

"What's wrong?"

She smiled.

"Charlie's awake," she said and turned. Behind her, Charlie was sitting up on the mattress, drinking water from a metal cup. She smiled when she saw me.

The showers still worked so we washed ourselves for the first time in months. I had never felt so clean. My beard had grown, so I searched for a razor but Charlie stopped me. No, she said. It suited me. I had never thought of myself as someone who could carry a beard, but when a woman says she likes something, you keep it. That is a fairly good rule to live by.

After our showers, we took some clothes and boots that had been left behind, and when Charlie stepped out in her military fatigues, I almost mistook her for an intruder. She looked half the woman she had been beneath her mass of jumpers and coats.

"It feels strange," she said.

"It suits you," I replied, and she blushed. So that is a rule that works both ways.

We spent one more night in the base. Then there was only one thing left for us to do. In an empty mess hall littered with paper, I knelt before Aisha.

"Do you still have that photograph, young lady?" I said. She pulled it from her pocket and showed me the back.

*Gorndale, Bistlethorpe, Yorks.*

MAGDA. X

Yorkshire.

I found a map. We packed supplies and headed north.

That night we lay on the musty bed of a ghostly M1 Travelodge, with Aisha asleep between us. I asked Charlie if she wanted to find her husband.

"No," she said, looking at Aisha. "I really don't. What about your brother?"

I thought for a moment, stroking Aisha's hair. "Maybe some other time," I said. "There are more important things right now."

After a careful pause, Charlie turned to me. "Reginald, what happened to your wife?"

So I told her.

On the day that Isla left us, Sandra left me too. In the bathroom of the hospital relatives' room she had found a badly misplaced packet of painkillers, and used them to end her agony before it had truly begun.

I had wanted to blame her—for cowardice, for leaving me alone, for anything—but I found it impossible. Our grief was the same, it just behaved in different ways. Hers was brutal and decisive, whereas mine stretched out in sick tendrils years in length.

The next day I had returned to our home, finding the half-unpacked boxes, toys, and clothes with which we had been about to start our new life. I had wandered through that empty flat, with the traffic, heatwave, and all the world's problems still churning outside, unaware of my own. I had searched through the boxes, feeling a decision being made somewhere deep inside of me: this needed to be buried, quickly. I would wrap these two terrible days in sackcloth, tie it tight, and abandon it in the most desolate part of my being.

As I had felt myself closing in, I had come across a box. Inside it was a video tape that Sandra had given to me as a birthday present the year before. *Classic Matches: World Cup Italia 1990, semifinal, England vs. West Germany.* I had put it on and watched it, and then I had watched it again.

I told Charlie all of this, and when I was finished, she cradled my face and kissed me.

"I'm sorry, Reginald," she said.

Then she lay down beside me and fell asleep, holding my hand. I loved her for not saying anything else.

Grief may be the end of all worlds, but as all worlds end, others begin. I still love my wife and daughter, but now I love Charlie too. Love does not divide, you see; if you let it, it multiplies, and in the end, how far it multiplies is down to you. I believe you can call the whole world by its real name, if you only let yourself.

I watched Charlie and Aisha dream in peace, lost in the stillness and the ripple of their eyelids. I thought back to those moments that had flashed before my eyes as I choked beneath the gallows, and I was certain that when death finally did take me, this moment would be added to the reel.

The next day we packed and found water and crackers in the hotel kitchen.

"We should locate a car," I said. "I could easily get one working."

Charlie smiled and stroked my beard. "If it's all the same with you, Reginald, I think I'd rather walk."

So walk we did, and later that morning we arrived at the remains of the M25 motorway. I paused at the edge and looked down at the cracked lip of road.

"What's wrong?" said Charlie.

"Nothing," I said. "I just haven't…"

I let the words dissolve and looked up. Before me was an unfathomable land full of fields.

I once met a man who told me he mourned for England. He said that the country he belonged to and that belonged to him was gone, and he yearned for it to return. But England is not a place you belong to. No country is. The place you belong to has no name. You cannot speak it, you cannot see it, you cannot touch it. But you can hear it sometimes. You can hear it in rustling hedgerows and distant birdsong. You can hear it in the wind's wild howl across a moor, a place upon which you have never set foot, but you swear you know by heart.

"Reginald?"

Charlie looked back at me, frowning, with Aisha by her side. "We should get going. We have a long way to go."

I used to be afraid. Afraid of touch, afraid of water, afraid of my past, afraid of crossing invisible boundaries in case I fell apart. But I am not afraid anymore.

"Come on then, hound," I said, smiling down at Lineker. He

looked up, his right eye obscured by a bandage. Then we stepped across, and the land opened its arms to greet us as it does anyone who places their feet upon it.

No, England is not a place you belong to. England is just a place you walk through. And if you do happen to walk through it, as we did during those early spring weeks when the cities burned and the forests yawned with new life, then I can tell you from experience that the walk is infinitely more enjoyable in the company of a dog.

# EPILOGUE

**LINEKER**

So.

I should explain.

(This is embarrassing.)

It turns out that repetitive cranial trauma *can* lead to certain psychological phenomenon like hallucinations, autoscopy, and delirium. In other words, getting a few wallops on the old noggin can make you see things, feel things, believe things.

Like you're dying and a host of golden geese are descending from heaven to carry you away into The Howl. I know, I know, embarrassing, *excruciating*, like I said.

Thought I was dying, wasn't, actually very much alive, fine, good, thanks for asking.

I mean, you can hardly blame me. These past few months have been a little—shall we say—*trying*, after all, and would it be an understatement to say that I have not been my usual self? Probably. But I'm all right now. Back on track. Right as rain.

I've still got it, though. The Killer. It strains inside like the ringing in my ear. You can never untaste blood.

THE LAST DOG ON EARTH    429

Strange. It doesn't really feel like it was me, looking back, although I know it was. The me before, the me between, and the me after: three different versions, but somehow all the same. You're not just one thing all your life, are you? You're not just one story but lots of little ones, endlessly told. Hard to keep track of them all.

Probably explains why you're such cunts.

Keep your hair on; I'm not getting all wolfy again, and I'm not saying that it's a bad thing. It's just the truth. You're cunts.

You. Are. Cunts.

There's no getting around it. You, sitting there, reading this right now, are an A-grade *See You Next Tuesday*. Just like me, Reg, and every other thing that walks or swims or slithers or crawls upon this rock. This planet—this pale blue dot—is populated entirely by cunts.

And that's all right. That's *fine*.

You've just got to accept it.

Let's pick someone at random. I don't know...fucking *Gandhi*. Mr. Mahatma Gandhi to you, leader of the Indian Independence movement, supporter of the underclass, pioneer of passive resistance, and all-around top bloke. Now, do you honestly think he got that virtuous without realizing that, deep down, he was a bit of a tit?

Do you not think there was a moment when he leaned before the bathroom mirror, took off those glasses of his, shook his head, and muttered, *What have you done this time, you stupid twat?*

Martin Luther King Jr., Mother Teresa, Nelson Mandela, Florence Nightingale—all the same. They had to realize what they were before they could change. That's how it works.

And who probably never had that moment before the mirror? Adolf—I bet he never thought he was a cunt. I bet he thought he was the *fucking bomb dot com*. Hitler, Stalin, Genghis Khan—none of them ever took that simple step of accepting they were anything more than a struggling mammal trying and failing to make sense of the world. No, they just thought everyone else was.

Plus they all had mustaches. So that's something to watch out for too.

Mind you, so did Gandhi. And Dr. King.

And Mother Teresa, come to think of it...

Still got this fucking ringing in my ear; it's like a gnat. I can't fucking *shake it off*.

What I'm trying to say is *own up*. Admit it. Confess. Stand naked on the rooftops and scream it to the sky, shout it loud, shout it proud: I AM A CUNT.

But—and this is important—one with potential. Because you can be nature's worst nightmares *and* the best of its dreams too; you only need to watch a child to see that. Take this one here. She's running up that hill, laughing, eyes streaming with happy little tears. At the top of the hill is some kind of enormous farm, a conglomeration of fascinating buildings (which I bet are absolutely *crawling* with rats), a babbling brook (I thought they were made up!), a mill, and a bunch of people strolling about in the courtyard, sawing planks, building walls, cooking food, playing with their kids. Dogs too. Lots of dogs. I can already smell the shape of the pack I am about to gloriously disrupt.

There's some old bird standing at the gate, and she's crying too; she can hardly believe what she's seeing—this brave warrior charging toward her. She knows who she is. She's special to her. Important.

But halfway up the hill, this brave warrior stumbles to a halt. Her chest still pumps, her hands still reach for the gate, her eyes still lock upon it, but something has made her stop. Slowly she turns to look down upon Reg, Charlie, and me, waiting at the bottom of the hill. We watch her dazzling in the sun, and with that bright, elusive smile of hers, she calls his name.

"Reginald!"

Her voice explodes, ringing like the bells of a hundred cathedrals, following her back down the hill and into his arms.

"You saved me, Reginald," she whispers into his ear, and tears squeeze from his eyes; the second time I have ever seen my master cry.

He smiles and says, "Other way around, I believe, young lady. Other way around."

I witness something happen to my Reg just then, and I could spend centuries trying to explain it, but some things are beyond the reach of words. Even poetry is just a grasp at the truth. All I will say is this: when he knelt to embrace her he was one thing, and when he stood he was another. That's all you need to know.

He lets her go, and I swear I can hear the hills sing as she runs back up to the gate, double speed—this furious heart that burned through a snowstorm, who saved my life, whose glorious scent streams behind her in ribbons and waterfalls. I know what it is now, that smell of hers; those pebbles on cotton, cut grass, glacial water, and peanut butter. It's home. The burning heart has found her home.

I think of *our* home sometimes—the flat, the window, my endless bird-filled dreams—but it all seems so dim and far away. Now we're here in this space, with fresh air filled with a thousand ghosts. The wood, the smoke, the rivers, the hills, the honey, the strawberries, the apples, the bracken, the maggots, the shit, the cocks, the cunts, and everything in between. It's all out there waiting for us. Heaven on Earth.

Still got it—*killer*. It tries to escape sometimes. It overwhelms me, and I feel the old fear bubbling, the hatred, the certainty—but I push it back, I lock that fucker down. Because hatred, fear, and certainty are the most woeful of things, the very worst stories you can tell.

So I close my eyes, count to ten, and let myself drift up from the long grass like downy spores on a summer breeze. Before I know it, Reg is calling my name, and—*bosh*—my eyes snap open and I'm away.

Free from Hate, free from Time, free from Gravity.

Into the Wind, into the World, into The Howl.

# READING GROUP GUIDE

1. *The Last Dog on Earth* introduces two very different narrators: a happy-go-lucky dog and his shut-in master. In what ways do their unique voices complement each other, and why do you feel the author chose to give two different perspectives? Between Reg and Lineker, who did you feel a stronger connection to?

2. In an age full of political upheaval and social tension, what echoes of history—or today's world—did you see on the pages of the book?

3. One of the book's explorations involves not ignorance but disregard—failure to take responsibility, the dismissal of threats, or turning a blind eye. How do you see Reg transform and grow in this regard, and can you envision yourself reacting any differently?

4. Reg has some very particular thoughts about heroism: "I am not a hero. Altruism does not exist. There are the things a man wants to do and there are the things he must do, and the things

he must do must be done, because if he does not, then the consequences linger. That is really all there is to altruism: the avoidance of bad feeling." What strikes you most about this statement, and how would you connect this belief with the world you see around you? What defines a hero, and would you say there are any heroes in this story?

5. Reginald's London is a very diverse and cosmopolitan city, so the way it fell to an alt-right dictatorship is very different from how it would be in other parts of the world. How do you envision your town, county, or region reacting, and how would it differ from London?

6. After the fall, those who are persecuted are not profiled by their religion, skin, or privilege but by their allegiance. What does that say about what sort of society is developing with the BU, and how do you envision "their" Britain?

7. Lineker is connected to The Howl, a force that calls to him as a domestic dog, a wild wolf, or a battle-ready beast. What do you believe your own Howl is, and how has it changed from our more primal times to now?

8. If you have a pet, what do you believe their voice sounds like, or how would you describe their attitude? How would they help or hinder your survival?

9. What are the possibilities of where our world will be in 2021?

# A CONVERSATION WITH THE AUTHOR

**What was your inspiration for *The Last Dog on Earth*?**

I knew I was going to write another end-of-the world book, but I wanted to write it from the perspective of a character who was not so caught up in the events, for whom the dystopia was actually an adventure. I tend to write about what I've been thinking about or doing most in the previous year, and I'd been spending a lot of time with my dog and her "pack" on Peckham Rye. The idea for Lineker emerged fairly quickly from that.

**Did you plan for the book to be this culturally relevant as you were writing it?**

Nope! My original idea was "alien invasion through the eyes of an East London rescue dog." But then the world started doing its current thing, and…you know.

**How did you envision the rest of the world reacting to the fall of London in 2021? Do you think the coup would have happened any differently in North America?**

The implication is that what happened in London happened

everywhere, and I think this wildfire effect is what concerns a lot of people right now. In the book, Reginald wants to detach from the world and live in his own controlled space with well-defined borders, but that's not as easy as it sounds. Our hyperconnectivity means that ideas and ideologies can and do spread in an instant. You only have to glance at Twitter on a bad day to see that.

**Where did you find insight for writing the inner workings of a dog's mind?**

I read some books (most notably *In Defence of Dogs* by John Bradshaw) and talked at length with a good friend of mine who's an expert dog trainer. But mostly, I just stared at my dog staring back at me. If you pay dogs enough attention, they tell you what they're thinking. I'm fairly sure mine thinks she's psychic.

**Do you ever look at your pets and wonder what their voices sound like? Would they be good companions during a violent political coup?**

Ha, all the time! My family and I developed a "voice" for Bronte, and I, er, *developed* that for Lineker. Dogs are noble and wonderful animals, but their rough and dirty side is often overlooked in fiction, so I tried to make Lineker's voice as close to how I believed Bronte and her mates would sound if they could speak.

I think a dog would make an ideal companion in any kind of dystopian experience. They wouldn't think anything had changed.

**As a novelist, did you discover or insert bits of yourself or your own journey in Reginald?**

Reginald's character is an extreme version of how I sometimes feel about the world. With everything being so connected and instant, I find myself wanting to detach from it all—to hide away and pretend it's all happening to somebody else. I often think of Peter Griffin in that episode of *Family Guy* when he fits a TV around his head. I'm sure it's not just me…

It is just me, isn't it?

**How did the experience of writing *The Last Dog on Earth* differ from your first book, *The End of the World Running Club*?**

In two ways—the first was that writing Lineker was much more fun. The second was that the final scene of *The End of the World Running Club* was clear in my head before I wrote the first line. *The Last Dog on Earth* evolved as I wrote it.

**What would you like to write next?**

I'm sticking with speculative fiction for the time being, and I've just finished two books. One is a twist on the reincarnation myth, and I won't say much about the second, but it's set in the future and I'm very excited about it.

The next one I write will, I think, be about parallel worlds. The idea of multiverses has always niggled me a bit, and I'd like to explore why!

**What book is on your nightstand, and what book is next on your list?**

The brilliant *The 7½ Deaths of Evelyn Hardcastle*. Next up is *Moby Dick*.

**Is there a lesson to *The Last Dog on Earth* or any conclusion you hope the reader walks away with as they turn the final page?**

Hmm… I don't think books should necessarily teach lessons, but they should ask questions. If there's one in *The Last Dog on Earth*, it's "Can you ever truly escape from the world?"

And, obviously, there's a fairly important message about squirrels in there too.

# ACKNOWLEDGMENTS

I would not have written this book without the help of my dog, Bronte, who bounded from a pickup one humid day in Texas and has been in my life ever since. She spends a good deal of her time staring at me, and I think she believes we are telepathic. Perhaps she is and told me this story.

This book is dedicated to her and all of her pack in Peckham Rye Park, but I want to thank their owners too—interesting folk with whom I have spent many happy hours chatting. Special thanks to Amey Markham, who has taught me a lot about dogs and why they behave as they do.

I'd also like to thank my editor, Emily, for laughing when I told her my idea and for pushing me to find the heart in the story, and to the wonderful Grace Menary-Winefield and her team at Sourcebooks for bringing Lineker to North America.

Lastly, as always, I want to thank my wife and first reader, Debbie, without whom I could not write any book.

# ABOUT THE AUTHOR

Adrian J. Walker was born in the bush suburbs of Sydney, Australia, in the midseventies. After his father found a camper van in a ditch, he renovated it and moved his family back to the UK, where Adrian was raised. Ever since he can remember, Adrian has been interested in three things: words, music, and technology, and when he graduated from the University of Leeds, he found a career in software.

He lives in France with his wife and two children. To find out more, visit adrianjwalker.com.